CRITICAL ACCLAIM FOR

THE MIND PALACE

"An ingenious use of fiction to penetrate some of the darker mysteries of the Soviet Union, particularly intramural struggles within the leadership and the use of psychiatry as an instrument of political punishment and coercion."

    —**Strobe Talbot,** author of *Deadly Gambits: The Reagan Administration and the Stalemate in Nuclear Arms Control*

"A chilling story of Kremlin intrigue by a former State Department doctor who knows inside out the Gulag of Soviet psychiatry."

    —**Joseph Kraft,** syndicated columnist, television commentator, and author

"Like *Gorky Park, The Mind Palace* is an intriguing portrait of the world hidden behind the Kremlin's walls. *The Mind Palace* raises the informational ante on *Gorky Park*, taking the reader inside the cultish practices of Soviet psychiatry. Pieczenik writes with a true insider's knowledge of both these fascinating worlds."

    —**James Grady,** author of *Six Days of the Condor*

"This is a great book on the deepest mysteries of Russia! Chekhov would be jealous of this brilliant American psychiatrist's deft plunge into the mind and 'intelligence' of the Russians."

    —**Georgie Anne Geyer,** syndicated columnist, and author

THE MIND PALACE

STEVE R. PIECZENIK

PaperJacks LTD.

TORONTO   NEW YORK

PaperJacks

THE MIND PALACE

PaperJacks LTD.

330 STEELCASE RD. E., MARKHAM, ONT. L3R 2M1
210 FIFTH AVE., NEW YORK, N.Y. 10010

Simon and Schuster edition published 1985
PaperJacks edition published May 1987

US ISBN 0-7701-0506-8
CAN ISBN 0-7701-0587-4

ACKNOWLEDGMENT

This novel is a work of fiction based on a history of psychiatric repression in the Soviet Union. Although the places described in the novel do exist, the events and characters are completely fictional. . .but possible.

I would like to acknowledge the invaluable assistance of the following people:

Robert Gottlieb of the William Morris Agency, agent extraordinaire, whose faith in me and commitment to the project were inspirational;

Herman Gollob, my simply awesome editor, a writer's dream—persistent, patient, and demanding;

Deborah Gordis, his literary assistant—forthright, dedicated, and meticulous;

Birdie, my wife, whose loving support and critical comments were indispensable.

To my dearest mother, who entrusted me with her love of books, and to the memory of my father, who taught me the necessity of discipline.

PROLOGUE

TBILISI, GEORGIA, 1984

Memories of a more flamboyant time swept across Anatoly Sukhumi's mind. Once, long ago, he thought, before there was a need for the Revolution, Rustaveli Boulevard, with its majestic sycamore trees, harbored all the colorful human elements who would now be considered anti-Soviet. Gangsters, wearing pinstriped suits with wide lapels and baggy pants, exhorting Jewish merchants to buy stolen goods. French-speaking aristocrats dismissing dark-eyed Georgian street urchins hanging on their sleeves. He recalled the melodious chant of the Greek street vendor demonstrating his wares to the Rumanian middleman, who simply walked across the street and sold it to a Bulgarian tourist sitting at the café beneath the shade of a lush acacia. Occasionally Sukhumi heard the sounds of Georgian hustlers hawking American blue jeans or Japanese radios and was grateful that corruption and the underground economy could still flourish beneath the oppressive weight of conformity and fear. How strange, he thought, as he gazed at the ornate building that once echoed the readings of Pushkin and Shota Rustaveli, the greatest of all Georgian poets, that he, Anatoly Sukhumi, general secretary of the Central Committee of the Communist Party of the Soviet Union and president of the Presidium of the USSR Supreme Soviet, should yearn for the sights and sounds he had helped to eradicate.

Eyes glistening, Sukhumi turned abruptly and returned to his *dacha*, to the surprise birthday party organized by his friends in the Politburo. He opened the door and was greeted by the raucous sounds of a lively celebration, the metallic precision of three balalaikas played by brothers from Smolensk who were offically assigned the much coveted unofficial designation of court musicians. Sukhumi loved the sound of the balalaika. It could arouse in the listener a series of emotions so varied, so rich, that all at once he found himself crying while exuberantly dancing the *kazatsky*.

Sukhumi grabbed Misha Kostenchik, the scrawny seventy-eight-year-old Party theoretician and dignitary, by the neck and embraced him warmly. "Misha, are you, my oldest friend, going to disappoint me on this, my sixty-eighth brithday? Look at you!" He pinched Kostenchik's cheek. "Only one glass of vodka. And no dancing."

Kostenchik pushed Sukhumi's hand away, unaccustomed to people daring anything more intimate with him than the salutation of a comrade.

Sukhumi clapped his hands to the rushing cadence of the music. "Misha! Misha! Just this once. For me. Forget the women here. They are like Swiss cows. Dance with me. Like the old days — when we organized the workers during the day and went whoring with them at night." Sukhumi grabbed a bottle from the table.

"Here, Misha. Our elixir of courage. Drink!"

Kostenchik peered around the room, making certain that most of his colleagues were preoccupied, and drank the entire contents of the bottle without stopping, driven on by Sukhumi's hand clapping.

"Drink! Drink! Drink!"

Kostenchik threw the bottle to the floor. "*Zhigulev-skoye!* In the fifty years I've known you, you still insist on drinking that poor excuse for beer."

"Misha, place your left arm around my shoulder, as I place my right arm around yours. Now, bend your knees so we can move with some illusion of grace." Locked together, the two men moved to the center of the room, engulfed by a feeling of relaxed camaraderie.

It was, indeed, a rare sight to behold. The most renowned general secretary of the Communist Party since Stalin and the most austere ideological theoretician of the USSR, who had first been promoted to the Politburo by none other than Stalin himself during one of the major purges in the late thirties, dancing arm in arm through the smoke-filled, alcohol-reeked room, to the shrill ear-piercing whistles of the men, and the mocking catcalls and laughter of their female companions. Each complete turn brought a progression of faster rhythms, louder encouragements from the onlookers, and conspicuous expressions of physical discomfort on the faces of the two men who had for that moment disregarded their collective and well-publicized infirmities — three heart attacks, one pacemaker, one chronic gallbladder, two kidney stones, and one moderate gouty arthritis.

Suddenly, the music stopped. The musicians began to rest their instruments and leave their chairs. Sukhumi, panting and barely able to catch his breath, wiped droplets of sweat from his face. He walked over to the musicians. "Play, play," he shouted in a raspy voice. "What is this? A musical insurrection?"

The musicians' leader shrugged his shoulders as a woman standing behind the draperies emerged.

The woman applauded slowly, her eyes focused only on Sukhumi.

How incredibly beautiful she is, he thought, as he approached her with outstretched arms.

"So, it's you?" Sukhumi bellowed. "Grushenka, please! I've done what no other general secretary of the Communist Party as been able to do — what not even Stalin with his reign of terror could accomplish." He pointed to Kostenchik, retching on the floor. "Misha danced for the first time in fifty years."

The woman nodded her head, stepped down from the stage, and wrapped her arms around his thick neck. "My *bogatyr*," she whispered. "My hero."

The guests who were watching the couple started to clap in a slow rhythmic pattern. As if on cue, the three brothers from Smolensk took up their balalaikas and began to accompany the clapping with a sensual, lilting melody.

"You know, you're a true Georgian beauty," Sukhumi said. Three years earlier, when he had first met her at an official Party function, he had been instantly mesmerized by her emerald eyes.

Sukhumi knew he was still very attractive to women, vigorous and self-confident. He could usually manipulate them into compliance, no matter how willful they might initially appear. But it was different with the woman standing before him.

"And you've had too much to drink," she replied with a sardonic smile.

The couple swayed slowly back and forth to the music and the applause, like two lovers-to-be entwined for the first time.

"My beautiful little girl," he whispered. She was thirty years his junior.

Running her long, tapered fingers through his thick black hair, she sang quietly in his ear.

Sukhumi rested his head on her shoulder, his eyes closed.

"Grushenka . . ."

"Even my *name* isn't really mine," she interrupted with an edge of sarcasm.

"That's not fair." Raising his head, he became noticeably agitated and lowered his voice to a whisper. "Grushenka is my name of endearment for you. Please, let's not fight again. Not on my birthday. Your being here today among my friends, in the open for the first time, is the finest present I could receive. Doesn't it mean anything to you that I insisted Misha invite you to my very own surprise party? No more clandestine meetings! I promise!"

"You had to conceal me from all these wonderful people? These good friends of yours?" She shook her head. "Which one? Which one would dare to harm me? And how do you know that they may still not want to harm me? Or you?"

Sukhumi started to laugh. What he suddenly found funny was neither the childishness of her question nor the way in which her question nor the obviously provocative way she had asked it. It was the way in which her question underscored the incredible degree of uncertainty with which he lived. How tenuous his stewardship was, despite a ten-year rule of the Party and the Politburo. And, yet, he survived by respecting one reality above all others — *kto kovo*, who is on top of whom.

Drawing the woman by the hand, Sukhumi introduced her to a burly, short man in his late sixties, who was attempting to slip his thick, stubby fingers into the open blouse of an equally heavyset woman, easily twenty years his junior.

"Oleg, I'm sorry to interrupt you, but I want you to meet someone very dear to me."

Field Marshal Oleg Rusanov bowed his head, clicked his heels, and almost fell over. He was very drunk.

Sukhomi held him up. "Oleg, tell this beautiful woman how many full divisions we have on the western front."

Abashed by the impropriety of the question, Rusanov hesitated. "General Secretary, please, I find this question highly unusual under such circumstances."

"Oleg, I appreciate your discretion. But I assure you that you can trust her. Because I trust her!"

"Of course. Of course," Rusanov replied obsequiously. "I didn't mean to impugn her character. Please forgive me."

She nodded, smiling. How amusing he is, she thought. An old man who likes to play war.

"There are fifteen regular army units, Category One preparedness, stationed from the Balkan to the Baltic seas. On the eastern front we have another fifteen to twenty divisions, mainly Category One, some Category Two preparedness. With the fifteen Warsaw Pact divisions stationed in East Germany, Poland, and Czechoslovakia we have a full army complement of thirty divisions."

"Thank you, Oleg!" Sukhumi took the woman's arm, and as they walked away he whispered, "He is my field marshal who makes certain that our foreign borders are secure. So there can never be the possibility of another invasion of our homeland."

"How do you know he can be trusted?" She recalled Sukhumi's description of Rusanov as one of "Misha's minions," a group of Politburo members opposed to Sukhumi's vision of major changes in Soviet soceity.

"Come with me."

They crossed the room, and Sukhumi greeted a wiry, well-dressed man in his early fifties.

"May I present Leonid Donskoi, chief of Internal Security for the KGB. This man makes certain that I know as much as I need to know about the field marshal's stable of generals. What they do. Who they consort with. Comrade Donskoi is particularly talented at assessing potential problems — malcontents, dissidents, heretics — and informs me accordingly. He is also responsible for controlling civilian unrest — spotting it wherever it may arise and crushing it before it becomes unmanageable."

The woman disliked Donskoi immediately. He appeared too self-contained, too aloof, alone in a corner watching the rest of the guests enjoy themselves, as if he were above such mundane pleasures. There was also something too natty about him, almost foppish — a silk tie, a body-fitting shirt, and a stylish Italian suit neatly tapered to fit his trim physique. Something slightly effeminate, she concluded.

"You must be quite a busy little man," the woman said.

Donskoi smiled and nodded his head, seemingly oblivious to her remark. "This is a most unusual opportunity. To have the pleasure of attending the general secretary's birthday party *and* to have the pleasure of meeting his charming" — he paused, obviously hesitating to find the right word — "if I may say so, friend. Now I understand why you have been kept such a carefully guarded secret from his close friends."

"But, Comrade Donskoi, with the exception of yourself and one or two others, I'm quite familiar with his 'close friends,' " she replied, obviously lying.

"Ah, Grushenka!" Sukhumi said. "I regret not having taught you the art of diplomacy. But subtlety has never suited your temperament."

Placing her arm through his, she replied with a proud voice, "If you sleep with pigs long enough, you begin to act like one. Right, Comrade Donskoi?"

Nonplussed, he replied, "There's very little that the general secretary does not know about me, Miss . . ." He stopped, fearful of revealing the fact that he knew her real name. "He will, if he sees fit, explain to you that I am not a man who can be easily provoked. As a matter of fact, one might say that I enjoy provocation." Pausing for a moment to assess the surprise on her face, he continued. "Who and what I am to the general secretary remains strictly and, I might add, comfortably between us. Isn't that right, Comrade Secretary?"

For the first time in three years that she could recall, someone was speaking to the general secretary with the same authoritative manner that he consistently demonstrated toward others. She was eager to see how Sukhumi would handle the insolence of this *apparatchik*.

Sukhumi placed his hand on Donskoi's shoulder and replied in a gentle voice, "No need to become jealous. Our marriage is still intact."

In response, Donskoi embraced Sukhumi with a bear hug.

The woman pulled Sukhumi away, placed her arms around his neck, and began to sway to the lilting music. "Who watches your good friend Donskoi?" she asked nervously.

He laughed. "Grushenka, how little you trust people."

"You look wonderfully tired for a sixty-eight-year-old-man. You need some rest. Why don't we sit down?"

"I'm healthy and happy. Stop acting like my nursemaid." He kissed her forehead. "And if you want a serious answer to a serious question, you can't wander away from the topic."

"You mean Donskoi?"

"Yes."

"Well, maybe I don't want to know the answer. He's frightening. And whoever controls him has to be that much more so."

"You see Misha, that wretched soul?"

"You mean he controls Donskoi?"

"Yes. Frail but tough Misha."

"And who watches over Misha?"

Sukhumi whispered in her ear, "Yours truly."

"And, my handsome stallion, who watches over you?"

"Probably only you, my dear Grushenka. Only you! Now you know why it has taken me over thirty years to get here. I needed enough people to watch each other so that there would be no one left to watch over me."

He laughed loudly. And then stopped.

Resting her head on his shoulder, she sensed that something was wrong. Sukhumi's arms suddenly felt heavy, leaden. His movements slowed and became awkward. His breathing became rapid and shallow. And as she peered into his face, wondering what was happening, she saw his pupils dilate and his face break into a heavy sweat. Clutching his heart, Sukhumi fell to the ground.

Chapter One

DR. ALEXSANDR BORISOV — director of Inpatient Clinical Services at the prestigious Kashchenko Psychiatric Hospital in Moscow; associate attending at the Bekhterev Institute in Leningrad; associate member of the Academy of Science of the USSR; visiting clinical professor at the Pavlovska Invalid Home for Children in Leningrad; adjunct clinical professor at the Kalinovska Central Ryon Hospital in the Vinhitsa Oblast in the Ukraine; distinguished psychiatric consultant to the Ministry of Health; official USSR representative to the World Health Organization; executive member of the Scientific Psychiatric Association of the Soviet Union and its corresponding societies, including the All-Union Scientific Society Neuropathologists and Psychiatrists; coeditor of the *Textbook of Psychiatry*; and principal author of over two hundred published psychiatric articles — pushed past a series of heavy wooden doors with signs prohibiting any other than authorized personnel.

Borisov entered the Hydrotherapy Treatment Unit, a huge white-tiled converted bathroom containing two large fire hoses attached to one wall. A tall, lean, flaxen-haired man in his early forties, Borisov greeted the chief nurse, an obese woman with a cherubic face. The nurse nodded toward two male orderlies holding a naked female patient between them, and announced that therapy could proceed.

Borisov walked toward the frightened, emaciated, middle-aged woman. "How do you feel this morning?"

The patient struggled unsuccessfully to free herself from the painful grasp of the orderlies. As Borisov neared, she controlled her agitation long enough to look straight into his face, cock her head back, and spit. "Satan!" she cried. "Godforsaken heathen! You and the rest of these Christ-killers will find damnation and purgatory. You are nothing but agents and political dupes of Anatoly Sukhumi and his Politburo stooges!"

Borisov wiped the sputum off his face with a stained lab coat sleeve. According to the patient's medical record, she had been initially diagnosed as having "recurrent" schizophrenia, where bouts of mental illness were interspersed with extended periods of normalcy. From time of admission, barely three weeks ago, she had lost fifteen pounds by refusing to eat. Over the past three days she had been force-fed through a nasogastric tube which she had once pulled out, seriously damaging the mucosal lining of her throat and nose. Since then, her mental condition had worsened and she was rediagnosed as a "progressively deteriorating" schizophrenic.

Borisov decided to assess her present mental status. "Tell me, do you know today's date?"

"Today's date?" the woman replied contemptuously.

"Yes, what day of the week is it? And what date? What year?"

"You must think me a fool, doctor!" She emphasized the word "doctor" as if it were an insult.

"No, I don't think you are a fool. I simply want to know how you think. It's a type of examination. Like a blood test."

"Here is what I think of your test." Thrusting her pelvis forward she tried to urinate on Borisov. "There, take my urine sample and tell me how well I'm doing." She laughed boisterously, looking for support from the snickering attendants.

"I see that you feel very upset today. Could you tell me why?"

The woman shook her head in disbelief. "I have lost my sable stole in the Kremlin and General Secretary Anatoly Sukhumi refuses to return it to me. How is that for a reason to be upset? You idiot! How do you expect to treat me if you don't know what's wrong with me?"

"I would like to be able to help you, but I would appreciate your cooperation."

" 'Appreciate my cooperation,' " she mimicked in an unctuous tone of voice.

Borisov leafed through the scribbled handwritten charts the nurse carried and discovered that, except for an alcoholic husband whom she detested, the patient's entire family consisted of a twenty-two-year-old son.

"I see your son is a corporal in the army."

" 'I see your son is a corporal in the army,' " the patient mimicked him again. "Tell these hooligans to let go." She wrenched her body forward in an attempt to break the grasp of the orderlies. "My son! My son! My son!" she screamed. "Why did you have to take him?"

"How did I take him?"

"You know! You bastard! You know!" She spat at Borisov again.

The nurse walked toward the woman and slapped her across the face. "Keep silent. You must have respect for the doctor. Stop this foolishness."

"Thank you, nurse. But I think we will be able to manage her without the slapping." He turned back to the patient. "Tell me again, how did I take your son away from you?"

The nurse coldly interjected, "Her son was killed in action one month ago. He was stationed in Afghanistan."

"Yes, yes, yes," the woman screamed. "You and Sukhumi and that gang of murderers in the Politburo killed my only child. For what reason? So that they can kill again — more people, more Russians. Murderers! My son! You son-of-a-bitch, you ask me what is wrong." Breaking away from the attendants, the woman grabbed at Borisov's face with her fingers, inflicting a few superficial scratches.

The attendants turned toward the nurse, who waited several seconds before giving the order to restrain the patient. They placed her in one of the white-tiled shower stalls, fastening her arms with two leather manacles.

"You see, you are the Christ-killer," the patient yelled to Borisov, "for he died like I am, chained to the cross."

Borisov nodded to the nurse to proceed with the normally scheduled therapy, and the assistants opened the hot- and cold-water valves on their respective hoses.

A deafening siren of pain exploded from the patient as her body slammed against the wall under the force of thirty pounds of water pressure per square inch traveling at sixty miles per hour.

Borisov turned his face away. That such a seemingly cruel procedure could have a calming therapeutic effect on a schizophrenic patient was one of those paradoxes he had learned to accept. And what about electroshock therapy, he wondered. A treatment that gave the impression that the patient was being tortured. And, yet, for psychotically depressed patients it was essential.

Checking his watch, Borisov cursed himsef. Dr. Dimitry Zoubok, director of the hospital and his superior and mentor, had probably already begun his opening remarks to the doctors assembled at grand rounds.

"Nurse, I think she has had enough. Let's wrap her up now."

"Are you sure she shouldn't have the full ten minutes?"

"No." Borisov was impatient. "Wrap her up."

The attendants unfastened the patient's arms from the leather straps, draped her exhausted body over their shoulders, and placed her, face up, on a plain wooden table.

Borisov took a stethoscope from the pocket of his lab coat and bent down to examine her chest for broken ribs. As he leaned over her, she reached up and grabbed his throat with a viselike grip that made his face turn crimson. The more he tried to pry open her hands, the tigher her grip became. He could hear himself gasp for air as the nurse jammed her fist into the patient's stomach. With a scream of pain, the woman released her grip and clutched her midsection.

"Thank you," Borisov said, massaging his throat. "You were right. Next time she'll receive the full ten minutes. Give her the twenty-minute wet-pack treatment and, if needed, repeat it again. At your discretion, of course."

"Of course, doctor." Pleased with her victory, the nurse bowed her head. With the help of the attendants, she wrapped the patient tightly in a sheet soaked in a phenol-based chemical solution that made the fibers shrink at a faster than normal rate. The patient squirmed within the contracting ersatz straitjacket. Eventually she would succumb to a comforting feeling of constraint. At least, that was the theory.

Borisov walked out of the hydrotherapy room, leaving behind the fading strains of the patient's moans. Scanning the expansive grounds of the seventy-five-acre hospital complex, he shook his head in disgust, embarrassed that the most famous psychiatric hospital in the Soviet Union looked so singularly unimpressive. It was an assault upon his sensibilities: crumpled remnants of *Pravda* and *Izvestiya* strewn across the grass; beer and liquor bottles, some broken; discarded items of clothing (one plaid woolen glove, two mismatched ear muffs, a pair of feces-stained underpants, several torn undershirts).

He rubbed his hands together, trying to maintain circulation on the cold October day. Several patients, bundled up in a pastiche of clothing, wandered aimlessly from one defoliated bush to another, bending over and pushing the branches aside, as if looking for something. What was it, he wondered, that made them walk past each other without the least acknowledgment or greeting. Occassionally they exchanged cigarettes and matches, or for the more enterprising, cigarette paper and pouches of tobacco. But there was no attempt at verbal communication. Yes, he knew the professional answer. These patients were regressed schizophrenics who suffered from an organic disorder. But watching them walk about like zombies, Borisov harbored his doubts. There was, indeed, something seriously wrong with these people. But something characterological as well as physiological. Something had gone out of their personalities. They seemed to suffer from a lack of will power and the discipline needed to order their lives. They had lost, or, better yet, relinquished their individual responsibilities.

Borisov sighed and exhaled, watching the trail of

warm air vaporize in the morning's brilliance. Glancing at his black-market Japanese digital wrist watch, he was reminded that he was already twenty-five minutes behind schedule. He tripped over a bundle of rags and paper, and fantasized what it would take to get rid of the chief grounds attendant. First, he would obtain Zoubok's approval. Then he would go to all the directors of the eleven neuropsychiatric dispensaries in Moscow to obtain their consent to fire someone they never had met. From there he would speak to four health administrators, who would forward their recommendations to the *oblast* — the regional health director. The *oblast* would take from six to nine months to review the attendant's case and then would forward his recommendations to the Health Ministry of the Russian Soviet Federated Socialist Republic (RSFSR). The ministers would then meet with officials of the Republic Gosplan, the central financial agency responsible for the allocation of personnel and other resources for the RSFSR. Because of the chief attendant's senior level of authority, the Gosplan recommendations would go to the Cabinet of the Republic. Once a decision had been made, it would be forwarded to the Ministry of Health of the entire Union of Soviet Socialist Republics. Borisov laughed to himself. All this for a man who refused to do his job and pick up some goddamn garbage. He kicked the bundle into the bushes.

Borisov strode toward the main building. The cement driveway was littered with partially filled sand and gravel pits. Its great gates of black iron, now pockmarked with patches of orange rust, were falling off their hinges, forcing the guard, a frail man dressed in a drab gray woolen uniform, to keep them half-opened. It hadn't taken Borisov very long to realize that those gates and the spear-shaped fence links surrounding the entire hospital were designed to keep the outside world away from the fearful patients rather them to prevent patients from escaping. Originally built in 1894 by Czar Nicholas II as a public charity institution for five hundred patients, the hospital was purposefully located in a poor section of the outskirts of Moscow where the attendants and guards frequently lived in little more than corrugated huts.

Borisov entered the dark corridors of Building 15, one of a handful of decaying, four-story T-shaped red-brick buildings. Sixty beds were crowded into each twenty-by-thirty-foot room. Patients lay cramped together amid a cacophony of unintelligible sounds and the pungent odors of urine, carbolic acid, cleaning fluid, and cheap perfume. The vertical part of the T housed the long corridor of individual seclusion cells, totally barren rooms with naked concrete floors and walls, and chicken wire embedded in the glass of each room's single window.

How could those *apparatchiki* in the Ministry of Health, Borisov wondered, expect anything from an overcrowded, undersized hospital straining at its seams to accommodate fifteen thousand to seventeen thousand admissions per year. True, well-intentioned civil servants had created Directive Number 702 of the Russian Soviet Federated Socialist Republic Management Plan, which stated that each psychiatric ward would receive major structural renovations every six years. But it had already been a multiple of six years since Directive Number 702 had been written and revised, and the overcrowding had become much worse. It appeared as if the mere writing of directives was sufficient to ameliorate the problems.

Directive Number 816, requiring each ward to have new furniture every five years, made no sense at all, having been written in 1932 and never changed to accommodate the realities of increasing patients and bureaucratic inertia. Staffing patterns looked impressive on paper — 175 psychiatrists, 100 *uchastok* family doctors, 750 nurses, 1,200 orderlies, and 300 *feldshers*, or paramedics. But as Borisov looked around the warehouse of twisted, spastic bodies, empty stares, and incomprehensible gibberish, he wondered what the staff was doing besides handing out medication.

Borisov peered into the day room, a cramped fifteen-by-ten-foot area accommodating a broken black-and-white twelve-inch Phillips television imported from East Germany, a truncated, three-legged Ping-Pong table complete with squashed Ping-Pong balls and plywood paddles without handles; a slanting card table, six metal chairs, and two torn sofas. On the far side of the room was a tiled bathroom, stained with feces and vomit. Four basins, over which hung four cracked mirror, faced four open stalls. The combined stench of the open stalls and the stagnant drainage, which filled the entire day room, was enough to make him gag.

The marble arch over the entrance to the main therapy building announced the *INSTITUTE OF PSYCHIATRY AND SOVIET ACADEMY OF MEDICAL SCIENCES*, words that implied that patients entering these portals were being entrusted to the care of very noble and knowledgeable doctors. Borisov knew those words to be intimidating but misleading. Of course, in every hospital there were doctors who were only interested in research. But at the Kashchenko, most doctors would not put in any effort beyond that which was necessary to stabilize the schizophrenic patient. Psychiatry, unfortunately, provided them with a specialty that required little exertion. Unlike surgery or internal medicine, one could treat large numbers of patients with medication and achieve impressive results; "impressive," defined as keeping the patient quiet and undemanding.

There *were* men like himself, still holding sacred what he described mockingly to his friends as the "holy trinity"; patient treatment, clinical teaching, and applied research. Doctors Ternowsky, Tsarev, Zeleneyev, and Zoubok all had that clear sense of commitment and purpose in treating and understanding schizophrenia. Of course, each approached it from his own personal predisposition or, more accurately, peculiarity. Zeleneyev, the youngest, the most eager, and ostensibly the most dedicated, would spend countless hours making certain he had the correct diagnosis. Then, after checking the diagnosis with three other doctors, he would check it again with Zoubok. Ternowsky, the bawdy peasant, would dismiss the fine points of a diagnosis, not because they weren't important, but because they imposed an unnecessary intellectual constraint on what he considered simple matters of the spirit. Schizophrenia was, for Ternowsky, a manifestation of a troubled mind and a "disturbed soul." Just as his peasant parents had learned to understand the "dumb animals" on the farm, he considered schizophrenics to be "helpless creatures" who needed care and understanding. Tsarev, the one pure researcher on the clinical staff, would, if he could, spend his life with the mice, hamsters, and rabbits in the laboratory, simulating schizophrenia with drugs. One day he was hoping to proclaim proudly that "we have the perfect model of schizophrenia with which to uncover its biological mysteries." Although Tsarev's approach to schizophrenia was closest to Zoubok's biological orientation, Borisov knew that Zoubok mistrusted Tsarev's findings, if only because Zoubok mistrusted any scientist intent on proving some original "truth." In fact, Zoubok treated both his doctors and his patients as if they were part of a personal fiefdom; the baronial lord who dispensed favors for acquiescence. As long as the patients were diagnosed and treated according to his theories, reflected Borisov, and the doctors obeyed Zoubok's rules of treatment, he would remain loyal to them.

Borisov walked past a line of patients seated on a wooden bench. Some were agitated. Others sat as if in a trance. Each patient was waiting his turn for therapy while the accompanying ward attendants stood together laughing or trading cigarettes. Borisov was well behind schedule, but felt compelled to take a few more minutes to check his division. Today he felt less anxious about stalling his colleagues; he had prepared a clinical surprise for them that would be well worth the wait.

As Borisov pulled back the heavy metal doors, emblazoned with the red letters ORGANIC THERAPY DIVISION, he was reassured by the familiar sweet pungent aroma of paraldehyde, one of the safest sedatives and sleep inducers in the panoply of psychotropic drugs. Organic therapy, he thought, would provide the answer for the treatment of schizophrenia. Despite admirable advances in neurophysiology and biochemistry, Borisov, like many other Russian psychiatrists, felt that schizophrenia was caused by an abnormal state of brain functioning. And following that assumption, certain therapies were appropriate, depending on the nature of the brain disturbance.

Four unfamiliar young men and an older woman dressed in white lab coats lowered their heads as he approached, and in a deferential tone of voice said, "Good morning, Dr. Borisov." One young man with thick eyeglasses and a nervous smile added, "I am Dr. Sirotkin from the Moscow Neuropsychiatric Dispensary, Region Fifteen. I and my four colleagues are here to observe your well-known methods for the treatment of schizophrenia."

Borisov flinched at Sirotkin's deliberate enunciation of "well-known methods," implying that there was some doubt of their efficacy. Perhaps I am still too thin-skinned, thought Borisov, a trait he suspected he had inherited from his mother, who despite professional accomplishments as a civil engineer and an active member of the Communist Party, was always defensive about her second-class status as a woman. Borisov's accomplishments were equally formidable: the youngest graduate of the gymnasium, highest ranking student in his class at Moscow University Medical School, and now chief of Inpatient Services at Kashchenko. Yet the organic therapies he espoused, although studied for over fifty years, were still met with skepticism and derision, particularly by nonpsychiatric doctors in the neuropsychiatric dispensaries and the polyclinics scattered around Russia, who felt that most psychiatric patients could be treated on an outpatient basis.

Nodding his head at Sirotkin with perceptible impatience, he walked toward a woman patient lying in bed.

"Dr. Borisov," someone called to him, pushing through the group. It was Dr. Zeleneyev.

"Yuri, what are you doing here? You're supposed to be waiting on tenterhooks for me at the clinical grand rounds," Borisov teased. "Have my grand rounds become so boring? Is that what you're trying to tell me?"

"Oh no." The young man with the hatchet-shaped face and bushy eyebrows flushed red with embarrassment. "I just knew you wouldn't start without first checking in on the patients in the Organic Therapy Unit."

When Borisov first noticed Zeleneyev some six years before, he had been impressed by the aptitude of the then twenty-three-year-old psychiatric resident at Kashchenko Hospital. His stocky build, broad shoulders, and large hands belied an acute emotional sensitivity and professional intuition. His ability to elicit scientific data from an agitated schizophrenic patient was impressive. He could ingratiate himself with disturbed patients in such a way that, by the end of the interview, the patients would invariably feel as if they had just shared confidences with a friend. He never abused the newly acquired trust, but simply used it to pry more deeply into the patient's life. He was, as Borisov often said to Zoubok, "clinically gifted." And, equally important in Borisov's esteem, Zeleneyev had decided to hitch his professional fate to that of his mentor, Borisov.

So Borisov had made Zeleneyev director of the Division of Organic Therapy — a department that consisted of Zeleneyev and two other psychiatrists, four nurses, five orderlies. The comfortable, clean room of eight beds, each painted white and separated by a night stand on which there was a handmade doily and a vase with fresh yellow flowers, had been designed to make the patients feel that their descent and ascent into and out of coma would be as pleasant as possible.

"Dr. Borisov, it would probably be of some value to you if we explained our particular interest in your special therapies," said Dr. Sirotkin, imposing himself between Zeleneyev and Borisov.

Borisov looked at Sirotkin's thick, curly, black hair, and immediately disliked him.

"As you may know, our neuropsychiatric dispensary is one of the largest in Moscow. We cover three to four hundred thousand people on an outpatient basis with an average of one hundred thousand clinic-hour visits per year, including ten thousand home visits by our twenty-eight staff psychiatrists. I am the director."

"Of course." Borisov smiled to himself. He would have guessed. "I'd like to learn more about your dispensary, but I'm already late . . ." Borisov checked his watch and started walking away from the group.

Dr. Sirotkin grabbed firmly onto Borisov's arm. "Perhaps I did not make myself clear. Not only do we have one of the largest urban outpatient departments, but also on my committee" — he gestured to a short, bald man with a gold front tooth — "is the head of Polyclinic Number Seventy-seven, the largest rural region covering Dherzinsky Ryon."

Borisov nodded to the bald man. Sympathetic type, he thought. How did he ever get connected with this son-of-a-bitch. Borisov had once visited Polyclinic Number 77 to investigate a spate of unusual admissions to the Kashchenko, each with similar unexplained symptoms of confusion, disorientation, somnolence, and stupor. He was impressed by what he had seen. Unlike the eleven other neuropsychiatric dispensaries, the polyclinic incorporated several medical specialities, dividing an area of forty thousand people very cleverly into thirteen smaller districts, each serviced by nurses, *feldshers*, general practitioners, and medical specialists. It was in these small districts that mental problems were detected, usually through a routine exam. The patient was then referred to the neuropsychiatric dispensary for a more extensive evaluation. If the patient required hospitalization, he or she might be hospitalized for a brief period in the neuropsychiatric dispensary and then sent to the corresponding psychiatric hospital, the Kashchenko, for further treatment. Zoubok expected Borisov to nurture this referral network so that the Kashchenko had a respectable patient census.

Sensing the tension between Borisov and the visitor, Zeleneyev led Sirotkin and his entourage to a bed where a heavyset woman in her mid-thirties, with red tinted hair, lay undisturbed, eyelids closed, with an intravenous tube extending from her black-and-blue left arm to a glass bottle hanging from a metal pole. Ordinarily, the woman would have been in extreme pain from the saline infiltration into her arm. But it was a measure of the strength of Borisov's organic therapy that she lay smiling peacefully, comatose.

"This thirty-five-year-old, recently divorced mother of two children, was referred by Polyclinic Number

Sixty-six for evaluation and treatment of a sudden, unexplained outbreak of abnormal behavior at the Likhachor Motor Factory in Moscow, where she works," stated Zeleneyev.

"What happened, did she decide to drive a Volga instead of a Zil?" asked Sirotkin. The three male doctors in his party laughed. Only the middle-aged female doctor shook her head in disapproval.

Borisov glared at Sirotkin and tried to pinpoint the geographical origin of this man's rudeness. Born and bred in Moscow from five generations of Great Slavs also born and bred in Moscow, Borisov had been imbued with a sense of the cultural and ethnic superiority of the Russians, Slovaks, Czechs, Poles, and Ukrainians, in that order, a group now barely the majority population. At the bottom were the Turkish groups, including the Attay, Azerbaijani, Balkar, Bashker, Chuvash, Crimean, Tatar, Uzbek, and Yakut. Sirotkin's dark curly hair, sallow skin, light brown eyes, and sharp features clearly placed him in the middle amidst the Ugric-speaking people, Hungarian. No, Moldavian. Only Moldavians imposed themselves on a stranger's hospitality and then made certain to demonstrate that whatever had been given was not quite sufficient.

"She was transferred directly to our hospital," Zeleneyev continued, "because the polyclinic was unwilling to provide inpatient hospitalization."

"Had she been at Polyclinic Number Seventy-seven, we would never have sent her on. We could have handled her," Sirotkin boasted.

Zeleneyev looked at Borisov, silently questioning whether he should continue. He, too, was beginning to dislike Sirotkin.

"The underlying assumption of what you see here," explained Borisov — "the induction of a comatose state through the use of intravenous insulin, or what we call 'organic therapy' — is that any altered states of consciousness provide different pathways to improved mental health. The proper dose of insulin obliterates pathological processes that create the confused thought patterns so typical of schizophrenia. We believe that coma induced by insulin encourages and activates healthy mental health processes by affecting neuronal pathways and mechanisms."

"Like eating fish makes you smart," interrupted Sirotkin with a smile.

Borisov ignored the attempt at humor. "We can also induce coma by other methods, all of which are represented here in one or another patient." He pointed to an elderly man lying motionless on a bed at the end of the room. "That patient is in a modified coma, what we call a 'sleep state.' You know it as narcosis therapy. That 'sleep state' will last twenty hours each day for a total treatment duration of three months. But, we'll save him for your next visit to this unit.

"Throughout the ages doctors have used everything from alcohol to opium, chloroform, ether, barbiturates and, as in this case, insulin. Sixty years ago it was believed that mental patients who were in good physical condition had a better chance to recover from their psychological problems than did physically debilitated, enervated patients. So insulin was given in very small doses to induce mild hypoglycemia — lowered blood sugar — which, as you know, induced the patient to eat more and gain weight. But doctors noted that it had a mild sedative effect, as well. In the 1930s, when the Soviet Union was pioneering the clinical use of insulin for the detoxification treatment of alcoholic delirium tremens, doctors also began to use insulin's sedative effect for the treatment of acute anxiety states. Phobic reactions, traumatic neurosis resulting from war experiences, toxic confusional states, and, eventually, schizophrenia." Borisov paused, making certain that none of the visiting doctors looked either bored or distracted.

"The basic principle for its treatment of schizophrenia is quite simple. We induce a state of coma after producing a state of hypoglycemia. By administering the insulin directly into the patient's veins we are able to control the amount of insulin that goes in and determine how much we want to lower the blood sugar. To induce a deep state of coma we simply administer more insulin. When we want to pull the patient out of the coma, we administer sugar or glucagon, a chemical that facilitates the production of sugar in the bloodstream."

Borisov raised the comatose patient's arm and pushed it slowly toward her body. "Notice the cogwheel rigidity." He raised the other arm and pushed it back also. "Same thing here." Taking a handful of the patient's flabby thigh, he squeezed it with all his strength. "Any alert patient would have been in excruciating pain by now." He then began to pinch the skin around both sides of the trachea. Her face suddenly flushed red. "What you see are the signs of the second stage of coma; an unconscious patient, unable to respond to pain, dilated pupils which respond to bright light, facial flushing — a vasodilation reflex to pain, extrapyramidal rigidity, tachycardia, brisk hyperactive bilateral reflexes. We call this the 'green phase' of coma."

Borisov took a bottle of insulin and withdrew one hundred units into a syringe and injected it into the woman's intravenous plastic tube. Within two minutes, the patient's body erupted into a fanfare of musculoskeletal spasms. Sirotkin watched incredulously, eyes transfixed by the huge body jerking in rhythmic sequence as if possessed by a demon, shaking the steel-framed bed with such ferocity that the group of visiting doctors stepped backward.

To the uninitiated, some invincible power seemed to be manipulating strings attached to the patient, forcing her to move in a way that was grotesquely farcical. Her left cheek twitched continuously, while her lips moved in and out like the mouth of a goldfish extracting its quota of oxygen from the water. Her arms and legs contracted in counterpoint, bending back and forward without any intended purpose or obvious means of locomotion. Her feet displayed the Babinski reflex — big toes bent upward and backward with the other toes splayed out as if pleading with some imaginary intruder to stop tickling her feet.

"Stage three, or yellow coma. In this phase," Borisov pointed to the appropriate parts of the body as he talked, "one sees positive bilateral Babinski in the feet, tonic clonic contractions in the arms and legs, and if you look carefully in the eyes, independent eye movement. These signs indicate that the coma is more profound than in stages one and two, and that deeper parts of the central nervous system are affected. But there is only one conclusive way to know that you have entered the yellow phase."

Taking the cocked knuckle of his right hand, Borisov screwed it into the bony lid overhanging the patient's right eye. She remained unchanged.

"If we were in a stage two coma, this patient would have felt this and either moved her head away from the pain or grabbed my hand and tried to pull it away."

Borisov withdrew another hundred units of insulin from the bottle, raised the syringe in the air, and squirted out a little bit of liquid to rid the syringe of any potentially harmful air bubbles.

The curiosity on Zeleneyev's youthful face had evolved into an expression of bewilderment and fear. What was Borisov doing? They had already lost one patient the previous week.

Borisov noted Zeleneyev's concern. He smiled and nodded, determined, however, to go on with the experiment. The sooner he felt comfortable with bringing a patient into and out of stage four coma, the sooner he would be able to pair this technique with his newly refined method of using the EEG — the electroencephalogram — to detect sluggish schizophrenia. Borisov was to present both of these discoveries, evolved over two years of experimentation, at grand rounds today.

Borisov looked down at the woman lying in the bed. It was a selfish approach, he thought, but acceptable from a professional point of view. This woman afforded him the opportunity to try his treatment techniques without having to worry about diagnostic purity. Mr. Nekipelov, the perfect patient for his demonstration, was undoubtedly waiting for him at grand rounds. And Nekipelov was invaluable because of his diagnostic uniqueness as a sluggish schizophrenic. Each served a function. Both contributed to a better understanding and treatment of schizophrenia. And Borisov was, above all else, a clinical-researcher. Not simply a clinician or a researcher. But a clinical-researcher. Part of a hyphenated breed of doctors who treated more than one disease entity, more than one type of problem, and more than one category of patients. Zoubok called him a "secular prince of psychiatry." Unlike the other doctors at Kashchenko Hospital, he could pick and choose patient, disease, and technique. He had been given the option, the mandate, to push the boundaries of biological psychiatry as far as they would go.

Injecting the insulin into the Y-shaped joint of the plastic IV, Borisov watched the second hand on his watch, ticking off in his mind the seconds that would lead to the brief minutes in which the patient would begin to enter stage four coma. He watched her chest. She was still breathing in a slow, rhythmic fashion. No irregularities yet. He was conscious of Sirotkin watching him intensely. Then suddenly there it was. He looked at his watch. Exactly two and a half minutes after he had injected the insulin. The patient's chest began to heave rapidly. Her breathing became frighteningly loud, raspy, and erratic, as if someone were trying to strangle her.

"Cheynes-Stokes breathing," Sirotkin said in amazement. "This is the first time I have ever seen it. We must be low down in the central nervous system."

"Look at her pupils," Borisov handed Sirotkin the flashlight and percussion hammer.

Sirotkin flashed the light in her eyes. "The patient has bilateral fixed pinpoint pupils."

Borisov took a handkerchief from his back pocket, rolled one of the corners into a fine point, and deliberately poked it into the corners of each eye to see if they would blink. They did not.

"No corneal reflexes. She has complete extensor rigidity in all four limbs."

Borisov examined the patient's newly acquired posture: all four extremities were stretched out and locked into position, as if in anticipation of jumping down from some considerable height. He felt her throat around the Adam's apple, and turned toward Zeleneyev. "Quickly, she's in laryngeal spasm and will soon stop breathing. Get me fifty cc.'s of thirty-three percent glucose. And an intubation kit."

Borisov took the glucose and injected it into the Y-sharped joint. The woman's breathing became more shallow. Her coloring turned pale gray. Alarmed, Borisov reached out for the metal tray that Zeleneyev wheeled over to him and grabbed a pocket-sized instrument shaped like a scythe, with a small light shining brightly from its base. He cut a small hole in the patient's throat. With his other hand he took a six-inch rubber tube, slightly bent in the middle, and inserted it into the hole. The patient's respiration started to improve. Color began to return to her cheeks.

Borisov checked her pulse. It was climbing rapidly to

sixty-five beats per minute. He breathed deeply as he withdrew the intubation apparatus from her throat and said, "That was red coma. Stage four."

Chapter Two

THE OLD WOMAN picked up a hand mirror from the counter, raised it to eye level, and turned it from side to side. All she saw were hordes of bundled women shoppers, kerchiefs wrapped firmly around their apple-shaped faces, tightly clutching the string handles of their brown paper bags. Nothing out of the ordinary.

What a Gothic monstrosity, she thought, looking around the GUM, the largest department store in the Soviet Union. A complex of low metal arches supported its V-shaped glass-roofed arcade. Really nothing more than a common marketplace. It probably hadn't changed since it was built in the late 1800s for the independent merchants who wanted to hawk their wares away from the vagaries of the brutal Moscow winter. Unlike the stylish boutiques of Paris and Rome, which she had visited many years ago, the GUM offered only plain, unfashionable clothing piled atop counters as if remaindered.

"Do you want to buy the mirror?" the salesgirl asked.

The old woman did not respond. She needed a few more seconds to determine whether she was safe. If they were to block the entrance she would have to choose another exit.

"Are you going to buy that mirror?" the salesgirl repeated curtly.

"What is the matter, young lady? My kopeks will be as good as anyone else's." The old woman glanced once more into the mirror and saw the two middle-aged men in dark raincoats.

The mirror fell onto the counter and shattered into pieces. The two men walked quickly past the shrieking salesgirl and followed the old woman out of the store.

She moved briskly over the slippery cobblestones of Red Square, past the massive somber pyramid of red granite guarded by two Russian soldiers standing erect with rifles at their sides, to the bronze doors in front of Lenin's mausoleum.

She affected a stooped posture and ran her gloved fingers lightly over the layers of makeup. The nose was broad and fleshy; her cheeks, full and rouged; the eyebrows thick and dark; her lips heavily covered with glossy lipstick that strayed liberally from the natural line of her mouth. Like many older women who try too hard to appear attractive, she looked almost grotesque.

She walked past a simple white marble platform, making certain that the gait beneath her thin black cloth coat was measured, even halting, but not slow enough to let them catch her. How often had she been here before? It seemed so peaceful, so innocent a place. And yet, she remembered how her *bogatyr* had solemnly told her that on this stone, the Lobnoye Mesto, the Place of the Skull, hundreds of Russian peasants had been hanged or tortured to death. The poor victims would have hot molten lead forcibly poured down their throats while Ivan the Terrible would lie in bed reading some piece of "religious nonsense" (those were his exact words), and then, when feeling sufficiently purified, would come to watch the torture. She remembered that the only concession Anatoly had ever made to any "holy man," as he sarcastically referred to them, was to his childhood friend Father Vakhtang Gorgasali, named after the Georgian king who had first founded the capital city of Tbilisi. She recalled Anatoly's instructions that if anything happened to him, she must immediately return to Tbilisi and see Vakhtang. He would tell her exactly what to do next. Only three weeks, Natalya thought anxiously, until October Revolution Day, November 7. The day the plan must be activated. As she heard her own steps on the stones she wondered what torture the men following her would employ if she were caught.

She turned right at 25th of October Street into Kitai-Gorod, the Chinese City, a sector consisting of tiny streets, a maze in which she might lose her pursuers as she made her way to the train station. Like the Kremlin, Kitai-Gorod was once a walled enclave of sanctuary for merchants, scholars, and foreign dignitaries who lived in Moscow during the 1500s. Much of the original city had been destroyed during the Stalinist reconstruction period of the 1930s. But she knew the area well. Often, when waiting to meet Anatoly, she would explore these sinewy, delightfully named streets: Khrustalny Pereulok, "Crystal Lane," Rybny Pereulok, "Fish Lane."

She stepped into the doorway of one of the many official-looking buildings lining the street — aseptic concrete boxes where thousands of bureaucrats spent their days. Peering around the corner she saw the men several streets away, obviously searching for her. She looked around. There was nowhere to go. If she went out onto the street they would see her. If she went into the building, the security guard in front of the elevators would request her identification. And she had none. At least none that would be acceptable to them. She decided to retain her present identity — an unobtrusive old lady without official papers. Otherwise, she might never get to the Byelorussian railway station, from where she could head south to Tbilisi and to Father Vakhtang.

"May I see your passport?" a deep voice asked, a finger tapping her on her shoulder.

She turned around and faced the determined expression of the young guard. His leather pistol case was strapped loosely to his side.

"Passport? Passport? Why do you need my passport?" the woman replied in a frail, faltering voice.

"Babushka, I have seen you standing in our doorway for several minutes. Why are you not going anywhere?"

"When you are my age, young man, you will be grateful for every corner that provides some shelter from the biting winds."

"I still must see your passport." He led her through the glass doors into the building's lobby.

The woman opened her handbag, a large, worn, black leather case, and thrust her gloved hand deep into its contents.

The internal passport, a document more precious to Soviet citizens than their very ancestry, contained her name, date and place of birth, address, occupation, nationality, and, most incriminating of all, her photograph. She knew that if the guard saw the passport she would be immediately arrested. And if he didn't see it, she would be arrested, too.

"Hurry up, Babushka. I don't have all day." The guard grabbed the bag away from her and dumped the contents onto the scuffed marble floor.

"How dare you?" the woman said indignantly, raising her fists in a gesture of contempt.

"Ah, there's your passport." As the guard reached down to pick up the familiar document, the old woman saw the two men outside the glass doors. The taller one flashed an identification card and beckoned her to come outside. Beads of cold sweat broke out on her forehead. Her knees flexed involuntarily. She fell to the ground.

The guard noticed the tall man and, from his peremptory demeanor, surmised that he was KGB.

"Wait here, Babushka. I'll be back in a minute. Don't leave, or I will throw you in jail."

The woman was grateful. Now, at least, she had a chance. She grabbed her passport and billfold, which contained rolls of ten-ruble bills, shoved them inside her coat, and jumped to her feet, heading toward a bank of waiting elevators. Seconds later, the guard and the KGB rushed into the building, frustrated as they watched the elevator she had entered climb to eight. They entered the second elevator and pushed the button for the eighth floor. Just as the shiny metal doors closed they saw the old woman run past them toward the front door. Her elevator had come right back down to the lobby. But it was too late. By the time their elevator stopped on the mezzanine and they had run down the stairs the sprightly old woman had disappeared.

The security guard watched the KGB run from the building, wondering why they would be interested in an old woman. The two KGB officers had said nothing to him. They had been instructed to apprehend her, but to make certain that she was not injured in the process. They ran down a maze of narrow lanes muttering to themselves. More than a full day's work lay ahead. If they failed in their assignment, they would pay dearly.

The old woman crouched in the doorway of the Ararat restaurant. She was out of breath. Her heart raced wildly. Holding her hand against her pounding chest, she recalled that day almost two weeks ago when her *bogatyr* had died in her arms. A heart attack they said. Hah! He may have had a heart condition and maybe he needed those patches of nitroglycerin on his chest to prevent chest pain. But he didn't die from his heart. She knew it. Liar! she screamed, when the KGB security officers had pulled her away from his body and the doctor at the special clinic servicing only the members of the Politburo informed her that Anatoly Sukhumi had died from a sudden heart attack. Liar. He was murdered! The doctor insisted that she was agitated and didn't realize what she was saying. Then why, she replied, was he wearing two nitroglycerin patches instead of his usual one? He had been ordered to wear the extra patch because of a recently detected problem with his cardiac functioning, was the reply. What problem? she screamed. He was fine! Perfectly fine. We had been making love frequently. No, you convinced Anatoly that his condition was getting worse. You knew he was a hypochondriac and you intimidated him into wearing the extra patch. And then it was so easy. Just a little extra pressure against his chest, two patches release more nitroglycerin that one body can take, and his cardiovascular system collapses. Don't forget, she had screamed at the doctor and surrounding KGB officers, I, too, know medicine. I am a doctor's daughter!

After that scene in the secluded hospital in Tbilisi, her life was no longer her own. She had been taken back to Moscow and placed under the tight supervision of her political-lackey husband, Zhores Vartanian. But despite her house arrest, she gloated, she was still able to escape from Vartanian's KGB thugs. Now, more than ever, she had to return to Tbilisi — for herself, for Anatoly, for Russia.

She regained her breath and composure and entered the restaurant. The room was inordinately dark, decorated with painted murals of Mount Ararat and the surrounding farmlands, once known as Armenia. Twenty-odd tables were covered with stained tablecloths, on each of which a lit candle burned in a small glass jar. She looked around the crowded room, squinting to focus beyond the flickering orange lights. She was relieved. She recognized no one.

A handsome middle-aged man with deep-set eyes, wearing a black suit and bow tie, led her to an empty table in the back of the room. "Would you like to order?"

The woman buried her head in the menu.

The waiter stared at her. Something bothered him. She looked to be in her late sixties. Her face was appropriately wrinkled around the eyes. There were deep furrows around her mouth and broad, deep lines in her forehead. But there was something about her eyes: too bright, too alert. Strange, he thought. "If there is anything on the menu that you don't understand, please feel free to ask me."

The woman sensed that the waiter was staring at her. She considered handing him back the large cardboard menu, but noticed the two KGB men entering the restaurant.

Her hands began to tremble. She raised the menu to cover her face, determined to keep the waiter at her table as long as possible. Certainly someone being chased by the KGB wouldn't spend her time ordering a meal. Defying the obvious and making certain that she could benefit from that defiance was her personal forte. And one of the reasons for her present predicament. She had entered into a relationship despite warnings that it would be dangerous for her and for him. And she had proved the relationship could work. Yes, she thought, she had defied the obvious and would continue to do so.

"Now don't look so worried," she said with an exaggerated quiver in her voice, "otherwise you will get as many wrinkles as you see on this old face."

"They are lovely wrinkles," he replied with well-trained diplomacy.

The old woman peered over the edge of her menu.

The two KGB men were now checking the credentials of the diners. Her only chance was to elicit the trust of this Armenian waiter. At least, she hoped he was Armenian. If so, she had a chance to appeal to his sympathies for a fleeing victim. Scrub the veneer off any patriotic Armenian and you will find an irreverent capitalist who mistrusts and detests the central authorities, whomever they might be.

The old woman grabbed the waiter's arm and pulled him down close to her face. "If you don't want to see a fellow Armenian killed by the contemptible KGB," she whispered, "you will allow me to accompany you through the kitchen and out the back door."

Placing her hand into her pocketbook, she withdrew thirty rubles.

"These are yours when you get me outside."

He nodded his head in agreement and steered her through the busy kitchen. Grabbing the money, he pushed her out the back door.

The woman looked around, orienting herself to an alley filled with garbage cans overflowing with empty bottles, bulging brown paper bags, and rusted nails sticking out of the brick wall. She smiled as she adjusted her coat and babushka. Nothing instills greater sympathy and fidelity than ethnic pride and the ungodly love for money, she thought. She laughed all the way down the garbage-littered alley, until she saw two soldiers approaching.

Were they searching for someone? If it were her they would have already drawn their weapons and ordered her to stop. So she would have to take the initiative.

She began to cry, placing her hands over her face. The younger of the two soldiers walked up to her. "What's the matter, grandmother?" he asked solicitously.

Yes, she thought, it might just work. But she had only a few minutes before the KGB would be coming out the back of the restaurant.

"I went into that Armenian restaurant, and . . ." she paused, sobbing. "I ordered a very nice meal."

The older soldier was growing impatient, but the younger one seemed interested in what she had to say.

"Armenian pie, pilaf, and this wonderful sweet wine, Algeshat."

"Grandma, I'm glad you had a lovely meal, but why are you crying? And . . ."

"And why are you coming out the kitchen exit?" the older soldier inquired brusquely.

"Well, that's what I was about to tell you."

"Hurry up, grandmother, before winter comes," said the other soldier.

"Don't be so smart, young man," she said as she jabbed her index finger into his shoulder, "it won't be too long before you find yourself forgetting what you've just eaten minutes before." This was her moment. But she had to play it just right. She felt the strong fingers of the youthful soldier tighten around her arm.

"Don't be in such a hurry with an old lady. Russian soldiers should have better things to do." She noticed the waiter peeking out the back door of the restaurant, curious to see what had happened to the old lady.

"That's the man!"

"What do you mean, grandma?" The younger soldier asked as he motioned the frightened waiter closer.

The woman pointed to the waiter slowly approaching them. "That man took my thirty rubles, placed them in his pocket, and then threw me out claiming that I hadn't paid the bill. Can you believe that? You know what these Armenians are like. They have absolutely no shame in taking advantage of a Russian citizen."

The old woman pulled loose from the grasp of the

two soliders and gestured toward the waiter's inner jacket pocket. "You'll find the rubles in there."

The young soldier walked up to the waiter. "Please fold your hands and place them above your head."

"What? Why? I haven't done anything." The waiter's voice trembled.

The older guard withdrew the Makarov pistol from his leather holster. "Do as my colleague suggests. Otherwise you'll be in worse trouble than you can possibly imagine."

As the younger soldier searched his pockets, the waiter guessed that the old woman had concocted something about the money. "What has that old bitch told you?" he asked.

Searching through the man's pockets, the younger soldier was annoyed that he found nothing. Apprehending a thief, especially an Armenian thief, would have been something to be proud of. Promotion came to those who showed some initiative in enforcing the law against one of the hundred and twenty minorities — particulary those ethnic upstarts who were usurping the rightful privileges of the Muscovite Slavs.

Having searched the waiter, the younger solider turned toward the old woman. "I found nothing," he said, shaking his head in disgust. "He's clean, grandmother. I'm sorry. Your story doesn't make much sense."

Frightened by the reference to his "story," the waiter pointed an accusatory finger at the old woman. "Did that senile old bitch make up some story about me? What did she say, that I tried to rape her?" he asked mockingly.

The old woman peered at the waiter. She was starting to worry. Where could he have put the bills she had given him? Taped to his chest? Inside his clothing? But the soldier had just turned all the pockets in his jacket

and pants inside out. His shoes? She stared at his feet.
The laces on his right shoe were loose, as if they had
been hurriedly tied. Of course, she thought, of course!

"Young man, if you take off that man's right shoe,
you will find the rubles."

"You liar!" the waiter shouted, as he started to run
away.

The young soldier turned toward the old woman and
shouted. "Babushka, you wait here till we come back."
Then he and his companion ran after the waiter.

As soon as the waiter and the soldiers disappeared
down the alley, the old woman began running in the opposite direction. As she turned the corner out of the
alley, a cluster of rusted nails protruding from the
bricks tore through the worn fiber of her thin overcoat
right into her shoulder. The throbbing pain was dizzying. She leaned against the wall and closed her eyes.

Please, don't let me get caught. Not now. Not this
way! Please, Anatoly, help me . . .

Blood from the wound in her shoulder began to seep
through her coat. She yearned for the comforting embrace of her *bogatyr*. She recalled the evening only a few
months after they had met when she had twisted her
foot leaving a performance of Chekhov's *Uncle Vanya*.
Later that night he had massaged her ankle, wrapping it
alternatively with warm and cold packs, never certain
which temperature was the appropriate one for the
treatment. He was so gentle, she thought, so caring. By
the next morning her ankle had felt much better. She
smiled when she thought how he had jestingly accused
her of purposely injuring herself in order to justify this
attention from him. She yearned for his firm, comforting hands. He had so much to give — so much patience,
so much tenderness, so much understanding. And, yet,
like the Russian hero for whom he was named, he could
flash from gentleness to unrelenting cruelty. The latter
she wanted to forget. She only wanted to remember the

happy times, those summer days in Tbilisi, seemingly endless days of making love. But how she worried about his health — his heart, his angina. He had to take so many pills, and had to wear twenty-four-hour nitroglycerin patches on his chest. She almost smiled as she recalled how he used to declare angrily that his glorious life depended on a piece of medically saturated "toilet paper."

Stuffing a handkerchief under her blouse against her wound, she moved into the center of the surging crowd of shoppers. She wanted to lose herself in the mindless intensity of those overweight housewives moving in and out of food stores, cursing the interminable lines. At that moment she envied their prosaic concerns — shopping, cooking, children — all of which she herself had considered lacking in purpose and meaning, compared to life in the theater and a love affair with her Anatoly. To her, life was an exciting struggle, a challenge, a defiance of the well-known Russian aversion to spontaneity. She never held to the popular notion that to be Russian was to be enamored of suffering. She wanted to live. But, more important, she had to live, if not for herself then for the legacy with which Anatoly had entrusted her. The secret she carried. Everything would be over, even her life, if they caught her.

She retraced her path back toward Red Square. Although it would be tightly guarded, she had a chance . . . first the metro, then the Byelorusskaya railway station for trains bound for the south.

As she approached the steel-framed kiosk covering the entrance to the Revolution Square metro, she noticed an inordinate number of uniformed policemen and plainclothes KGB officers checking identity cards as people entered the station. She started to walk in the opposite direction but suddenly stopped. The two KGB agents and the two uniformed soldiers were only five hundred feet away. She quickly turned around again.

Should she take a chance with the guards covering the entrance to the metro? Somehow, she would have to make certain that the soldiers wouldn't want to interrogate her.

She pulled the handkerchief from her bleeding right shoulder and for a moment felt faint, realizing that she had lost so much blood. She then sucked the handkerchief, swallowing some blood clots, holding one or two clots in her cheeks. She walked up to the group of guards, her bloody handkerchief covering part of her face.

"Identification card," ordered a policeman with a scar on his right cheek. He nodded toward his colleagues, an unspoken sign that this, finally, might be the fugitive woman. The description seemed to fit. A woman in her mid-sixties, dressed shabbily in a black cloth coat.

Stay calm, she thought as she broke into a spasm of coughing and spat large globules of blood into her handkerchief and onto the officer's khaki uniform.

The officer jumped back, startled.

"I'm sorry," she said, "I am a sick woman. I ran out of my tuberculosis medicine and am on my way to pick up some more. And stop this curse of a cough before someone else catches it."

"Catches it?" the officer asked, stepping backward. "What am I going to do with this?" he pointed to the red spot on his jacket. "Get to the hospital as quickly as possible," he said, pushing her toward the escalator. "Make sure you cover your mouth," he yelled after her. "Next time I will arrest you for being a public nuisance."

Without turning around, she raised her right arm in a sign of gratitude. She smiled to herself as the escalator descended into a black cavern. What a wonderful Russian trait — fear of illness. But the guard's grasp had reopened the wound and she could sense the blood running more quickly down her arm. She held on to the black moving belt of the escalator as she pressed her handkerchief into the wound. She could feel its ragged edges. How insignificant in size, she thought, compared to her *bogatyr's* massive body scars. Years of fighting first the czarist soldiers, then the radicals, and then dissidents within the revolutionary movement had caused enough damage to his left kidney to require surgical removal under the crudest conditions. Now that was a scar which signified aggression, initiative. Hers was merely the result of an attempt to escape.

The startling cathedral splendor of the subway station jolted her from her musings. The bright lights of five crystal chandeliers hanging from a Gothic vaulted ceiling were irritating. And the pain in her shoulder was increasing. She leaned against a wall bearing a stunning window mosaic of yellow flowers weaving throughout multicolored circles and listened intently for the rush of oncoming trains. She closed her eyes and admitted to herself that she was tired. No, not just tried. Depleted. But she knew that in spite of her fatigue, her wound, her loss of blood, she had to survive. Survive! Her life had been a continuous series of challenges, most self-imposed, but all based on the certainty that tomorrow would be better than today.

She waited for the green-line train that went to the Mayakovskaya metro station and then on to the Byelorusskaya train station. As the bright headlights of the train came closer she began to relax. Once inside, she felt relatively safe, and was able to close her eyes and rest her head against the vibrating metal siding of the subway car. Little children screamed. A cantankerous old man complained about their behavior to an indifferent mother. A round-faced, bulbous-nosed peasant woman wearing a red babushka and laden with grocery bags, stared at this disheveled eldery woman whose face was streaked with sweat and powder base and who had a dark wet spot on her right shoulder that was rapidly growing larger.

She was oblivious to all. Only the commotion of people leaving the car for Mayakovskaya station woke her up. Groggily she opened her eyes. The peasant lady with the grocery bags nodded her head and in a sympathetic tone of voice announced the station. The woman nodded her head in gratitude and looked through the connecting doors into the next subway car.

There they were! The two KGB officers were at the far end of the car, bending down before each rider to scrutinize each face. The woman looked around her car. It was nearly empty and the doors were about to close. In a few seconds the KGB officers would find her. Then she would be trapped.

She could feel the weight of exhaustion tie her down to the seat. No! Get up! she silently pleaded with herself. Get up before it is too late. Get up! Holding her right shoulder for fear that it might hemorrhage, she ran though the closing subway door and into Mayakov-skaya station, large enough to have accommodated a massive Communist Party rally during the Nazi siege of the city.

The subway doors closed before the heavyset KGB officer could squeeze through. He looked like a drowning man reaching out for help that he realized would never arrive. Natalya saw fear in his face. She had eluded his reach and now they both knew that he would pay for having let her escape.

She turned around to make certain that no one else was following her, and then looked at the signs. The unrelenting pain in her shoulder made her feel faint. She did not want to pull out the handkerchief, for fear that she'd be unable to stop the bleeding.

She looked around the cavernous structure, its drab gray walls unadorned except for pictures of Karl Marx and Lenin. Photographs of Ernest Hemingway were being sold from the souvenir kiosk. Strange, she thought, how Russian men were so obsessed with the American writer. He appealed to all those traits that Soviet and American men apparently shared: a chauvinistic hedonism based on degrading women, drinking themselves senseless, and endlessly testing their courage, strength, and "manhood."

She bought a one-way ticket to Tbilisi and without incident boarded the bright red train bound for Kharkov and Rostov-on-Don. The conductor wouldn't be checking the passengers' tickets until the train was well on its way. Only one of the four seats — the one near the window — was unoccupied in the second-class coach compartment she entered. She sat down and felt the train start to move slowly away from the platform. Yes, escape *was* possible. Kharkov. Then Rostov-on-Don. Pyatigorsk. Tbilisi. Then she would worry about the next phase of her escape route. Now she needed to rest. And the hypnotic clicks of the train passing over the rail ties felt reassuring.

She drifted into a reverie, comforted by the peace of a moment without fear. And so she didn't notice when the train, less than ten minutes out of the station, stopped abruptly. The door to her compartment was flung open and a man dressed in a red policeman's uniform shouted, "Come with me!"

Chapter Three

STANDING IN THE rear of the amphitheater, Borisov could appreciate how small the room really was. Ten rows of uncomfortable wooden pews, arranged in a semicircle around a shallow pit from which a scarred lectern arose, seemed to shrink the space. From his usual vantage point as biweekly lecturer, the arching rows of seats made the room appear to be in the process of expanding its boundaries. Today fifty doctors squeezed against one another, sitting obediently in their dirty, rumpled lab coats, some wearing white surgical caps with strings hanging down over their necks, trying valiantly to keep their heads upright and appear attentive to the words of admonition spoken by Dr. Dimitry Zoubok, chief psychiatrist. As always, to make certain the official records would be set straight, Zoubok insisted that a stenographer take notes at all grand rounds.

A haze of smoke swirled through the room, collecting

around the simply framed photographs of grim previous directors of the hospital, which hung along the upper part of the cinder-block walls.

Borisov knew that Zoubok would be discussing the rules of conduct governing patient care, trying to cover for Borisov's tardiness. He watched as this large, heavyset man, with his shock of curly gray hair, walked comfortably around the pit, addressing the doctors in a deep, relaxed voice. His last words, thrown out with almost lackadaisical slurring, would be the essence of his point. Zoubok was very much like the room — deceptive. In a strange, almost spiritual way, the fates of Borisov and his mentor had been intertwined. Before Zoubok took over the hospital, some thirty years ago, the amphitheater was an academic arena in which the doctors at the hospital congregated on an informal basis to share common experiences on the wards or to discuss an unusual medical problem. It served a pleasant, if unimportant, function. In contrast, Zoubok had allowed the physical appearance of the room to deteriorate, but had made it both the intellectual and administrative center of the hospital. Large sheets of light blue paint peeled away from the walls. Residual brown stains from years of leaking pipes decorated the ceiling. The blackboard was so faded from old chalk marks that only the new residents were foolhardy enough to use it.

Rather than make his office the core of hospital operations, Zoubok had decided to deliver his own rules of conduct, as he called them, from this amphitheater. It was perhaps the very deliberate asceticism of the room, highlighted by four large light bulbs covered only by metal lampshades hanging from the ceiling by rusted metal chain links and frayed electric wire, that allowed Zoubok to convey his fundamental message: it is from me, doctors, that you will learn the true meaning of mental illness and the proper way to treat it. Here, in the stark sanctity of this room.

Zoubok was gracefully arching his nicotine-stained fingers into the air, making some point about admissions procedure, as he worked his eyes systematically across the room, up and down each aisle, memorizing who was there, who was alert, and who was taking notes. He ignored Borisov's presence. A man in his late sixties, Zoubok looked easily ten years younger. He had thick, white, bushy eyebrows, brushed upward, and insouciant hazel eyes that settled on, then wandered away from the listener. His ruddiness was due to a fair complexion, a not too modest drinking habit, and a morning regimen of swimming in an ice-cold lake next to his house on the outskirts of Moscow. The hard lines of his Great Slav features were balanced by a rounded, soft chin, and small, slightly protruding ears. His hair was meticulously groomed.

Sitting languidly in a chair in the back row, Borisov allowed Zoubok's words to enter his consciousness, but knew he wasn't processing the information. He didn't have to. He knew the words by heart. So did everyone else in the room. But the first unspoken rule of grand rounds was never to inform Zoubok that he was repeating himself. Rule 2 dictated that any physician present must sit attentively, appearing interested and concerned, preferably scribbling Zoubok's words in a notebook which was kept in the left-hand pocket of the lab coat for instant referral. Borisov peered over the shoulders of two doctors who were sitting in front of him, one of whom was writing "bullshit" in a battered black notebook.

Zoubok's sonorous voice rang in the air. "Once again I repeat that you must become intimately familiar with the directive on civil procedures for forcible confinement."

Borisov moved his lips in silent synchronization with Zoubok's words, seeing how close he could come to mouthing the speech. Who knows, he thought, someday he might have to deliver the same lecture.

"The directive is your professional handbook. Its title spells out its purpose, and the words contained within clearly define its intent. *On Emergency Confinement of the Mentally Ill Person Who Represents a Social Danger. Issued on August 26, 1971, by the Ministry of Health in Agreement with the Procurator General.*"

Funny, thought Borisov, Zoubok always left out the end of that title — *and the KGB*. It had become an almost ritual omission. For Rule 3 dictated that no one would mention the participation of the KGB in all operations of the hospital.

Neither national security nor organizational imperatives interested Borisov. As far as he was concerned, these were incidental to his own research and clinical practice. In most civilized societies, rationalized Borisov, the police or national security apparatus must become an integral part of its systems. A political necessity to maintain social order.

Zoubok began to enumerate three conditions under which a patient could be incarcerated into a psychiatric hospital against his own will: if the patient constituted a danger to himself, to others, or was psychotic. Watching the doctors in front of him pretending to be absorbed in his recital, he wondered how different he and they were from the *muzhiks* and *kulaks* who accepted the presence of an authoritarian ruler, much like himself. Concerned, yes. Even caring. But always ready to use the concealed gauntlet. Like the czars of yesterday, Zoubok had been anointed by the system with complete authority to do whatever he wished to do within the system. At a minimum, he had to provide for the mental health of its people and contribute to the social order by treating those citizens who would choose to disrupt it.

Although Zoubok never explained the genesis of his preeminence, Borisov, like every other psychiatrist in the hospital, had pieced together a history from fragments of conversations, hearsay, and the mandatory reading of Zoubok's 350 published articles. That was Rule 4 of the grand rounds: become conversant with Zoubok's rise to power. Borisov understood Rule 4 to be the most important of all because it taught the astute learner two lessons. The first lesson was that pure, unadulterated power is obtained by "playing" with those who are also intent on garnering it. The second was that Zoubok was not above resorting to any means necessary to obtain the ends desired.

Yes, Zoubok was professionally and politically ruthless, but he had also earned an impressive medical reputation through hard work. As a student in the 1920s of the then father of Russian psychiatry, I.M. Balinsky, Zoubok first trained at the Bekhterev Institute in Leningrad where psychiatry was in the process of divorcing itself from the field of neurology. Then on to Moscow to the Korsakov School of Psychiatry, preeminent in the study of the organic basis of mental illness. In the early 1930s he made his first major intellectual contribution to Soviet psychiatry. Clearly not the only one working on the problem, Zoubok was, nevertheless, the only psychiatrist credited with integrating Pavlovian teaching into the practice of psychiatry. He had a talent that was just becoming recognized — a talent for integrating and synthesizing disparate elements of conflicting ideas. The natural agent for Marx's dialectical materialism.

Zoubok posited a theory of personality that corroborated Communist political theory and bolstered it against the advances of Freudian psychoanalytic theory and capitalism. He simply emphasized the demands of the group over the importance of the individual. It was his genuis to understand that communism would need a scientific theory of personality development that emphasized conditioning man, as did Pavlov his dogs, by stimuli within a controlled social environment.

When Borisov worried aloud that he might have missed his opportunity to make a major discovery, Zoubok reminded him that a necessary part of his "work" had to be neutralizing potentially threatening competitors.

Zoubok had not only brought Pavlov to the forefront of Soviet psychiatry, but he had made certain that Freudian psychoanalysis would be considered "simplistic," "idealistic," and "self-indulgent." His first articles had attacked Freud's unconscious determinism as arbitrary and unscientific, a Western European indulgence distracting the Russians from the more important problems of mental health prophylaxis, epidemiology, and public health.

Zoubok also had made certain that he was appropriately appreciated by both the psychiatric community and the politicians in the Kremlin. Borisov needed, according to Zoubok, to be more "personally accountable." More willing to trade favors. It wasn't, as they both knew, that Borisov was naïve. He wasn't. Otherwise he could not have reached the professional prominence he had as director of Inpatient Services. It was simply that Borisov was not "sufficiently" political. Zoubok, with great pride, explained one evening over several shots of schnapps, that early in his career he had mapped out a strategy to accumulate power that was reflected in increasingly more important committee and conference assignments: section chief of the Committee on Organic Diseases at four Congresses of Russian Psychiatrists; director of the Executive Committee of the sections for Nervous and Mental Illnesses at three Congresses of Russian Physicians; opening speaker and organizer of four All-Russian Conferences of Psychiatrists and Neuropathologists. Twenty years before, he had appointed the chief psychiatrists for three of the four areas. All were still alive, productive, and treated him as their benefactor. Only forensic psychiatry remained beyond his immediate range. The directorship of the infamous Serbsky Institute and the other "special" psychiatric hospitals was not "his" appointment. Perhaps this one fact, more than any other, allowed Borisov to trust Zoubok.

The Serbsky Institute, organized in the 1920s as the

principal center for examination and research in forensic psychiatry, was under the direct supervision of the
minister of health with the collegial assistance of the
director of the KGB. It was the hospital where the most
dangerous mentally ill patients were sent for evaluation
and treatment, and a KGB prison for political
dissidents.

Borisov felt relieved as he heard Zoubok's voice grow
louder, the unmistakable sign that he was about to conclude. "The directive states specifically," Zoubok continued, "that the patient must demonstrate symptoms
of mental disturbance, either hallucinations, illusions,
delusions, or a distinct pattern of chronic deterioration
in behavior for admission to this hospital."

Borisov smiled as he thought about Rule 6: the more
evident the demonstration of mental symptoms, the less
appropriate the patient becomes for admission to the inpatient research unit. Increasingly, Zoubok encouraged
Borisov to admit schizophrenic patients who did not appear disturbed or agitated, in order to study the
disease's many manifestations.

But it was Rule 7 that made these biweekly grand
rounds bearable and working in the hospital enjoyable:
the cherished Russian tradition of *vranyo* — lies. Those
doctors sitting attentively in the amphitheater had all
played out the time-honored charade, practiced for centuries between the serf and the landed gentry, the repentant sinner and the priest, the patient and the doctor, the
Soviet citizen and the *apparatchik*, the *apparatchik* and
the senior Soviet official. *Vranyo*, a word that allowed
Borisov to accept the maddening discrepancies of the
psychiatric system without despair. Zoubok could say
whatever he wanted, in whatever manner — ordering,
dictating, pontificating, demanding, imploring, revealing. And, in turn, Borisov would ostensibly agree with
Zoubok in order to avoid any further time-wasting
discussions; and, then, he, Borisov, would continue to

do whatever it was he had initially intended to do. *Vranyo* was simply a tradition of allowing the authority to lie without losing face.

Zoubok finished his lecture and invited Borisov to the lectern. Borisov walked slowly down the steps toward the stage. Along the way he nodded toward Dr. Ternowsky and Dr. Tsarev. He saw Zeleneyev smile, assuring him that everything was in place.

Moving slowly, Borisov made certain not to lose eye contact with anyone in the audience. When he reached center stage, he continued walking about in a circle, measuring each step, taking advantage of his colleagues' heightened interest in his presentation. He could feel the eagerness mount. Rule 8 of the grand rounds said that doctors, like any audience, would rather be entertained than instructed.

"Today I would like to address a basic question that has plagued Russian psychiatry for thirty years, since our good Dr. Zoubok first described the problem." Borisov paused to add emphasis to his statement and glanced at Zoubok.

"How can we, as scientists and clinicians, prove scientifically the existence of sluggish schizophrenia? For too many years we have been unfairly subjected to the criticism of our colleagues in the West who claim that sluggish schizophrenia does not exist and has been 'discovered' by us as an excuse to incarcerate in a psychiatric institute dissidents who are perfectly well. As you all know, the World Psychiatric Society in 1977 in Hawaii accepted the majority of our classifications for schizophrenia, developed by Dr. Zoubok. Dr. Block, president of the American Psychiatric Association, agreed that 'continuous' schizophrenia is easily diagnosed by its prevalent symptoms: a distortion of reality, overflow of sensory stimuli, auditory or visual hallucinations, delusions of grandeur and persecution. A disease with a progressively downhill course, without remissions, resulting in a vegetablelike, catatonic patient, physically, intellectually, and emotionally disorganized."

"Leading to the physical, intellectual, and emotional collapse of us good doctors," shouted Ternowsky, good naturedly.

The audience laughed. Ternowsky had hit a responsive chord. Only Zoubok was not amused. He didn't like Ternowsky. He rarely laughed at Ternowsky's jokes. He reminded Zoubok of an uncouth Russian peasant. Big, brawny, round faced, doe-eyed — almost Oriental-looking — his calloused hands always red and chafed. Ternowsky represented much too much of the past Zoubok had left behind in a small village fifty miles north of Leningrad. Ternowsky spoiled the image of the modern Soviet psychiatrist — lean, elegant, graceful in manner and speech. In short, Borisov.

Thank goodness the Soviets were appreciative of Zoubok's efforts. Anatoly Sukhumi, general secretary of the Communist Party, had personally commended him for his "extraordinary insights and contributions to the preventive mental health care of the Soviet system," specifically his contribution to the diagnosis of sluggish schizophrenia. The zenith of his professional and political career. But, the true genius of his findings, as everyone in the Politburo and KGB had recognized instantaneously, was that sluggish schizophrenia occurred in seemingly normal people, who were disgruntled with the Soviet system and attacked it through personal letters to friends, the *samizdat* (the underground press), or in public demonstrations. Zoubok's findings were, as even the West had realized, a formidable tool for the political system.

The American Psychiatric Association forced the World Psychiatric Society to denounce the diagnosis at the meetings in Hawaii in 1977. Eight years later, there still remained the need for a scientific, indisputable test for the diagnosis of sluggish schizophrenia. With such a test, Zoubok would be personally and professionally exonerated. The leaders of the Soviet Union could respond with impunity to world pressure.

Zoubok leaned his head against the back of his chair, momentarily savoring the nostalgia of Borisov's account of the Hawaii meetings and the victory that he, Zoubok, had single-handedly wrested from the worldwide condemnation of his system. Zoubok was particularly proud of the fact that he had persuaded the Americans to accept certain aspects of his system. And now, Borisov could broaden the scope of that acceptance.

"The World Psychiatric Society also accepted our category of periodic schizophrenia. Here, the constellation of symptoms occurs in discrete episodes of unusual behavior, after which the patient appears completely normal. In this form, there is no evidence of a gradual deterioration of affect or mental acuity."

Borisov paused to see if he had lost any of the doctors to boredom. Most were expecting an electrifying announcement. Good, he thought. They all sat straight on their benches, glancing in turn at Zoubok and then Tsarev.

"The third type of schizophrenia is the 'shiftlike form' where, like the periodic form, there are acute episodes of deteriorating behavior and thinking. But . . ." — he paused, then clapped loudly — "but unlike the periodic form, the shiftlike form becomes progressively worse. Each time the patient emerges from his bout of symptoms with increased deterioration of his mental faculties. Eventually there is no chance for remission or improvement. No matter what we do."

Dr. Tsarev raised his hand to interrupt Borisov. Tsarev was in his mid-fifties, wisps of gray hair falling over piercing gray eyes. His bifocal steel-rimmed glasses sat below the bridge of his nose. His disheveled appearance was a calculated affectation. In both his personal life and in his laboratory he was an incredibly meticulous, thorough man who would brook no sloppiness. He was still exploring new applications of the once fashionable Filatov's tissue therapy for the treatment of mental illness. The son of a famous clinical pathologist, Tsarev had always been fascinated by the use of tissue cells prepared in the laboratory for the treatment of various physical and mental disorders. The staff, including Borisov, had learned to tolerate the role of distracted scientist Tsarev felt compelled to play.

Zoubok turned to Tsarev and nodded his head in quiet encouragement. Tsarev was useful. He could give Borisov a difficult time. He still felt slighted that he had lost out to Borisov four years ago as director of Inpatient Services.

Tsarev, like Borisov, knew he was being used by Zoubok but he played along. Partly because he had no choice. Partly because he still held out the hope that if Borisov were promoted he would have a chance to become director of Inpatient Services.

Borisov ignored Tsarev's attempt to interrupt him, concerned that if called upon Tsarev would spend twenty minutes quoting from an esoteric article in an outdated issue of the *Karsakov Journal of Neuropathology and Psychiatry*.

"And within each of these categories of schizophrenia," continued Borisov, eager to finish, "there is a subcategory of abnormality which, as you know, we call 'sluggish' schizophrenia. To the untrained eye it remains the most difficult mental illness to correctly diagnose, evaluate, and treat. Primarily because the patient appears so normal." Borisov motioned to Zeleneyev, indicating that he was ready.

"I will now present a patient, one Vladimir Nekipelov, who was brought to this hospital several weeks ago by our distinguished colleagues in the KGB." A smatter of snickering broke out in the audience.

Zoubok scowled, angered by the patronizing, sarcastic tone of Borisov's voice. He had warned Borisov about these innuendoes. Comments like "our distinguished colleagues" or the one he had made last month, "the KGB astutely observed that the paranoid patient was suspicious," or the proposal he'd made the month before that the KGB receive a special certificate licensing them to treat patients, would not help Borisov's career. Borisov was a good Communist; he was a nominal member of the Communist Party but consistently argued that he was "not political by nature." Yet Zoubok felt that his political cynicism would one day get Borisov into trouble. Didn't he realize that at every grand rounds there was at least one person who informed the KGB daily of "occurrences" at the hospital? The KGB was more than willing to build a file on anyone who had been mentioned or cross-referenced. Borisov's only response to Zoubok's warnings was a smile accompanied by a shrug. The problem had continued long enough for Zoubok to take a measure of self-protection. He had already started to accumulate his own file of anecdotal material on Borisov. One never knew how handy that might be in the future.

Borisov paused to look at Zoubok, who seemed to be sneering, and continued to present the patient's history.

". . . was brought to us six weeks ago for violation of Article Seventy of the 1961 Russian Soviet Federated Socialist Republic Criminal Code — vagrancy, panhandling, and hooliganism. This patient demonstrates the characteristics of a well-defined case of sluggish schizophrenia — including the classical duo of a demonstrated abnormality of rational thinking accompanied by a lifestyle that has progressively deteriorated over twenty years."

He took a deep breath before stating the reason for today's excitement. "I think that I have discovered a scientific test that can prove the existence of sluggish schizophrenia."

There were gasps of surprise from the doctors, and subdued words of encouragement. Angered that he had not been kept apprised of the recent developments of Borisov's research, Zoubok's eyes widened and his face turned crimson. But he could not help admiring his protégé. Borisov was ambitious and calculating, but above all brilliant.

Beckoning the awaiting orderlies, Borisov turned and acknowledged a patient seated in a wheelchair. The man was pale, unshaven, disheveled, and easily ten years older than his alleged age of thirty-five.

"This is Vladimir Nekipelov, who was found wandering about Dzerzhinsky Square in front of the KGB headquarters at Lubyanka Prison."

Nekipelov gazed around the room nervously. He had never seen so many doctors in one room. Something was expected of him. As Dr. Borisov had explained, he was simply to act natural, tell the good doctors exactly what had happened to him, say a few things about his past life, perhaps add one or two phrases about why he thought he was not successful — and allow Dr. Borisov to do the rest. He liked Dr. Borisov. In the beginning he had been frightened of him. But Dr. Borisov had always acted kindly toward him. Especially since that day the doctor had looked disheveled, apparently up all night working in his laboratory. He had come to Nekipelov's ward for one "final try," as if sentencing Nekipelov to a fate worse than death. But the doctor had not wanted him to do anything except what he had been doing all along — lie still in his bed or sit up straight in his chair while Dr. Borisov fastened a rubber band around his head to which were attached a series of different colored wires (red, green, yellow, and blue). All of the wires led into a funny-looking machine that Dr. Borisov had frequently wheeled into the room. The machine's thin metal fingers squirted ink onto a red-lined moving page, making wavy lines. Nekipelov remembered that Sunday well because, after having examined the paper carefully, Dr. Borisov's tired faced broke out into a broad smile. So ecstatic was Dr. Borisov that for the first time in their relationship his disconcerting official coolness suddenly disappeared and he became quite informal, visiting Nekipelov sometimes twice a day. Dr. Borisov had told him to keep the experiments with the EEG machine strictly confidential. No one had ever before taken him into their confidence. It made him feel very, very important. He wasn't like the other patients anymore. There was something very different and special about him.

"Why did you stand in front of KGB headquarters?"

"I was hungry and cold," Nekipelov answered in a cracking, dry voice.

Dr. Ternowsky, seated in the rear of the room, shouted, "Alexsandrovitch, since when have we become a foundling home for orphans and beggars?"

Some of the doctors in the room snickered. Zoubok turned around and glanced angrily at Ternowsky, who had gone too far. The patient, after all, was entitled to respect.

"I apologize, my colleagues," Ternowsky said quickly, in response to Zoubok's stern look. If Borisov had not frequently intervened on his behalf when he became facetious, Zoubok would long ago have sent him back to the hospital in which Borisov had found him. They had met five years ago, during Borisov's two-week visit as distinguished attendant at the Kalinovka Central Ryon Hospital, in the northern part of the Ukraine, the area in which Ternowsky had grown up. At that time, Ternowsky was in charge of recruiting consultants from Moscow, Leningrad, and Tbilisi to develop a fifty-bed inpatient psychiatric unit. So engrossed was Borisov in everything from the architectural layout to recruiting the psychiatrists, developing new admissions policy, and creating new therapeutic programs, that Zoubok had to telex him from Moscow to return to Kashchenko or stand to lose his position as director of Inpatient Services. In those two weeks, Borisov and Ternowsky had become friends, taking hikes through the lush green forests of the Carpathian Mountains, ambling aimlessly through golden fields of wheat, and discussing everything from the future of Soviet psychiatry to the more important concerns of love. Ternowsky had opened his heart to Borisov and spoken about the different loves in his life — the farmgirls, the shop maids, the nurses, and, finally, his wife, a *feldsher*. From time to time, he admitted to Borisov, he would fool around. But his wife understood. Borisov was more reticent about his own ex-wife.

Ternowsky was impressed by Borisov's obsession with his position at Kashchenko Hospital and the need to solidify it through more and better clinical research. He remembered the day that Borisov turned toward him in a farm field covered with cow manure and bright yellow daffodils, and spoke the words that changed his life. "Andreivitch, you are a good man and a good doctor. If you stay here you will never be appreciated. Come with me to Moscow. I promise you a continuous, stimulating challenge. It will never be professionally boring. And, we can nourish our friendship." Without pausing, Ternowsky had grabbed Borisov in a bear hug.

Yet Zoubok was not pleased by his arrival. Ternowsky could never decide whether it was a personal prejudice against Ukrainians, or peasants, or both. In return, Ternowsky never liked this somber, pretentious Great Slav who dominated his fiefdom with a fist of steel. He felt awkward and insecure in Zoubok's presence, and did his best to avoid any confrontation that might lose him his job at the hospital. Now, after five years in the claustrophobia of Moscow, he had decided to return to the Kalinovka Central Ryon Hospital as chief of the Psychiatric Division.

Yes, he thought as he listened, Borisov has taught me the importance of making professional advancement one's number-one priority. He had learned to enjoy the intellectual stimulation of a forward-looking research center. He had learned to appreciate the prestige of being a clinical attendant at Zoubok's Kashchenko Hospital. And now it might mean double his seven hundred rubles per month salary upon returning to Kalinovka. Being able to buy his own house and possibly a little *dacha* high in the mountains, where once again Borisov and he might walk and discuss life. But that was a dream for the future. He would put in two more years of quality medicine at Kashchenko and then ask for a letter of recommendation from Zoubok. And he knew with a clear sense of inevitability that Zoubok would be pleased to write him such a letter. Zoubok would understand it to be in his own self-interest, his desire to extend his influence beyond the borders of his hospital.

Borisov's words came filtering through his ruminations. Nodding toward Ternowsky, Borisov continued in a deferential tone of voice, "In many ways, Dr. Ternowsky is quite correct. We psychiatrists should be able to distinguish between those patients who are truly ill and those souls who find their lives a series of unfortunate losses — of jobs, friends, opportunities, and self-esteem."

"Self-esteem? Alexsandrovitch," Zoubok interrupted in a startled voice. "What do we have here, a disciple of Freudian metaphysics?"

Borisov turned toward Nekipelov and proceeded with his questioning, determined to choose his words more carefully. Self-esteem. He should have known better. That concept had long ago been translated by Zoubok into Pavlovian operational terms. Positive and negative stimuli. Inhibition and stimulation of the nervous system. Not self-esteem.

"Why were you hungry and cold? Didn't you realize that the KGB would pick you up?"

"Why was I hungry? Because I hadn't eaten in a week," Nekipelov replied with a quizzical expression on his face.

"But why didn't you eat? We have soup kitchens all around the city. You could have gotten some bread and soup."

"Dr. Borisov, please. I, too, have my pride."

Borisov smiled. "Are you saying that you didn't want a handout? Then why were you panhandling? You seem to find the soup kitchens more offensive than begging."

"That is simple, doctor. Panhandling allows me to use my own skills. At the soup kitchen, I simply ask and they give."

Again, snickering broke out in the audience. Was he losing them? Borisov's case for sluggish schizophrenia was not convincing.

"Then why did you go to KGB headquarters? Certainly you didn't expect them to feed you?"

"Why not? That afternoon was very unproductive. I was only able to get three kopeks. You can't buy even a slice of bread for three kopeks. At KGB headquarters I would at least have someone to talk to. I had nothing to be afraid of. I had committed no crime. I knew no state secrets. I had no reason to fear them. And they certainly had no reason to fear me."

"Are you sorry now that you went there?"

"No, doctor. They brought me here. And you and everyone else at this hospital have been very nice to me."

"Tell me a little about your past. What happened to you over the years that forced you to end up here?"

Nekipelov's delivery sounded practiced. "I think all of my problems — my drinking, my wandering, my begging, began ten years ago when I married a bitch." He paused, watching several of the doctors in the front row smile and nod in agreement.

"She wanted me to become someone — make more money, buy more things. I worked hard just like she wanted. But soon I began drinking. I started as a machinist in a turbine factory. Then I became a carpenter. I was good at both. But each time I got a new job I realized I didn't want to go home. I drank more and worked less."

"How many jobs have you held?"

"I was a truck driver, street cleaner . . ."

"Do you have any desire at present to become anything besides a drifter?"

Nekipelov turned toward Borisov with hurt in his eyes. "Why? What's so wrong with what I am? At least I'm trying to do something on my own . . . for myself. If I get into trouble, the state will be there, I know."

Without looking at Zoubok, Borisov knew that his expression now must be intolerably smug, that he must be inordinately pleased that Borisov was having a hard time demonstrating that this patient was schizophrenic, let alone a sluggish schizophrenic. But, of course, that was the very problem! Sluggish schizophrenics frequently looked, sounded, and acted normal. It was their very appearance of normalcy that made them problematic. Yet the first time he saw Nekipelov, Borisov had sensed that intangible "quality" that Zoubok had first described in his now classic paper, "The Nosology of Schizophrenia," written in 1958. It was during Borisov's sixth and final year at the Medical School of Moscow University, where he was obligated to follow ninety-six hours of psychiatric lectures with a two-week clinical clerkship at Kashchenko Hospital, that he became aware of sluggish schizophrenia, for him the most exciting variety. And he liked the unusual. The unique. The difficult. In all honesty, he was not a creative researcher; Tsarev was far more original. Nor was he one to defy traditional concepts and assumptions. He had always done application research. During his three-year psychiatry residency at Kashchenko Hospital he had developed a new therapeutic modality called "cyclic prolonged sleep." The accepted procedure called for prolonged sleep — twenty-two hours daily — for seven to eleven days. Borisov had modified the plan to one forty-eight-hour period of sleep, interspersed with a forty-eight-hour pause, the pattern to be repeated five to six times. Borisov believed that the sleep state he had designed was more effective in eliminating the noxious agent, whether infection, toxicosis, or psychic trauma, that precipitated the schizophrenia. Zoubok had been impressed with his experiment, had pronounced it "appropriately innovative, respectful to the basic tenets of sleep therapy, and scientifically sound," and invited him to stay on at the hospital and do two years of *Aspirantura*, a clinical fellowship. During this period Borisov became interested in Zoubok's classification of sluggish schizophrenia. At that time the scientific community was having difficulty deciding what types of organic therapies would work. It didn't require much of an innovative leap for Borisov to go from sleep therapy to investigating the use of insulin coma. Systematically, he had gone through the barbiturates, carbon dioxide, chloral hydrate, and alcohol, until he finally came to insulin.

After some reflection, and discussions with his colleagues, Borisov decided to remain at the hospital after his two-year *Aspirantura*. He moved up quickly from instructor to assistant professor to associate professor, to full professor, and then to the highly prized clinical directorship of the Inpatient Service, all the while studying Zoubok's favorite problem — sluggish schizophrenia.

Over the past six weeks, Borisov decided that he had finally found a sluggish schizophrenic who should be tested on a specially modified EEG machine. Nekipelov had been that patient. The results had been no less than remarkable — slow, irregular wave patterns on the frontal cranial leads, a schizophrenic EEG reading on a sluggish schizophrenic. He then wanted to present the clinical results at grand rounds without first informing Zoubok of his conclusions. It would be the right occasion to place his own imprimatur on his findings and start to break away from Zoubok's control.

"Do you know what it means when someone says 'People who live in glass houses shouldn't throw stones'?"

Nekipelov was eager to prove his sanity. "Of course, of course. It means that the glass will break."

"Thank you." Borisov turned toward his colleagues. "Is there any doubt in anyone's mind that this is a case of sluggish schizophrenia?"

The doctors were silent.

"What we see is a man who appears lucid and sounds nonpsychotic. But it is that very appearance of normalcy that makes the diagnosis of sluggish schizophrenia difficult. Here is a man who is unwilling and unable to accept the ordinary responsibilities of everyday living, a man who abandons his wife, his family, numerous jobs, and who finds comfort and solace only through the bottle. His life is a series of contradictions between wanting to take care of himself and allowing the state to take care of him." Borisov paused and smiled, "With all due respect, one must question the basic judgment of any citizen who presents himself voluntarily to the KGB for food and lodging."

"Why?" asked Tsarev, restless in his seat, anxious to discredit what he already sensed might be a significant discovery. "He told you quite clearly that he had no reason to fear the KGB; and, they had no reason to want him. It's simply a matter of different perspective. Not necessarily schizophrenic."

Borisov listened attentively. There was nothing else he could do. Theirs was a long-standing competition. Tsarev had a point. But Tsarev did not care whether this patient was schizophrenic or sociopathic. He was simply reaffirming his self-anointed title of true scientist — by questioning and doubting.

"If you recall the patient's interpretation of the proverb, Dr. Tsarev, you will note a hallmark of schizophrenia — the concrete interpretation of proverbs."

"My God!" replied Tsarev contemptuously. "You mean every time someone interprets some fairy tale differently from you, he is automatically schizophrenic? Nonsense!"

Borisov felt the rush of adrenaline pump through his body, but had to maintain his composure else Zoubok would consider him volatile, immature, and unable to handle a simple professional disagreement. Borisov would also be admitting publicly to the existence of rivalry.

Tsarev stood up, adjusted his lab coat, and walked toward the stage. Rule 10 of the grand rounds allowed any physician to confront the lecturer face-to-face about any point of disagreement. On the surface, the rule appeared relatively innocuous. In fact, it had been invoked less than a dozen times in five years. Entering the "arena," as the area around the podium was affectionately known, was a clear statement of defiance. A test of intellectual prowess. It was one of the few places of psychiatry where one could take a risk.

Tsarev introduced himself to Nekipelov, then turned toward Borisov. "May I?" he asked in a cold, perfunctory tone.

"Yes, of course," replied Borisov. He had no choice.

"Mr. Nekipelov, do you know what today is?" Tsarev was solicitous as he hovered over the wheelchair.

"Is there a holiday today? Was I supposed to know there was a holiday?" Nekipelov was bewildered by the question.

"No, don't worry, Mr. Nekipelov." Borisov patted his arm in a reassuring manner. "Dr. Tsarev wants to know if you understand where it is that you are. He's trying to find out if you have some problem with your memory."

"You know, Dr. Borisov, I don't have any problems with my memory."

"Then tell Dr. Tsarev what day of the year it is."

"I never know the days. I never need to know what day it is." Nekipelov looked at the audience, thinking that the best course to take was to appeal to their compassion. "I move around the city one day at one corner, another day at another corner. It never really matters which day I am at a particular corner. On Monday I might be in front of the Metropole Hotel on Number one Marx Prospekt. On Tuesday, Gorky Street. Understand, I am a man of no consequence to anyone. I don't have meetings or appointments on days which I should remember."

"Do you know where you are? And who I am?"

"Of course," replied Nekipelov proudly, "that's obvious. I am here."

Borisov suppressed a smile. Good work, Nekipelov. Give that son-of-a-bitch a run for his money.

"But where is 'here,' Mr. Nekipelov?"

"Here is here. Not over there." Nekipelov pointed to the audience.

"Not bad for a Russian education," Ternowsky shouted.

Without turning his head, Zoubok exclaimed, "For the first time in your life, Dr. Ternowsky, you might be right."

The entire audience laughed. Except Zoubok, who rarely laughed at his own jokes, and Tsarev, who felt increasingly frustrated. Perhaps this man's obstinacy *was* a sign of some underlying schizophrenic process.

"Did you ever hear any voice that instructed you to hurt yourself?"

"You mean like commit suicide?"

"Yes. You understand, don't you?"

"There were times when I felt I could no longer go on. Sometimes on a street corner, cold and hungry, I would feel terribly humiliated and ashamed that I had accomplished nothing in my life. Then I would say to myself, 'Vladimir, why don't you just quietly walk across the street against traffic. The impact is fast and hard. And no one will miss you.' "

"Well what stopped you?"

"Nothing really. Nothing. Only the possibility of thinking about it some other time."

"You mean you have thought about suicide on a number of occasions?"

"Of course . . . of course. It's an enjoyable game when I am alone and hungry. But, good doctor, for all the times that I may have thought about it, I never once attempted to do it. Not once. And I wouldn't," Nekipelov added with determination.

"Mr. Nekipelov," Borisov interrupted, "do you think other people might have it out for you? Try to harm you in any way?"

"Oh no, Dr. Borisov. You know that I can't answer that question."

"Why not?" Tsarev was piqued by the evasive response.

"Dr. Borisov knows. You have to ask him. I can't tell."

"May I share it with the doctors in this auditorium?" Borisov asked, knowing what Nekipelov would answer.

"Oh, you are very kind, Dr. Borisov, but I cannot have you do that."

He had promised to maintain the confidentiality of the doctor-patient relationship, so Borisov remained silent. Tsarev deserved a hard time, he thought, even though his questioning was becoming counterproductive. Borisov's presentation with the EEG was waiting. But first he had to make certain there would be no doubt in the audience that beneath Nekipelov's amiable facade was a mind that was having serious problems accommodating to reality.

"Mr. Nekipelov, tell Dr. Tsarev what you think the proverb means when we say 'Don't cry over spilled milk.' "

"Spilled milk? You shouldn't spill milk — it's not good for the tablecloth and your clothing. And of course, you won't have any more milk to drink."

Tsarev turned toward the doctors in the audience. "The literal interpretation of proverbs in itself is not a sign of schizophrenia. We need more clinical and objective evidence that Mr. Nekipelov is first a schizophrenic and secondly a sluggish schizophrenic. We don't have any results on his T-lymphocyte agglutination test — whether it was positive or negative."

"Jews . . ." blurted Nekipelov.

Tsarev looked startled. "Jews . . . what about Jews?"

"Jews. You asked me if there was anyone who had it out for me. Well, I know it's not very nice to say. And, Dr. Borisov kept his word that he wouldn't say out loud what I told him in private. But, I am pretty certain that almost every one of my bosses who had fired me was Jewish."

"How did you know?" Goddamn, thought Tsarev, I've been set up. Now the patient is becoming paranoid.

"I can tell a Jew. They are usually the ones running the place. Almost every one of them, except for one foreman, had blond hair. The rest of them have dark hair, dark eyes, and as everyone knows — big noses. But, you have to understand," interjected Nekipelov apologetically, "I don't personally dislike them. They are very smart. And some of them can be very kind. But they are after me. I have never been successful working for them."

Nekipelov was obviously uncomfortable. He stood up and started walking around Borisov in smaller and smaller circles.

Borisov turned toward Tsarev. "What do you make

of this psychomotor perseveration? Doesn't it denote some form of mental restlessness?''

"Wrong interpretation of proverbs and walking around in circles does not denote schizophrenia," Tsarev replied provocatively.

"And the paranoid delusion of persecution by Jews. What do you make of that?''

Dr. Zeleneyev raised his hand and spoke, "Dr. Borisov, let us assume that the majority of us believe the patient is a sluggish schizophrenic. How do you prove it scientifically?''

"Very good question, Dr. Zeleneyev," shouted Ternowsky from the back of the room. "Even you can't provide a definitive test for sluggish schizophrenia, Dr. Magician. You're not addressing medical students. Everyone here knows that the diagnosis of sluggish schizophrenia is stricly subjective. There are no blood tests. No x-rays. No tests that definitively prove the presence of sluggish schizophrenia. Isn't that right, Dr. Zoubok?''

Zoubok nodded his head in agreement. He knew that the doctors wanted him to intervene, to make some definitive statement about whether the patient was or was not a sluggish schizophrenic. But he would allow Borisov to continue. Borisov's presentation would be of value to him in the near future, of that he was now sure. Borisov may have inadvertently presented the perfect solution to an ugly political problem that had been plaguing him.

With the assistance of two orderlies, Borisov sat Nekipelov down in the wheelchair, strapped a one-inch rubber band around his head from which several multicolored wires dangled, and attached them to a portable EEG machine which had been wheeled into the amphitheater.

Obviously frightened, Nekipelov reached up to grab

Borisov's hand, "Please, doctor, this won't hurt me, will it? I haven't done anything wrong. All I want is a place where I can eat and sleep."

"Don't worry," Mr. Nekipelov. This procedure is absolutely painless. No one will do anything to hurt you."

"Thank you. Thank you." Nekipelov kissed Borisov's hand in gratitude.

After several minutes of testing with the EEG, Borisov ripped off from the machine a piece of paper on which wavelike patterns had been scratched by elongated metal fingers. He looked toward Zoubok first, and then to the audience.

"For many years, psychiatrists around the world have felt that the EEG is too crude a method to record brain wave patterns distinctive to schizophrenia. But Dr. Zoubok, in his already classic studies, hypothesized that there were distinctive high-voltage irregular slow-waves on the cranial leads that would indicate an unusual volume and quality of activity occurring in schizophrenia." Raising the paper in the air, and then passing it around among the doctors in the audience, Borisov announced his *coup de grace,* "As you can see, those same wave patterns are found in this man, who is suffering from sluggish schizophrenia."

The audience remained silent. Only the sound of shuffling papers could be heard.

"Why?" Zeleneyev asked, eager to make certain that Borisov had not simply uncovered some electrical artifact.

"Because"— Borisov's response was slow and deliberately modulated —"the EEG patterns have never before remained consistently the same in the sluggish schizophrenic under induced hyperventilation, photic stimulation, or carotid pressure."

Zoubok could no longer constrain himself. Political expediency gave way to jealousy — and disappointment. He had expected to be kept informed of Borisov's research findings. Perhaps his protégé was becoming ungrateful. He would have to teach him a lesson.

"Dr. Borisov, we are all very pleased to be sharing your recent discovery with you. But, we must remember the old Russian proverb that warns us that one swallow does not make a spring. Similarly, one EEG reading does not conclude a diagnosis, and certainly does not constitute a diagnosis."

The room became silent.

"I presume that in addition to your EEG studies, your *preliminary* studies, you were able to get corroborative evidence from hyperventilation studies which show a paroxysmal series of slow activity?"

"Well . . . I haven't yet had the time . . ."

Zoubok interrupted in a tone clearly intended to humiliate. "I know in your careful preparation of the case that you have completed photic stimulation of the brain with a strobe light. That you have evidenced the characteristic abnormal response of bilateral synchronous or focal paroxysmal spike-and-slow-wave patterns that would corroborate your diagnosis of schizophrenia."

Borisov was speechless. There was nothing he could do now. He had brought this envious tirade on himself. He had made one mistake by not informing Zoubok of the degree to which he was coming close to making a significant clinical breakthrough. He had made a second by allowing his own vanity to prevail over meticulous checking and rechecking before bringing his findings to grand rounds.

Zoubok left his chair, whispered something to a doctor seated next to him, walked determinedly toward the patient and forced him into an upright position in the wheelchair. He reattached the rubber band with the dangling wires around Nekipelov's head, turned on the machine, and placed his right hand firmly around

Nekipelov's right carotid artery. He began to squeeze it with the force of a man intent on killing.

Nekipelov struggled, trying desperately to pry Zoubok's hand from his throat. "Please God! Please God! Help me!" He looked frantically to Borisov, who stood by helplessly. Zoubok would extract his vengeance from poor Nekipelov.

"Why do you look so concerned, Dr. Borisov? Don't you think a carotid compression is required in a patient with a history of vagrancy, hooliganism, and total irresponsibility?"

"I know that with a history of vagrancy and sociopathy one is required," Borisov chose his words carefully, "to determine if there is a carotid occlusion, a mechanical defect in the internal carotid artery which might be contributing to such antinormal behavior."

Zoubok realized that was the first time that Borisov had used the word *normal* in referring to societal pressure. He had always avoided the concepts of "antisociety" or "nonadaptive" because these were terms that were judgmental, prejudicial, lending themselves too easily to political discussion of what constituted appropriate behavior.

"Also, Dr. Borisov, if we look at the printout, I believe we will see something quite interesting." Zoubok released Nekipelov's neck and Borisov handed Zoubok the paper from the machine. As Zoubok reviewed the machine's printout, Borisov broke open a vial of ammonia and placed it under Nekipelov's nose.

Revived, the patient pleaded to be allowed to leave the room.

"I understand your fears," Borisov was reassuring. "But as a result of these tests we will know much more about you. The better to help you." Of that he was certain. The tests that he and Zoubok were performing were absolutely necessary — not only from a theoretical point of view but also from a therapeutic perspective.

They would allow him to continue his research on the organic therapies of sluggish schizophrenia with relative impunity.

"Look at the tracings with the compression of the carotid. Slow waves in leads one and two. What does that tell you?" Zoubok asked Borisov.

"That there is a possibility of a psychiatric disease entity other than sluggish schizophrenia," shouted Tsarev from the audience, brimming with confidence.

"Thank you, Dr. Tsarev. And there is one more test that we can conduct to make certain that we were not dealing with some other disease."

The doctor to whom Zoubok had previously whispered brought him a large syringe filled with dark fluid.

When Nekipelov saw it his mouth opened, but no sounds emerged. His throat tightened and his arm rushed with pain as the sudden thrust of a metal needle, easily three inches long, insinuated its way up his forearm. Then came the sudden burning sensation. Nekipelov screamed.

Zoubok turned his back on both Borisov and his patient and addressed the audience. "What you are about to see will confirm to you both by clinical observation and EEG reading whether or not we have sluggish schizophrenia, or some other psychiatric disease."

Without warning, Nekipelov slipped off his chair onto the floor, smashing his head as he fell. As the blood trickled down his face from the open wound, his body contorted on the floor, arms flailing in circles, legs kicking up and down, his tongue pierced by his teeth.

Zoubok walked calmly about the room, seemingly unconcerned about the patient's safety during the convulsive seizure. He eyed his audience coldly, daring them to challenge either his methods or his reasoning. No one spoke. He turned toward Borisov and asked the inevitable question. "What do you think?"

Borisov was bending down, wiping away the blood

from Nekipelov's face. He felt this patient's chest straining for air. It reminded him of the desperate sounds of the woman he had earlier treated with insulin — hissing a sibilant cry for help, gasping for the last molecules of air. The rhythm of Nekipelov's breathing became more labored but less functional. His face was turning blue. His eyes began to water, and glaze over. Respiratory distress. In a few seconds — death.

Reflexively, Borisov reached into Nekipelov's mouth and pulled his tongue from the back of his throat. Immediately he could hear and feel the sounds of relief as air rushed back into Nekipelov's chest. A smiling Zoubok held the EEG reading for Borisov to read. "Schizophrenic. Sluggish schizophrenic," he repeated, in a voice smoldering with repressed anger. "Very good, Dr. Borisov. Very good. You have an interesting find there. Keep experimenting."

Chapter Four

THE LATE AFTERNOON light pierced the half-painted windows of the Organic Therapy Unit. The patient Vladimir Nekipelov was agitated. He moved from side to side, trying to find a position where he could inhale what he considered an adequate amount of oxygen. His nostrils flared, his mouth was agape, and he flailed his chest as if practicing some religious ritual of self-flagellation. He detected a flicker of motion near the window, where the light of the window broke into the closed shutters. Yes, there was someone there. Someone who wanted to stop him from breathing.

"I see you," he shouted, oblivious to the patients around him who were too submerged within different phases of coma to make any sense of his rantings.

"No, I won't let you do that to me," he screamed, certain now that Dr. Zoubok was about to strangle him again.

He raised himself and looked around. He had to get

out of bed immediately. Otherwise, he would die lying helplessly. Turning toward his left arm, he pulled on the intravenous tube entering his arm, causing more insulin to drip into his veins. His breathing became more labored. He could feel his chest heave with desperation. The room began to contract and expand as he became disoriented.

Suddenly a man in a white shirt and pants appeared over him. "Ah, thank God," Nekipelov said with a sigh of relief. "Thank God you've come, Dr. Borisov. Get me out. Please! They're trying to kill me."

"You idiot," the man in the white shirt and pants replied brusquely. "Shut your goddamn mouth."

"Get out of here," shouted Nekipelov at the shadow. "You're here with Dr. Zoubok. You're both going to kill me!"

The burly man in the white uniform, a hospital orderly with unsavory features and manners, slapped Nekipelov across the face and tied his hands with the leather restraints attached to the sides of the bed.

Nekipelov resisted and tried to punch the orderly.

"Listen, you bastard, just because you're in this goddamn hospital bed, acting like you're sick, doesn't mean you can get away with it. At least not with me." He took off his black leather belt, wrapped it halfway around his fist, and began to hit Nekipelov with the shiny bright metal buckle.

Nekipelov screamed as welts formed on his face, neck, and chest.

Zoubok hurried into the room as the nursing attendants went to call Borisov. "Stop! Get off that patient immediately."

Borisov ran into the room, trailed closely by Zeleneyev. Without hesitating, he pulled the orderly away, knocking him backward onto the floor.

Borisov went to Nekipelov and examined his pupils, checked his respiration, and tested the reflexes on both knees and ankles. "Give me a five cc. IV of glucagon. And prepare a debridement kit," he shouted at the nurse who stood cringing in the doorway.

The orderly stood up groggily, placed one hand on Borisov's shoulder, and swung him around. Borisov cocked his right fist, ready to strike the orderly. But he heard Zoubok yell angrily, "Stop! What do you think this is? An American cowboy movie? Dr. Borisov, may I remind you that you're chief of a service here at Kashchenko Hospital." He told Zeleneyev to take the orderly out of the room and place him on administrative leave without pay. And then he turned toward Borisov.

"What's wrong with you, Alexsandrovitch? Have you lost your sense of decorum?"

Borisov was furious as he placed a poultice saturated with antibiotic cream over Nekipelov's swollen eyelids. "Why in God's name do we have an orderly on this ward who beats up one of my patients. He's not even one of our orderlies. He was not assigned to us by . . ." Borisov stopped short.

"That's right," Zoubok smiled sardonically. "He was personally assigned to the unit by me. This is a very special ward to me, as you well know, Alexsandrovitch. And you know we've been short of our quota of nursing orderlies for quite some time. You should be grateful that I sent someone to you."

Borisov concentrated on suturing the minor cuts over Nekipelov's eyebrows. How was he to answer Zoubok? Yes, it was true that Zoubok himself had ordered additional staff for his unit. And that Zoubok himself picked the staff. It was not accidental that this orderly, and perhaps one or two others, were ex-convicts from various prisons around the country — including Lubyanka Prison at KGB headquarters. Were they ordered to monitor Borisov's activities? Did Zoubok want to send a message through the system by the use of physical intimidation? Too incredible to be true,

Borisov thought. Zoubok was neither stupid nor self-destructive. Nekipelov was the patient by which he could prove Zoubok's theory of sluggish schizophrenia.

Zoubok grabbed Borisov by the shoulders and turned him around. "Alexsandrovitch, listen to me. You're upset. I don't want you to say or do anything foolish. There's too much at stake — your career, your research, your reputation."

Zoubok knew the threat was totally unnecessary. But he wanted to reaffirm his authority quickly and loudly so that Borisov, and the nurses and doctors watching from the doorway, would have no doubts as to who was really in charge of the Organic Therapy Unit, the Inpatient Service, or, for that matter, Kashchenko Psychiatric Hospital. If he wanted his orderlies to beat up patients for behavioral infractions, then that was his to order. Of course, he would never do that. There was no need for brute force. This was a new orderly, recently released from prison, and he wasn't yet accustomed to the frightening behavior of the insane. So he panicked. Zoubok would see that it would never happen again; otherwise, the orderly would be sent back to prison. But there was a definite advantage to employing ex-prisoners in strategic positions, assuming they were given little responsibility. They provided an invaluable service — surveillance. It was their job to make certain that Zoubok was kept informed of everything that transpired in the hospital. The fact that they were criminals acted as a silent deterrent to anyone who entertained the grandiose notion that they might usurp Zoubok's power or position. These hooligans were a cheap and realible insurance policy against certain administrative problems. Zoubok had introduced the idea of using ex-criminals as hospital orderlies despite the stated objections of his hospital staff, who found the concept repressive and professionally degrading. So Zoubok provided an economic and administrative rationale — it was inexpensive (costing almost nothing except lodging) and allowed him to hire more professional staff without jeopardizing the annual hiring quotas. His plan was eagerly approved by the KGB because it allowed them to collaborate with an institution which, until then, had been denied to them by the powerful Academy of Science. And by that time, Zoubok was a driving force with the august Academy.

"We can no longer afford to keep these orderlies. Next time, a patient will die." Borisov had always quietly protested the presence of these orderlies because it would too closely identify the hospital with the Serbsky Institute or with the special psychiatric hospitals where it was standard practice to use criminals as both nursing attendants and guards and to give them the authority to beat patients at their discretion.

"Please excuse us." Zoubok flushed red and waved away the group standing in the doorway. When they had all left, he turned toward Borisov. "Are you telling me how to run this hospital?"

Borisov realized that he had crossed the fine line between controlled irreverence and outright insubordination. Jealous, Borisov thought. He's jealous. This entire charade was because he didn't want me to admit the patient in the first place. He can't handle competition. He recalled the story of how Zoubok had denounced his mentor in order to advance his own career.

"What happened? Why was the patient agitated?" Zoubok tried to shift the focus away from an imminent confrontation.

"What happened?" Borisov regained his composure. He took the patient's blood pressure. "Ninety over sixty, regular pulse, rhythmic breathing."

"Hypotension?"

"Probably. Cerebral ischemia secondary to hypoglycemia or hypotension. I think the insulin was either dripping in too fast or there was too much insulin.

Or simply an unexpected rebound phenomena from the hypoglycemia.''

"Is that how that patient died six months ago?"

Borisov nodded, surprised that Zoubok had finally mentioned it. Now, when he was most vulnerable. On the other hand, why not now, when he was on the defensive. Be patient. Wait. And, at the right moment — strike.

"That is correct. As I recall, he had sluggish schizophrenia. He died from either cardiac arrhythmia or a massive myocardial infarction.''

"What did the autopsy show?" Zoubok asked nonchalantly, knowing full well the answer. He had to teach Borisov some humility. He had become too rambunctious. Too arrogant. And worst of all — too independent. A change that had evolved gradually over the past six months since the death of the sixty-five-year-old vagrant admitted for sluggish schizophrenia. At the time he was surprised that Borisov had not mentioned the death in his weekly census. That was his mistake — he had tried to deny the importance of the death. Worse yet, he assumed that Zoubok would not learn about it. How presumptuous. How foolish.

"There was no autopsy, Dr. Zoubok." Borisov adjusted the intravenous tubing in Nekipelov's arm. "There was no need for an autopsy.''

Zoubok remained silent. Calling Borisov a liar wouldn't serve his purpose. Right now he needed Borisov for something far more important than this problem.

"I think the problems are similar. Perhaps your insulin therapy is too aggressive. Start with lower doses. And work up more gradually," Zoubok replied gently. He had detected a note of repentance in Borisov's voice.

"I've tried that. It doesn't work. It places the patient in a type of twilight sleep, half in coma, half out. I'm convinced that the very process of rapidly inducing the coma is an essential ingredient for the recuperative process of sluggish schizophrenia. I saw it in Nekipelov. I pushed the insulin in at a fast rate, the coma was induced quickly, and he came out of it with fewer symptoms. His apathy, negativism, and some of the paranoia disappeared."

"If you can repeat those results then you may really have something very impressive."

"Thank you." Borisov was pleased that a confrontation had been avoided, but he didn't have to wait long to know what Zoubok really wanted.

"I have a new patient for you. Someone you might be able to try your insulin coma therapy on. Come with me."

They walked out of the room with Zoubok's right arm on Borisov's back, signifying to the waiting staff that everything was as before — friendly and collegial. Or so it appeared.

She awoke with the groggy remembrance of a car ride past the somber statue of stern-faced Felix Dzerzhinsky, which stood before the singularly unimpressive neo-Renaissance façade of the headquarters of the Komitet Gosudarstvennoi Bezopasnosti, Committee for State Security, or the KGB. She had been dragged by two men down lengthy corridors and taken to a small room. Was it a small room? It was important that she remember. Was it an interrogation room containing one large wooden desk with a bright naked light bulb? No, that wasn't it. She was resisting the image. There was something unusual about that room. Men playing balalaikas? Men and women intertwined in various positions of love? Her *bogatyr*, tall, handsome. Nostalgic bitterness made that room recede, and yet the memory of the room would not vanish. Perhaps it wasn't the room at all but the person in the room. A person whose face she never saw. A disembodied voice;

high pitched, deliberate, controlling, authoritative. What did he want from her? She had fought to keep her eyes open, to retain consciousness while the pain in her right shoulder, the loss of blood, and her enveloping fatigue forced her to succumb to a restful darkness.

He was asking questions. Where was I going, she had repeated to herself each time the question came, holding onto the sounds of the syllables as a way of reaffirming her existence. Was I going to Tbilisi? She had replied that she wasn't certain. "Uncertain about what?" he asked persistently in a voice that was incredibly familiar. She had strained her eyes to look beyond the brilliant yellow halo around the light and for a fleeting second thought she had seen his face. A long, tight face. But it was his voice that lingered in her memory.

Why did you flee the police like a common criminal? She had mustered enough energy to shout back — Common? There is nothing common about me. If you don't know that then you don't know anything about me. She recalled that he laughed. A mean, knowing laugh, which assured her that he knew exactly who she was. Then he had continued. Why did you run away that day? She didn't answer. There was no answer. The answer would reveal the very source of her secret. The secret that lingered in some shadowy chamber of her mind, awaiting release. She knew it was there but she didn't know how to unlock it. What combination of words, associations, memories? Something Anatoly had told her. Perhaps something he had shown her.

Were there any papers? Documents? Then he assumed a solicitous air. Are you feeling all right? Does your shoulder hurt? He seemed concerned about her blood loss. She resented the way he cynically phrased the sentence, as if she had purposefully torn up her shoulder in foolish protest. And then he continued, his line of questioning, always going back to that day in the *dacha*. Who was there? What did she say to the guests? How many were there? What was the occasion? It seemed to her that he repeated the questions endlessly. What did you say to them? Did you notice anything unusual about the guests? Were there any irregularities?

She looked around the room she was now in. It was bare. A room a little larger than her bathroom at home, but without the amenities of a sink or toilet. She was lying on a white metal-framed bed, one arm in a sling, the other tethered to the bed by a leather wrist band. She tried to pull her wrist away but the pain in her shoulder intensified. She stopped and lay still, and became aware of the awful screams that filtered through the barred windows.

Pskhushka, she muttered to herself. I am in an insane asylum. Her mind began to swim in a turbulence of impressions and fears. Madness was something that genuinely frightened her. In the town of her childhood, some ninety kilometers northwest of Moscow, there was an old woman who insisted upon sleeping in a different doorway each night. In summer, she nestled in a cardboard crate on a park bench where children would often taunt her. She was one of them. And she recalled a winter twenty years ago, when the men of the village went hunting for a rabid dog that had bitten and killed two little girls. Uncontrolled dogs and uncontrolled behavior terrified her.

Zoubok nodded to the two men dressed in plainclothes guarding the patient's room and whispered to Borisov, "She's the wife of an important party official."

"Are they KGB?"

Zoubok didn't answer. The answer was implicit in the question.

Borisov was disturbed. In the past, Zoubok certainly had admitted members of the Party or the Politburo. But never to the isolation unit where only the most suicidal, most dangerous patients were sent. And certainly never under arrest, with KGB agents at the door. Zoubok had always been powerful enough to resist KGB interference in the operation of this hospital. Why these unusual procedures, Borisov wondered, as he approached the patient.

He watched the woman struggling with her restraints, totally ignoring his presence until he bent over to unfasten the leather.

"There. I think you'll feel more comfortable now. I'm Dr. Alexsandr Borisov, director of the Inpatient Service, and this is Dr. Dimitry Zoubok, the director of this hospital."

She raised her head and looked defiantly up at the men. What nerve they had, to call themselves doctors. Jailers. Torturers. KGB. Certainly not doctors.

"This is Mrs. Natalya Vartanian, the wife of Zhores Vartanian, executive administrator of the Secretariat for the Politburo. He's in charge of all the paperwork that flows in and out of the Politburo."

"Nikitchenko," she interjected.

Looking contemptuously at the two men, she adjusted her position in her bed so that it looked as if she were granting an audience to supplicants.

"Nikitchenko?" Borisov asked.

"Yes, Nikitchenko. I use my maiden name," she replied defiantly.

"She's a very angry young lady," Zoubok added.

The woman glared at Zoubok. Suddenly, Borisov realized how incredibly beautiful she was. She had almond-shaped green eyes and long, dark eyelashes. High, sharply edged cheekbones, the kind seen in fashion magazines where the sculptured lines were achieved through makeup and lighting. But she wore no cosmetics. Her skin was a smooth, olive color of exotic beauty. He tried to resist staring at her.

"What's your name?" she asked.

"Dr. Alexsandr Borisov," he replied. Perhaps she

has a short-term memory loss. He made a mental note to test her memory function.

"Does *your* name change when you get married?"

"Well, no . . . of course not."

"Neither does mine," she replied with cool anger.

Borisov wasn't sure whether to assume that it was all right to call herself whatever she wanted, or simply to laugh. He turned toward Zoubok, who looked impatient and irritated.

"My name is Nikitchenko. And if you wish to address me, then please use that name."

"Are you still married?"

"Why, are you propositioning me?" she asked.

Borisov laughed.

"Dr. Borisov asked you a very straightforward question: Are you or are you not married? Answer it accordingly," Zoubok said brusquely. He didn't intend for her to control this initial interview.

"Only on paper."

"What does that mean?"

"It means exactly that," she replied.

"Your husband brought you here." Zoubok waited for her response.

Natalya said nothing. It was obvious who had brought her here.

"Is that right?" Borisov asked.

Natalya turned onto her side and looked through the window, dismissing both doctors.

"Answer the question, Mrs. Vartanian," ordered Zoubok. "May I remind you that you are in a mental hospital and we expect all our patients to cooperate fully with us."

She quickly turned toward him, and grimaced from a spasm of pain. "And if I don't cooperate, Dr. Zilberg, what will you do?"

Borisov couldn't resist smiling. The woman knew exactly how to irk Zoubok — mispronouncing his name to make it sound Jewish.

"Are you frequently this angry and suspicious?" Zoubok asked.

"Yes, Dr. Zilberg . . ."

"Dr. Zoubok, Mrs. Vartanian, remember, Dr. Zoubok."

"Well, Dr. Zilberg . . ."

"Mrs. Vartanian, we have . . ." Zoubok stopped suddenly, realizing that he might say too much. More than he could justify to Borisov. So he whispered something in Borisov's ear and turned toward the patient. "A fond goodbye, Mrs. Nekipelov. I will see you again, rest assured. As for now, Dr. Borisov will be taking care of you." He walked briskly out of the room, more certain now of his next course of action.

Natalya's bitter smile bespoke a sense of satisfaction from having frustrated the chief of the hospital. But she knew that it would be a short-lived victory and a dangerous one. In time she would pay for humiliating Zoubok in front of his subordinate.

She stared at the doctor standing before her, and took a quick reading: attractive, intense, distant. But when he smiled his cold blue eyes became warm and inviting. He clearly enjoyed her defiance.

"Mrs. Nekipelov?" Natalya asked, "Who is Mrs. Nekipelov? Is that the old doctor's mistress?"

"I'm sure that was just a mistake." Borisov flushed slightly.

"That's what you in psychiatry call a Freudian slip, isn't it?"

"Yes, an unconscious slip of the tongue. But we . . ."

"Do you believe in the unconscious?" she interrupted.

He heard her question, but, for the first time since he had been in the room, he noticed how extensively her right shoulder had been bandaged.

"May I take a look at your shoulder."

"It's fine. Please, I'm fine." She drew back, fearful.

"Please," Borisov sat down on the edge of the bed

and gently pressed her shoulder to feel for any moisture.

"How did this happen?"

"I was walking down the street, minding my own business, and two strangers decided to take a shot at me just for fun."

He looked at her incredulously. She shrugged her shoulders and smiled sheepishly. "It's true there were two hooligans. But I was wounded while trying to run from them."

He looked at her closely now. She had the vivid, vigorous expression of someone who was very much involved with life. She was neither innocent nor indifferent. She was, however, hiding something.

She watched him as he touched her shoulder. He had long, thin fingers, gentle fingers, like a pianist. At times his movements seemed awkward. She could always sense when men felt slightly uncomfortable around her. "You haven't answered my question." Her tone of voice was warm.

"What was that?"

"Do you believe in the unconscious? In Freud?"

Borisov brought a chair from across the room and placed it next to her bed. "I'd like to take those bandages off your shoulder. Who sewed you up?"

"You don't like to answer questions, do you?"

"We seem to share that tendency." My God, he thought as he gazed at her slim form underneath the loose white hospital robe, it's been a long time since I've flirted with a patient. Once during the time he had been an intern, and twice when a resident, because of inexperience and the simple exhilaration of the experience. But he'd never consummated these aroused feelings — that would have been a serious breach of professional protocol. From the time he had arrived at Kashchenko Hospital, he had resisted any temptations. It never seemed worth incurring Zoubok's disapproval. But he'd never had a patient so lovely. He realized she had managed to detour him from the main issues. Why was she here? How could he help her?

"I'll make a deal with you. I'll answer one question if you answer one question." She extended her left hand.

He took her hand. "All right."

"My question is: How can I get out of here? And why am I in here, as opposed to anywhere else the authorities might want to place me? And before you say anything I will give you one free answer. The two men who followed me . . ." she paused, about to tell him of the KGB, but decided against it. "They were robbing the theater in which I was starring."

"You're an actress?"

"No . . . no. Remember our bargain. One question followed by one answer. You've already asked your one question."

"Okay. A deal is a deal. I'll give you a free one. No, I don't believe in Freud — in the unconscious. I believe very strongly in economic determinism and free will. We have the absolute right and capability to choose our own destinies, unencumbered by fairytale stories of the past or beliefs and ideas we cannot measure." It was an incomplete truth. It wouldn't look too good if the director of Inpatient Services harbored doubts about Pavlovian theory, or had any fascination for those intellectual theories that attempted to explain the spiritual malaise of the soul.

"As for your other question, the sooner you can help me figure out why you're here and explain to me the type of mental problems you've been having, the sooner we'll be able to tell what's wrong with you and treat you accordingly. I can't do any better than that."

"Fair."

"Then why don't we start from the beginning?"

"Which is where?"

"Anywhere you want to begin."

Where should she begin, she wondered. Certainly not

with her falling in love with Anatoly. Nor with his death. Nor with the party. Wherever she began she had to be very careful, for he would try to probe for the answers he really wanted. The ones Zoubok wanted. But if she gave him enough history to interest him in her background, perhaps she could deflect attention from her current situation, long enough for her to survey the hospital and develop a plan to escape.

"Let's start from the beginning. For the record. Name. Age. Occupation. And the reasons you were admitted to the hospital."

Her green eyes sparkled with the eagerness of an understudy who has been informed that the lead actress has just fallen ill. Running carefully manicured fingers through her auburn hair, she thrust her head backward like a privileged woman who has been pampered by the attention and affections of admiring men. Even in this bruised, disheveled state she knew she was attractive. And she was eager to speak in hope that he might find her role as the sensitive, misunderstood, abused wife sufficiently convincing to help her get out of the hospital. "My maiden name is Natalya Nikitchenko, born December 7, 1953, which makes me thirty-one. On the surface I am expansive, gregarious, and dramatic. I make friends easily. I like the company of interesting men who are physically, intellectually, and emotionally attractive. And I expect them to fall in love with me. Failing that, I expect them to invest a considerable amount of their time, energy, and money in me." She paused, assessing his reaction. None. "I see I haven't made myself insufferable yet."

Borisov smiled.

"I have a firm knowledge of what I like and what I dislike." She gazed at the door. "I don't like your colleague. I don't like people who lie. But I like people who can look me straight in the eye and tell me the most incredible lies about their feelings toward me." She laughed. Then abruptly she became quiet.

"What wrong? You look sad," Borisov asked.

Now she appeared distracted. "Oh, nothing." Smiling unconvincingly, "Nothing."

"Were you thinking of something that made you sad?"

"Doctor, your question doesn't sound like good Marxist psychiatry. Where's your economic determinism?"

He felt embarrassed. He had been caught short. He sat up straight in his chair and started to ask perfunctory questions.

"Where were you born?"

"Oh, I'm sorry," she responded. "I didn't mean to embarrass you." This man, she thought, is far more sensitive than he appears. But she realized that he would now resist her. She had made a mistake by allowing him to recognize that she had been playing with him. Her Anatoly had always warned her that it would not be her blatant seductions that would cause her trouble, but her need to demonstrate how much in control she was. A little more humility, he always said. A little less flippancy.

"I was born in Tbilisi, Georgia. I was an only child. As you can imagine, spoiled rotten by an incredibly handsome father whose life was devoted to me and to his work — he was a general practitioner in one of those little polyclinics on the outskirts of town. He was the kind of doctor who spent his evenings, when not at home, at the small peasant homes of his patients, delivering babies or treating heart attacks. I loved him very much. He often took me with him to those straw-thatched houses, and he taught me how to use the various medical instruments he carried in his black bag — the sphygmom . . ."

"Blood-pressure machine," Borisov replied with a smile.

"No . . . no . . . What is the real name? The fancy medical name for that machine."

"Sphygmomanometer."

"Sphygmamon . . . mamameter. Right?"

He nodded.

"No, that was not right!" She realized that she was overdoing it. She had better back off quickly. Her tone became matter-of-fact. "We were very close. Of course, he had a secret agenda. He never quite said it, but I always knew that he brought me along in the hope that one day I might become a doctor, too. He never encouraged me directly but he always asked me if I wanted to take care of people. And I would answer that the only person I really wanted to take care of for the rest of my life was him. I was a little girl, terribly in love with this kind and gentle man." She became visibly upset, pressing the bridge of her nose in an attempt to keep from crying.

"Are you all right?" Borisov was unsure whether this was a demonstration of her acting skills or a true expression of the depth of her feelings for her father. "What happened to your father?"

"He died when I was eight years old." Her eyes glistened and her voice was subdued. "After a long day's work at the polyclinic, he simply laid his head on his desk for a quick nap. And he never woke up."

Borisov could see she was trying to hold back tears. She suddenly looked so vulnerable. He wanted to put his arm around her shoulders. To comfort her. But such feelings were totally inappropriate. She was a patient who was in pain. She needed him to find a way of helping her to alleviate that pain from within. Today he had witnessed two different emotional responses to the loss of a loved one. The psychotic woman in the hydrotherapy room had expressed the pain of losing her son in violent behavioral outbursts accompanied by a loss of contact with reality. But here, he was witnessing a woman who was very appropriately responding to the tragic loss of her father. Why was it that one set of stimuli — loss and pain — set off two totally separate behavioral and emotional responses in two different people? Pavlovian theory would explain that two basically different stimuli appropriately created two different responses. But it was an explanation lacking texture and sophistication. What he was witnessing was far more than a Pavlovian stimulus-response reaction. How do I help these patients handle the pain of loss, he wondered, without using drugs, or numbing them or placing them in a coma? He needed another explanation. Another way of asking questions about pain and loss that would not threaten patients and, he hesitated as he said it to himself, not threaten him. Zoubok would be outraged if Borisov pursued the line of questioning which was most directly related to the emotions that Natalya was feeling. So far he had not heard or seen anything that required her to be a patient at this hospital. She evidenced no thought or emotional disorder. At least not yet. Was Zoubok of a mind that she was a sluggish schizophrenic? It would take time to uncover.

"Tell me about your mother. Did she raise you when your father died?"

Her face froze for a split second. "My mother." She looked as if she were trying to grasp an image in some faraway place. "My mother was born in Moscow in the early years of the Russian Revolution. Her family were, as it was explained to me much later, part of the landed gentry who owned much property on the outskirts of Moscow. All of which, of course, was confiscated by the Bolsheviks. She resented my being my father's favorite, and would take it out on me — slapping me when he wasn't looking, threatening to leave if he continued lavishing attention on me instead of her. Do you have any idea of what it is like to continuously compete with your mother — for attention?"

"I imagine it must have been quite difficult."

"Difficult! Difficult is when your mother ignores

you. That would have been a salvation for me." Her voice became more animated. "She was tall, stately, strict. After school she made me come directly home to practice the piano, a minimum of one hour. No wonder I hate classical music. I'm a great admirer of the Vyzcheslav Ganeļin Trio from Lithuania. Do you like jazz?"

"I enjoy it." Borisov was unenthusiastic. "I don't really understand jazz. Too much spontaneity. Too uncontrolled."

"Too spontaneous. Too uncontrolled," she repeated. Perhaps he was as tight as he appeared.

"Tell me more about your mother," Borisov interjected, determined not to let her stray from the point.

"Did you ever hear of Nikolai Levinovsky's allegro group? They are really quite good. If you prefer piano improvisations you should listen to Leonid Chizhik; or Alexei Kozlov if you like a good saxophone. And then there is a wonderful singer, Larissa Dolina. What a voice!" She paused for his reaction. He is a good listener, she thought. But she knew that he was waiting for her to return to the subject.

"My mother, right?" she sighed.

Borisov nodded.

"My mother." Natalya leaned her head back against the pillow. "Did I tell you she was born in a small town about one hundred kilometers west of Moscow on the Ochakovskoye Highway called Novobrat?" She withdrew her arm from the sling, grimacing with pain, and extended her fifth finger, on which she was wearing a finely handcrafted silver ring designed as a garland of flowers, lily pads, and fruits. "I've had it since I was a girl. My mother gave it to me. It was made in Novobrat. That's where we lived after my father died. Myself, my mother, and my endlessly drunk nanny. Novobrat is famous for skilled silversmiths."

She suddenly stopped, as if she had remembered

something important that she didn't want him to know about. Borisov made a mental note to ask her later about Novobrat, silver rings, and her nanny.

"My mother had all the typical contradictions of a Russian mother. She wanted me to be anything I might want to be — as long as she approved. She insisted that I didn't go out to play with my friends or take my drama lessons until I'd practiced the piano. Her father had played the violin, so she wanted me to play something."

"How would you describe your mother?"

"She was a very haughty, elegant woman who demanded all the comforts of nobility in a communist society." She smiled. "And that's not easy to live with. Believe me."

"What do you mean?"

"My father made an adequate salary, enough to afford a modest two-bedroom cooperative, a Zhilga, and occasional vacations to Warsaw and Dubrovnik. We were by no means wealthy. My father was a very scrupulous man — hard working, honest, with no pretensions. But *she* forced him to open an illegal private practice, charging the more prominent people in Tbilisi for private house calls. Then she would take the money and buy antiques and icons and elegant haute couture clothing from the black market."

"Why did she stay with your father?"

"I don't really know. Maybe because she was afraid to leave him."

"I don't understand."

"Separation. Fear."

"Fear."

"Possibly. Although she may have had a more exciting life with other men, some of whom I now realize were probably her lovers, none had as prestigious a position in society as my father. He provided her with a necessary illusion of security."

"Why 'illusion of security'?" Borisov was fascinated

by her facility at analyzing people. But he wondered how much of what she was saying reflected an actual representation of what her parents were like and how much was a distortion — a product of her own disappointments, hurts, and wishful thinking. She was unlike any patient he had interviewed before. Beautiful, articulate, manipulative.

"Where is your mother?"

She stared at Borisov. Where is your mother, she repeated the words to herself. My mother. Goddamn my mother!

"Where is your mother? Is she living in Tbilisi still?"

"Yes, she's in Tbilisi. She's not well."

"What's wrong?"

"She's sick."

Suddenly her composure dissolved. She glanced nervously around the room, as if her mother's presence lurked somewhere within its barren confines.

"Is she mentally ill?"

"What do you mean?" Natalya's voice cracked with apprehension.

"Is she in a mental institution for, say, severe depression or schizophrenia?"

"Why did you ask that?" She realized that she had just made two serious mistakes. First, she had completely forgotten about the incriminating nature of her mother's illness. Second, she had underestimated Borisov. She had always simply regarded her mother as "sick." At first, it was only a matter of mood swings — one day happy, the next day depressed. Her father had often given her mother a bromide elixir, a brown, foultasting fluid that burned the tongue. Later on, in the years following the death of her husband, her mother's depression became severe.

"Are you all right?" Borisov noted that her distractions were increasing in frequency and length. She had difficulty staying with one idea, allowing tangential thoughts to intervene. A sign of schizophrenia. Not a strong, convincing sign, but definitely a clinical clue. What about her mother? If this woman does have a mother with a documented history of schizophrenia, there is clearly a genetic predisposition. Natalya could have strong latent tendencies for schizophrenia. Borisov would have to find out what happened to her mother.

"Is your mother in a mental hospital?"

"She's in the Tbilisi Neuropsychiatric Hospital, on the outskirts of the city."

"All psychiatric hospitals are on the outskirts of some town. Otherwise, the townspeople would be contaminated by the infection of insanity."

Natalya laughed, as Borisov hoped she would, and her face brightened. Beautiful, he thought. White teeth, perfectly aligned, so rare to see with such poor dental services in the Soviet Union.

"Do you know what her diagnosis was?"

"Yes and no."

"What do you mean?"

"The doctors explained to me that she had a problem with mood swings. She might be joyous one day and then severely depressed the next day."

"Did they say she was a manic-depressive?"

"No. A few years ago they noticed that she became easily distracted. Eventually, she started talking to herself."

"What did she say?"

"I don't know."

"Does the term 'schizoaffective' mean anything to you?"

"Yes. It was said to me on several occasions. But I don't really know what it means."

"That's reasonable. Neither do we doctors. We use it as a catchall diagnosis for a deteriorating mental process that is accompanied by serious emotional problems. It is usually treated with phenothiazine medications."

"I know she is still taking medication, but I don't know what."

"Tell me what happend to you after your mother became sick."

"I was around fourteen or fifteen. I think the pressures of living alone, without my father, precipitated her emotional problems."

"But I thought you said she was an independent woman, who had a number of different lovers."

She smiled and shrugged her shoulders. "Perhaps you can tell me how an outwardly independent woman could fall apart when her source of security, which I think my father was to her, disappeared. We moved to Novobrat when my father died and, then, a few years later returned to Tbilisi where she was, finally, hospitalized. And quite frankly, I left home in order to get away from her demanding, controlling ways. Had I remained at home I would have been an emotional invalid. It was unbearable, making breakfast in the morning, serving her in bed, dressing her in the fashions of twenty years ago. Shopping. House cleaning. I did it because she felt that she had to be treated like nobility, which in her mind she had become. From time to time she insisted that I call her a Romanov. I would then give her a pill and she would spit it out, cursing me." Natalya stopped, and began to cry, wiping her eyes on her sleeve.

"I became interested in the theater. I imagine in that way my mother was helpful. She drove me away from her, and I discovered a life of my own."

"How did you do that?"

"When I was about nineteen, I ran away with a regional theater group that traveled around from Moscow to Tbilisi presenting good Russian plays — Chekhov, Pushkin. I learned the fundamentals of acting, make-up — and survival. Looking back, I was probably no different from any other Russian girl of that age. Eager for romance. Contemptuous of my mother. Totally ignorant of the realities of sex and contraception. So I fell in love, became pregnant, had the first of several abortions, and married the father for exactly one hundred and twenty-one days, after which the nineteen-year-old-boy — that's really what he was — ran away from marital bliss and eventually went into the army. To serve the motherland. I have never heard from him since. But I learned quickly that young love is exactly that — immature, with no sustaining power in and of itself."

"You sound cynical."

"No, Dr. Borisov, I am not cynical. Perhaps a little bitter, but definitely not cynical. The proof is in what transpired afterward. At no time was I disillusioned with love. On the contrary, I realized that if I wanted to enjoy it, I would have to learn much more about sex. Mind you, at no time was I promiscuous or indiscriminate. I simply sought the companionship of older men, in their thirties or forties, who had experience and who were willing to teach me. You can well imagine that I was not at a loss for male companionship. But I chose very carefully. Unfortunately, no matter how strongly they professed their love and trust, most of them were jealous and possessive."

Borisov had never met anyone who could discuss her past so forthrightly. The Russian women he had known were far less insightful. True, the system provided little sex education. Most Russian women, it seemed, were awkward and unsure in bed, knew almost nothing about contraception and absolutely nothing about orgasm. Russian psychiatrists, upon whom the system had implicitly come to rely for information and expertise in sex, had totally abrogated that responsibility by denying its significance. They had relegated it to a regional division called Family Guidance which spent most of its time treating alcoholics and their families. Women feared the diaphragm because it was too complicated to insert. A rumor had been spread which claimed that the prophylactics used in the USSR had tiny perforations and could not be trusted. So the only reliable contraceptive was abortion. Borisov had learned to accept ten to twenty abortions as a norm. It was not unusual to treat a twenty-two-year-old girl for a septic infection because some *feldsher* had unintentionally botched the procedure, not realizing the young woman's uterus was already scarred from previous abortions.

Yes, sex in Russia was a significant problem. He had heard countless complaints that Russian men were sexually inept. They were frequently so drunk that they had difficulty acquiring an erection. And, if they weren't drunk, they ejaculated too quickly. Newlyweds had to live in cramped quarters with their parents, or they married simply for the chance to acquire a separate apartment in Moscow. Without privacy, newlyweds could not spend the time necessary to develop the intimacy needed for a meaningful emotional and sexual relationship. And in a country where everyone was supposedly equal, women were required to work in the general economy for significantly less pay than men in comparable jobs. They had to wait in long lines to shop and they had to take care of children with only occasional help from a state-financed daycare center. They had to maintain their household and take care of a husband who spent most of his time resting on the sofa. One of his patients had described her husband as the "Emperor of the Armchair." Borisov understood that what Natalya was describing — the series of immature loves, the multiple abortions, the need to run away from her parents to establish her own identity — was not particular to her, but to a whole society. He had never heard it so articulately and unabashedly described by one woman. In many ways, she was like his ex-wife Sonya, a survivor, never waiting for permission to grab what she wanted. She simply went out and took it. But there was something wrong with Natalya, although he could not put his finger on it.

"What happened after you left home and joined the actors' group?"

"Are you an Aquarius?" She noticed a warm, sympathetic quality about him when he relaxed his mouth.

"What do you mean?"

She sat up in bed, enthusiastic. "Astrology? Don't you know anything about your horoscope?"

Borisov smiled self-consciously. Although a technical specialist, he prided himself on the breadth and scope of his knowledge on subjects extending from ants to zoophilia. As an atheist he felt no need to engage in studying the supernatural, the latest fad among the intelligentsia in Moscow. But astrology was a subject that was gaining importance in Russia, especially for post-Revolutionary second and third generations, children who had never experienced religion directly.

"I'll tell you my birthday — January twenty-third."

"Ah, there you are. That explains your formality and restraint."

"Formality and restraint?"

She was satisfied. But she had to be very careful if she were to forge an alliance with one of the enemy. Yes, the enemy, she thought. For the first time she allowed herself the luxury of saying that word to herself. It reminded her not to lose sight of their intent. She had to keep her wits about her to survive. Yes, she would survive in this madhouse. Her Anatoly had taught her that "with a golden hammer one will break down an iron door." Charm and guile, for now, would be her golden hammer.

"You are very much an Aquarius. They are supposed to make excellent teachers and physicians. And they are not very good at mathematics. Is that true of you?"

Puckering his lips, Borisov nodded his head not so much in agreement as in a pensive evaluation. "Perhaps."

"Which part is true, doctor? Let's see how modest you really are."

He smiled at her, refusing to fall into a well-laid trap that would make him sound self-important. "It's true that I am a poor mathematician."

"That's part of the Aquarius personality. Very practical. Uses a lot of common sense. Rarely makes impulsive responses or decisions." Her green eyes sparkled. "Often they are bachelors who live alone. Their best companions are Sagittarians, who you can see are charming, presumptuous, arrogant, skeptical, temperamental, and expansive. Well, would you agree?"

"I agree that you certainly *act* charming, expansive, arrogant, and all those wonderful adjectives you just mentioned. But as you yourself said, we Aquarians do not form opinions or judgments very quickly. We remain skeptical, uncertain, and particularly inquisitive. What would you say about that?"

"I would say" — shaking her head in approval — "that you are one very smart doctor." Without thinking, she spoke unguardedly. "My *bogatyr* would have liked you. But he also would have warned me that not everyone who snores is sleeping."

"Thank you. But who is he?" Borisov was surprised at her use of the word. In Russian history a *bogatyr* was a powerful, heroic figure. For a woman it would connote a very powerful man in her life, someone who not only influenced her but in fact dominated her completely. Who could this man be? Her father? She clearly loved him, but he sounded too gentle, too kind. A lover? Apparently she never became very attached to any of them. Her husband? She had said very little about him. And she had said that their marriage existed more on paper than in reality. Then why had she married him? And how did this *bogatyr* fit into her marriage?

"My *bogatyr?*" She repeated the words with only the slightest evidence of discomfort. "Just an old friend. A dear, respected old friend."

"Where is he now? What does he do?"

She replied slowly and nostalgically, gazing beyond the bars of the window. She restrained her emotions. "He was a friend. A very special friend."

" 'He was'? You say it in the past tense. Is he no longer alive?"

"Yes, he's alive." She was irked by his persistence. "He's alive and well."

"What does he do?"

"Why is he so important?" she snapped, annoyed with his probing manner. "I'm the one who is in here. Not him."

"You seem very angry. Is there anything that I've said to make you so angry?" Normally Borisov would have ignored her anger and simply demanded to know who this man was, what he did, and what relevance he had for her life. It would have been as crude and direct as that. Except that she was different, very different. Whatever she would reveal would have to come out in her own time and her own way.

"How silly of me to play games with you." Recomposing herself, she smiled broadly, and was no longer defensive. "My husband, Zhores Vartanian, is a decent man fifteen years my senior. When I first met him I was acting in a small theater near the Kitai-Gorod. He was a handsome *apparatchik* who worked in one of those buildings near Red Square. He was ambitious, smart, and in his own way, very tender. When we first met, like all new lovers, there was nothing he wouldn't do for me. He pampered me with gifts — French lingerie, Swiss chocolates, Italian shoes. He had been married once before and had recently divorced his wife. In the beginning, as you can imagine, everything was possible — my career, his promotions, our life together. Then *he* was my *bogatyr*. He made every day seem filled with hope. As if everything were possible. For the first time in my life, I wanted to have children. With him. For him. For us." She began to cry uncontrollably. "But things didn't work out that way." She paused. "Do you have a handkerchief?"

Borisov reached into his hip pocket and pulled out a clean white handkerchief. "What happened?"

"My husband left me. I don't mean physically. But spiritually, emotionally. We began to settle into a deadly routine. I worked. He worked. I rarely saw him until very late at night or on the weekends. I became pregnant again. But I suspect that I may not have wanted the baby."

"Why?"

"Because I had a spontaneous miscarriage."

"How was this one different from your other miscarriages?"

"Abortions, doctor. Not miscarriages. Specifically requested by me but performed by someone else in a clinical setting. This one, and the few that followed, were all self-induced."

"Do you mean you forced yourself to miscarry the child?"

She looked away, hurt. "You could say that. The effect was the same. For all pratical purposes, I might as well have used a coat hanger. But, no, I think my mind did it for me. Without any implements. Just simply the fact that I wasn't sure I wanted to have a child, not the way the marriage was going. Anyway, the marriage got progressively worse and that's why I am here. Severe depression. Pathological melancholia, I think you call it. I haven't been able to overcome the death of my marriage and the deaths of my unborn children."

"What kept you in the marriage for so long?"

"Inertia. Fatigue. Depression. Zhores treated me all right. He provided me with daily comforts. As a government official I didn't have to worry about starving or going without nylons.''

"Why do you say you were admitted for depression?"

"My husband was always threatening me that if I didn't pull out of my lethargy he would admit me to a psychiatric hospital. I guess I just wasn't able to pull myself together.''

"And your shoulder injury. Where did you get it?"

"I told you. I knocked into something. Two men were trying to prevent me from running away from home and I injured one of them when he tried to stop me.''

"What did you do?"

"I hit him over the head with a bottle of Georgian wine. There was a big cut. He was bleeding a lot. I was afraid and I started to run out of the apartment. The other man warned me several times to stop. My husband begged me to cooperate. But I did what I wanted and started to run. They caught me and brought me here. Well, what do you think?''

Borisov didn't answer. He no longer knew which part of her history was true. Whatever had happened certainly did not result from her running away from either the KGB or hospital orderlies. There was something wrong with the latter part of her story, he thought, especially the reasons for her coming to the hospital. It wasn't convincing. Her emotion wasn't bound to the words in the same way as when she had been describing her father or her mother. It was almost as if she were trying to placate him. But why? If it turned out that she didn't belong here, there was no need for such games. But what if these were not games. What if all that she said were true? Then how would he diagnose her?

"It's a little too early for a diagnosis. Even for a patient who has been so cooperative and insightful.'' Borisov stood up, took a stethoscope out of his coat pocket, and began to examine her chest and back.

"I am going to ask you some standard questions I ask all my patients. Do you know what today's date is?"

"October something or other. I've lost track of the days."

"The name of this hospital?"

"You won't believe this! But I don't know. No one told me when I was brought here."

"Do you know what kind of a hospital this is?"

"Of course," she laughed, "it's a madhouse. Tell me, doctor, how long do I have to remain here?"

"Do you know the meaning of the proverb 'A stitch in time saves nine' ?"

"I prefer 'Measure the cloth nine times before you cut it,' " she countered.

"Do you hear voices?"

"Only yours."

"Did you ever hear any voices that told you to hurt yourself or anyone else?"

"No. What I did or did not do came out of my own impulses. My own thoughts and desires."

"Have you ever felt so depressed that you wanted to kill yourself?"

"I know the answer is self-incriminating. But I would have to answer truthfully — yes."

"Have you ever tried to commit suicide?"

She paused. And thought about how much she wanted to tell him about her *bogatyr*. How much she had loved him. How . . . she stopped and thought again. No . . . Borisov is one of them. She would have to keep her secrets to herself. Or is he? He had been so nice and concerned about her. But, no. Trying to establish trust and mutual understanding was an old KGB trick. Anatoly had warned her that they were always pleasant, even gracious, in the beginning. They had nothing to lose. After that they could always resort to their more time-tested methods of interrogation and torture.

"No," she lied. "I never tried to commit suicide."

Borisov heard the words but ignored them. This woman was not likely to commit suicide. Beneath whatever pathology may or may not exist was abundant self-love and self-centeredness, he thought. People who love themselves as much as she does, do not kill themselves. On her lower back he had noticed two café au lait spots about two centimeters in diameter with a cluster of black hairs growing from them. They were located in the center of the vertebral column, spaced one inch apart. He made a note to order a spinal tap to rule out neurological tumors, which could produce serious depression or schizophrenia. Maybe Zoubok was right. He was an astute clinician.

"Tell me, have you ever had any dizzy spells, seizures, or abnormalities in your hands, feet, walking, or talking?"

"Oh my God, you make it sound very serious. No! I've never had such problems."

"Are you aware that you have some moles on your back?"

"Yes. I have some beauty marks along my spine."

Putting away his stethoscope, he started to walk out of the door. "I am ordering a series of tests — blood tests, an electroencephalogram, a spinal tap, and some psychological tests. Hopefully they will be done within the next day or so. I will see you tomorrow."

Natalya now looked concerned. At some point his aura of concern and empathy had vanished. What had she done wrong? Maybe she had assessed him wrongly all along. But there was no way for her to know now.

"You never answered my question, Dr. Borisov. How long will I be here?"

He looked at her fixedly and replied, "As long as it takes."

Chapter Five

ZELENEYEV ENTERED THE private room at the far end of the hospital, accompanied by two burly male nursing attendants wheeling a metal cart draped with a green sterilized sheet. He was looking forward to meeting the beautiful and mysterious Natalya. How lucky Borisov is to have her as a patient, he thought, observing her as she lay sprawled out on the bed, her coal black hair splayed over the white pillow, her eyes closed. What a tragedy for such physical beauty to be marred by a mental infirmity.

"Hello," Zeleneyev said gently, fearful of waking her too abruptly.

"Who are you?" She was startled to see someone in her room.

"I'm Dr. Yuri Zeleneyev, Dr. Borisov's assistant."

"What do you want?"

"Several tests were ordered for you. In cases like this I'm usually the one who performs them."

"What do you mean, 'in cases like this'?" She sat up in bed and ran her fingers through her hair.

"Well, I meant . . ." he stammered, embarrassed. Women, in general, and beautiful women, in particular, made him feel awkward. How would he explain, without frightening her, what he was about to do?

"Well, what do you want?" She watched the two attendants move toward her bedside. "What are you doing? Stop it!" she shouted.

"We must turn your bed in the other direction so that your back is facing the door. Then I will be taking some fluid from your back." He spoke gently, trying not to alarm her.

"Fluid from my back? Oh no. No . . . no you won't. I won't allow it."

He motioned the two orderlies to move the bed. Either approach he might take, gentle or tough, would lead to the same outcome — resistance. Her back was now parallel to the entrance and she was facing the far wall.

"What are you doing? Dr. Zeleneyev, please, what are you doing?"

He had no other choice but to explain the procedure. Unfortunately, for many patients, the description elicited more anxiety and fear than the actual procedure itself.

"What I am about to do is called a spinal tap. I will insert a metal needle into your back." He paused for a moment, thinking about how terrifying the procedure sounded when described. "The needle, a long, well not that long . . . We insert the needle in between the spaces of your vertebrae, and then we let a few drops of spinal fluid flow out the needle into a glass tube. Then we take it to the laboratory to analyze it for any abnormal sugar, protein, or tissue cells. This will tell us a lot about your condition."

"Are you sure this is necessary?"

"If Dr. Borisov thinks so, then I can assure you it's very necessary."

"Please, be gentle . . ." Natalya was afraid.

As Zeleneyev was spreading the dark brown Betadine antiseptic over Natalya's spinal column, a nurse walked into the room and whispered something into his ear. He apologized to Natalya, telling her Zoubok had an emergency on another ward and his help was required. He would return as quickly as possible. The attendants remained.

The two KGB agents at her door smiled cryptically at each other as Zeleneyev turned the corner of the corridor.

Natalya rested comfortably on the bed, waiting for Zeleneyev to return. At best, she knew it would be an unpleasant experience, but she suspected that Zeleneyev would do everything possible to mitigate her pain. She heard the door close and the sound of footsteps coming toward her.

"That wasn't very long for an emergency." Her voice was resigned.

The two nursing attendants held her down on the bed. The one facing her, a pock-faced man in his early fifties, explained to her that she must not turn over or she would contaminate her antiseptically cleaned back.

"Was your patient all right?" she asked Zeleneyev.

There was no response.

"You know," she added seductively, "even a lady can get tired of lying in bed all day."

Again, no response. But she could hear Zeleneyev preparing the instruments on the metal tray. "Can you tell me what you're doing now? It would help me to know."

She heard a rustling sound and the stretch and sudden snap of someone putting on rubber gloves.

Without warning she was given an injection in her left shoulder.

"Dr. Zeleneyev, what is that all about?" No answer. "Zeleneyev!" she shouted loudly. "What are you doing?" She felt breathless, unsure which was more painful, the viselike grip of the orderlies, or the sharp pain shooting down her left arm.

Suddenly her concentration became difficult as she fluctuated between consciousness and a restless stupor. The intramuscular injection of scopolamine, conducive to questioning and interrogation, gave her a strong desire to close her eyes and sleep. Yet when she closed her eyes, she became anxious.

Natalya felt a cold wetness as concentric circles were painted on the top of her coccyx. The sensation became increasingly intense until she felt the most profound pain she had ever experienced. She felt herself stabbed by something sharp. No, it was worse than that. It was as if a serrated knife were ripping the tissues and muscles of her lower back.

"You're killing me," she screamed.

There was no response other than a tightening of the orderlies' grips on her. "What are you doing?" She grew panicky at the continued silence. Only minutes before, Zeleneyev seemed so solicitous for her well-being.

Suddenly the pain was accompanied by the probing path of a metal instrument. First downward, and then upward. The rim of her anus felt as if it were on fire. She tried to move her hands backward to relieve the pain, but they were pinned more firmly against her body.

The sharp instrument now ground downward, seeming to have no clear destination.

"Why . . . why are you doing this to me? Goddamn it, speak!"

This time a disembodied voice replied in a controlled, dulcet tone. "I have just inserted into your back a seven-centimeter-long needle, about one one-hundredth centimeter in diameter. If my knowledge of anatomy is correct, it is presently located between the fourth and fifth lumbar vertebrae.''

She tried to concentrate, but was no longer certain of what she heard or what she felt. The searing pain was bcoming increasingly more acute and pervasive. That voice, she thought. Deliberate, soft spoken. She had heard it before.

"The spinal tap needle is an incredible instrument of discovery,'' the voice persisted. "Think of it, Natalya . . .''

Natalya. The pronunciation of her name brought recognition of the voice. It belonged to the man who had interrogated her when she was taken half alive from the train. And where had she heard it first? Her mind was torn between the lulling rest induced by scopolamine and the excruciating pain of that prying needle in her back.

". . . a needle about the size of those used by our sweet Babushkas to knit a sweater for their beloved grandchildren. That same needle is being used for the greater glory of scientific truth. Here I am, inserting a needle, a simple needle into your back, in order to elicit some truths. Some of which are scientific and some of which are, should I say, subjective? So ingenious.''

"Who are you?'' Natalya heard herself shout, exhausted by the effort.

"It's a pity you can't see what I am doing. Right now I am touching the nerves which control your rectum and your feet. Do you feel it, Natalya?''

"Oh my God,'' she screamed, as she felt her right leg begin to twitch reflexively from the sharp pains radiating downward. "Please . . . stop. What do you want?''

"I like that, Natalya. It is so important that patients ask the correct questions. Otherwise they will never know what's wrong with them.''

Natalya felt the needle move farther downward into a complex of nerves and blood vessels.

She began to writhe on the bed, now more forcibly restrained by the nursing orderlies.

The needle was withdrawn a few centimeters.

"Natalya, please," the voice said indignantly, as if reprimanding a child. "You've spoiled a perfectly good clinical experiment. I have inadvertently cut into a minor blood vessel and blood has begun to seep out slowly around the the needle's entrance hole. Oh, what a pity. What a pity. I'm sorry to tell you but I'm going to have to start all over again. You see, I could never submit a specimen of cerebrospinal fluid filled with blood to the pathology laboratory. That's just not possible."

"No, God, no," she cried as she felt the needle suddenly withdrawn from her back. Some liquid trickled down toward her rectum. She was unable to turn around and see her interrogator. But she knew it was not one of the doctors. The voice belonged to one of her interrogators. One of those at KGB headquarters. Or at least, wherever she had been taken that day. It was so hard to remember. She could only recall the sounds of voices — and questions and more questions.

The man moved his fingers delicately over Natalya's vertebrae until he found a location not unlike the first one — a chocolate colored discoloration covering the space between vertebrae three and four. Once again he painted the spot with Betadine antiseptic, making certain that there were no untoward discolorations anywhere else. He was extremely careful and took great pride in being able to emulate the physician's proficiency and concern for antisepsis. After all, he had been taught well by Dr. Zoubok, who had always appreciated Donskoi's morbid fascination with medicine and its more intrusive procedures. In certain ways, he was now far more proficient than his mentor, who had not done a spinal tap in quite a while.

With mathematical precision, he found the exact center into which he wanted to insert the needle.

Spreading the first two fingers of his rubber-gloved left hand over the new site, the man held the needle with his right hand and began to push it in gently, breaking through the skin. He paused. Natalya's body jolted against the needle, forcing it in even farther. "Now, now Natalya, please remember that I need a clean specimen of cerebrospinal fluid. No blood, and hopefully, no other contaminants." He pushed in just a little harder.

"You know, Natalya, you have given us a very hard time. Needlessly so. We thought that if we were accommodating to you we wouldn't have any problems. Instead, you try to leave the country and force our men to chase you around the city. My, what a problem you've become."

That arrogant, self-assured voice. She had heard it before in a setting where it had made a distinct impression. She was trying as hard as she could to keep her eyes open and her mind alert to stimuli other than pain. Recognition was within her reach.

"Natalya, I must compliment you. You have an incredibly sensuous back. It's a pity you can't feel the subtle undulations between each vertebral arch. You are in the finest sense of the word an attractive creature." He pushed the needle in farther. She screamed.

"Oh, I am so sorry. I am afraid we may have spoiled another clinical sample."

"Oh no . . . no . . . please . . . no . . ." she pleaded with an acute sense of futility. No matter what she would say, it would not matter. But she would defy him, every step of the way. At least she had defiance to hold on to.

"Wait . . . wait. I may have some good news. Let me see." He pulled back on the needle. "Well, we certainly are lucky. No blood." He pressed his thumb deeply into her vertebrae. "You are very lucky, Natalya . . . very lucky. I don't think you appreciate how lucky you really are."

She heard his words clearly enough to understand the implied message. But she would not concede. He would never extract the secret. Certainly, not willingly. Yes, it was the secret he wanted. Why else would he keep her alive? And afterward? She couldn't think that far ahead.

"Your *bogatyr*, Anatoly, tell me about him. About your relationship with him."

"My *bogatyr*?"

"Don't sound surprised, Natalya, it insults my intelligence. That piece of information was well known in your august circles."

"I loved him. He loved me. That's all there really is to say."

"Yes, if this were a short love story. But it is not. He told you a great deal! Much more, I suspect, than most lovers tell one another. What did he tell you about the plan?"

"The plan?" She tried to reply without any trace of emotion in her voice. The pain in her back was a good distracting focus. The plan, she thought to herself. The plan. Anatoly would never have been that pretentious. Idea. Secret. Conspiracy. Yes. That was more akin to his skeptical, earthy nature. But not a plan. It made things sound so aseptic and rational. None of the characteristics that would apply to her Anatoly. She felt the needle enter deeper into her back. This time there seemed to be no hesitation.

"I love to do spinal taps. I learned to do them quite some time ago when I . . ." he stopped abruptly. There was an awkward silence. "I learned the procedure from my physician friends, who knew that I had a particularly morbid fascination with the mind and the nervous system." Pause. "In case you are not aware, I am not a doctor. Or at least not a professionally trained one. I consider myself somewhat related to the medical profession, however, because of my unusual personal interest and patronage." The voice became egregiously solicitous. "Please don't worry about my lack of official credentials. I can assure you no harm will come to you . . . inadvertently."

Natalya said nothing. She understood that words from her could only provoke him.

"You know why I particularly like the spinal tap as an instrument of clinical investigation? Because it combines a multitude of talents — clinical curiosity, meticulousness, precision, perseverance, and, I might add, an innocent delight in discovering new truths." He paused, placing digital pressure on the tip of his needle. "What did he say about the Politburo?"

"The Politburo?" She knew he would continue this torture, no matter how she answered. "The Politburo," she repeated, taking her time. She felt a sharp pain shoot straight through from her back to her abdomen. She reflexively bent her legs to relieve the pain but attendants instantly straightened them.

"Don't!" screamed the man. "Don't move like that. I don't want you to hurt yourself foolishly. Like truth, the spinal tap is most effective only when you pierce the layers of protection covering the soft central core." He pushed on the needle with the full thrust of his hand and extracted a clear cerebrospinal fluid, the fluid that fills the nervous system, from the bottom of the sacrum right up into the center of the brain. The fluid came rushing out the end of the needle, and the man began to transfer it to an empty test tube.

"I must congratulate you. It looks quite clear. No gross signs of infection, abscess, or hemorrhage."

Natalya did not respond.

"However, I must qualify my clinical impression by stating that we won't know for quite some time what necessitated your hospitalization here. The pathology lab might discover that you have some abnormal protein, like taraxen, often found in schizophrenia. Given your history of sexual promiscuity, you might have a latent case of what we, in medicine, call tertiary syphilis — which could account for your obviously erratic, paranoiac behavior.''

The message was clear. If she decided not to cooperate, she would face a lengthy hospitalization — or torture. Now she knew that she was initially right in her own diagnosis. Borisov, Zeleneyev, and Zoubok all worked together, in collusion with this man and the KGB.

"You still don't remember me, do you?'' The voice had changed unexpectedly. It was now soft and almost plaintive.

"Why do you presume that?''

"Because if you had remembered me, you would have called me by name. That's common courtesy. Manners. I've called you by your first name. Not by Nikitchenko or Vartanian. But by Natalya, your lovely proper name. I've received no equal consideration. I am hurt.''

She tried, unsuccessfully, to recall his identity, their meeting.

"Such a pity. I know it is hard for you to believe this, but I am quite a sensitive individual, whose feelings are easily hurt. Here I am, in effect told that not only have I not left a favorable impression on a very attractive woman, but I've left no impression at all. As if I did not exist. As if I were totally insignificant . . .'' He paused to collect himself. "That, Natalya, is really quite hard to accept.''

As she listened to his words, her head began to throb. She felt nauseated and dizzy.

"My head hurts.'' She was uncertain what to expect from the complaint. He was clearly a sadist who wouldn't give up until he had obtained what he wanted.

"Oh, my poor Natalya. I'm sorry I didn't tell you before about one of the minor, but nastier side effects of this procedure. It is exactly what you are experiencing now — a relentless, pounding headache. Taking aspirin, even codeine, doesn't really help. It's one of those special headaches that isn't caused by the stress of a poor marriage, or a dangerous liaison, or by playing unnecessary, childish games with an authority. No, it's caused, listen carefully, by too much cerebrospinal fluid leaving your nervous system, and particularly your brain, too quickly. Any amount of fluid loss through the hole in your back that I have just created would give you a headache. More fluid loss, more headache. Until you lose so much fluid that you fall into a coma and your brain literally begins to sink — falling through the hole at the bottom of your skull. It's called a herniation. And that, I'm sure I don't have to tell you, is a very ugly situation. Almost totally hopeless and uncorrectable. If you're very lucky, you die quickly. If you are not so lucky, the brain herniates gradualiy and the headache becomes so unbearably intense that you feel the only way out is to kill yourself. But don't worry, I'm sure you're too smart for that."

"Please," she implored, "I feel as if I'm going to throw up."

"Now don't be shy, Natalya. If you feel you must vomit, don't hesitate. But please try not to aspirate. Because you could literally suffocate. And then there is little, if anything, I can do for you."

"Please . . . do something. My head is hurting so."

"At the party, did Sukhumi talk to Comrade Kostenchik?"

"Kostenchik? Kostenchik? He saw so many people that day. So many."

"An old man in his late seventies. The Party theoretician."

"Misha?"

"Yes, Misha."

"I need something, my head . . ." Her voice was desperate. She had visions of the liquid in her brain pouring out of her back, her head falling into her shoulders. She needed relief, even if it meant answering some of his questions. Selective, she repeated to herself. She would answer selective questions. Only those that would not compromise her or her Anatoly.

"I've stopped the flow of the fluid. That should diminish the amount of pain you will be feeling over the next few minutes."

"Thank you." She resented the gratitude she felt.

"What did he talk to Misha about?"

Now he sounded officious, and she was impressed with how quickly her interrogator could switch attitudes. She began to think of him as *her* interrogator. He was sadistic and merciless. But like all victims of torture, she derived some personal gratification from taking a proprietary interest in the torturer. And she was determined to survive the interrogation.

"He wanted to dance with Misha. He said that he had never seen Misha dance and for his birthday he wanted Misha to do that for him."

"Anything else?"

"I find it very difficult to keep talking. I am hurting all over. My head. My back." She paused to see if he would respond.

"I'm giving you an injection that will relieve the pain in your back for a short while."

Natalya held her breath, praying that this was not another gambit to make her talk. She felt the soothing, cool sensation of the liquid dissolve the sharp pain of the spinal tap needle. "There was one other man he introduced me to."

"Who was that?"

"A general of some sort. A cute man, fat. I don't remember his name."

"Marshal Oleg Rusanov."

"Yes, that was it. Rusanov. Seemed very sympathetic."

"Extremely so. At times too talkative."

"Well . . ." she stopped herself.

"He spoke too much, didn't he?"

"He simply mentioned something about troops. That our glorious troops were prepared everywhere and anywhere for any dangers that might confront the Soviet Union."

"Did he mention anything about their state of preparedness? Or their deployment?"

She recalled the reluctant conversation with the field marshal, which had meant nothing to her at the time. "No, he simply talked about how wonderful his soldiers were."

"Are you certain?"

"Yes."

The interrogator pushed the spinal tap needle deep into the spinal cord, beyond the zone of the anesthetic freeze.

She screamed. "Oh no . . . please . . . take it out."

In response, the needle was moved about the cavity, causing even greater pain. Natalya screamed again and the orderlies leaned on her, with their full weight, so that she would stop moving about.

"Oh, please . . . give me something to numb it."

"Are you certain that Field Marshal Rusanov said nothing else?"

"Yes."

He moved the needle again. "Are you certain?" he asked.

"Ugh . . . huh . . . "

"I'm sorry, I can't hear you."

"Yes." She gasped with pain.

"Nothing about Troops One, Two, or Three? Or our state of preparedness?"

"Yes, he mentioned them. But I don't know what they meant."

"Did he tell you where they were being deployed?"

"No. He just said they face our enemies on the west

and . . ." — she tried hard to recall the conversation —". . . and China."

"Anywhere else?"

"No . . . no . . ."

"Did he mention anything about a new military plan?"

"No, he didn't say anything about a plan."

The needle continued to move.

"No, he didn't say anything else," she screamed.

"Please, Natalya. The sooner you tell me about Sukhumi's plan, the sooner we can terminate this . . . nonsense."

"I don't know anything about his plan or anyone else's."

"You certainly are stubborn." He paused, deciding to redirect his line of questioning. "What happened to the general secretary at the party?"

She was confused by the question. Only someone who had been there would have known enough to ask that question. Wait! There was someone else she had met. Someone whose appearance and demeanor had made her dislike him immediately.

"There is another person my *bogatyr* introduced me to. That's why the KGB placed me under house arrest and then followed me . . . because of . . . *you*. Donskoi. Chief of . . ."

"Chief of Internal Security. That is right. A little late. But nevertheless, I am delighted that you remembered me."

"Yes, I remember you . . . well."

"Unforgettable." He was sarcastic once again.

"I assure you no offence was intended."

"And that's how it shall be taken. Now, tell me about Sukhumi's death."

"I know nothing more about it than you."

"Have you told anyone?"

"No. Misha had asked . . . instructed me to say nothing to anyone, for there would be much internal fighting among the politicians if they knew he was dead. So I have said nothing. I don't pretend to understand these matters."

"Oh, please, Natalya. Do you think you can make me believe you have no interest in Party politics? It would serve both your purposes and mine if you would presume that my intelligence is significantly greater than that of your standard *apparatchik*."

Natalya could visualize him in her mind. A wiry, diminutive man, well coiffed, well manicured. Nattily dressed in a silk body shirt with the letters LD sewn onto the cuffs. Thin silk tie comfortably tucked in between the wide lapels of his Italian suit. Self-assured and composed in manner. She recalled now what Anatoly had said about him. "Comrade Donskoi is particularly talented at assessing potential problems — malcontents, dissidents, heretics. . . . He is also responsible for controlling civilian unrest — spotting it wherever it may arise and crushing it before it becomes unmanageable." She also remembered that embrace — what she now considered the fatal embrace. The one that released all that extra nitroglycerin into Anatoly's bloodstream.

"How did Anatoly die?" she asked, wanting to make certain that her suspicions were right.

" 'Die'?" For the first time he hesitated, recalling that day in Tbilisi, only two weeks before, when she accused Sukhumi's personal physician of having been an accomplice to his murder. Yes, she was smart. Too smart. He never would have expected her to notice the extra nitroglycerin patch. Even Sukhumi accepted it with only minor grumbling, asking facetiously whether he could now make love twice as vigorously as before. Perhaps it had been a mistake to place Natalya under house arrest in her husband's care. Gentle discussions in a nonthreatening surrounding had not persuaded her to reveal the key names and whereabouts of the co-conspirators. He had even hoped that after she escaped she might have led him to her contact in Moscow. Instead, she fled to the train station, a fact that alarmed his colleagues in the Politburo.

But the real error, Donskoi realized, took place when Kostenchik and Rusanov, his immediate superiors in the Politburo, had overreacted after learning that Sukhumi had developed a systematic plan for taking complete control of the government, a strategy that would have eliminated each member of the Politburo who had opposed Sukhumi's attempts at liberalizing the Soviet Union. They had prematurely ordered Sukhumi's death. Donskoi's advice to first arrest and then interrogate Sukhumi about the details of the planned coup on November 7 had been overridden by Kostenchik's emotional argument that Sukhumi would prefer to die rather than reveal his plans. And without Sukhumi's personal intervention, Kostenchik had reasoned, there was no possibility of successfully implementing the coup.

Donskoi could not agree. The evidence indicated the contrary. Sukhumi had specifically chosen Natalya, his trusted mistress, as a courier, so that the plan could be implemented by co-conspirators in case he died. She was his insurance policy. Convinced, finally, by Donskoi's arguments, Kostenchik and Rusanov assigned him the task of uncovering the identity of the co-conspirators and the details of the plan before November 7.

For the present, his orders were simple: Under *no* condition was she to leave Moscow. Donskoi had argued persuasively to allow him to admit her to Kashchenko Hospital instead of the Serbsky Institute or Lubyanka Prison. In the other places, Donskoi insisted, Natalya would have been treated as a routine political dissident and charged under Article 70 of the Soviet Code of Criminal Procedure. Her case would have attracted offensive lawyers and ineffective judges. Too much unnecessary legal documentation of the charges. Worse yet, possibly a protracted courtroom trial, the outcome of which he could not control. There would be leaks. And anything that she said would tie her to Sukhumi — to his whereabouts, to the future of the Soviet Union. Yes. The decision to admit a well-known, volatile personality to a prestigious psychiatric hospital for a mental cure had been a stroke of genius. He, personally, had total control. Whatever news might leak out could be immediately discredited as the product of a raving madwoman. He could keep her here at the hospital until he extricated all of the information he knew she had. Especially the name of her contact, the only other person who knew the contents of the plan — or at least where a blueprint was hidden.

"How did he die?" Donskoi repeated her question. "He died the same way we all do, through the inevitability of physical decay."

"Who killed him?"

"If one could say that anyone killed him, I think it would be fairest to say that he killed himself. Rich foods, stress, and . . ."— he paused to choose the right word —". . . intemperance."

"Why was he killed?" she persisted.

Leonid Donskoi stared at the spinal tap needle. Should I plunge it in again? She will not be easy to break. The more pain inflicted, the more defiant she becomes. How typically Russian. He had to admit to himself he was beginning to admire her. She seemed to possess many of the attributes with which he felt he was endowed: loyalty, self-assuredness bordering on arrogance, shrewdness. But she underestimated him. If Sukhumi's plans were discovered by the wrong people, they could place Donskoi and many key members of the Politburo and Central Committee in mortal danger. And if the plans were implemented, they could radically alter the nature of the Soviet Union. So Sukhumi's death had to remain a secret for as long as possible, and this plan had to be aborted. And Sukhumi's mistress was the key to the entire process.

"Once again, Natalya, tell me who else knows about the plan besides yourself?" He gently fingered the needle.

"I don't know what you're talking about, Comrade Donskoi," she replied contemptuously.

His fingers pushed forward on the needle, and Natalya screamed.

Blood started to trickle through the needle. He watched patiently as it fell drop by drop onto the dirty linoleum floor. She could only endure this pain for a few seconds — not more.

His composure was disturbed only by the orderlies, bending over with their bodies, pulling back on her legs. "Stop her. Don't let her bend her legs. Otherwise she will perforate a blood vessel and start to hemorrhage."

Natalya grimaced with pain as she tried to force her legs into a fetal position. Her head began to throb. She knew she was again losing spinal fluid. But it was worth a try. She might be able to force Donskoi to pull the needle out. Otherwise it would have done sufficient damage to her spinal cord and blood vessels to injure her beyond the point of torture. She smiled through her pain as she realized how much of Donskoi's effectiveness depended on her remaining intact.

Please, my *bogatyr*, she whispered to herself, give me part of your strength so that I may survive and avenge your death.

Chapter Six

FOR BORISOV, THE Komsomolskaya metro station was a fascinating anachronism of architectural styles. Fanciful plaster curlicues on vaulted ceilings and oxidized gold-plated chandeliers cast an iridescent white light over sparkling marble floors, arched columns, and walls containing stained-glass mosaic windows. It was a Russian marriage of styles. The ornate and the somber. The foyer of the twentieth-century Hotel Moskva enveloped the central nave of the eleventh-century Byzantine cathedral of St. Sophia in Kiev. All that was missing, he thought, grasping the black rubber handrail as the brass-toothed escalator carried him slowly toward the surface, was a shimmering gold mosaic of the Praying Virgin, like the one that commanded the apse of the central church of the Russian Orthodox Holy Communion. How reluctant we are to enter the twenty-first century without some tribute to the past.

And how different from the Americans. Their trains

and subways were nothing more than dull aluminum crates. No religious pictures or ornaments or murals commemorating social or political themes decorated the walls of their stations or subway cars. He smiled. Yet on his way back from Hawaii in 1977, while stopping over in New York, he had been shocked by the license that the authorities, and he presumed the public, granted those hooligans in New York to paint obscene words and symbols throughout the subways. Incredible. A total disintegration of social and political norms. If nothing else, the graffiti symbolized the inevitable decadence of anarchy resulting from a self-indulgent emphasis on the individual and his rights. Of course, those filthy marks were immediately interpreted by his host, Dr. Block, as the "creative and enthusiastic products of Spanish youths who were not yet acculturated." For all their ingenuity, he thought, the Americans were still unable to discover a way to prevent the defacing of public property. So the authorities had simply raised their hands in disgust and proclaimed the obscenities to be "art." Borisov felt great pride that never once had he seen even a child's crayon mark on the walls of the stations in Moscow. It was simply not possible. Certainly the fine for defacing public property by drawing or expectoration was prohibitive, more than one month of a laborer's wages. But, more important than that, it was not in the Russian character to place one's personal imprint on public property. Our citizens, he thought, have too much respect for the collective integrity.

After a day's work Borisov looked forward to the ritual of return to his apartment on the corner of Gorky Street and Marx Prospekt — the subway ride, an extended walk that provided time to reflect on the day's activity, and then a stop at the bar at the National Hotel near his apartment. The pattern could vary, but not very much. Borisov was a creature of comfortable habits. He enjoyed the rhythm of a predictable life-style. There was enough excitement and diversity in one day at Kashchenko Hospital to excuse what his fellow colleagues would complain of as the "boring periodicity of life." He enjoyed an occasional romantic tryst, or a night of drinking with his friends, or a good game of *gorodki*.

His apartment was conveniently located near his major interests. The Moscow Music Conservatory usually presented at least one concert every month which featured the works of Prokofiev, Shostakovich, or Bartok, his favorite composers. He frequented the Mayakovski Theater particularly to enjoy the romantic works of Pushkin and Lermontov, their dramas depicting isolated heroes engaged in great personal conflicts. Every other month, if he had the time, he would visit the Zoological Museum with its impressive collection of amphibians, reptiles, and insects. He believed in his ability to entertain himself. To be so fully self-contained that there was very little need, or little room left, for indulgences that were not self-directed.

The subway ride home afforded him an opportunity to travel around the Soviet Union without leaving Moscow. It was a tired man's excursion. Like the game he had played with himself earlier that day, trying to determine Sirotkin's origins from his appearance and speech, Borisov only had to look across the aisle in the train, or at the faces to either side of him on the escalator, to see the variety of his country's people. He would give himself ten seconds to determine the geographical origins of the stranger.

On the descending escalator to his left, Borisov saw a young couple holding one another tightly around the waist, laughing and jostling each other in a mocking attempt at pushing the other off the steps. They each had broad faces with high cheekbones, slanted Oriental lines to their eyes, thin lips, ectomorphic bodies. From Alma Ata, Kazakhstan, he thought.

A short, attractive woman with black hair, a sallow complexion, broad face, high cheekbones, and full lips stepped to Borisov's side.

Moldavia, he thought. With those beautiful, big, brown, slightly slanted eyes. Kishinev, Moldavia.

Borisov left the station, adjusting the wool-lined collar of his heavy brown Yugoslavian leather coat against the October cold. He walked at a brisk pace down the potholed streets toward the Moskva River, where the night mist settled on its banks. Moscow was the city of his youth, the city of his passion. At one or another time, by attending different psychiatry conferences, he had visited most of the major cities of the world. But none could compare to his beloved Moscow. Less manicured than Paris, less organized than London, not bustling, like Tokyo, or quaint and charming, like San Francisco, Moscow was a city of immense historical vitality.

Borisov stopped walking when he reached a familiar bridge, with hooded yellow lamps. He stood at the rusted metal railing, listening to the river rushing beneath him. The tensions and anxieties of the day seemed to ebb as he watched the white foaming tips of the river's waves surge upward and then disappear into the darkness. So much energy was required to sustain a day's activity at the hospital. Aching muscles in arms and legs. Tightened ligaments in his neck. Burning, reddened eyelids, tired by dim incandescent lights and the strain of maintaining eye contact. Borisov stopped short of admitting to himself that he might be "burnt out." A disturbing phrase that denoted a collapse of his soul as well as his body. He could accept the fact that he was physically run down. But to admit to some form of spiritual exhaustion would force him to reexamine the choices he had made in the past: psychiatry, an unsuccessful marriage, an unwillingness to find another woman to whom he could commit himself. Yet what alternatives had there been for him? This was not America, where they called a major change in a person's life a crisis in development. In Russia we call it self-indulgent and irresponsible, he thought.

Looking upward, he saw the gold and silver spires of the cathedrals reach skyward, stretching over the crenelated walls of the Kremlin with its massive stone towers and bastions. He felt truly Russian. Not Soviet. Not communist. Not socialist. *Russian.* The Kremlin reminded him that the Borisov family dated from the late 1400s, when members accompanied Ivan III in his campaigns against the rapacious Pecheneg tribe of the Mongol horde. His grandmother had spoken proudly of the Borisovs as great warriors and builders. He laughed, remembering how she used to boast that the three distinctive characteristics of church architecture had all been developed by the Borisovs: the onion dome, the "trapeza" or gallery with open sides that gave protection from the elements to the worshipers outside the door, and the "Kokoshnik gable," named, she claimed, after her great-great-great-grandmother, who wore the winged headdresses of that time that were suited for the heavy snows. She claimed further that in the sixteenth century Ivan the Terrible, with the help of the Borisovs, constructed the most impressive church in all Moscow — St. Basil's — celebrating another Russian defeat of the Pechenegs. However, this time Ivan the Terrible blinded Borisov the builder so that he would never produce anything more beautiful. Even then, the Borisovs had sacrified themselves to the whim of the authorities.

He had always been close to this maternal grandmother. Wary of sending him to the state-run daycare center when they left for work, his parents had dispatched him to "Baboo," his diminutive term for Babushka, who lived down the street. She would sit with him at the kitchen table, before him a glass of hot milk with its residue of cream floating on the surface, and a thick piece of homemake babka, embedded with rich nuggets of dried fruits and stale nuts. She waited until he had eaten everything on his plate and then proceeded to tell him stories of the "famous" Borisov family, and explain that he must use his gifts in science to carry on a centuries-old heritage. As a devout Greek Orthodox, she had always disapproved of his parents' membership in the Communist Party, reviling any beliefs that supplanted the concept of the Holy Trinity. But she was smart enough, he realized in retrospect, never to impose her beliefs on him. The likelihood of Mother Russia ever returning to the status of a free Christian state was minimal. So she was determined never to poison his mind against a system that could cause problems for him in the future. But she did insist, above all, that Borisov never forget to believe in himself. No one, not even Lenin or Stalin can take your name away, she would say. It belongs to you. Some day, she would warn without elaboration, you will need it.

Old Baboo, Borisov thought, had certainly left her mark. He had become a man who did not belong to the system. He simply worked within it. He joined Komsomol, the Young Communist League, when he was only sixteen years old, and then the Communist Party, when he was twenty, not because he was an ideologue or because he believed in Marxist-Leninism, but simply because he was encouraged to do so by his mother, at least out of respect for the memory of his real father, an ardent Communist and genuine war hero. He shared neither his parents' enthusiasm for their participation in a major "social revolution" nor his grandmother's cynicism toward "the corrupt communist system." He regarded authoritarian control in Russia as a legitimate extension of the Russian need for strong moral and political leadership. Never had he felt that his life betrayed the Borisov tradition of individuality and professionalism. So far, the political and professional system had been good to him. It had allowed him the opportunity to develop his natural talents for science and obtain a high position within his profession. Even under the strict control of Zoubok, he felt sufficiently independent. He opposed the myth of the free man as propagated by the social philosophers, psychiatrists, and politicians of the West. Democracy, he decided, was antithetical to the basic nature of man, a nature vested with a strong need to belong to a social group and an equally powerful need for limits and controls imposed from without. The individual had to subordinate his personal needs and responsibilities to the collective good. His professional commitment to improving the diagnosis and treatment of schizophrenia was merely a logical extension of his personal desire to maintain the social order for the common benefit. But the individual case must be diagnosed according to scientific, not political criteria. This was why his colleagues thought him a purist, and at times unbearably self-righteous.

Borisov continued walking slowly across the bridge. The night air was becoming colder. The mist had dissolved. The stars sparkled brilliantly in the clear dark sky. Still, Borisov disliked this time of the year. It was in the late fall that he first met Sonya. He married her one year later and divorced her five years after that.

They had first met as students at Moscow University some fifteen years before. She was twenty-five, exuberant, brash. And gorgeous. Her beautiful gray eyes and tiny snub nose were typical of the area in which she was born, the city of Rovno in the Ukraine. Even now, as he recalled her half-pouting, half-daring seductive smile, inviting him to seduce her and implicitly challenging him, he felt a surge of adrenaline flow through his body. In the beginning, she seemed to share his dreams and his ambitions. But after a few years she became bored by his colleagues and his profession. Soon every sexual encounter became a contest of self-interests. He had been unable to constrain her extramarital activities, and had even begun to learn to adapt himself to her promiscuity. But the smirks and innuendoes of his friends and colleagues had eventually become intolerable. Why had he stayed in the relationship so many years? He understood the obvious points of attraction — her vibrance, her physical attractiveness, her sexual provocativeness, her urbane pretentions and posturings. Something within him needed that relationship, its superficiality and casualness. It absolved him of personal responsibility and commitment to her. All of his intensity, involvement, and intimacy could be legitimately channeled into his professional life.

Borisov walked down a block lined with newspaper kiosks, wooden benches, and denuded elm trees, past the Moscow Art Theater with its billboard announcements of Anton Chekhov's *Three Sisters*, and entered the lobby of the National Hotel, a handsome building erected at the turn of the century and renovated twenty years previously under an ambitious five-year plan to make Moscow more attractive to tourists. There was something decadently comforting about the lobby, with its worn Persian Bokhara rugs and the peeling leather armchairs propped against cracked marble columns. The hotel's employees, some dressed in ill-fitting black tails, nodded to him familiarly. Borisov entered the caged elevator, closed the golden latticed door and got out on the tenth floor.

Ternowsky's gruff peasant voice, shouting Borisov's name, rang like a welcoming clarion call across the darkened barroom. Borisov followed its sound through the cluttered, smoke-filled room that Zoubok had once called an "ill-advised" meeting place for the hospital staff. But he had applied no pressure and they enjoyed the hustle-bustle pretense of Western decadence. Early Art Deco had remained the motif, with circular blue mirrors covering rounded walls, silver-framed pictures of thirties roadsters, and a brightly shining brass handrail leading up curved stairs to another level.

Borisov walked over to a table beneath a color photograph of Moscow at dawn. The usual crowd was there — Zeleneyev, Tsarev, and Ternowsky. These weekly meetings were a ritual, like confession or personal prayer, in which each participant could speak to one another *dusha-dushi*, soul to soul. They sought and received each other's support and encouragement, but only after much good-natured derision, mockery, competition, and jealousy. The rule of the "Round Table," as Ternowsky called the group, was that anyone could say anything, but nothing was to be repeated outside of the "meeting."

"Yuri, move over!" Ternowsky grabbed Borisov's hands and pulled him toward the table. "Let Alexsandrovitch sit down. It's not often we have a distinguished scientist and innovator with us."

"Nothing has yet been proven," Tsarev replied.

"Jealous!" chortled Ternowsky, raising his hand in the air, as if summarily dismissing Tsarev. "He has just told a horrible anecdote, and has no right to speak until our next round of jokes."

Zeleneyev, clearly inebriated, stared at Ternowsky with glassy eyes. "Tell him the joke about communism."

Everyone nodded their heads in approval, including Borisov, who grabbed Ternowsky's Black Russian and drank it down in a gulp.

"Son-of-a-bitch," Ternowsky shouted at Borisov. "Order your own. You get paid more than I do."

"Please!" Zeleneyev's speech was slurred. "Tell him the joke."

"Okay, you thief. Listen, Alexsandrovitch. Three professors from Kiev were discussing the present state of communism in the Soviet Union. The first one said that it was still in the early phase of postrevoluntionary bourgeois turmoil. The second professor replied to the first professor that he was totally wrong and that, in fact, the Soviet Union had just entered its most perfect final form of socialism. Just prior to communism. The third professor turned toward both of them and said, 'You're both completely wrong. If you have indeed studied the society carefully you will notice that the Soviet Union has just entered an intermediary stage not described by Marx, called alcoholism.' ''

When Borisov began to laugh, Zeleneyev, always eager to appear appropriately irreverent without being too disrespectful, leaned over the table. His voice was low and conspiratorial. ''Three doctors who are attending an international medical conference are sharing their different clinical experiences. The Spanish doctor complains: 'The problem in Spain is that we can successfully treat a patient's rheumatism; but, nevertheless, the patient dies from a cancerous complication.' The Italian doctor agrees. He says, 'We have the same type of problem. We treat a man for cirrhotic jaundice, but, he then dies of a heart attack.' But the Russian doctor protests. He says in disgust, 'Everything you say is nothing but bourgeois double-talk. We, in the great Soviet Union, are true to our word. When we say that we treat our patients for pneumonia, then I can assure you that they die exactly from that — pneumonia.' ''

There was a momentary silence. Zeleneyev looked around anxiously, concerned that he might have overstepped some invisible boundary.

''Not bad! Not bad!'' Ternowsky patted him on the shoulder, throwing him inadvertently into a coughing spell.

Tsarev, who had already finished off a few Cognacs, placed his arm around Borisov's shoulders. ''The truth is that you gave a pretty good talk. And you stood up to that bastard Zoubok — with guts.''

"Enough," shouted Ternowsky, "this is not a dance hall where you're trying to seduce some whore. Love each other somewhere else. Not here and not tonight. It's your turn."

Uncomfortable in the limelight, Tsarev asked in a stilted voice, "Who invented socialism? Workers or scientists?"

"Scientists?" Ternowsky shouted, loud enough that the people seated next to him turned around. "Scientists," he repeated angrily. "Can't you ever leave science and the laboratory back at the hospital? What are we to do with you?"

Embarrassed, Tsarev grabbed Ternowsky's hands in his own. "Listen, please, for a moment. This is not a bad joke. I promise."

"You swear?" Ternowsky was skeptical.

"Yes," Tsarev crossed his heart with his left hand. "Again, I'll ask you, who invented socialism — workers or scientists?"

"I give up," Borisov replied. "I don't know which one invented socialism."

"Workers, of course," Tsarev said. "Scientists would have tested it first on hamsters."

The response was less enthusiastic than Tsarev had expected. Borisov saw the disappointment in his face, and started to laugh.

"Don't patronize me. No one liked the joke." Tsarev sat back petulantly, as if he had just been denied access to the Academy of Medicine.

Borisov looked around the table. This evening he wanted to forget their rivalry. He understood that humiliation at grand rounds was gnawing at Tsarev. Borisov had not only achieved a professional coup, but had allowed Tsarev to make a fool of himself.

"I enjoyed the joke," Borisov replied.

Tsarev dismissed the comment with a flick of his hand.

"Alexsandrovitch, it's your turn," said Ternowsky.

"Give us something even more irreverent than what you said today at grand rounds. Oh, I love you, Alexsandrovitch, you stood up to that blowhard tyrant."

"Yuri, one day you're going to make one of your smart-ass comments and I won't be there. Then what will happen to you?"

"I'll go back to the luscious gold wheat fields of my Ukraine — to eat our wonderful, black sourdough bread and not that chewing gum you Muscovites dare to call bread. Anyway, my loved one, it's your turn. The winner of the best joke receives free drinks from all of us." Ternowsky looked around the table to see if he received confirmation for a game and a rule he had just made up.

"You bandit," Zeleneyev replied affectionately, "why not make the worst joke teller pay for everyone else's drinks?"

"All right. Is everyone in agreement?" Ternowsky asked.

Borisov thought for a moment. He was not by nature a raconteur. He preferred being an appreciative audience. When it came to telling jokes he always felt awkward, anxious that he might forget the punch line. Nevertheless, he leaned over the table and began.

"An American psychiatrist who was visiting the Soviet Union boasted to his Russian counterpart that 'We Americans, on the average, own three different cars. One car we use to go to work, the other car we use for summer vacations, and the third one we use for traveling into other countries.'

"The Russian psychiatrist, someone like Yuri here, replied with all the Russian self-confidence that he could muster, 'Well, we Russians don't even need a car. Not at all. For the most part we travel to work by subway. And we go to our summer homes on our beautiful and extensive rail system.' " He paused for effect. " 'And when we take foreign trips, we all go by tank.' "

"Terrible. That was a terrible joke." Tsarev giggled.

"You didn't like that joke, Josef?"

Shaking his head from side to side, Tsarev reaffirmed his dissatisfaction.

"A joke is a joke," shouted Ternowsky. "Now that deserves a round of drinks."

Borisov stood up, raised a glass in his right hand, and said to Tsarev, "That was the finest statement of the day, made by anyone, bar none, including myself. And I propose, since by consensus I have just made the worst joke, and Josef made the best one, I propose that I buy all the drinks. What do you say?"

Everyone broke into applause and Borisov asked the waiter to bring over another round of drinks.

Ternowsky grabbed the new bottle of Stolichnaya vodka and poured some into everyone's glass.

"Wait." Now Ternowsky stood up and raised his glass. "On this auspicious occasion of reconciliation" — he tipped his glass toward Borisov and Tsarev — "and the new discovery of diagnosing sluggish schizophrenia."

"Now . . . now . . . let's not forget the purpose of this evening's celebration," Ternowsky interrupted. "Tonight we should have a vodka befitting the august importance of the evening." Ternowsky beckoned the waiter. "Give us a bottle of Starka vodka . . ."

"Why not Zubrovka?" Borisov demanded.

"Okay, one bottle of Starka and one bottle of Zubrovka. Anything else?"

Without having to say more, they all knew that to order both Starka or Zubrovka meant that the evening's festivity had just attained a new height of importance. Starka was an aged rye vodka with a noticeable caramel color and a sharp taste. Because it was difficult to obtain, the National Hotel served it only to their preferred customers. Zubrovka was Ternowsky's favorite, a strongly flavored vodka created by dipping buffalo grass into the bottle, a popular drink in the Ukraine.

The waiter brought over the bottles of Starka and Zubrovka and four small, thick, thimble-shaped glasses.

"Bring us ice and one bottle of Narzan," Borisov ordered.

"And a plate of herring and dish of black caviar."

When the waiter returned, Borisov grabbed a herring and threw it into his mouth, followed by a small glass of Starka and a glass of Narzan.

"Now look at Alexsandrovitch — that's the way a true Russian drinks." Ternowsky banged the table with gusto.

"True Russian, huh! A true Muscovite."

"Okay, my friend. If you Great Slavs weren't such good drinkers I would have ignored you a long time ago."

"Good drinkers? We Slavs are great drinkers. But you *kulaks* . . ." — he paused, not wanting to offend a good friend — ". . . you are better drinkers." Borisov stood up and made a mock bow, enjoying the jocosity. So much of a premium was placed on control, sobriety, and intensity at the hospital. He glanced around the table, relishing the camaraderie. Throughout his life he had had only one or two close friends who shared any intellectual interests. His Pioneer Camp days were far behind, along with skiing, ice fishing, pistol shooting, ice skating — all hobbies he had pursued through the camp. What was lacking in his recent adult relationships was a certain spontaneity of activity or desire. In the past there were very few times when he or a friend might suddenly suggest they do something unusual, disruptive, or adolescent. Perhaps that was why he enjoyed the Round Table so. It was an opportunity, perhaps the last one, for true revelry. Here he could parody the day's events without concern that Zoubok would reproach him for his faux pas, snide comments about the KGB, or aggressive professionalism. And here he could speak his mind about Zoubok to an audience of sympathizers, without having to worry that one of them might be an informer. In any case, Borisov reasoned, he had seniority and was least susceptible to blackmail. He hated the deep-rooted paranoia that was a prerequisite of survival. Paranoia: the imperative of mental health in the Soviet Union. He glanced at Zeleneyev, who sat with his hands folded over his lap like an obedient schoolboy. In his eagerness for advancement in the hospital, he might be tempted to report to Zoubok about Borisov. But Borisov had come to the conclusion that he could always initiate a countercampaign. Perhaps deprecate him for fictitious misconduct, or replace him as a deputy, when Zoubok was away, or send him off for a sabbatical. No, no danger there, he thought. Tsarev was even easier to handle because their rivalry was so transparent to so many people. Anyone would consider Tsarev's mutterings the result of an adversarial relationship. A natural part of their ongoing conflict. Ternowsky was certainly the hardest one to maintain an effective vigilance against. There was very little that he could hold over Ternowsky. Certainly neither his drinking nor his boorish manner. His unsophisticated diagnostic skills? His limited interest in research? To the best of Borisov's knowledge, Ternowsky didn't even have a mistress. Anyway, Borisov concluded, he could not foresee an occasion where he might have to turn against his friend.

"Alexsandrovitch, you're drifting away from us. Why are you so distracted?" Ternowsky shook Borisov by the shoulder.

"What do you think it would be like if one of us were disloyal to the rest of the group?"

Borisov's friends were startled by the question.

"What do you mean? Why would we be disloyal to one another?"

Only Zeleneyev was not truly surprised. He knew the signs of Borisov's *tristesse*, as he had once labeled it. A distracted sadness. But Zeleneyev had noticed that Borisov was evidencing these periods of *tristesse* more frequently over the past six months. Borisov would simply leave the Organic Therapy Unit and take long walks around the grounds. Zeleneyev had brought up his concern on several occasions, but Borisov would dismiss it with a joke, suggesting that Zeleneyev break the reverie by splashing cold water on his face or scaring him. But Zeleneyev knew that whatever was bothering Borisov could not be dismissed by a moment's distraction. It required an in-depth analysis, which he did not feel equipped to undertake, a psychological understanding more sophisticated than that provided by Pavlovian conditioning, or organic therapies, or Zoubok's nosology. Zeleneyev suspected that Borisov was contemplating a question that had been troubling him for some time.

"What do you mean?" Zeleneyev asked.

"Yuri, leave him alone," Ternowsky said. "What truer emotion can one Russian expect from another when drinking Starka, than good old Russian melancholia? Especially from a Muscovite."

"Yuri, it's a good question." Borisov addressed Zeleneyev with seriousness in his voice. "I was thinking about what had happened between me and Josef today at grand rounds." He turned toward Tsarev. "I apologize, my good friend, for the shame I put you through."

Tsarev stood up, holding the table with both hands. His tie hung askew from his open shirt. Wisps of his hair stuck straight out from his scalp. "Alexsandrovitch." Tsarev, definitely drunk, spoke in a stentorian voice. "I hold no grudges. It was I who was presump . . . presumptuous enough to question your . . . your . . ." — he paused — "brilliant discovery."

A round of applause broke out at the table. Borisov walked around the table and grabbed Tsarev in a bear hug.

Only Zeleneyev recognized the fact that Borisov's

warm embrace once again masked the seriousness of Borisov's question about disloyalty. Borisov sat down, but this time he surprised Zeleneyev.

"Yuri," Borisov continued, "did you ever wonder what it is that allows Zoubok to do what he has been doing?"

"What do you mean?"

"Why does he have such power?"

"Alexsandrovitch, do you realize what you are asking?" Ternowsky was incredulous. "Please get such foolish questions out of your head. You're not some adolescent who has to find out where babies come from. Zoubok is Zoubok. Leave it at that."

"Do you think that, for his own sake, one of us is capable of turning against the others?"

"For what reasons?" Zeleneyev asked.

"Fear. We never talk about fear. We're never allowed to." Borisov waved his hand around the room. "There's too much of it . . . everywhere."

"Oh my God." Ternowsky was exasperated at Borisov's indiscretion. "Before you talk any more, we'll have the KGB all over us."

"Do you know the difference between a Russian optimist and a Russian pessimist?" Zeleneyev interceded, concerned that some further loose talk would get them all into trouble.

Ternowsky replied, appreciating his help, "No, what is the difference?"

"The Russian pessimist claims that the Soviet Union has become a shit hole. Everything is so bad that it couldn't get any worse. But the Russian optimist says in response to the pessimist, it can get worse. And it certainly will."

"I am a free man." Borisov raised his voice. "A Borisov. My family were generations of . . ." He tried to find the right word, feeling good to be so unconstrained.

". . . of . . ."

"Ungodly drunkards!" Ternowsky replied in anguish.

"I beg your pardon, Dr. Ternowsky. I must ask you to take that back. Your insult to my family."

"Excuse me. I retract the word 'ungodly.' "

"Not ungodly. We were . . . are . . . Greek Orthodox atheists. We believe in the church as long as the church believes in communism." Borisov paused. "Noblemen. That's right. We were noblemen. How do you like that one, Yuri?"

"Alexsandrovitch, I like that one very much," Zeleneyev replied.

Ternowsky watched Borisov closely and decided that he had to do something about Borisov's drunkenness. "Gentlemen, it's time for *gorodki*. But first, let's sober up. Everyone drink more mineral water . . ."

They left the bar chanting with annoying persistence, *"Gorodki . . . gorodki . . ."* bidding the various waiters and guests at different tables adieu. They stood at attention as they passed two military officers in the hallway and saluted them as they walked by.

Borisov led the procession down to an empty ballroom large enough to accommodate three full-sized crystal chandeliers. Ternowsky took a wooden chair from a stack against the wall, raised it above his head, and brought it crashing down onto the newly polished floor.

Borisov marked off an imaginary line and paced thirteen meters. He grabbed the five broken pieces of wood from the floor and arranged them in the shape of an arrow.

"Who has forgotten the rules?"

"Forgotten the rules?" Ternowsky replied sarcastically. "You are always changing them. Last time the distance between the throws and the target area was six and a half meters. Now you've just made it thirteen meters. How can you talk to us about rules?"

"The person who has the wood makes the rules."

"Aha, so this is the man who wondered only a few minutes ago about Zoubok's arbitrariness. Interesting, isn't it?" Zeleneyev joked.

Borisov picked up the wood and rearranged them only six and a half meters from the line. "Is that all right? Do you have any other grievances?"

"The rebellious troops have just lost their first round," Zeleneyev shouted.

Borisov turned toward his friend. "Let's agree for today. The purpose of this game is to take one wooden stick, called the *beeta*, and throw it sideways, not overhead, and try to dislodge the *gorodki* — the arranged pattern of wood pieces — in this case the arrow formation. Each one of us will get two tries. The one who is able to knock the most number of wooden pieces out of the target area wins."

"And the prize?" asked Tsarev.

"Don't worry, it's a prize befitting your short status," replied Ternowsky.

Everyone laughed.

"You take the first one. Show us how the champions do it." Borisov threw the *beeta* at him.

Ternowsky stood behind the imaginary line, took careful aim, and threw the jagged stick sideways. It flew through the air, landing at the tip of the arrow. Borisov picked up the stick and threw it back to Ternowsky.

"You can do better."

Ternowsky took aim as if he were about to throw it at Borisov. He flung it and dislodged the arrow formation, but failed to displace it from the area.

"Okay, old man, take another shot." Borisov threw the stick back to him. "You're getting the hang of it."

Ternowsky picked up the stick and flung it in disgust, barely missing Borisov's feet.

"Josef, show us how a true scientist plays this game."

Tsarev looked around the group, nodding his head, acknowledging the challenge. Even in a game, he thought, the competition between him and Borisov continued. "First, you, Alexsandr, then I. This way I'll have something to emulate."

"Well said." Borisov took the stick and watched as it flew completely past the target area. While Tsarev went to claim it, Borisov rearranged the *gorodki* so that the wooden pieces no longer formed an arrow, but a cannon. The new target consisted of five sticks piled one on top of another.

"That's not fair," shouted Ternowsky. "You've got to hit the same target as we do."

"Do I?" asked Borisov. "You know that the only rule is that you have to hit the *gorodki* out of the target area. There is nothing in the rule book that prohibits you from changing the type of target, as long as the same five pieces of wood are used in a recognizable configuration. The cannon, the star, the sickle. All are interchangeable targets."

Borisov took careful aim and scattered the target.

"Now I know why you're Zoubok's successor," Tsarev muttered to himself.

"What did you say?" Borisov asked.

"I said that you play by the rules."

"I try to, Josef."

"As long as there is a possibility to twist them around to suit your needs."

"Okay, fellows." Ternowsky tried to intercede. "This is not the amphitheater." He turned toward Borisov with disgust. "Couldn't you leave well enough alone?"

"Okay, Josef." Borisov threw the stick at Tsarev. "Prove to the group that you had no intention of changing the target as I did."

"What do you mean?" Tsarev knew he had been caught. Borisov had guessed his intention and had simply been faster. There was nothing else for him to do except hit the same target. He took careful aim and threw the stick. It went spiraling through the air and smashed the target beyond recognition.

Borisov went over to examine the sticks and found that only three of the five pieces of wood had been dislodged from the target area. He bent down with his back toward the group and gently nudged the two remaining sticks out of the target area. He stood up and flashed a broad smile. "The winner and champion of today's match is Professor Tsarev."

"Wait a minute," Zeleneyev said. "We didn't get a chance to play yet."

"Oh, yes you did. You don't remember. You forfeited your turn. Didn't he?" Borisov turned toward Ternowsky.

"Sorry about that. The harmony of the game is more important than the rights of the individual players. Is that not right, Professor Borisov?"

"Absolutely. It's an excellent Ternowsky rule."

"Alexsandr, may I please have the *beeta?*" Tsarev's voice was quiet.

"The game is over. You're the winner, Josef."

Tsarev took the stick and flung it up at the chandelier. The fixture shook pieces of crystal to the floor. Tsarev went to retrieve it for another fling.

"Stop!" Borisov shouted. "Why don't you all go home. I'll take care of this matter." Zeleneyev went to get the hotel manager.

"We'll make sure he gets a good night's sleep." Ternowsky took Tsarev by one arm.

Zeleneyev walked in with the manager, a slender man in his late fifties who, although upset by the extent of the wreckage, was more than happy to negotiate the cost of damages for rubles and the promise of free medical services for his family. In turn he would report only that an accident had occurred during a cleanup. He knew from experience that Borisov and his friends were occasionally rowdy, but always true to their word.

Borisov bid the manager and Zeleneyev good night and walked soberly to his apartment down the street. He was pleased that it had only cost 150 rubles to resolve what could have become a protracted and nasty fight, possibly ending up in criminal court. Which would have required Zoubok to appear personally in front of the magistrate and testify on behalf of his staff, all of whom he probably would have dismissed afterward. Yet, the hotel manager had, as usual, been reasonable.

Borisov opened the door to his apartment and turned on the light. He was fortunate. The apartment was small, but it was all his. As a member of the Communist Party, and, perhaps more important, as a senior staff member of Kashchenko Hospital, Borisov was entitled to rent an apartment in a relatively modern building, twenty years old. Unlike his neighbors, who were assigned to three-bedroom communal apartments that they were expected to share with parents, grandparents, and children, Borisov was able to come home and be alone.

A hand-carved wooden coat rack, made by a grateful patient, was bolted to the wall. Borisov placed his shoes on a rack below his coat. Although small, the apartment bespoke Borisov's privileged station. On the wall to the left of the entrance hung a telephone, a highly prized commodity obtained after three months of flirting with the clerk at the telephone office. A mirror with an antique gilded frame hung over an oak stand on which was placed a metal dipper, allegedly made in the late sixteenth century, given to him by his grandmother who told him that it had been handed down to her from her mother — a Borisov legacy. The *kovsh*, as his grandmother had explained, was a low boat-shaped dipper designed originally in the 1300s for ladling *kvass*, beer or mead. The original *kovshs* were made of wood. But his, like those later refined by the Russian nobility into highly decorative ladles covered with precious metals, was inscribed with highly stylized Slavonic lettering on its side. Borisov had long suspected that his *kovsh* was counterfeit, duplicated some seventy years ago by forgers who commonly trafficked in such historical memorabilia.

Borisov reflexively touched the *kovsh* as he walked by it, a superstitious gesture designed to ward off evil spirits, a gesture he had vowed to relinquish. But it maintained his identification with past traditions. His apartment was filled with memorabilia, the greater part of which he had collected from family heirlooms disposed of on the black market.

Borisov sat down on the flower-patterned sofa, a cheap Russian imitation of a Scandinavian design, and placed his feet on a laminated brown coffee table. He was exhausted. It was this main room, an all-purpose room that served as the living room, dining room, study, and, if needed, extra bedroom, that allowed him to feel privileged.

A credenza, a dinner table with four metal chairs, and a small desk filled the floor space. The walls were covered with wooden shelves overflowing with books and journals in psychiatry, and volumes of colored photographs of Russian icons. Also on the walls, as in many houses of cultured Russians, hung Borisov's most valuable rugs, four small signed Persian red-and-blue Bokharas bought on the black market.

He got up and walked over to the window, raised the venetian blinds, and opened the double sets of windows that were standard equipment for a Russian apartment attempting to outlast the Russian winter. From the sixth-floor apartment he saw only one car, a black Zil, parked across the street.

The doorbell rang. Borisov opened it to find an embarrassed neighbor asking whether he had any green vegetables he might spare for her children. He smiled and invited her in. She preferred to stand in the hallway so she could hear if her baby cried, and also to monitor her four boys. Borisov knew and accepted the ritual. Every third day, this neighbor would ask him for either a vegetable, or some milk, cheese, or eggs. Each time she presented herself as "just having fallen short" of that particular item. But he knew that, like all Russian mothers, overburdened with the care of several children at home, and a husband who worked two jobs (in the evening he was a *shabashnik*, a moonlighting mechanic who fixed private automobiles), she had little or no time to wait in line daily for the necessary staples. She knew he was important, and, therefore, had access to the KGB Gastronom.

He asked her to wait and he walked through the bathroom into his tiny kitchen. His refrigerator contained two cucumbers and a small head of lettuce. If this didn't last him for the week, he would be obliged to wait on interminably long lines. What the hell, he thought, as he gathered up all his remaining vegetables and added a prize delicacy, a jar of East German red Bulgarian cherries marinated in sweet liquor. He put them in a brown bag and closed the top so that she wouldn't be placed in the embarrassing position of having to accept more than she requested. As he gave her the bag she muttered "thank you very much" and walked to her apartment. He heard the shrill cries of her joyful children as they discovered his surprise. Smiling, he closed his door and went back to the kitchen. For a fleeting moment he wondered what it would be like to have a child of his own. But he quickly dismissed the notion. It was too late in life to begin a family now.

He took out a pot, filled it with water, and emptied a half box of dark brown coarse *kasha*, buckwheat, into it. That would be his dinner. Outside the kitchen window, the black car had disappeared.

He felt restless. He walked into his bedroom, a room containing a bed two inches too short for his size, an imitation Scandinavian dresser, and a mirror with a small nightstand. He opened his closet, which contained all the paraphernalia of a confirmed bachelor: rusted leather-bound ice hockey skates from his days in gymnasium; woolen, heavy knit sweaters made in Yugoslavia that Sonya had bought for him two birthdays in a row. Reaching to the highest shelf, Borisov took a package and brought it to his desk in the living room. He unfolded the coarse brown wrapping paper with meticulous care and peeled away thick sheets of oilcloth soaked in the pungent aroma of terpin hydrate. Everything was in its proper place. The small brushes, toothbrushes, tightly sealed bottles, and the perforated wooden icon of the Virgin Mary holding the infant child. The Virgin Mary was shrouded in a brown veil marked with two golden stars, one on her forehead, and one painted on her right shoulder. The left shoulder was hidden behind the flowing gold robe of the infant Jesus. The icon, made some five to six hundred years before, was a remarkable copy of the original Virgin of Fladimir, created by a Byzantine artist in the twelfth century. Like the original, with which Borisov had fallen in love when still in his early teens, this icon portrayed the essence of what all true Russians felt was sacred — maternal tenderness.

Borisov placed the worn icon on the oilcloth, arranged the brushes and bottles, and contemplated his approach. He decided to concentrate on restoring the golden filigree lines along the forehead of the black veil, that portion of the lines that heightened the sensual aestheticism of the Madonna's eyes.

First, he passed the toothbrush lightly over the area of restoration, making certain to eliminate any large particle of dust or clumps of paint that would prevent him from matching the antiquated gold color of the icon with his gold paint. Clearly, he thought, there is no way I can restore the entire icon to its original beauty. There was one part, just above the bridge of her nose, that was giving him a particularly difficult time. Taking the longest, thinnest brush, he dipped it into the bottle of aqua regia. This mixture of acids had the elegant property of being able to test for true gold by dissolving other particles which were sensitive to the eroding properties of hydrochloric and sulfuric acid. He touched the golden filigree border over the forehead, making certain that he could count the number of drops lazily descending from the brush. When the drops dried, he took another delicate brush, dipped it into the gold paint, and watched the heavy globules slowly drip to the tip of the brush. With a slight flick of his wrists, he unleashed the gold droplet onto the line, reaffirming a spiritual lineage that began several eons before the concept of a nation-state had ever entered the consciousness of the Great Slavs. Although a confirmed atheist, Borisov could appreciate the sacred tradition of the icon painter who toiled for years over one representation. He could respect the artistic code laid down by the Greek Orthodox church which was as strict and formalized as the religious rituals of the church itself. How similar religion was to the profession of psychiatry, he mused. Both required dedication to a calling beyond the immediate requirements of personal satisfaction. Both required working within a given set of rules, transmitting a body of knowledge from one generation to the next, which bore witness to the divine nature of man. They each demanded total dedication and, for the most part, anonymity. The church required that all icons remained unsigned so that they would reflect the spiritual quality of the religious subject matter and not the idiosyncrasies of the individual artists. In psychiatry, the individual doctor was subordinated, for the most part, to a consensus diagnosis and to a body of knowledge that had been developed through an individual's initiative but had been subsumed into the sterile anonymity of scientific knowledge. The clerics of the fifteenth century had actually issued edicts to the icon makers for the proper conduct of their lives: they should be chaste, live with few possessions of their own, and remain dedicated solely to the art of ressurrecting the spirit of Christianity through the concrete respresentations of holy personages. Any suggestion of three-dimensional art was to be strictly eschewed and considered sacrilegious. Borisov knew full well the oil-based paints that he was now using to restore parts of the icon were totally forbidden until the eighteenth century because they were too redolent of the sensuous, secular Western artists. As in psychiatry, the tools and materials of the icon tradition were simple and ascetic. Figures were to be drawn only on a well-seasoned wood without knots, such as cypress, pine, birch, or oak. Once the wood was chosen, a woven linen was attached to it with some type of glue, and the material coated with two to nine layers of gesso, made from ground alabaster. When a design had been decided upon, after numerous consultations between the artist and the priest, it was stenciled onto the dried and polished gesso. Next the icon maker prepared his paints, composed of pulverized mineral earths ground in a liquid mixture of egg yolk, water, and *kvass*, rye beer preservative. Figures were drawn in two-dimensional planes to avoid the proscription against statutory idolatry, and the backgrounds were highlighted in gold leaf, especially the halos and sinewy gold lines that often ran down a vestment. After days of drying, a protective coat of boiled linseed oil was applied, adding the extra touch of a golden sheen over the entire icon. Since his icon had lost most of its golden background, restoring it had become Borisov's major project since his divorce.

Borisov inserted a finger beneath a loose edge of cloth and suspected that it was saturated with only half the amount of gesso needed. Maybe next week he would strip the cloth off the wood and add more gesso. What could you expect from an icon bought for eighty kopeks from a farmer at the Sunday market near the train station? He had claimed it was a family heirloom. Borisov suspected that its value on the black market had increased several fold. But financial appreciation was not his primary interest. Rather, it was a chance to physically connect with a spiritual tradition that had once been sacred and meaningful to the Russian people. Yes, he believed in the Marxist dialectic and the importance of the proletariat revolution. But these were man's fabrications, and easily dissected, discarded, or reformed. Like many, Borisov yearned for something that allowed him to believe that there might be a grand design that was not dependent simply on man's will. A force beyond, which even he could not comprehend. He wasn't ready to accept the arcane concept of a God, but he did believe in the sacred tradition of divine inspiration. So for the moment, he was willing to believe in the Russian people's most divine artifact, the icon. Later? Who knew.

Chapter Seven

BORISOV SLEPT FITFULLY. He dreamed of Natalya, dressed as a religious Arab woman shrouded in a chador, at once beckoning him to look beneath the hooded veil and accusing him of moral infidelity. Since he didn't believe that dreams had significant psychological meaning, he dismissed it as a superficial reflection of the previous day's events. Yet he had never before been so eager to visit a patient. As he walked down the bleak corridor to her room, he decided that she was probably not schizophrenic, but suffered from a mercurial personality. How much of her history was accurate? Every patient distorted the past to highlight aspects that, at the time, seemed inordinately important. Natalya had mentioned marital problems as a precipitant for her admission to the hospital, but Borisov was not convinced. There hadn't been enough emotion or conviction behind her statements. What she had unwittingly said about her *bogatyr* had seemed more important, not so much what she had said, but the way she had said it. He would have to find out who this *bogatyr* was and what he meant to her. He also made a mental note to check her mother's hospitalization in the central mental health registry book, a daily tally of all inpatients admitted to a psychiatric hospital anywhere in the Soviet Union, distributed by the Ministry of Health to Zoubok and the other regional mental health directors.

The same two KGB security agents guarding Natalya's door greeted Borisov with unusual warmth. When he entered the room, he understood why; Natalya was missing. The guards laughed when Borisov asked about visitors to the room and they began to cite the names of famous Soviet citizens who might have entered and left. There was very little he could do except to allow them their few minutes of fun. When he finally pointed out that he would have to lodge a complaint against them for negligence, pranksterism, and insolence, their joking ended, as Borisov knew it would. The underbelly of all security agents was their personnel file, with a section for citizens' complaints, which gave the appearance that the system was sensitive to outside criticism. They told him that she had been taken for hydrotherapy.

Borisov rushed down the corridor, brusquely pushing aside several nurses, and ran across the hospital grounds. Why was she receiving hydrotherapy? Only the most agitated, the most violent, the most disturbed were taken there. Just yesterday she was fine. Her tests were not completed. Who would have ordered therapy?

In the hydrotherapy room Borisov was greeted by the same nurse who had assisted him the previous day. She was supervising two nursing attendants, whose hoses were pinning Natalya aginst the white tiled wall by the force of the criss-crossing high-pressure streams of hot and cold water. Each pulsating thrust of water tossed Natalya upward and sideward, reinjuring her shoulder.

She was trying desperately to grab some imaginary handle that would allow her some modicum of stability. Her screams were muffled only by the rush from the savage jets. The Scotch douche, a procedure that Borisov knew improved the condition of many patients, suddenly appeared barbaric.

"Stop this at once."

The nurse looked at him, bewildered. "May I remind you about yesterday's patient? The one whose therapy we stopped too soon. May I remind you, doctor . . ." — she paused to monitor his response — ". . . you regretted that decision soon afterward when she caught hold of your neck and started strangling you."

"Stop this therapy immediately." Borisov's eyes were cold and penetrating.

"I can't. It's an official requisition by a superior. Only he can cancel it."

"A superior?" The words rushed through his mind. That was not possible. There was only one official at the hospital who was empowered to countermand or supersede Borisov's orders, and he had no reason to do so.

"I'd like to see the order sheet."

Clearly disgusted, the nurse handed a paper to Borisov. On the bottom of the page was Dr. Zoubok's signature. Borisov took out his pen, crossed out Zoubok's name, and replaced it with his own. "Dr. Borisov cancels the therapy." He handed back the chart and shouted to the two nursing orderlies. They turned toward him but looked at the nurse for final orders. The nurse looked at Borisov. If she wanted to she could refuse, and the nursing assistants, by order of proper hospital protocol, would have to follow her orders because they were signed by Zoubok. Both she and Dr. Borisov knew that he had no legal or moral authority to rescind the orders. That was the way of Kashchenko Hospital. But if she defied Borisov, he could make her job at the hospital very difficult, to the extent of forcing a voluntary resignation for all sorts of legitimate reasons — poor health, the stress of the job, a need to be with her children. Worse yet, he could have her reassigned to one of those dreadful institutional warehouses for the chronically disabled, where she would probably spend the rest of her life cleaning up the excreta of incontinent patients. Looking at his angry, determined face, she knew he would eventually get his way. The crucial question was whether she would be better off suffering at Zoubok's or Borisov's whim. Both could be difficult. It has always been the same, she thought. Her parents and grandparents were all feudal serfs on an estate outside of St. Petersburg. What difference did it make to them who ruled, when one master was as unforgiving as the other. She decided to accept Borisov's order. She certainly had presented sufficient outward resistance. If called to account for her actions by Zoubok sometime in the future, she could always summon the two nursing orderlies as witnesses on her behalf.

Anyway, the patient was beginning to bleed through the bandages on her right shoulder and she did not want to be held accountable for any accidents.

"I agree with Dr. Borisov's clinical assessment. The patient has had enough hydrotherapy." She nodded her head, signifying to her orderlies that they desist.

When the water was shut off Borisov grabbed Natalya's bathrobe and walked over to her with it. She had barely enough strength to stand up.

"Son-of-a-bitch," she spat. Her olive skin glistened. Her coal-black hair was matted against the sharp angular lines of her face. Her green eyes gleamed with rage.

He handed her the bathrobe but she had difficulty putting it on. When she slipped to the floor the second time, Borisov lifted her up and carried her to the examining table.

The nurse brought a suturing kit, a small metal tray bearing needles and nylon threads. Borisov removed the blood-soaked bandages from her right shoulder to inject the reopened wound with 2 percent Zylocaine anesthetic.

Natalya's eyes opened and she started to scream.

"No, not again. Leave me alone. You've tortured me enough."

"Natalya. I have to sew the wound. It has opened up again."

"Let it bleed. It is a lot less painful than your 'treatment.' "

"I don't understand." Borisov's voice was slow and gentle. "Clearly, something has happened to you and you think I am responsible. But I will not know what I am accused of until you tell me."

Natalya stared at him incredulously. She gritted her teeth and hissed, "Get out or get me out of here."

"I must sew your open wound."

"No. I want *you* to get me *out* of this crazy house. Now!"

"I can't do anything unless you first let me sew that wound."

"No, I'll bleed."

Borisov motioned to the two orderlies to hold her down. They, in turn, looked at the nurse, who nodded her approval.

Natalya offered no further resistance. She watched as Borisov inserted the needle of the syringe into the raw, rough edges of her wound and injected the anesthetic. She stared at the point of the insertion, remembering it, fixing it in her mind so that she could rehearse it over and over again until she would no longer be afraid of seeing a needle go into her shoulder, her back . . . or anywhere else those bastards would decide to put it.

"I hope that didn't hurt you," Borisov offered.

Natalya didn't reply, concentrating instead on the hooked needle as it passed through the flaps of the wound.

She watched with fascination. A sharp, piercing pain radiated down from the suture site along the lines of her neck. She grimaced. But the pain was no longer frightening. It had become a known quantity. A predictable companion. Something upon which she could now count for a sense of control over her life. She accepted that her life had become discrete episodes of trauma and pain. How different from the halycon days when she and Anatoly would spend every possible moment together devising techniques to give each other physical pleasure and emotional gratification. After an evening of passionate lovemaking, he would surprise her with some bauble, silver earrings, a bracelet, a ring. She flexed her fingers to feel whether the sons-of-bitches had left her with any of her rings. They had.

How perverse, she thought. Pain now substituted for love and tenderness as a way of relating to her surroundings, to herself. And yet the physical pain she was experiencing resonated with feelings that she had always had, but had submerged. Sukhumi's death . . . her father's. She tried to dismiss the terrible thoughts flooding her mind, that frightening word she always associated with trauma and pain. Abandonment. No, no. She corrected herself. Not abandonment . . . but death. Death and abandonment. What was the difference? In either case the person departed, leaving behind an emotionally scarred victim filled with anger, disappointment, and mistrust.

"There. That looks elegant." Borisov tied the last suture. "If we leave it alone for a week it will heal quite nicely."

Natalya didn't answer. Borisov watched as she carefully moved her fingers toward the wound. Would she purposefully hurt herself, just to spite him? To make him feel ineffectual? He would give her the chance to prove that he could trust her.

Her fingers ran along the ridge of raw flesh, gingerly touching the coarse elevations of the nylon thread. She glanced sideways and saw Borisov waiting for her reaction. Her long, unmanicured nails hooked into the spaces beneath the nylon suture. Before she could reopen the wound, Borisov jerked her hand away.

"You're hurting me."

"No, I'm stopping you from hurting yourself."

"You stupid *apparatchik*. I prefer this pain to your torture. At least I control it."

"What are you talking about? I know you don't believe me, but I really don't know what you mean."

"Liar."

The nurse looked critically at Borisov. By now Zoubok would have had her secured in a straitjacket and placed in solitary confinement for such insolence. Seizing the initiative, she nodded at the two nursing orderlies to prepare to take her away.

"No, let her alone. If she wants to rip her shoulder, that's her business."

"Will you need us any longer, doctor?"

"You can go. I'll take care of her. Just leave the wheelchair here."

"As you know, Dr. Borisov, the wheelchair belongs back on the ward. It is my duty to bring the chair back."

"Leave the wheelchair here."

Grimly, the nurse handed Borisov the chart, asking him to sign it and release her from personal responsibility.

Borisov sat Natalya on the table after they left.

"Oh, my head," she said, squeezing her temples tightly.

"What's the matter?"

"My head, my head. You know what's the matter."

He grabbed her head and held it upward, brusquely pushing aside her hands. He took a pinlight flashlight from his lab coat. Every time he brought the light near either her right or left pupil she jerked her head away.

"You idiot. Don't you understand that my head feels as if it is going to explode?"

"Mrs. Vartanian, I strongly suggest that you stop calling me names, if you want me to help you."

"Your head would hurt too if someone jabbed a needle in your back that practically reached your skull."

"Oh, you mean a spinal tap. Unfortunately, a headache is one of the side effects."

I was right about him after all, she thought. He had ordered the spinal tap. He, Donskoi, and Zoubok are in collusion.

"The spinal tap is one of a series of clinical tests that are part of our standard workup for a patient admitted under the circumstances that you were."

"Do you always send the chief of Internal Security of the KGB to perform your spinal taps?"

"Of course not. One of our staff doctors performs the procedure. It's complicated . . . and dangerous if done improperly."

"So I was told."

"And why did you say that?"

"What do you mean?"

"About the chief of Internal Security."

"What about him?"

"Stop playing games with me." Borisov was becoming angry. "You just told me that the spinal tap was performed by the KGB's chief of Internal Security. Did you actually see him?"

"No."

"Then how do you know? And masquerading as a doctor?" She was becoming paranoid. Perhaps he should rule out neurological problems, like a sudden swelling of the brain due to a blood clot.

Borisov took out an opthalmoscope and peered into each of her dark black pupils. Both optic disks looked flat and round and refracted a normal color. He counted the number of vessels crossing the border of the optic disks — twenty-one in the left eye and twenty in the right eye. Normal. No evidence of papilledema or hemorrhages anywhere in the retina. No neurological lesion is causing her headache, he concluded. Next he checked the cranial nerves, one through twelve. He had her stick her tongue out and wiggle it from side to side, puff out both cheeks, close and open her eyelids quickly, move her neck up and down and from side to side. Everything looked normal. Her symptoms all pointed to a primary psychological disturbance, characterized by persecutory auditory hallucinations.

"Does that hurt?" Borisov gently tapped the vertebrae in the lumbar region with this fist.

"Yes."

"Where?" Now he pushed on the vertebrae. She groaned only when he touched both café au lait spots. He examined the areas but found only two very small, normal puncture wounds from the spinal tap. He checked her ability to bend and move her legs to the sides, asked her to squeeze them together, and observed no limitation of motion sometimes occurring after a spinal tap. He moved Natalya's head up and down, side to side. Despite her protests of an unremitting headache, he could find no evidence that anything was physically wrong. Psychosomatic, he concluded. Her body, primarily her lower back and head, was responding to whatever emotional stimulus she was feeling — probably anger and anxiety. According to Pavlov's theory of psychophysiology, Natalya's emotional agitation and paranoia were the independent variables that could be monitored by the dependent variables of her physiological responses, such as the tone of the muscles in her lower back or cortical brain-wave activity that could be monitored by the EEG machine. Perhaps Zoubok's imperious assertion that this woman was a sluggish schizophrenic was correct. Clearly, she did not trust Zoubok. If left untreated, her anger might lead to an extremely paranoiac condition.

Borisov considered her possible treatment. Very frequently, especially with exceptionally bright and verbal patients, "talking therapy" could be quite useful. Certainly, as an adjunct to the use of drugs or insulin. In any case, it was important that he win her confidence. Otherwise, she would never allow him to complete his tests in an appropriate way. If he needed physical restraints to calm her, he might distort the EEG test, since agitated patients produced a brain-wave pattern that confused the distinctive pattern of the sluggish schizophrenic. He had to find out who she really was, why she was at the hospital, and which parts of her history were truthful. Also, who was this *bogatyr?*

Borisov wheeled Natalya past a nurses' station. He opened the medicine closet and withdrew some ergotamine and aspirin to relieve her headache. She swallowed the pills only after he had assured her that if he had wanted to poison her, he could have done it much sooner. They continued down the corridors and exited into a brilliant morning sun.

"If you are taking me to my death or to another torture, I would like to spend a few minutes in the sunlight."

Borisov laughed. "All right, if that's the way you want it."

Natalya found it hard to believe that this doctor could be associated with brutal men such as Donskoi. She recalled Anatoly's admonitions, "Beware of any man who belongs to the system — he has already martyred his soul to survival or advancement." Borisov must be very ambitious, she decided. Yes, there was something in the sharp angles of his face that suggested a restless intelligence. It was the face of a man dissatisfied with his present condition. And a man consumed by professional ambition might do anything required to get ahead. No, she would not be deceived by his moments of kindness. They had competing interests. She would have to figure out how to take advantage of the situation. She smiled ruefully when she thought about how smart Anatoly was. He had tried to prepare her for the dangers he knew she would encounter simply as a function of her association with him, to teach her the rules of survival within the system he had helped to create.

Her headache and shoulder pain began to subside as Borisov wheeled her into a dilapidated building that included a ward of women between the ages of eighteen and forty-five. Each woman had been admitted for either alcoholism or drug abuse. Unlike other wards, this one had a feminine atmosphere. The walls were papered with a splashy pattern of daisies and violets. The sofas in the day room were covered with a pastiche of cloths sewn together to disguise their deteriorating condition. Eight women were seated in a circle, and Ternowsky conducted group therapy.

Borisov stood and listened. Ternowsky presided over the group with an ease of command akin to that of a Moslem sheik listening patiently, if somewhat condescendingly, to the problems of the women in his harem. This was one of the major incentives, he knew, that kept Ternowsky at Kashchenko. He enjoyed "his women," as he called them. Borisov knew that Ternowsky lacked enough sophistication to interpret their problems with the proper sensitivity and insights. But he did provide them with the patience, authority, and leadership they needed to express their problems and help each other out. And that was, of course, what a group was all about.

Borisov was proud of the inpatient alcohol rehabilitation services they had created together. First they had initiated a nationwide campaign to change the attitudes of Russian officials toward the problem of alcoholism. As in many Western countries, the Soviet officials had for a long time refused to admit there *was* a serious problem. So, Borisov, Ternowsky, and the other doctors at the Kashchenko went into office buildings, factories, and schools and began to lecture on the physical and psychological dangers of alcohol. After several years the bureaucrats accepted the fact that alcoholism was a medical disease that should be treated as a mental illness. Now public drunks who were picked up by the police were not incarcerated, but placed in a division of the prison that was staffed by a physician and a *feldsher.* If they required hospitalization, they were transferred to a psychiatric hospital and placed under the personal care of a narcologist, a physician trained specifically to treat the physical symptoms of the alcoholic, such as physical debilitation, insomnia, irritability, and visual hallucinations. In the second stage of therapy, the narcologist and patient would work on specific ways of overcoming the need to drink, including persuasion, self-hypnosis, and behavior modification. The third part of the therapy combined a drug and psychotherapy program that enabled the patient to maintain the gains made in the second stage of therapy.

A short, pale woman with long black hair, in her early thirties, had been speaking in an impassioned voice. She stopped when she saw Borisov and Natalya enter the room.

"Go ahead, Tamara," Ternowsky said, "you were talking about the futility of dreaming if there's no chance to see your dreams through. You're still among friends."

Tamara looked around the group for support. The others nodded silently and she continued. "It sounds so obvious and simple. But there are no women in the Soviet Union who rule. Or who have any power. Any real power. It's a man's society that doesn't officially recognize any difference between a woman or man's achievements and status. But the truth is, we have equal responsibilities for earning a living, added responsibilities of being mothers and wives, and we still receive less pay, no job advancement. No power.''

How familiar this sounded, Natalya thought. She had often complained to Sukhumi about this dismal situation and he had promised, on his mother's soul, that he would soon change it.

"I'm a union member at my factory," Tamara continued. "At the senior levels of my union, where the decisions are made, there are no women.''

"Same thing in the upper levels of the army, the Communist Party. No women," added Katya, a robust woman in her late twenties, with short-cropped blond hair and metal-rimmed glasses.

"Of three hundred and thirty member of the Central Committee of the Communist Party, only thirty-five are women. Ten percent in a population where over fifty percent are women. And there are no women at all in the Politburo or the Council of Ministers.''

"Who cares whether there are thirty-five or seventy women?" Tamara was angry. "The point is that there are no women in any position of power.''

"I was only trying to illustrate the point more clearly.''

"You're always trying to illustrate the point more clearly. Can't you let someone else make a simple point without always having to elaborate on it with numbers?''

"Why is she always picking on me, Dr. Ternowsky? I was only trying to help her.''

"Perhaps you shouldn't try to be so helpful.''

"Thank you, Dr. Ternowsky. She can sometimes be too helpful. In fact, a pain-in-the-ass." Tamara glared at Katya. "I'm a college-educated factory worker.''

"We know," Katya replied.

Tamara looked toward Ternowsky for guidance, but received none.

"I live in one room in a communal apartment about fifteen square meters in size, which is not bad. I share the apartment with one other family. We try to see as little of each other as possible."

"How were you able to obtain your own room?" Ternowsky asked.

"I have a three-and-a-half-year-old son. The law allows a single parent to live with her child in a single room. But that is part of the problem that brought me here. Because I work from seven in the morning to seven in the evening, I rarely see my son. He stays in a state nursing school while I am at work."

"What about your parents? Can't they help you?" Ternowsky asked.

"No! When I left their house I left them for good. I was determined to live my life my own way. But since I left, everything I touch has spoiled."

"What do you mean?"

"Well, I'd been seeing the man who ultimately fathered my son for several years before I got pregnant. Neither of us really knew very much about contraception. We relied on the rhythm method. But I guess we weren't very good at mathematics."

Everyone in the group laughed.

"We tried the condom, but like anything that's made of rubber in the Soviet Union, there are always some defects."

"That's also true for the IUD, the diaphragm, and the pill," added Lidia, a pretty woman in her mid-thirties, dressed in faded blue jeans and denim shirt, both highly prized possessions within the Soviet Union. "The only thing that works is this." She raised her middle finger, moving it in a clearly masturbatory fashion. "Who needs them anyway?" she asked, laughing.

"Without them you turn to the bottle. Which is what I did." Tamara glanced at Katya. "Or to some other woman."

"What do you mean, you bitch?" Katya stood up.

"Sit down, and apologize to her, Tamara," Ternowsky interjected. "You were saying that you started to drink because your fiancé left you."

"I started to drink because I was fed up with all the shit — a job without a future, a child who didn't even know his mother, a selfish boyfriend, and a life that was going nowhere."

Natalya looked around the group. This was the first time in a long while that she'd had the chance to hear about someone else's problems. She couldn't recall ever having sat down with a group of women to share her feelings, her dreams, her disappointments. Her mother had cautioned her to keep her hopes and discontents to herself, and not to expose herself unnecessarily to someone else's sadism. Her *bogatyr* had told her that only in the intimacy between two lovers could there by any real expression of longing and anger. Here she saw a group of women expressing anger with their jobs, the system, with themselves.

"The most depressing part of my life is the fact that I no longer question the reasons why things are the way they are."

Katya peered through her glasses at Tamara, like a frightened child awaiting approval from her older sister. "Once I was inquisitive. I used to ask a lot of questions. Why do so many people live in one apartment? Why can't I do the things I've always wanted to do, like write poems? Personal poems. Poems that allow me to say what I feel."

"Stop dribbling, you crybaby! I've read that crap you call poetry."

"You're terrible! Cruel!" Katya began to cry. Lidia walked over and placed her arm around her.

"Okay. That's all for today. We'll meet tomorrow at

the same time." The group dispersed. Ternowsky then greeted Borisov. "Alexsandrovitch, why is that you have all the beautiful women?"

"This is Natalya Vartanian, a recent admission. I wanted to show her that there are parts of the hospital in which we don't torture patients, but actually try to find out what concerns them."

"I'll tell you a little secret." Ternowsky's eyes sparkled. "I used to be a lion tamer before this, so I am well prepared for my present job."

"Nice meeting you," Natalya said, making an effort to smile.

Borisov wheeled Natalya out of the room, passing a row of workshops where men and women were engaged in different types of activity. The men were seated at metal work benches making small wooden boxes. The women were sitting at antiquated sewing machines, pumping the foot pedals monotonously.

"They look like automatons."

"These are chronic schizophrenics who are being taught some basic manual skills that they can use on the outside. Many of them are heavily medicated, so their movements are slow, robotlike. But, believe me, they enjoy it."

"How do you know?"

"They all volunteered for this program."

"Volunteered? You mean a Russian volunteer or real volunteer?"

Borisov did not respond. He smiled to himself and pushed her into a room filled with electronic equipment.

"So you're trying to frighten me. Well, you've succeeded."

"This is the room in which we try to figure out what's going on inside of your mind by scientific methods. We perform certain tests on our patients." Borisov tried to sound reassuring. "Tests that involve picking up brain waves. And we give written tests, as well."

"In short, it's a torture chamber."

"Please, don't be frightened. There is nothing here that will cause you pain." Borisov extended his arms. "Here, let me help you up." As she took his hands, Natalya looked into his eyes. They seemed warm and sincere, but underneath she sensed a calculating individual who would be pleasant merely to obtain what he wanted. He had brought her to view the group psychotherapy to demonstrate that this was really a psychiatric hospital concerned about the well-being of its patients. But now she realized he was only softening her up for the tests that he wanted to perform.

With encouraging words, a female technician helped Natalya into a seat and strapped a band with wires onto her head. Even if she had wanted to resist, Natalya was too exhausted.

Borisov equilibrated the electroencephalogram machine, checking its leads. He attached the polygraph machine to the EEG reading, so that he could also obtain a measure of her veracity. The polygraph was frequently unable to detect patterns of distortion or lying with many schizophrenics and sociopaths, but it was worth a try. He looked at Natalya, sitting with multicolored wires emanating from her head. She looked almost surreal, a face of pristine beauty beneath a grotesque crown.

Natalya felt serene. There was very little Borisov could do to her that she had not already experienced from Donskoi — humiliation, degradation, fear, intimidation, threat, violence.

"Natalya, I'm going to ask you some questions that are not too different from the ones I asked you before."

"It's a pity you can't think up new ones."

"Maybe you're right." He smiled. "What questions would you ask yourself if you were in my place?"

"What am I doing here?"

"That's a good question. What are you doing here?" He watched both the EEG tracings on the large console and the adjacent polygraph tracings on the smaller machine.

"I am a political prisoner."

"In what way?"

"I am here for reasons other than mental health."

"We don't admit people for reasons other than those of mental health." He looked at the paper tracing. No unusual patterns.

"I have been admitted for reasons other than insanity. I am not mad. You know it. I know it. And your stupid machines, if they are any good, will tell you the same thing."

"No one said you were insane."

"Then why am I here?"

The polygraph showed increased activity. Nothing specific. The EEG tracing was picking up background activity.

"You're here because you have had some recent emotional disturbance."

"Like what?"

"Like the problems in your marriage." Still no changes in the tracings.

"My marriage? I told you there is no marriage. There has never been a marriage. It has simply been an alliance of convenience which turned out to be neither convenient nor an alliance." She paused. She had to be very careful just how much she could reveal to him. "He was part of the plan." She hesitated to use the word *conspiracy*.

Borisov glanced at the machine tracings. The cranial leads in the EEG tracing revealed clusters of long- and short-wave activity. The polygraph machine demonstrated some increased anxiety but nothing that was characteristic of major distortion or lying.

" 'Plan'? What plan?"

"A plan they have to bring me to this hospital and keep me committed here for as long as necessary."

"Who are 'they'?"

Natalya hesitated.

Borisov watched as the polygraph machine began to show increased bursts of electrical activity. She was definitely becoming agitated, and approached the GSR boundaries for lying.

"A group. A group of men you know well. And with whom you work, I am sure."

"Which group?"

"Listen, does that machine tell you what I am thinking about if I don't answer your questions?"

"Yes." He lied. Part of the effectiveness of the polygraph test lay in the myth that the machine could distinguish between boldfaced lies and the truth.

"Does this group, the one that wants you committed, involve doctors at this hospital?"

"Yes."

"Dr. Zoubok?"

"Yes."

"Me?"

"Yes."

"Dr. Zeleneyev?"

"Yes."

The EEG pattern began to evidence the characteristic slow, irregular waves that he had seen in Nekipelov's tracings. Sluggish schizophrenia, he said to himself. But he needed a more sustained tracing.

"Why would Dr. Zeleneyev want to hospitalize you?"

"Because . . ."

The polygraph machine became more active. A little more anxiety perhaps, but no evidence of lying, thought Borisov.

"He wants information."

"What kind of information?"

"Information."

"Had Dr. Zoubok ever met you before yesterday?"

"No."

"So on the basis of never having seen you, or examined you prior to your admission to the hospital, Dr. Zoubok wanted you committed to this hospital in order to elicit certain types of information that you are not at liberty to reveal. Is that right?"

She nodded her head. He had trapped her into admitting what sounded even to her like a fantasy.

"I'm sorry. I can't hear you. Was that correct, what I just told you?"

"Yes. That was right."

"Who else is involved in this conspiracy to commit you to a mental institution?"

"Leonid Donskoi."

"Leonid Donskoi? Who is that gentleman?"

"He is no gentleman. He is a torturer."

"Who is he?"

"Chief of Internal Security of the KGB. And he enjoys giving your patients spinal taps."

Suddenly the polygraph machine stopped moving. Borisov looked at her. Could it be possible? Even in her agitated state, could she be telling the truth? He glanced at the EEG machine. It was still showing its pattern of slow waves. He felt reassured. He had just acquired one more clinical confirmation of this powerful new diagnostic tool. Yes. She was indeed a schizophrenic. A sluggish schizophrenic. Zoubok, as usual, was right.

"Dr. Borisov, I assure you I am not crazy. I am a political prisoner. And you are about to sign my death warrant."

The seriousness and intensity with which Natalya spoke was disquieting. A disturbing thought entered Borisov's mind: In spite of the test results, what if she were right? He tried to dismiss this doubt, and he ordered the nurse to call some orderlies to take the patient back to the ward. But if she were right. . . . His heart wouldn't listen to his mind. If she were telling the truth she would be placing him in direct opposition to Dr. Zoubok. She must be wrong.

Chapter Eight

"THAT'S REALLY WHAT it comes down to." Borisov had the test results laid out on the desk in front of him. "The EEG pattern shows a consistent series of short waves, just like the ones we saw in Nekipelov's tracings. But the galvanic skin response from the polygraph shows marked electrical activity in every response that involves persecution, commitment, or attack. She even accused Dr. Zoubok of being in the conspiracy to commit her here — yet, she'd never met him before yesterday."

"Why would Zoubok want to commit her?" Zeleneyev was incredulous. "This is not the Serbsky Institute. She wasn't brought here on Article Seventy for anti-Soviet activity. Zoubok has kept this hospital clean of any political involvement for over twenty years. He's not going to jeopardize his professional standing for this woman. Or anyone else. You saw what a hard time you had getting Nekipelov admitted, and he's a far better candidate for schizophrenia."

"Then why was she admitted?"

"Maybe Zoubok owed some favor to a self-important *apparatchik* who wants to keep a shaky marriage and a volatile woman under control. And Zoubok suspected she was a sluggish schizophrenic with strong paranoid features."

"Why the KGB guards? Why the hydrotherapy?"

"The *apparatchik* is nervous. He has a seductive, temperamental woman on his hands who has caused him embarrassment. He really doesn't trust Zoubok, or this hospital, but his career can't resist a paranoid woman running around screaming obscenities and weaving tales of mysterious plots and conspiracies. Not bad, huh?"

"She thinks that you and I are part of that conspiracy." Borisov smiled. Zeleneyev might be right. Although Natalya might not have looked sick or disturbed on admission, she certainly had revealed a schizophrenic predisposition over the past forty-eight hours.

"I don't know about you, but I can assure you that I'd never met her before last night. And although she's an incredibly attractive woman, I haven't the desire to court her or incarcerate her."

"I know. I know. But there are so many pieces that just don't fit together. You, yourself, told me that you were prevented from entering the room and completing the spinal tap."

"That's true." Zeleneyev picked up a lab sheet. "But someone must have done it because the results came back negative for cells, negative for sugar, negative for protein or any microorganisms."

Borisov grabbed the lab sheet. Zoubok's name was clearly printed as the physician in charge of the test.

"She claimed a man by the name of Leonid Donskoi, chief of Internal Security for the KGB, performed the spinal test."

"Look, I'm not crazy about the KGB. And I believe that from time to time they do unpopular things to make certain the system runs smoothly. But spinal taps?" Zeleneyev laughed. "Remember, she thinks you and I are in collusion against her."

"Then why did the GSR results show that she may have been telling the truth?"

"Alexsandr, what are the EEG results?"

"Short-wave patterns."

"In other words, sluggish schizophrenia."

"I know. I know."

"You know that GSR results are often unreliable with schizophrenics and sociopaths. And between me and you, I am not sure that our fair damsel in distress doesn't have more than a touch of both."

"What do you mean?"

"Alexsandr, I have never seen you so distressed by data that at any other time would have elated you. Another patient has provided you with clinical and EEG data to show that there is a legitimate category of sluggish schizophrenia that can be picked up in an objective test."

"That's only two cases."

"With only one case you didn't hesitate to present the findings at grand rounds. With two cases you have become uncertain."

"Uncertain?"

"Well . . . reluctant. You have become reluctant to accept the importance of your finding. That's not like you."

"So?"

"Something has changed in you in the past forty-eight hours. And I think it's related to your feelings about the patient."

"What do you mean?"

"Alexsandr, please!"

"No, please tell me, Yuri. I'd appreciate it."

"Alexsandr, I think you're letting your heart rule your mind."

"How?" The protest was weak.

"How?" Zeleneyev laughed. "Listen to yourself. You have been trying to find a reason why she doesn't belong here, after you've shown me evidence that proves conclusively she *should* be here. A paranoid history, paranoid behaviour, paranoid thoughts, all coupled with data that shows an underlying schizophrenic process. On top of that, you and I are part of her delusional system. Alexsandr, how do you explain it all, other than another irrational process like . . ." Zeleneyev stopped short.

"What irrational process, Yuri? Are you alluding to a non-Pavlovian concept like love?"

"Not necessarily. I am not sure we have a technical term for what I mean. But in the argot of Western psychiatry, Freud would call this 'countertransference.' "

"Countertransference?"

"Feelings a therapist has for a patient that are not necessarily explained by what is actually transpiring between them."

"Why?"

"Why does it occur? Or why are you demonstrating it?"

"Why . . . both."

"As I understand it, there are certain feelings within each of us that are not apparent in everyday activities, but that result from previous intense emotional experiences. Countertransference refers very specifically to those feelings a therapist has for his patient that may be due to unresolved feelings he may have had toward his parents, in your case more particularly, your mother. For example, Natalya is a beautiful woman.

Perhaps she reminds you of your mother. And your desire to help Natalya may be based on how you related to your mother when she needed your help.''

"But how does that relate to the way I treat my patient?''

"Somehow she is stirring very strong feelings of caring and concern in you. What the Freudians call 'rescue fantasies.' ''

"This sounds like some sort of fairy tale. Old loves and present dangers.''

Zeleneyev smiled sadly. He sensed Borisov's sarcastic edge of resistance. He had said too much. Borisov was obviously overwhelmed by this fanciful theory of human behaviour — a theory that depended more on a sense of human proportions and dynamics than on any measurable variable of behavior.

"Please . . . my friend. I'm sorry. I find it a little bewildering because . . .''

"Because it's frightening to know that there may be uncontrollable forces within us?''

"Exactly.''

"I had that very feeling the first time I read about it. A professor of philosophy gave me several books on the unconscious and ego defense mechanisms while I was in college. Then, on my own, I started to read books by Freud, Adler, Jung, Sullivan, Horney.''

Borisov, of course, knew the names of these prominent psychoanalysts. He had read some works of Freud on the unconscious and dream interpretation. But more as an object lesson about all those theories to which Russian psychiatry was singulalry opposed. "Fairy tales," "self-indulgent," were the words Zoubok had used before he had all the books on psychoanalysis removed from the hospital library, and set the trend for the other psychiatric hospitals in the Soviet Union. The only books currently available could be procured on a random basis from the university libraries and small bookshops in out-of-the-way places. What startled Borisov most of all was how little he really knew about his protégé. The first time he had met Zeleneyev was when the younger man was a medical student doing a rotation in psychiatry at Kashchenko Hospital. Both of them had shared a singular dedication to organic therapy and biological psychiatry, the total antithesis of psychoanalysis. Yet Zeleneyev must have been secretly following psychoanalysis, studying the writings of its principal teachers. Was he also applying it to the care of his own patients? Borisov felt a twinge of envy. Zeleneyev was familiar with an area of psychiatry that he, Borisov, had always dismissed as irrelevant and insignificant. But the envy turned to anger. If Zeleneyev could keep this secret about himself for so long, what else had he been harboring? Borisov had the uncomfortable feeling that from now on he could never fully trust Zeleneyev.

"We are complicated creatures. You . . . and I. Secretive. Possessed of forces and motives we don't understand. Or want to accept."

"Why not?" Zeleneyev replied matter-of-factly. "We are Russians. That is our basic character, Alexsandr. Secretive inside. And emotionally effusive on the outside."

"With the help of Stolichnaya."

"We give of ourselves whenever our friends nee help."

"Yes, thank you. Perhaps at some point you will teach me more about psychoanalysis and its operational dicta."

"There are very few. The psychiatrists spend a lot of time watching and supervising one another. And then critiquing each other's interpretations and approach."

"So now that I have a psychoanalytic problem of countertransference, what am I going to do about it and my patient?"

"As long as you are aware that the reason you are resisting the conclusions of your EEG data may lie in your own unconscious, or your feelings for the patient, you should proceed as you normally would. Despite your underlying conflict."

"So understanding my problem psychoanalytically doesn't necessarily mean that I have to change my behavior."

"Only if you want to. Understanding unconscious behavior is not specifically geared to changing it, like in our Pavlovian and organic orientation. It is simply a tool to better understand yourself, so that you have the option of deciding what you may want to do about your behavior."

"So here I am. Now that I am aware . . . I still want to do . . . what I normally would have done anyway . . . without my newfound understanding."

"All right." Zeleneyev laughed, and was joined by Borisov.

"I want you to administer the Eighteen Personal Factor psychological test."

"The Eighteen PF, Alexsandr? Why?" Zeleneyev was surprised. It was a test that psychologists in the Soviet Union considered more objective than the psychoanalytically oriented ones like the Rorschach Projective Test or the Thematic Apperception Test used in the West. It measured eighteen variables, including suspiciousness, rebelliousness, anxiety, dominance. A profile of the patient would emerge on the basis of an elegant statistical analysis, called multivariate factor analysis. But it was one of those tests of which Zoubok disapproved. The test was not based on any of his theories, or even on Pavlovian constructs. And Zoubok did not understand statistics.

"Alexsandr, you know it's not admissible evidence for either the psychiatric board or Soviet courts."

"I know, I know. But I want it anyway. It's a good backup to have."

"You mean a good control on the EEG readings."

"No . . . not good control. Simply an interesting control. And I am not even sure she will let you administer it to her."

"All right. I'll try. But remember, those tests don't lie."

"Neither does my countertransference. And I'm not yet comfortable with what I feel."

Zeleneyev left the room relieved that they had ended their discussion on a positive note.

Zoubok's office was a large, spartan, immaculately neat room. A framed black-and-white photograph of Karl Marx hung over the mahogany desk. Zoubok was leaning back comfortably in a wooden swivel chair as if he had been waiting all day for Borisov.

"Come in, Alexsandrovitch." He stood up with outstretched arms. "Let us sit here." He walked Borisov over to a plain wooden dining-room table, where a tray with a pot of hot water, two glasses in metal holders, tea bags, lemons, and cookies waited for them.

"Take one, Alexsandrovitch. My wife baked them."

Borisov took a cookie, although he knew Zoubok's wife was for the most part, on any given day, too inebriated to bake cookies. It was a sore point for Zoubok, who rarely invited any of his staff to his home. Nevertheless, he maintained the facade of a happy domestic life.

"What brings you here?" Zoubok poured the tea. He hoped the question didn't sound as rhetorical as it was.

"Natalya Nikitchenko Vartanian."

"Ah . . . a beautiful woman. Yes, what about her?"

"She claims she is a political prisoner, and that you are keeping her against her will."

"Does she also include you in this accusation?" Zoubok's voice was quiet and his tone solicitous.

"As a matter of fact, she does."

"So?" He leaned across the table. "We have a clearly paranoid patient."

"Yes . . ."

"Why the uncertainty, Dr. Borisov?"

"The EEG pattern shows slow irregular wave patterns on the frontal cranial leads."

"Wait a minute," Zoubok interrupted. "Did you say she demonstrated those same patterns as that patient . . . what's his name?"

"Nekipelov. . . . Yes, the one in grand rounds."

"That is very exciting news." He paused, noting that Borisov didn't share his enthusiasm. "You've made a great discovery, my son. I can't tell you how happy I am for you . . . for me . . . for this hospital. When you first announced your findings . . . I was a little envious." He stopped and looked at Borisov with great pride. "No, I will tell you the truth. I was more than a little envious. I was very envious . . . and very proud. You, my protégé, had uncovered scientific proof of my theory. But I was hurt that you did not tell me before. But I forgive you. Better yet, I forgive myself for such petty indulgences. Tell me again about your new patient."

"Her EEG waves demonstrated a clear pattern of sluggish schizophrenia."

"Then why, Alexsandrovitch, do you look unhappy?"

"Unhappy? No, sir. Bewildered. But not unhappy."

"What could you be bewildered about?"

"She seems quite normal on clinical exam — no obvious delusions, hallucinations, behavior. Even the way she lived her life is not unusual . . . for an actress."

"Why did she tell you about her life-style?" Zoubok's face didn't hide his intense concern.

"I'll get to that in a moment. I'm most concerned about some very bizarre accusations."

"What do you mean?" Zoubok asked brusquely.

"She doesn't know why she's here. She claims she has been brought to the hospital by you, personally, to be tortured."

"Preposterous! Who is supposed to be torturing her? Me? You?"

"No, a Mr. Leonid Donskoi, head of the Internal Security Division of the KGB. She claims he performed a spinal tap on her. "

"Donskoi? Donskoi?"

"Does that name mean anything to you?"

"No. There is no one here either on the professional or administrative staff." Zoubok rose and began to pace in a small circle. "Donskoi. Donskoi. Did she see him?"

"She seems to have a description of him, but is not clear whether she had ever met him before."

"What type of man is this Donskoi, according to her?"

"Sadistic."

"Of course." Zoubok laughed. He walked over to Borisov and placed his arm around Borisov's shoulders. "Obviously a fictitious character. Are there any other paranoid delusions?"

"There's you, me, Zeleneyev."

"Anyone else?"

"She keeps mentioning her *bogatyr*. Clearly a nickname. But there doesn't seem to be a delusional quality to it. Whoever he is, she certainly felt very close to him."

"Bogatyr?"

"I really don't know very much about him. But I have a distinct impression that he must be an older man. She talks of him much as she would a father — powerful, knowledgeable. I think he was a lover who may not be with her anymore. Perhaps he died."

"Why do you think that?"

"A very nostalgic, forlorn tone of voice whenever she talks about him. As if he were dead."

"Did she specifically say that he was or was not dead?"

"No. It's simply an impression I have. Call it my clinical sense."

"What about her history? Anything suggestive of sluggish schizophrenia?"

Borisov hesitated. On one level, the multiplicity of boyfriends, the life of a bohemian actress, the inability to develop a meaningful steady relationship, suggested a type of regressive history compatible with schizophrenia. On the other hand, she was beautiful, free spirited — an equally plausible explanation for her life. He didn't want to prejudice Zoubok's clinical judgment, so he tried to balance his remarks. He told him about her mother at the Tbilisi Psychiatric Hospital, the beloved father who died unexpectedly, the multiple marriages and love affairs, the vagrant creative life.

Zoubok nodded his head as Borisov spoke. "Of course, on the surface it sounds unstable — progressively deteriorating. But one must never jump to hasty conclusions, particularly in as complicated a case as this one. I admit, your EEG and GSR results are very impressive. They certainly corroborate a history — particularly with a mother in a mental institution — of hereditary schizophrenia." Zoubok watched Borisov's face as he explained his hesitancy. I must not overplay it, he told himself.

"Why was she admitted to the hospital?" Borisov asked matter-of-factly.

"Because she needed to be admitted." Zoubok's reply was markedly defensive.

"She claimed that KGB agents had followed her. Why would the KGB be following a prospective patient?"

"For that very reason."

"What reason?"

"She was extremely agitated and paranoid on the day that she was admitted. She became violent and started to attack the hospital attendants and security officers who accompanied her to the hospital."

"Why were there security officers? What was the need for them?"

"I told you before, Alexsandrovitch." Zoubok was now irritated. "They were there because her husband is often accompanied by KGB guards." He floundered for a brief moment. "On that day, he specifically requested their presence because he knew he would have problems with her."

"What type of problems?"

"Indiscretions. Obscenities. Violence. He wanted her admitted as discreetly as possible. *En famille*, as the French would say. That's why he asked that I admit her under my personal supervision. I, in turn, gave her over to you to implement the standard workup and treatment for sluggish schizophrenia."

"If you transferred her to my care, why was she given hydrotherapy treatment before her workup was finished?"

Zoubok placed his arm around Borisov's shoulders, sensing that his question was related to injured pride. "She is still my patient, Alexsandrovitch. I am, as you may recall, still the chief of this hospital. Every one of the patients, attendants, physicians, *feldshers* — anyone who walks on these grounds — is . . ." — he slapped his barrel-shaped chest — "my singular responsibility. Not yours. Mine! My sole responsibility. You are, as you may also recall, my deputy. One day, I hope, my successor. But for now you are here to implement whatever plans or ideas I might have, and treat whatever patients I might assign to you. Even though I have given you the responsibility to implement a treatment program, it did not in any way absolve me of a more fundamental responsibility. Mrs. Vartanian remains my responsibility. Does that seem reasonable?''

Borisov nodded his head. ''Why did she receive hydrotherapy?''

''She received hydrotherapy because she was extremely agitated that evening. Delusional, paranoid, screaming, accusing us of all types of ridiculous tortures. I didn't want to spoil your clinical workup, particularly your EEG readings, with any of the antipsychotic drugs. So I ordered a therapy which would at once calm her down, and at the same time not affect any of her brain chemistries.'' He paused to watch Borisov's reaction.

''Then what you are telling me is that you will do with her whatever you decide will be necessary, at whatever time of the day you might decide. That puts me in a pretty awkward position, doesn't it?''

''Your position at the hospital remains unchanged, as I see it.'' Zoubok's statement was meant to conclude the discussion.

''How long will the KGB agents be here?''

''As long as they are needed.''

''I want to meet her husband.''

''That can be arranged.''

''I want no further interference in my workup of her. Whatsoever.''

''May I remind you again that I am still the chief of this hospital? And that I have the right — no, more than the right — the duty, to intervene at any point, for whatever reason?''

''I'm not questioning your authority . . . or your clinical prerogatives. I'm simply requesting — suggesting — that we implement a closer system of consultation between us.''

''Damn it, Borisov. Don't push me!'' Zoubok stood up and slammed his fist on top of the table. ''Don't play games with my authority. I do what I want without asking you or anyone else for permission or approval or consultation.''

"Dr. Zoubok, I'm only trying to clarify the status of my patient and my relationship with her. So far I've been told that she was followed by the KGB for being unruly and potentially violent and admitted to this hospital for some unspecified marital difficulties. Suddenly this woman receives a spinal tap from some stranger . . .''

"I performed the spinal tap. Her husband called me up urgently, requesting my immediate assistance. He had heard these stupid horror stories about the complications that can arise from a tap so he asked me to do it myself. I am sorry I forgot to tell you.''

Borisov paused. "Dr. Zeleneyev has done over one thousand spinal taps without any complications. Why wasn't he allowed to continue?''

"He wasn't needed!''

"Then how am I to proceed with the workup and care of this patient if there is to be interference?'' Borisov shouted, unable to contain his anger any longer. Zoubok's peremptory manner was disturbing and his explanations not credible. If Zoubok wanted to do spinal taps himself, or order hydrotherapy, there was no real need for Borisov. So why didn't Zoubok simply take him off the case?

"You have my word that you can evaluate and treat the patient as you wish.''

"Then I request an immediate convening of the psychiatric commission board to present Mrs. Vartanian's case and to decide, after a formal presentation to my fellow colleagues, whether Mrs. Vartanian should or should not be here.''

Zoubok was startled. How stupid, he thought, not to have anticipated Borisov's request for a commission hearing. He had forgotten how enamored Borisov was of those hearings. Ever since the commission's inception, almost ten years before, Borisov had initiated at least a dozen hearings, no doubt a result of his righteous character.

Ironical, Zoubok thought. He was, in part, to blame for creating the mechanism, authorized by the Ministry of Health in conjunction with the Ministry of Internal Affairs and the Ministry of Justice and the Procurator's Office, under Directive 1076. It stipulated that anyone accused of anti-Soviet activity under Article 70 of the Russian Soviet Federated Criminal Code was allowed the right to a psychiatric hearing, composed of at least three psychiatrists and the chief of staff of a psychiatric hospital, to be held either in the hospital or anywhere within the criminal justice system. The request for the hearing might be made either by the physician treating the patient, by the defense counsel, if there was one, or by any family member. At the close of the hearing, the board had to decide whether the patient or accused should be incarcerated in a mental institution or in a prison. Zoubok knew all too well that the real purpose of the commission was to provide a legal imprimatur to the commitment process of a psychiatric patient. It had been, once again, Zoubok's attempt to deflect criticism by Western psychiatrists over patient hospitalization that seemed to them to be autocratic and arbitrary. Of course, less than 20 percent of the patients were released as a direct result of the commission's hearings. But Natalya . . . it was a loophole he should have anticipated. He was getting sloppy.

"All right! You can have the commission." Zoubok knew that if he refused Borisov the opportunity of a psychiatric hearing he would raise suspicions.

"I want Zeleneyev, Tsarev, Ternowsky to join you . . . within two days."

"Two days? How do you expect to find this girl not psychotic, when your own laboratory tests show that she has sluggish schizophrenia?"

"Two days." Borisov tried to hide his own anxiety. Why had he said two days? He could have asked for a month. Was it because he didn't trust Zoubok? His hesitancy, defensiveness, evasiveness. It wasn't like Zoubok. An unusual quality of uncertainty. If he had asked for more than two days, Zoubok would have found some excuse to usurp the case and displace him. At least, he would now have two more days to try to resolve the discrepancy between his scientific data and what all of his senses were telling him.

"Two days," Zoubok repeated as they bade farewell. "The hearing will be held here. No lawyers or prosecutors will be present. All right?"

"There seems to be no reason for them. She was never formally charged with Article Seventy of the RSFSR Criminal Code. Correct?"

"That's right."

"Then I see no need for lawyers."

"Good." Zoubok watched Borisov leave his office. "Remember," Zoubok called after him, "treat her as you would any other schizophrenic. Forget politics. It has no place in psychiatry . . . at this hospital."

Chapter Nine

ON THE PERSONALITY variables of dominance, impulsivity, rebelliousness, imagination, Natalya scored a nine out of a possible ten. A free, rebellious spirit laced with a generous amount of histrionics, Borisov concluded. It would certainly explain her acting talent. She was an artist. But the perfect ten out of ten on suspiciousness, shrewdness, and anxiety worried him. These variables frequently suggested the presence of a paranoid personality, and in this case offered more objective corroboration for his EEG findings. Borisov studied Natalya's sculptured face. No, he simply could not believe it. She was too bright, too vibrant, too spirited to be a sluggish schizophrenic.

Natalya sat on the edge of her bed, bemused by Borisov's serious expression.

"What's the matter, Dr. Borisov? Do you detect some terrible thoughts in the dark recesses of my mind?" Natalya asked.

"Dr. Zeleneyev, I would like to be alone with the patient now." Borisov handed Zeleneyev the results of the Eighteen PF test. "Make certain that no one sees these papers."

As soon as Zeleneyev closed the door behind him, Borisov sat alongside Natalya. He felt hesitant, uncertain, anxious.

"Well, doctor, it looks as if one of us needs help."

How should he answer? He had won her a reprieve. Perhaps in the long run, a Pyrrhic victory. But at this moment, a victory of sorts.

"Do you understand what I told you about the psychiatric comission?"

"I understand that you are upset by the test results . . . and by me."

Borisov wanted to reach over and hold her hands reassuringly. Be careful! he thought. Paranoids have an uncanny ability to sense other people's weaknesses and use them to their advantage.

"The commission will allow you to argue your case. To demonstrate why you should not be hospitalized. After, of course, all the data are presented."

"Of course." Natalya mimicked his serious tone of voice. "After all the data are presented."

"You asked me for a chance to get out."

"Please, Dr. Borisov. Do you really expect me to believe that I have a chance to escape this *pskhushka?*"

"Yes. If you are really as sane as you claim."

"As sane as I claim?" She paused and her voice filled with anger. "Tell me, doctor, why are you so concerned about me and my case? Why help me at all if your stupid tests prove that I belong here?"

Borisov resisted the impulse to grab her by the shoulders and shake her until she understood that she should be grateful for what he was doing. That he was doing it because . . . because he cared for her. Instead, he replied almost inaudibly. "It's a chance. Not a great chance, but still a chance. Will you help me to help you?"

"Help you to help me?" she shouted. "Do you know how ludicrous your words sound to someone who has been tortured by . . . one of you?"

There was no use arguing with her, he thought. She was still too angry.

"What if we can uncover information that might help you get out? What would you say to that?"

"Information? What information?"

"I don't know. That's where you have to help me. You claim you were brought here for reasons other than mental health. Tell me how I can verify that."

"What's the matter, Dr. Borisov? Don't you trust your capability to make a diagnosis?" She watched as his neck, his ears, then his face became increasingly red. Even the sadistic *apparatchiki* have a sense of professional pride, she thought.

Borisov spat out his words " 'Diagnosis'? I have my diagnosis. As a matter of fact, I have several diagnoses. Would you like me to list them for you?"

She nodded her head, satisfied that he was provoked.

"When you first came in you were hostile, suspicious, angry. On interview you appeared cooperative, reciting your life history with the ease of a high-school student reading Pushkin. Then on mental examination I found evidence of paranoia, hysteria . . ."

"Paranoia . . . hysteria . . . not bad diagnoses. But not strong enough to keep me here, correct?"

"The laboratory tests showed that you were impulsive, delusional. My diagnosis could be sluggish schizophrenia with strong paranoid elements."

"I like that. I really do." She clapped her hands. "Did you make up that name, sluggish schizophrenia? It sounds like a term that would justify slumping around all day long in pajamas and slippers."

"Stop it!" Borisov shouted. "It's not funny."

"Being in this institution is not funny. Being followed by the KGB is not funny. Having a needle twisted into your spinal cord until you pass out is not funny. Sluggish schizophrenia *is* funny."

She was ravishing. He wanted to seize her. To hold her. To caress her until she believed that he cared what happened to her. Instead, he stood up.

"Don't worry, Dr. Borisov, I won't bite." Natalya laughed a nervous laugh. Her captor was afraid of her. "I am sorry I can't offer you any comfort. But I do invite you to sit down again on my bed." She extended her arms to him. "Just make believe it's a seventeenth-century piece of French antique furniture. And that I have already offered you a drink. And we are making pleasant, light conversation."

Once again Borisov sat down next to her on the edge of the bed. Even in a stained hospital robe she is lovely, he thought.

Natalya returned his gaze, mindful that he was staring at her admiringly. Perhaps he was right, she thought. It might be her only chance.

"How can you help me?"

"I would help you the way I would try to help any of my patients. With complete professionalism."

"Do you really believe I am crazy? Or am I being kept here for other reasons?"

"I don't know." Borisov was gratified by the silence his words provoked."

"What do you mean?"

"Exactly what I just told you. I don't really know. You have a family history that indicates a strong genetic predisposition for schizophrenia. Your tests suggest that you have an underlying psychological problem. The conditions under which you came are suspect — lacerations in the shoulder, KGB security guards, an accusation of conspiracy. Even you can see that things appear strange."

Natalya stood up and walked slowly around the room, glancing nervously at the door. Then she approached Borisov. "Suppose I told you that Anatoly Sukhumi, general secretary of the Communist Party, is dead. What would you say?"

"What do you mean?"

"The great leader of this country is dead. Murdered!"

"Murdered? By whom?" Borisov was incredulous.

"By those who want to take over the government. Members of the Politburo, and others who have been in a major ideological struggle with him for some time."

"You mean you think that I and Zoubok and this Donskoi, whoever he might be, are . . . or were . . . part of a plot to kill Sukhumi?"

"I'm not certain. But you do seem genuinely surprised by what I've just told you. And I think there's a chance you believe that I've been telling you the truth. Why else would you be wasting your time with me, if you were so certain of your diagnosis?"

"You're right. I do have some doubts. But I can't resolve them unless you cooperate with me and tell me more about yourself."

"I have told you the most important things about me. I am sane. I do not belong here." She paused, unsure whether she would regret what she was about to say. "What if you discover that I am telling the truth? What would you do?"

Before Borisov could answer, the door flew open and the KGB guard informed him that he was urgently needed by a patient named Nekipelov. As Borisov strode out, he wondered whether Natalya's *bogatyr* could be Sukhumi. And, if so, what kind of a political mess was he getting himself into?

"Don't forget, I only have two days left," Natalya called after him. "If I am not proven sane, I will never get out of here alive." Her voice trailed off. "Two days left to prove me sane."

When Borisov reached the Organic Therapy Unit, Zeleneyev was already on the floor, pressing down with both hands on Nekipelov's chest. The nurse was having trouble slipping an intubation tube in Nekipelov's mouth. The larynx was in spasm. Borisov knelt and took over for the nurse. He yelled to her to bring him a tracheotomy set. She couldn't find one; the ward was in the process of ordering a new set. Borisov ordered her to bring a surgical knife and tincture of iodine. He watched the blue tint of death ascend over Nekipelov's neck, around his jawline, heading ominously toward his lips.

Borisov rubbed a cotton ball soaked with iodine around the skin an inch above and below Nekipelov's Adam's apple. He took the surgical knife and made a one-inch incision below the midpoint of Nekipelov's Adam's apple. The skin opened up, as if a zipper had suddenly parted a seam. Borisov heard the crack of the cartilaginous trachea breaking open. Small vessels began to bleed copiously, flooding the windpipe. Nekipelov started to gurgle; sibilant sounds of death came through his gaping blue mouth.

"He's drowning," Borisov shouted at the nurse. "Give me some more gauze pads, order the anesthesiology consult to get down here immediately, and give me something to keep this wound open."

"He's not going to make it," Zeleneyev said.

"What happened?"

"The same problem as before. At some point between yellow and red coma his breathing became labored. It does not seem to be dose related. I think it's idiosyncratic."

"It's the second time we've witnessed respiratory distress after the yellow coma period. I am afraid it's part of a pattern. Perhaps an unexpected buildup of insulin molecules beyond the blood brain barrier. The body can't seem to clear it out. We'll go back to our lab animals before we proceed on any other human subject." Borisov was thinking about Natalya. If it was determined that she had sluggish schizophrenia, she could become the next subject.

Borisov placed his hands over Nekipelov's ashen cold face. Whatever life remained was minimal. Should Nekipelov be placed on a respirator and intravenous fluids, or should Borisov, with two fingers, squeeze Nekipelov's nostrils shut for sixty seconds? An uncomplicated death. Borisov looked at Nekipelov and shook his head. He stood up and directed Zeleneyev to transfer Nekipelov to the Home for Invalids, called the "human warehouse" by patients and staff alike, located in one of the Moscow suburbs. Of the ten thousand beds, in the thirteen Homes for Invalids scattered around Moscow, one third were allocated to severely mentally retarded patients, one third to irreversibly neurologically damaged invalids, and the other third for the very old and crippled. Borisov knew that whatever days or weeks Nekipelov had left, they would be lived in respectful dignity.

"Make certain that you report this incident on the hospital's weekly morbidity and mortality sheet."

"Are you sure?" Zeleneyev was surprised.

"Yes, I'm very certain. This time it will be different. We will report it."

"You know what that means." Zeleneyev was disturbed by the orders. He knew that Borisov's clinical judgment was being influenced by his feelings for Natalya Vartanian. Dangerously.

The orange coal embers hissed as cold water was ladled into the black pan beneath the wooden benches. Donskoi stood up in his Finnish-style sauna, grabbed a wrapped bundle of birch branches, and began systematically to beat himself on the back, grimacing and shouting obscenities at the same time.

"What incredible joy a few whacks with some branches can give, Dimitry. You Pavlovians would say that my unconditioned stimulus for pleasure is pain. Is that right?"

"Yes, of course." Zoubok knew the answer Donskoi wanted, and resented the fact that he would acquiesce.

"I think that Freudians have you beaten on this one. They understood that the true essence of pleasure lies with the individual's ability to control the amount of pain he unconsciously desires. There exists at one and the same time both pleasure and pain. But you don't believe that, do you?"

"Well . . ."

"Come, come," Donskoi teased. "You don't have to be defensive. We are not conducting one of your megalomaniacal grand rounds."

"Leonid, please. There is no need for innuendoes and epithets. We have too much serious business ahead of us."

In another setting, Zoubok would have already dismissed Donskoi. But they needed each other, and Zoubok knew it was imperative to restrain himself. He would wait Donskoi out.

"Yes. Of course, of course." Donskoi ignored Zoubok's patronizing manner. In the twenty-five years Donskoi had served in the KGB he had rarely allowed his emotions free reign. As a graduate student at the prestigious Institute of International Relations, he had been enjoying the fast life with the children of the Party elite when he was recruited as a *stukach*, an informer, by the KGB. He had joined primarily because it was one of the few state institutions that would allow him to maintain his high standard of living. The KGB had promised — and to Donskoi's complete satisfaction had delivered — greater pay, large co-op apartments, exciting foreign travel, and lavish vacations. With one stroke of the pen he was able to obtain all the accoutrements of Soviet life which every citizen yearned for but was unlikely ever to obtain. Only once had he been dissatisfied: While stationed in the Russian embassy in Poland, he had come into contact with Western diplomats and military attachés, and he had relished the experience. This made him suspect to his superior, an old-line KGB operative who had been recruited by none other than Lavrenti Beria, Stalin's chief of the NKVD, as the KGB was then known. Anticipating irreconcilable differences, Donskoi approached the Glavnoye Razvedyvatclnaye Upravleniye, the GRU, Chief Intelligence Directorate of the Soviet military, and the KGB's principal bureaucratic rival. He was able to get himself transferred to its division of psychological interrogation, and spent more of his time there devising new interrogation techniques for ferreting out potential defectors on Russia's western front. He did such an impressive job that the KGB got rid of his superior and gave Donskoi the position of chief KGB operative in Poland, and then chief of the Section on Internal Disturbances for the entire Soviet Union. He helped develop the technique of internal exile for prominent political dissidents and was instrumental in developing the strategy of ridding the country of its Refuseniks. Now, as chief of Internal Security, he could afford to humor Zoubok.

"It's amazing how a simple piece of wood can be used to elicit such complicated emotions as pain and pleasure." Donskoi would make certain that Zoubok would not lose the point. "Take any object, let's say . . ."

"A needle?" Zoubok interrupted. He understood Donskoi's point quite well.

"Yes, very good. Take a needle for example. Look at

how many different uses you have for it in medicine —
giving injections, removing foreign objects . . ."

"Doing spinal taps."

"Doing spinal taps. What an incredible procedure,
Dimitry."

A half-naked Zoubok rose, stomach billowing over
scanty briefs, opened the door, and ran quickly across
the pine-covered wet ground into the freezing waters of
the lake. He flailed around in the water, enjoying the
solitude. He had forgotten just how much he disliked
playing the cat-and-mouse games that Donskoi always
insisted on whenever they were together.

Donskoi strolled leisurely down the path, purposefully
exhibiting his lean, taut, naked body. He knew that it
annoyed Zoubok, who considered him, according to
certain well-placed rumors, a "self-indulgent dandy." It
was a reputation Donskoi accepted and enjoyed. His
European-style suits, combined with meticulous attention to his physical appearance, allowed him an acceptable means of quietly defying the constricting norms of
the Soviet system. A small defiance, but an important
one for him. Anatoly Sukhumi had appreciated Donskoi's affected Western style. Unlike Zoubok, Donskoi
gingerly walked into the water, grabbing the foliage of
an overhanging tree limb for as long as he could hold
on.

"Dimitry, I don't know how you do it. So exuberantly.
And so early in the morning." Zoubok looks completely
out of place in the water, thought Donskoi.

"When you have my kind of thick covering you don't
worry about a little dish of ice water."

"You know, you never looked better, Dimitry. Work
suits you."

"I enjoy my work if I don't have to worry about unnecessary complications."

" 'Unnecessary complications'? My, my. That sounds
very serious."

"Goddamn it, Leonid! Stop playing games! Do I have to freeze my ass off before we finally get to the subject?"

"Now, don't get excited, Dimitry. You, better than I, know how dangerous that could be. We wouldn't want you to have a heart attack, right here on my estate, twenty beautiful acres courtesy of the KGB. People might think that I had lured you here, tortured you, and then killed you. What an incredible embarrassment that would be."

"Leonid, I thought we had an agreement. While she was in my hospital she would be under my personal care."

"But she is under your personal care. I haven't taken her out yet."

"You know what I mean. My hospital. My methods."

"Oh, you mean that unfortunate evening when I couldn't get the needle in between L-four and L-five."

"Precisely. You've put the entire project in jeopardy."

" 'Project'?" Donskoi's voice exhibited a mixture of indignation and sarcasm. "What is this, a five-year plan? What we have is a very simple problem — how do we persuade one recalcitrant woman to tell us certain names and facts. That is all."

"That is all? That is enough. The political future of the Soviet Union depends on what she knows and is willing to tell us. The fate of our colleagues in the Politburo, not to mention our personal and professional futures. Yes, we must *persuade* her to talk. But shoving a spinal needle into her back and possibly herniating her brain is not my idea of effective persuasion."

"Who taught me that elegant technique?"

"That's beside the point. It was not to be used . . . in my hospital."

"Ah, I see. A point of proprietary pride."

"Nonsense! And you know it." Zoubok angrily hoisted himself onto a dock. He picked up a towel and began to dry himself.

"All right, Dimitry. I'll admit it. I was overzealous." Donskoi joined him on the dock. "But no damage was done. So what are you fretting about?"

"You know very well I am not the Serbsky Institute. If you want to torture psychiatric patients, send them to my colleagues there. I am sure they will be happy to accommodate you."

Pathetic, Donskoi thought. Even now Zoubok deludes himself about his own ambitions and methods. How really different was his Kashchenko from the Serbsky? Both places tried to curry political favor from the KGB and Politburo. Perhaps the Serbsky did it more openly, less apologetically. They worked directly with us at Lubyanka Prison. Only this fat horse, Zoubok, has to keep pretending that he doesn't eat oats or fart in the stable. Fine, thought Donskoi. If that's what he wants, that's what he will get.

"Think of it this way. I was simply trying to facilitate your research project on sluggish schizophrenia. By doing the spinal tap myself, I could personally guarantee the integrity of the results."

They walked back to the sauna in silence. Donskoi took two large glasses and two teabags from an outside cabinet and brought them into the dry, suffocating heat of the sauna. He took a ladle of hot water and poured some into each glass, and wrapped each in a moist towel. They sat down on the wooden bench to drink the hot tea.

"You could easily have compromised me. Fortunately, my doctors are convinced that she is sufficiently paranoid and delusional to have imagined the spinal tap scene."

"I wouldn't do anything to compromise you or your scientific integrity. I think you know that, Dimitry." Donskoi's voice was less than assuring.

"I agreed to admit her as a regular patient and treat her according to routine hospital procedures . . ."

"But I have a time limit." Donskoi's voice sounded

cold. "Within the next few days I must find out what she knows. What he told her, if anything. His exact plans. The names of the people involved. And I must also find out who, besides her, knows about his death. I don't have to tell you that if the other members learn of it . . . That, in itself, would precipitate a serious struggle for power. And lead to the one thing we fear most . . ."

"Civil unrest."

"Anarchy. If we don't find out the exact nature of the plan, who was appointed to implement it, and who of us was designated to be eradicated, all of our efforts and ambitions will have been a waste."

"Are you sure?" Zoubok was suddenly concerned that he had been seduced into a conspiracy that might *not* lead to power that had been promised. Yet if this attempt to neutralize Sukhumi's plans proved successful? He dared not imagine — minister of Internal Affairs. President of the Academy of Sciences. Ministry of Health. The possibilities were dizzying.

But Zoubok's question had not been lost on Donskoi. He picked up the birch branches and began to whisk himself on the back. Sukhumi envisioned nothing short of a complete renovation of Soviet society, from major transformations in the Politburo to changes in the military, KGB, and the economy. More political freedom. More economic liberties. A decentralization program that granted greater autonomy to the individual Soviet states and increased managerial responsibility at local levels. In short, an emasculation of the centralized bureaucratic power which they, in the Politburo, would not tolerate. During the last few years, Sukhumi had tried, unsuccessfully, to implement some of these ideas. So in typical Sukhumi fashion he decided to bypass the Soviet bureaucracy and the Politburo and do no less than appeal directly to the people through his frequent radio talks. When confronted by the fact that his actions were unnecessarily provocative and inflammatory, he merely paraphrased Lenin's response to the chaos he had wrought with the October Revolution, "You can't scramble an egg without cracking the shell." And so this policy dispute had resulted in a deadly covert struggle for power between the Politburo led by Kostenchik and Rusanov and Sukhumi. *Kto kovo.* With the public acceptance of Sukhumi's death by natural causes, all that remained was to ferret out those members of the Soviet bureaucracy who were loyal to Sukhumi and were involved in a conspiracy to implement his grand visions.

Funny, thought Donskoi, looking at Zoubok. Even in so closed an authoritarian society as theirs, there were constraints on their respective use of power. First, entrenched bureaucratic factions would not allow the different powers to maneuver as readily as they would like. Second, the innate Russian fear of sudden changes possibly leading to chaos prevented the implementation of any drastic new programs. Even the sudden death of any of the members of the Politburo, but particularly the death of the general secretary of the Communist Party, had to be concealed until there was a consensus among the remaining members of the Politburo about who would be the successor and what course of action he would eventually take.

So rather than change the rules of the game, the Politburo had decided to kill him.

How typical of Sukhumi to personally draft a plan and then, to implement it, to secretly recruit a cadre of discontented *apparatchiki*, military officers, and security officials, known only to himself — with promises of increased power and prominence in a future administration. It was now imperative that Donskoi and his superiors discover the leaders of the conspiracy, and their intended course of action. Mass incarceration and interrogation was unthinkable: for one thing, the KGB lacked the manpower and resources such an operation would require; more important, the process would alarm the general public, who would immediately suspect that their beloved leader had been eliminated. Donskoi knew that the crucial link to the plan was Natalya. She was the key that would unlock the mystery of Sukhumi's great scheme. With or without Zoubok's help, he would find out what he needed to know from this woman.

The sound of a dog barking interrupted his thoughts. Two white Borzois loped through the woods toward the sauna. Their stately, arched bodies, curved tails pointing skyward, and high-strung restlessness irritated Zoubok.

Donskoi ran his hand through their shiny long-haired coats. "Aren't they beautiful? Unfortunately, they represent the last remnants of Russian nobility."

"Yes, attractive, aren't they?" Zoubok responded. "So lean and graceful. Weren't they specifically bred for hunting?"

"They were bred for the sole purpose of running down wolves. And now there are no wolves for them to hunt. What a shame."

"I'm sure dogs like these will always find something to hunt down."

"I would imagine that you prefer the Laika."

"As a matter of fact, I do. I used to have a Samoyed."

"Black and white?"

"Yes."

"They are so . . ." Donskoi hesitated purposely. "So common. So practical. So Russian. Useful but unattractive."

"They, too, were bred for hunting. But unfortunately, refinements were bred out."

"Tell me about Dr. Borisov. How much does he know?" Donskoi knew it was time to end their polite little game.

"Dr. Borisov is the son of a Russian war hero. His

mother, an engineer, was a member of the Communis'
Party.'' Zoubok was uncomfortable having to describe
one of his staff to a senior director of the KGB. No matter how much he thought he knew about Borisov, he
was certain that it would pale in comparison to what
Donskoi would soon find out.

"May I have some more tea, please? My throat is
dry.''

"Yes, of course.'' Donskoi poured hot water into the
glass and watched as Zoubok inhaled the steam. "I
think that tea should be officially declared the Soviet
remedy for all physical and psychological ailments.''

"Dr. Borisov is an honorable, loyal, extremely com-
petent physician.''

"Admirable traits. However, can we trust him?''

"I have trusted him for almost fifteen years — and
you know that I am not a man who trusts easily.''

Donskoi nodded his head. *Trust* was a relative term.
Even the cynical Zoubok was forced to trust Donskoi
because Kostenchik and Rusanov had ordered his
cooperation. Nevertheless, Donskoi felt relieved that he
never had to explain to Zoubok the evidence for incriminating Natalya as an essential link in Sukhumi's
plan. Zoubok had always presumed that the crucial
evidence against Natalya had been elicited from Donskoi's routine interrogations of suspected *apparatchiki*.
Donskoi had not disabused him of that notion.

"Does he suspect anything?''

"Frankly?'' Zoubok asked, having thought he could
avoid the question.

"You have already answered my question.''

"He feels that there are certain aspects of this case
that do not make sense.''

"Such as?''

"The diagnosis of sluggish schizophrenia doesn't
seem to be borne out by certain aspects of her
personality.''

"You assured me that there would be no problems

with the psychiatric aspects of her case." Donskoi became agitated. "That's the one area in which I had to trust you completely. Now you tell me that there is a problem." Donskoi paced the sauna. "Don't let me down, Dimitry. It will not be good for either of us."

"You asked me a serious question. I am trying to give you as direct an answer as possible."

"What else does he find unusual?"

"That the spinal tap was not performed by one of his subordinates . . . but by someone by the name of Donskoi. Fortunately, he feels that this person Donskoi is simply one of his patient's delusions, as I am sure you expected. But he was disturbed by the fact that my name was on a hydrotherapy treatment order."

"What did you tell him?"

"Simply that she had been agitated all evening and required a sedation therapy that didn't interfere with her neurohormones."

"Very clever, Dr. Zoubok. Very clever."

"Thank you, Commissioner Donskoi. However, my cleverness is diminishing in direct proportion to your interference with the case."

"Thank you for your assessment. May I remind you that I have as much as you, if not more, to gain if we can successfully keep her in your hospital."

"Then stop interfering with my hospital procedures."

"What else does he know?"

"I don't think he knows anything about her relationship with Sukhumi. He asked me about her nickname for him — *bogatyr*."

"What did you say?"

"Nothing."

"Good. Anything else?"

"Yes. On the positive side, I think we have had some luck. Results of Borisov's EEG tests showed her to have sluggish schizophrenia."

"Are you sure?" Donskoi couldn't conceal the joy in his voice.

"Yes. I'm certain enough to take the risk of allowing him to hold a psychiatric commission hearing."

"What?" Donskoi shouted. "A commission hearing with other psychiatrists on the board, and a defense lawyer, and a representative of the procurator's office? You fool! The whole reason for avoiding the Serbsky Institute . . . or prison . . . was this very problem. The legal . . . the stupid legal system! You've just undone everything."

"No lawyers, Leonid. No prosecutors. Only three of my staff psychiatrists and me. No family. No staff other than the ones who already are aware of her presence."

"And who might they be?" Donskoi relaxed a little.

"Dr. Zeleneyev, Borisov's assistant. Dr. Ternowsky and Dr. Tsarev. I guarantee you that they will diagnose her as a sluggish schizophrenic with strong paranoid features, requiring indefinite hospitalization and whatever treatment modality is required."

"How do I know?"

"You have my personal guarantee. They are my problems. Not yours."

Donskoi nodded his head in agreement, knowing that the last thing he would do from this point onward would be to trust Zoubok's judgment. He placed his arm around Zoubok's broad shoulders as they walked back toward his *dacha*. Only Felix Dzerzhinsky's dictum gave him solace: Trust is good, control is better.

Chapter Ten

THE MINISTRY OF Health on Rakhmanovsky Street, a massive thirty-floor skyscraper euphemistically known as "Stalin's birthday cake," was one of the typical neoclassical buildings built during the impressive construction period of the 1930s. It was the nerve center for health care in the entire USSR.

Borisov drove his 1974 Volga four-seater into a parking space reserved for senior medical officials. He had often dialed the building's restricted telephone number, 47-36-28, allowed access to every department through the Ministry of Health level. He shut off the engine and continued to listen to the radio. General Secretary Anatoly Sukhumi was finishing one of his monthly speeches designed to inspire his fellow citizens. This particular speech discussed the rampant problem of alcoholism and how it impaired national productivity. Sukhumi was recounting how he periodically walked the streets of Moscow incognito, watching citizens, already completely inebriated, going to work in the morning. Borisov was impressed by Sukhumi's courage to speak so openly about alcoholism. For over thirty years, every Russian leader had denied there was a real problem with drinking. Over the past year, Sukhumi's speeches had become increasingly innovative and provocative. His speech on corruption, Borisov recalled, had warned workers, politicians, and intellectuals that trading on a special status would result in criminal prosecution. He had gone so far as to name several regional Communist Party members who had been discovered skimming off the profits of their cooperatives and factories and selling their special privileges in the Party to the highest bidder.

This broadcast ended with a positive message in his deep, resonating voice: "Be not afraid to change what you believe should be changed. Trust in the future and . . ." — he paused dramatically — "and, more important, in each other."

Borisov turned off the radio. There was something very comforting about the messages. They lacked the harsh stridency of the speeches of all the political ideologues before Sukhumi. He seemed to understand the Russian psyche. The Russian's innate fear of chaos. His need for structure and order. Perhaps it was because Sukhumi was a humanist. A Communist humanist, at that. Borisov smiled to himself, recalling Natalya's words that Sukhumi was dead, killed by a group of men which included himself. How could he take her seriously? He felt foolish. Zeleneyev might just be right about countertransference — and Freud, too.

He took a branch off the roof of his car and remembered that he still had not done anything about the cheap East German car wax that he'd accidentally allowed to bake into the enamel. His beloved black car looked as if it bore the lesions of some automotive disease.

As he passed through the glass doors of the building, Borisov thought he recognized one of the KGB security officers who had guarded Natalya's room. He turned for a better look, but the man disappeared down the corridor.

The wall directory was the most progressive Borisov had yet seen in a government building. Departments were arranged according to their hierarchical position within the Ministry of Health. He wanted to get to the office of the Central Registry, where he would be able to find information on any patient admitted to any hospital or polyclinic in the Soviet Union.

He entered the elevator slowly, waiting to see whether anyone would follow him. A few people entered, busily chatting. None resembled Natalya's KGB guards. He chided himself for becoming paranoid as the elevator slowly worked its way to the twenty-fifth floor. Her malady was becoming infectious.

A sparkling, aseptic white marble corridor led him to Room 2532.

"Dr. Borisov!" A white-haired woman called jubilantly to him. She was seated at one of the many secretarial desks occupying the room. She rose to greet him, a frail, pale woman in her late sixties. "What brings you here to our bureaucratic mortuary?"

Borisov hugged her. In the five years since she had worked in the administrative records department at Kashchenko Hospital she had aged significantly. But she still retained her ascerbic wit.

"How are you, Manya? You look wonderful."

"You're still a charming liar," she replied, pinching his cheek. "I don't look good at all. But a lie from a handsome young man is always worth the inevitable disappointment that nothing could ever come of it."

"You've lost a little weight," he teased.

"A little weight? Try twenty-five pounds in two years. Cancer of the colon."

"I'm so sorry to hear that. Did you have it removed?"

"The butchers went in, cut something out, and then they told me I was fine. No metastasis. Ha. They wouldn't know a metastasis if it spread into the lung and I was spitting blood."

Borisov looked down at her tiny hand, which clutched a red-stained handkerchief.

"I'm truly sorry, Manya."

She replied jovially, hitting him playfully on the chest, "Come on now, Dr. Borisov. You didn't come here to pay a courtesy call."

Borisov drew her aside and lowered his voice. "I need some help."

She nodded.

"I want to find the psychiatric record of a family by the name of Nikitchenko. Whatever you might have on any of its members."

"Hospitalized where?"

"Tbilisi and Moscow."

"That sounds like trouble."

"Why?"

"Healthy Georgians are trouble enough. Crazy Georgians are intolerable."

He laughed. No, she hadn't lost her humor. She turned toward the back of the room, lined by metal stacks filled with records. "Follow me into my den of iniquity. Please don't feel offended if I don't introduce you to any of my cohorts. I'm sure that you would prefer that this visit be as discreet as possible. Is that right, Dr. Borisov?"

"You're always a few steps ahead of me."

"I have to be. I walk so much slower."

She turned to a section of bulky, thick black folders filed under the letter N.

"Believe it or not, these records are very complete and up to date. We have a record on anyone who has been admitted to any hospital, for whatever reasons, up till yesterday . . . and going back about ten years. If you need anything beyond that, those records are upstairs.'' Manya stepped onto a small stool, reached up to the top shelf, and pulled out a thick folder filled with computer printouts. She ran her spindly yellow-stained fingers down each page as if they had been programmed to stop at only one name.

"There it is, Laura Nikitchenko. Born December 19, 1919, right at the beginning of the Russian Revolution. She's no spring chicken, this one. You need something special on her?''

"Please keep reading.'' He appreciated the fact that she took pride in personally transmitting the patient's record to him.

"Born in a town called Novobrat.'' She looked up at him. "That's not far from here. It's on the Ochakov-skoye Highway.''

"How do you know?''

"I see you don't collect handcrafted silver jewelry. If you did you wouldn't ask about the name of the town. Novobrat silver rings used to be a favorite among Russian women.''

"What else?''

"Admitted in January 1970 to the Tbilisi Neuro-psychiatric Hospital for an attempted suicide, agitation, and paranoia. She had a string of diagnoses: severe depression, cyclothymic personality, manic depressive illness. Over a fourteen-year period she's been admitted and discharged twenty separate times. She's had every type of schizophrenia — chronic undifferentiated, schizoaffective, hebephrenic, catatonic. And it looks like paranoid schizophrenia has been the favorite for the past five years. They noted here that for the past several months she's been on very large doses of Thora-zine — almost eighteen hundred milligrams, by mouth, for increased paranoid delusions, visual and auditory hallucinations." Suddenly Manya stopped reading.

Borisov leaned over the chart:

Prognosis: Poor. Patient dying from malignant tumor. Suspected origin — neurofibromas. Radiation and chemotherapy have proven completely unsuccessful. Patient is expected to die within the month because of decreased resistance to infections and significant weight loss.

Family history: Dr. Vladimir Nikitchenko, general practitioner, left family in 1961. Never returned. Natalya Nikitchenko born December 7, 1953, in Tbilisi, Georgia. Married to Zhores Vartanian, 1980. No other related mental illness in family.

"Manya, how recent are these entries?"

"At our slowest, three days. At our fastest, I remember entries that had been posted within six hours of a patient's admission. Why?"

"Do you have a separate record on Natalya Nikitchenko?"

Manya slid her fingers down the index of names and then turned several pages. "Nothing. Why?"

"Are you sure?"

"Yes. You can look for yourself."

Borisov checked the list of names. "Could you look under the name Vartanian?"

After looking for several minutes at the names listed under the letter *V*, and in another section listing recent admissions, it was clear that Natalya's name was not in the records.

"That's not possible, Manya. Natalya Nikitchenko or Natalya Vartanian was admitted to my unit. She has to be listed on some patient registry."

"When was she admitted?"

"Three days ago."

"We would have had her posted by now. One of the sheets that is filled out by the physician on admission is automatically sent here. The only possible delay would have been due to our inability to enter the names. And I can guarantee you that this past week we had very few names to enter."

"Is it possible she is listed under any other category?"

"I don't think so. But, wait here. I can check one more place."

Manya returned with a thick black-bound book. "This book gives you admissions by hospital." She opened the page to Kashchenko Psychiatric Hospital and glanced over five pages of names. "Dr. Borisov, I hate to tell you, but there is no listing for a Natalya Nikitchenko or Vartanian."

Borisov glanced at his watch. He had fifteen minutes left before his next appointment. He leaned his head against the wall and wondered why Natalya's admission to the hospital was not recorded in the Central Registry. Bureaucratic ineptness. The admission paper was lost on its way over here. Possible. Given the nature of the bureaucracy — quite probable. The other possibility was that whoever had her admitted, namely Dr. Zoubok, didn't want any official record of her admission. But why? Borisov's mind raced over Natalya's accusations. A political prisoner? What could she have done that would have made her a threat to the State. She wasn't Jewish. She wasn't an intellectual. She was a beautiful actress with an exciting bohemian life-style. But was she crazy?

Glancing at the rearview mirror, Borisov could see the blue Zil trailing three cars behind him, but not the face of the driver. What difference, he thought. Someone wanted him watched. But who? And why? Was it related to Natalya? He made a right-hand turn and slowed down to see if the Zil followed. It did, always keeping a three-car distance behind. He turned several more corners and each time the blue Zil followed. Borisov reflected on Natalya's history. She had been relatively honest with him. Her mother, as she had said, was at Tbilisi Neuropsychiatric Hospital, quite ill. He wondered when she had last seen her mother and whether she knew that her mother was dying. The only major discrepancy in her history was her story of her father's death when she was eight years old. So he had abandoned the family. Was that a fact of her life she was still unable to accept?

Glancing at his watch, Borisov was relieved to discover that he was only fifteen minutes late for his luncheon appointment at Sokolniki Park. As he parked the car he looked admiringly at acres of white birch trees interspersed with luscious green pine trees.

"Dr. Borisov?" The voice was gentle, almost soothing.

Zhores Vartanian was a well-dressed, small-boned man of average height, with delicate facial features. Not the type of man Borisov would have chosen for Natalya. He had imagined her husband as robust, earthy looking. This man had a nervous twitch in his left eye, of which he was clearly self-conscious.

"How did you recognize me?"

"Dr. Zoubok gave me a very accurate description."

The two men walked past wrought-iron gates. On their left was a miniature amusement park with a small carrousel, bracketed by a funhouse decorated with undulating mirrors and an outdoor dance hall.

"Have you ever been here before?" Vartanian pointed toward a large clearing beyond the trees.

"Yes, when I was very young. I used to play in the woods here. But that was quite a long time ago."

"I like to come here several times a week. It is a very nice break from the stodgy atmosphere of the Kremlin.

When I look at these beautiful white birch trees, I'm reminded that there are things in life far more important that pushing sheets of paper across my desk."

"I understand you are the executive administrator of the Secretariat of the Politburo."

"Sounds impressive, doesn't it? Actually, I am merely a more efficient paper pusher than most of my colleagues."

They stopped in front of a moon-faced old woman bundled up in a variety of sweaters and a tattered coat, her head wrapped in several dirty babushkas. She was warming her hands over the glowing charcoal in the makeshift wooden pushcart from which she sold baked sweet potatoes.

"Two please." Vartanian handed one to Borisov. "I've tried them all. Take my word, hers are the best."

Borisov laughed. There was something surprisingly likable about this man, he thought.

"The old czars didn't have it bad at all here, did they?" Vartanian's arm swept the air. "They hunted with their falcons and then, when they'd had enough, they enjoyed a few wenches who waited for them in the forest. But you haven't come here to hear stories of the czars, have you, Dr. Borisov?"

Borisov smiled. "If you don't mind, I'd like to talk to you about your wife, Comrade Vartanian."

"Of course I don't mind. Whatever will help." He sighed. "We first met here many years ago at the Besna dance hall. As you well can imagine, she looked stunning. She wore one of those blouses that billowed over her shoulders, and one of those loose-fitting skirts that seemed to anticipate the movements of her body. I was a young man, a little less paunchy" — he patted himself, self-effacingly — "with a little more hair. Perhaps a touch more debonair. In any case, we met here one spring and several months later were married."

"What was she like then?" Borisov appreciated the sweet, sad quality of Vartanian's memories.

"You mean as a woman or as a potential patient?" Vartanian stopped to think of what he had just said. He added, laughingly, "Maybe they are one and the same."

"What was her personality like? Did she manifest any paranoia?"

"Paranoia, Dr. Borisov? Show me a Russian who doesn't exhibit paranoia, and I'll show you someone completely intoxicated. From the moment we're born we're suspicious — of having been born, of our mother's milk, and of our future." He paused to gauge Borisov's reaction. He thought he was accomplishing his desired effect; Borisov's stern face seemed to be relaxing. "But, to respond to your question, I would have to say that even for a native Russian, she was inordinately suspicious. Perhaps that's the prerogative of a very beautiful woman; to question a man's motives, his words, his deeds."

"How would you describe her paranoia?"

"Doctor, if you don't mind, I would prefer to leave the use of such words to professionals like you. As you know by now, she is a high-strung woman, extremely volatile and sensitive to every innuendo, slight, or blandishment. When we first met, she used to alternate between moods of profound joy and deep depressions. Literally, for days. If things went well, for instance, a theatrical role that she was enjoying, she couldn't be more loving and attentive. She would even talk of having children. But as soon as something went wrong with the part — a poor rehearsal, a poor performance — she would come home and become verbally abusive. Sometimes even physically abusive. She would accuse me of having ruined her career by consuming all of her. By making her work at home cooking. Scrubbing floors." Vartanian stopped and noticed that Borisov hadn't eaten his potato. "Please don't be embarrassed to ask for something else. I know this is a most unusual lunch. I apologize for my peccadilloes. I still remain very much a peasant."

"No, this is fine. Thank you." Borisov wondered whether Vartanian really was a self-effacing, misunderstood husband. Or merely an actor describing the troubles of another actor.

The two men walked over to a large outdoor ice-skating rink where even on a work day there were countless people skating, waving to onlookers, or pushing or holding each other in carefree camaraderie. "Now that's the way to spend one's life. With the great worry being how many times you can get around the rink without falling down. Quite frankly, I don't think even here I would be too successful."

"You were telling me about your wife's mood swings."

"Ah, yes! I'm sorry. Now you can see why I come here so often, how much I get carried away by the natural beauty of the place and the spontaneity of these people. Natalya's moods? Let me see. She would yell at me, and then start to throw things as she became more angry. I would actually have to grab her and hold her to calm her down, assuring her that she was a great actress and that one day she would be properly recognized. As long as I can remember she was always temperamental, incredibly sensitive to any form of rejection or diversion of attention away from her."

"What do you mean?" Borisov blew into his cupped hands to keep his fingers warm.

"You are cold," Vartanian said.

"No, I'm fine, thank you. How would you calm her down?"

"Well, she would invariably place me in the awkward position of having to denounce, by name, a list of real and imagined enemies who had caused her injury."

"Like the director?"

"That's where we would start, of course. Then she would force me to tell her how much I suspected the leading man, her understudy, the stage manager, the lighting man, of having purposefully gone out of their way to embarrass her on stage and make her look incompetent.''

"What do you mean, she forced you?"

"I know it sounds a bit histrionic, but the only way I could calm her down was to play her game of 'who-hates-me-and-why.' And with each offering of a name she became noticeably calmer.''

"Were they angry with her? Or against her?"

"You see how easy it is to succomb to her paranoia?" Vartanian laughed. "It's infectious, isn't it?''

Borisov was becoming annoyed with Vartanian's patronizing manner. "We have a saying in psychiatry that even paranoids have enemies. It's possible that different members of the cast could have been antagonistic toward her.''

"Dr. Borisov, I see you're getting cold. Why don't we move on toward the dance hall. We can get something to drink there.'' Vartanian took Borisov's arm and then started toward a massive, wood-framed, multicolored, octagonal building which looked as if it housed the largest carrousel in the world, instead of the largest dance hall.

They sat down at an outdoor café adjoining the building. Vartanian ordered a small bottle of Georgian white wine, Tsinandali Number 1, because, he said, it went well with the sweet potatoes. As they raised their glasses in a toast to good physical and mental health, Vartanian continued Natalya's history.

"Yes, doctor, it's possible that various members of the different casts resented her because of her high-handed ways, and were openly antagonistic. But, as you would know far better than I, there was an element of a self-fulfilling prophesy. The more suspicious she became, the more antagonistic she became toward her colleagues, and the more unpleasantly they behaved toward her. I was frequently interrupted during my work day to rush over to the theater to mediate some conflict between her and the director, or some other member of the cast. Invariably, when we were alone later, she would attack me for having taken sides with her adversary. On two different occasions she became so angry with me that she went to a polyclinic and, without even having told me she was pregnant, got an abortion." Vartanian stopped, his eyes glistening with tears. He poured himself another glass of wine and then another one.

Borisov began to sense how difficult it must have been to be married to Natalya. In many ways she was like Sonya, his ex-wife. Demanding. Forcing him to make impossible choices. Never satisfied. Both women portrayed themselves as helpless victims when, in fact, they were quite manipulative. And destructive.

"As you can imagine, our relationship became strained. By the two abortions, and the endless fighting and jealousy."

"Jealousy?"

"Yes. For example, many times when she would call at the office and my secretary would tell her that I was in a meeting Natalya would conclude that I was with some other woman. Which, of course, was totally absurd because I had no energy left to engage in a liaison. Taking care of Natalya was a full-time occupation."

Funny, Borisov thought. Sonya had also demanded more time devoted exclusively to her, while she, in turn, gave less. She falsely accused me of infidelity, which she herself was guilty of.

"The fights at home became more intense. The words became harsher. The violence more severe. Natalya finally took a butcher's knife and tried to stab me." Vartanian phrased his next statement unambiguously. "I had to commit her. I really had no other choice. I knew Dr. Zoubok from previous meetings. I knew of his outstanding medical reputation. He was someone who could be trusted. If you know what I mean."

"Yes, of course."

"I asked him to commit her without going through the official channels — without lawyers, without polyclinics — directly into the hospital. As few records as possible."

"That explains why she's not filed in the Central Registry."

"I would hope not. There were strict orders not to submit any papers to the Ministry of Health. As you must realize, discretion is mandatory in such a sensitive political position as mine. I must often work outside regular channels."

"Of course, I understand. You said something before about not blaming her. What did you mean?"

"Her mother was, or I presume if she is still alive, is quite mad herself. As a young girl, Natalya took care of her. Eventually she couldn't stand it any longer and ran away. She probably inherited some of her mother's illness. It seems like the whole family was unstable. Her father left them when Natalya was, what, about nine? Ten?"

"Eight."

"To this day she will not admit that he is still alive, somewhere." Vartanian's thoughts drifted only momentarily. "I don't know how to say this. It's self-incriminating. Well, during the past few years, while our marriage was deteriorating, I had a few liaisons."

"I thought you didn't have the energy."

Vartanian laughed nervously. "The truth is, she, too, was allowed to have her dalliances. Only in that way were we able to keep a pretense of the marriage alive. She took on the habit of dating older men, which I once told her was her way of finding her father. She screamed at me and called me a simpleton." Vartanian followed Borisov's gaze to an elderly couple holding each other tightly, swaying to the strains of some imaginary music.

"Why did she stay with you?"

"A luxurious cooperative apartment. A *dacha* on the

Black Sea. A black limousine with a chauffeur. Special privileges. Access to the senior levels of government . . . and freedom to pursue our individual lives.''

"And why did you stay with her?"

Vartanian smiled. "Natalya is an incredibly exciting woman. Unpredictable. Threatening. But, exciting. I think you understand."

Borisov nodded. "Let me ask you something else."

"Go right ahead."

"Do you think she's crazy?"

" 'Crazy.' " Vartanian looked distractedly around for a waiter. "Would you like some more wine?"

"No, thank you, I'm fine."

" 'Crazy.' " He repeated. "It's funny, how many times have I screamed at her, accusing her of being crazy . . . threatening to commit her . . . and now . . . and now when you ask me so coldly . . . so analytically . . . it somehow sounds different."

"You seem unsure."

"No, no, I'm quite sure. I just don't know how to say this." He paused. "There is something very wrong with Natalya, very wrong. Of that I'm certain. Maybe it's her Georgian blood that makes her so rebellious, so independent. Combine that with a touch of madness from her mother and you get a very troubled woman. Beguiling, enticing, beautiful — and troubled. At times, I can't believe that she really exists. . . . So if you ask me if, in my heart of hearts, I believe she's crazy, my truthful answer, after several glasses of wine, is no . . . I don't think she's crazy. Troubled . . . rebellious . . . defiant . . . but crazy, no . . . not in the sense you use it."

Borisov was not surprised by the answer. The man had fallen in love with a woman who was different from anyone else he had ever met. On the one hand, he couldn't let her go. On the other hand, if he stayed with her she would destroy his life and her own as well. He thought he knew the answer to his next question. "Why should she still remain in the hospital? I have an opportunity to get her out. Would you take her back if she is released?"

"I imagine, because of my weakness for her, that I will always take her back. I'm glad to hear she has an opportunity to leave. If she wants to come back to me, she is welcome. But I can understand if you choose to keep her there. I'm not sure a system like ours can afford to allow someone like her to run around so freely . . . so wildly . . ."

Borisov had heard enough. He glanced at his watch and stood up. "Thank you for your help. I must be going. I want to visit Novobrat. I have a feeling it holds a great significance for my patient."

"What makes you think that?"

"A clinical sense. Nothing more specific. The way she speaks about her mother and their years there. Perhaps a visit to Novobrat will help me to understand Natalya better." He paused and then continued, hesitantly, "Also, her jewelry. Her ring. She seems to be very attached to it. She hasn't parted with it once during her hospital stay. It was made in Novobrat."

"I am glad I could help. If I can be of any further assistance, please feel free to call me any time. Dr. Zoubok has my number."

"Thank you." Borisov took a few steps before he stopped and turned toward Vartanian. "Do you know whom she might be talking about when she mentions her *bogatyr?*"

Vartanian became visibly nervous. He picked up Borisov's half-filled glass of wine and drank it. "I'm sorry if I seem a little distraught. But it brings back the memory of a very painful period in our relationship. I'm afraid I can't really help you. I don't know who it was . . . or is. That was one of our more considerate discretions. We never told each other the identity of any of our lovers."

"She also keeps mentioning the name of Leonid Donskoi. Do you know him?"

"Yes. I'm sorry to say I do. A very unusual fellow whom she met once at a social occasion, and, I understand, immediately disliked."

"She also keeps on insisting that Anatoly Sukhumi is dead."

Vartanian laughed heartily. "And I can safely say, with absolute certainty, that he is alive. I saw him only this morning."

"I'm glad to hear that." Borisov was relieved. "I heard him speak on the radio this morning. Thank you once again."

Poor fellow, thought Borisov as he walked away. He has suffered a lot, struggling to keep a relationship alive that had, from the beginning, very little chance of surviving.

Vartanian watched Borisov walk toward the gate and spoke to no one in particular. "I think that was a very productive meeting."

Natalya felt better. She walked about the hospital grounds in the bright afternoon sun, trailed by the two guards she jokingly called Misha and Pisha, and treated with the patronizing affection she would have for two pets. She would test their effectiveness by speeding up her gait. If they fell too far behind, she would hide behind a tree and jump out before them, shouting "Misha, Pisha, Misha, Pisha." She was becoming comfortable with them. Perversely, she was beginning to think they were there to protect her. She liked that feeling. Anatoly had always made her feel safe. Not insulated, but safe. Incarceration in the hospital offered a certain protection from the uncertainties of her future. She now knew that they would do everything possible to keep her alive . . . for the time being. There were limits to how much they could torture her. That gave her a sense of security.

Suddenly the two nursing attendants who had held her down during the spinal tap appeared from nowhere. They motioned toward the two guards, beckoning them to bring her along with them. Natalya became anxious. Perspiration ran down her back. The secure feeling disappeared. The men in white were like angels of death. She looked at the front gate only a few hundred feet away, and bolted for it. She felt her legs leap with a surge of adrenaline. But the closer she seemed to approach the gate, the more distant it seemed to become. As she ran, she felt as if a harness had been strapped to her back and was reigning her in. Was it the medication that they had given her? Had Donskoi permanently damaged her body? A strong pair of hands grabbed her by the shoulders and forced her down toward the ground. She pleaded with Misha to let her up, lest everyone in the hospital think that they were passionately making love. When they stood, she was passed to a less playful nursing attendant.

As they walked through the empty corridors of the Speech and Hearing Center, bright fluorescent lights shimmered off the marble floors. What new torture have the good doctors devised for me, Natalya wondered. The attendants led her into a circular room about ten feet in diameter.

"What is this?"

The two attendants ignored her question. They sat her in a black leather chair above a rotary machine. Her hands were strapped down to arm rests and her feet were strapped to a foot rest. Behind her head were several black boxes with dials. Rising from the boxes was a long steel arm with a miniaturized television camera. Directly above her head, suspended from the ceiling, was a black metal cylinder with slits in its sides from which different colored lights radiated. She looked at the thick gray padding on the floor and around the walls and realized that the room was soundproof. Through a glass window she could see a technician sitting in front of a console of fluorescent computer terminals and bright red lights.

"Is anyone alive?" Her screams fell flat, as if devoured by the walls. There was no response.

"Which of you sons-of-bitches are going to work on me today?" She waited for a response she didn't expect.

A door opened behind her and she heard footsteps.

"Well, hello, Dr. Donskoi. It is Dr. Donskoi, isn't it? Or do they have a special title for people who only play doctor?" She felt his cold, slender fingers brush her wrists and legs, unfastening the leather straps.

"I'm glad to see you're in such good spirits. Oh, by the way," he said, pointing to a heavyset man with a pleasant smile, "I've brought along my assistant, Vladimir Panova, who is very interested in the practical applications of this impressive scientific instrument. He has for years been involved in many of my more interesting medical experiments." Donskoi was proud of having recruited Panova, who had acquired extensive experience in forging illegal documents and analyzing codes during his tenure in the clandestine or "wet affairs" sections of the Russian embassies in France, West Germany, and Spain. But it was his five years in the Thirteenth Department of the KGB, engaged primarily in covert assassinations, that made him particularly valuable.

"Every doctor needs a *feldsher*."

"You *are* in good spirits, aren't you?"

"I know it won't last too much longer. So I might as well enjoy myself. Isn't that right, Dr. Donskoi?"

"Is there anything I can do to make you feel more comfortable before we begin our next medical procedure?"

"Yes, it would make me quite comfortable and happy if you disappeared. Permanently."

Panova smiled as he went to the control booth. Donskoi walked around the chair and faced Natalya. His tone was professorial. "Let me tell you what this beautiful, expensive machine is." His fingers ran along the back of the chair and down the armrests, as if he were gently stroking a woman. "This is the only one of its type in the Soviet Union. I use it often in my . . . practice. And as a result, I am proud to say that I have become quite an expert. Imported from Switzerland. It is called a computerized vestibular diagnostic system, and what it does is to measure the integrity of your vestibular and ocular systems. Or those parts of your nervous system responsible for balance, coordination, eye movement and several other things that are really beyond the scope of our interest today."

"You seem to have an uncanny fascination with the nervous system, Dr. Donskoi."

"Very astute. I feel it is the one system that truly distinguishes us from the animals."

"Oh, I wouldn't say that. I think you've disproven that assumption."

"Anyway, Mrs. Vartanian, this elegant system will allow me to measure your vestibulo-ocular reflex arc." He paused and stepped back toward the wall. "Do you enjoy riding on a roller-coaster?"

"No, not particularly."

"What a pity," he replied, as he motioned to Panova in the booth.

"Aren't you afraid I might run out of the chair . . ."

Natalya's question was cut off as the entire chair tilted forward thirty degrees and spun quickly around ten times in less than ten seconds. When the chair stopped moving, Donskoi watched Natalya's eyes move from one end of their sockets to the other, in tremorlike oscillations called nystagmus. He held her head in both his hands admiringly.

"I wish you could see yourself. Those beautiful green eyes of yours are moving back and forth, back and forth like beautiful green marbles rolling aimlessly inside an empty skull. Can you now see the beauty of this machine? By simply moving this chair around quickly I have been able to override your brain's control over your body's equilibrium."

Natalya pulled her head away from his hands and extended it upward. Her stomach felt as if it were floating. But by concentrating on the light emanating from the technician's room she found that she could counteract her dizziness.

"Is there anything you would like to tell me?" Donskoi waited. "Well, let me give you some good news. Your horizontal semicircular canals are intact. And from a cursory — mind you this is only the beginning — examination, it looks as if your vestibular system is working properly."

"I never had any doubts, Donskoi."

"Oh, but I have. You see, anyone who is in proper balance would want to cooperate with me. Only those who are mentally and physically unbalanced have to be thoroughly and professionally evaluated. My dear, as I have explained to you before, this is all quite scientific. Take, for example, this test. I have just measured the movement of fluid called endolymph in the horizontal parts of your semicircular canals which are little cartiligenous tubes" — he touched her head — "right inside there, attached to your ear. If the fluid is any way disrupted by motion, direct stimulation, or sudden changes in temperature, it will induce those abnormal nystagmus eye motions and intense feelings of nausea and vomiting."

"Donskoi, do you have any friends?"

"Of course I have friends. Why don't you ask your husband?"

"That . . ."

"You married him."

"Yes, but you would be a far better mate for him."

Donskoi did not respond. He motioned to Panova. The chair tilted backward sixty degrees.

"Do you want to tell me anything?"

"Yes, I hope I vomit in your face."

Donskoi signaled Panova once again. This time the chair spun more than fifty times in twenty-five seconds. Natalya's eyes oscillated rapidly; her face had taken on a green hue.

"Who is the person in Moscow responsible for implementing Sukhumi's plan?" Donskoi needed only one name. With that he could begin his arrests.

"Get me up and I'll tell you."

Donskoi motioned to Panova to raise the chair vertically. As he bent down before Natalya's drooping head, she threw up on him.

"Cunt!" He jumped back, wiping vomit from his face, and disappeared into the technician's booth. He returned in a few moments with two large syringes with needles.

"I want you to know I feel significantly better."

He motioned to Panova to lower the chair backward sixty degrees and place one needle near Natalya's outer left ear. "As you might recall, had you been listening, any sudden rise in the temperature of the endolymph will cause rapid eye movements, usually away from the side with the change in temperature. So if I squirt this warm water in your left ear, like this . . ." He paused as he pushed the plunger of scalding hot water all the way in.

Natalya screamed, wrestling to get out of her chair but unable to move because of an incredible sense of vertigo. The room seemed to be spinning quickly around her and, yet, she realized by the fact that Donskoi was still standing next to her, she had not moved. Yet.

"What a pity that you can't see yourself. Your eyes

are moving slowly to the right, with a quick jerk back to the left. Now, I'm going to reverse the direction of your eye movements, completely overriding and confusing your brain. It will be interesting to see in which direction your eyes will move." He paused. "If you thought you felt poorly before, you can't even imagine what this will be like."

He picked up the other syringe and injected ice cold water into the left ear.

Natalya screamed in agony. She felt the water cut through her brain as viciously as if it were a cold blade of steel. The mounting waves of nausea were unbearable. Then the chair began to move again. Her surroundings became a blur of lights and movement. She thought she heard Donskoi ask again for the name of her contact. In Moscow. In Leningrad. In Tbilisi. But with one name he would be able to obtain all the names. Vomit welled up in her throat. This time she would try not to open her mouth. Instead she would aspirate it. She had no other choice. She had to remain silent for as long as possible. For herself. For Father Vakhtang. For her *bogatyr*.

Chapter Eleven

NOVOBRAT WAS LIKE every other small town in the Soviet Union. Its central core of concrete government buildings was surrounded by a phalanx of private residences with brown or blue wood siding and red corrugated tin roofs. Large posters of helmeted steelworkers urging their comrades to work even harder adorned the side of one of Novobrat's four Greek Orthodox churches. Old women draped in black dresses and black babushkas rushed past idle teenagers who loitered about park benches smoking cigarettes and combing their hair. The town had no more than five thousand residents.

Borisov parked his car along a side street and started to walk toward the center of Novobrat. The blue Zil that had followed him from Moscow was nowhere in sight. He walked past a stone obelisk chisled with faces expressing fear, anger, surprise. It reminded him of one he had once seen in Kiev. Perhaps many towns had one of these stone markers, depicting the three faces of Svantovit, a tenth-century Slavic god that the Slav peasant believed could ward off the evil arising from the four corners of the world. Borisov smiled. How typically Russian — to retain this memory of the infidel Tartars. To remind the Great Slavs that they were still vulnerable to attack, that if they weren't prepared they could once again be placed under the yoke of slavery.

As might be expected, the shop windows bespoke a shortage of merchandise. Borisov looked through the window of a candy shop. I can start here as well as anywhere, he thought, as he entered the store.

A middle-aged woman in a blue flowered dress sat behind the counter. She nodded to Borisov as he gazed at walls lined with half-empty shelves. Her tone of voice was indifferent. "Look around. We have some good Swiss chocolate."

"Swiss chocolate?"

"Are you shopping? Or interrogating?" Her reply was brusque.

"As a matter of fact . . ."

"Do you or do you not want chocolate?"

"I would like some information . . ."

"I'm no information center. You want the police station. I sell chocolates. Swiss chocolates. If you want to buy — fine. If not, get out. I want no trouble here. Do you understand?"

Yes, he thought, he understood. He took out a roll of money and the shopkeeper motioned him forward.

"Buy yourself a box of Swiss chocolates. You won't go wrong." Her tone was now seductive as she took several rubles from the roll. She handed him a sealed box. "What you're looking for is in here."

Borisov pulled off the heavy string around the box and lifted open the cardboard top. Inside were four pieces of chocolate wrapped in a flimsy tissuelike paper. He looked up angrily.

"Is there anything wrong?" The face of the store-keeper was unperturbed.

"You charged me fifteen rubles for four stale pieces of chocolate."

"Those chocolates were made in Switzerland."

He bit into one piece and grimaced. "Switzerland! It's nothing but charcoal." He walked out of the store disgusted. He should have known better. He was an amateur at bribery.

The cosmetic shop down the street appealed to him. It was cheerfully decorated with flowers, mirrors, and bright lights, a poor imitation of some American or Parisian boutique. A pretty young salesgirl dressed in the standard blue uniform smock approached him. She looked no older than nineteen.

"May I help you?" she asked.

"Yes, I'm looking for a family that used to live here."

"I've lived here my whole life and I know everyone in town." Her reply was spirited.

"Well, good. Then you might be able to help me." Before he could finish his sentence, he found himself being pulled toward a counter in the back of the store.

"I'm so glad you returned to our store." The salegirl's voice was purposefully loud. "I am sure your wife will love this fragrance." She held out a small crystal bottle shaped like the turrets of the Kremlin. "If there is anything Russian women love more than a handsome man like yourself, it is perfume. This is our most popular brand. Kreml." She opened the bottle, rubbed a few drops of the liquid on the inside of her wrist, and held her hand to his nose. "Won't you smell it?"

Borisov buried his nose in the heavy fragrance. "Our local KGB officer just walked in," the salesgirl whispered in his ear. "He hasn't visited us in quite a while. Be careful."

"Do you know the name Nikitchenko?" Borisov whispered back.

The salegirl thought for a few moments. "There was a family who lived here a long time ago with a similar name. I was very young. My grandmother would remember." As the KGB agent walked toward them, she continued in a loud voice. "Kreml perfume contains different floral extracts from the Caucasus — orange, jasmine, lavender, acacia. Combined with extracts from the Far East — ambergris, ylang-ylang, cinnamon. Back here we have some different types of perfumes. More exotic, more expensive. Do you think your wife would like them?"

"Perhaps," he said as he walked with her toward the rear door exit. The girl opened the door and pointed in the direction opposite the constabulary. "My grandmother owns a jewelry shop down toward the main square. I don't think the officer saw your cute face. Be careful. Listen, come by again if you're not married. Okay?"

"How much for your trouble?" Borisov took some money from his pocket.

"Three rubles?"

"Here, take ten. You've earned it."

The girl pocketed the rubles and disappeared.

Borisov decided that the jewelry store was probably back near the obelisk. He looked nervously behind him. No one was following him. Why should someone be following him? Was it standard procedure because he was taking care of a family member of an important government official? It was certainly not unusual for the KGB to check up on him from time to time, to find out about certain patients who were under his care. They would usually ask very simple, factual questions, the answer to which they could have found in the central patient directory. To the best of his knowledge, he had never been followed before. He was unnerved by the ominous atmosphere of surveillance that pervaded the town.

He retraced his steps to the main street and stopped in front of a very small jewelry shop with a few trinkets in the window. He would have missed the store completely if he had not been told of its existence. The word TRINKET, spelled out in gold stenciled letters, was peeling away from the glass of the front door. Toward the front of the shop was a roll-top desk, and rows of shelves piled with boxes lined the gray walls. Borisov wondered how the famous silversmiths of Novobrat could be represented by this hovel.

He rang a bell on the countertop. No one appeared. Maybe he had the wrong place. The air was stale and moldy — an oppressive smell that reminded him of his grandmother's living room. Once more, he rang the bell. Still no one came. He looked at the jewelry placed haphazardly beneath the glass countertop. Coiled wire earrings and tarnished bracelets. Amid a clump of bulky rings was one he thought he recognized. He walked around the counter and picked it up. It was an exact replica of Natalya's ring — a garland of flowers, lily pads, and fruits.

"May I help you?" A thin voice came from the dark.

"How much is this ring?" Borisov strained his eyes, and held the ring high up in the air.

"It depends." The voice responded with youthful defiance.

"Who are you? I can't see you."

"It doesn't matter. I can see you."

"How much is this ring?"

"I said it depends on who wants it. Why they want it. And for whom they want it."

"That's absurd. I only want to buy it, not marry it."

A stately woman in her late seventies walked toward Borisov. She adjusted her chignon. "You like that ring. Why?"

"I'm looking for someone who would know who else might like this type of ring."

"Who wants to know?" The lady took the ring back and examined it.

"My name is Dr. Borisov. I am deputy director of Kashchenko Hospital in Moscow. And I am looking for someone who might have known the Nikitchenko family. A mother and a beautiful daughter with olive skin, long dark hair, and green, almond-shaped eyes."

"A most unusual ring." The woman ignored his question. "Intricate craftmanship. If you look closely enough at the leaves, you can even see the veins. Take a look."

"Yes." Borisov examined the ring. "Very impressive. Did you do the work."

"No, I don't do it myself." She laughed. "There are silversmiths all over this region who bring me their work and I sell it on consignment." She paused to examine Borisov as scrupulously as she might examine a piece of jewelry. "You have an honest, intelligent face. Perhaps a bit too stern. But you are clearly a man who doesn't like to waste his time."

Borisov nodded his head in agreement.

"How do I know you are not KGB or police?"

He looked at her. She was testing him. "Because you know quite well that the KGB has been following me."

She laughed. "You are as smart as your blue eyes tell me you are."

"And you are as clever as your granddaughter is charming."

"Very good, Dr. Borisov." She drew him back toward the dark shadows of the store. "I think we will be a little safer back here." They stood huddled together. "Is Natalya in trouble?"

"She could be if I can't prove her sanity. She is my patient. I must know more about her past. Where she lived. With whom. What her neighbors thought of her. What she was like."

"You know she often came to visit us here in town. Her old nanny still lives in the family house."

"Really!" Borisov was not as surprised as he sounded.

"Yes. Natalya liked to buy jewelry. She bought one of those rings. She would always try to bargain me down on every item."

"That sounds like her," he replied.

The woman's silence was palpable.

"Follow me." The woman led him through the rear door into the back alley. She covered her head with her shawl and looked furtively around. They proceeded down the alley for some distance, to what appeared to be the edge of the main square. "Wait for me. I will return in a minute." When she came back she held a bottle of Stolichnaya vodka wrapped in a brown paper bag. "You will need this. Believe me."

They crossed behind a group of trees which hid them from the view of five uniformed policemen who were busy admiring a new Zil. They walked quickly, until the woman stopped, short of breath.

"I am sorry. I am an old woman. I can't go any farther."

"Sit down, Babushka. Don't worry. Where are we going?"

"When you get there you will know what you are looking for. You must continue down this road for about a mile. Then there will be another smaller dirt road. Make a right. Go another half mile and you will see a large log cabin. Tell the old woman inside that you are lost. She's quite hospitable. And very knowledgeable. You will have to use your guile, but if that fails, share this bottle."

Borisov kissed her forehead in gratitude. She grabbed his hand.

"Wait. Humor an old woman, sit down here, next to me."

Borisov smiled. He knew exactly what she wanted. His grandmother had been the same way. Whenever someone would leave on a journey of any length, she would invoke the timeless tradition of everyone sitting down together, wishing each other "good luck" and a "long life," and implicitly bestowing the blessings for a safe voyage, which no one would directly mention lest they foolishly tempt the gods. The tradition probably dated as far back as the first Russian grandmother who worried about her children going far from home.

Borisov sat down, squeezed her frail fingers in his hand and wished her "good luck." Then he took off. Down the road, according to her directions, he found the cabin. Dark black smoke rose from its stone chimney. He held the bottle tightly in his left hand and knocked on the door. The scene reminded him of Tolstoy's children's stories, where mysterious strangers rap on the door of some unknown house in the middle of the green forest. The sort of universal story that pits childish innocence against an unknown evil. Borisov would have been only partially surprised to see a witch open the door and invite him in with a seductive cackle. At his second knock the door opened slightly and a wizened woman peered through the crack.

"Yes, young man?"

"I've come to see the person who lives in this house."

"Yes?"

"Are you that person?"

"Yes."

"May I come in?"

"Yes." She replied without opening the door any farther.

Borisov started pushing, but the door was chained. "Can I come in?"

"Yes," she repeated, unremittingly.

She's senile, he thought. What should I do? "Is there anyone else in this house?"

"Yes."

Borisov raised the bottle up to eye level where she

could see it. The door opened and revealed a moon-faced woman with a bulbous red nose, the kind that only alcohol could produce.

"Yes," she repeated as she took the bottle and he let himself in.

The room was filled with torn and broken furniture and smelled of urine and feces. The windows were tightly closed. Except for a few lamps with weak, naked bulbs the room was dark. Borisov turned toward the woman, whose woolen nightgown was torn and stained. He estimated her age at about eighty-five. She walked with a shuffling gait, fingers rolling against each other, her gaze distant. Definitely senile dementia and Parkinsonism. From the looks of the room and her disheveled appearance, he knew that she needed hospital care. He would make a note to inform her regional medical director about her. Had she been Natalya's nanny? "What is your name?" he asked.

She nodded her head and gave him the bottle to open. He poured a drink into a white porcelain teacup with a chipped rim. The woman grabbed the cup and gulped the liquid down. Her eyes started to glaze as she lowered herself into a rocking chair.

"What is your name?"

She extended her cup, offering him her drink. Perhaps, thought Borisov, a drink will lead to trust. It tasted acrid, more like homemade ethanol than commercial vodka. He returned the cup and watched the old woman's head sink down onto her chest. She fell asleep. The cup dropped into her lap.

Borisov walked slowly around the dark, musty room. Except for a bookcase filled with dust-covered, frayed, leather-bound books, the room was bare. The mantelpiece, covered with dust, had a few clean areas, as if whatever had been there, possibly framed photographs, had been recently removed. He leafed through the brittle yellow pages of a book of Pushkin plays, the edges of which crumbled at his touch. Most of the other books on the four remaining shelves were also related to the theater. He found a large folder containing Natalya's reviews. Borisov laughed as he read one critic's description of her as "terribly vivacious and uncontrolled." Another one said ". . . she overpowered her role." A sheet of paper fell to the floor, a theatrical flier announcing the production of *Master and Margarita* at the Taganka Drama and Comedy Theater in Moscow, introducing Natalya Nikitchenko, with a full-face picture of her taken, he calculated, about six years ago. He folded the flier, and slid it into his pocket. As Borisov started to close the book, he noticed a brown-tinted photograph, folded and stuffed into the book's spine. He pulled it out and stared at it. The face looked familiar. The thick head of hair. The dark complexion. The deep-set eyes looking away from the camera. It was hard to be certain. But the barely legible writing across the bottom confirmed the man's identity. It was Sukhumi.

As Borisov began to slip the photograph into his pocket, a strong hand on his shoulder spun him around toward an oversized fist rapidly approaching his face. The handwritten words "With Love — Your *bogatyr*" raced through Borisov's mind as he sank to the floor.

Zoubok knew that he was being unusually pleasant and solicitous toward Zeleneyev. Was there anything more he could do for Nekipelov? He was terribly sorry that it had turned out this way. But he had warned Borisov not to admit him to the hospital. He walked slowly around the moribund patient, tapping his knees, his toes, his fingers with the pencil in his hand. He lowered his voice, wary of his own male nurses on the opposite side of the room.

"You know, between you and me, I have been concerned about Borisov's clinical judgment lately . . ." He hesitated, to emphasize the point. "Ever since he has been treating Mrs. Vartanian, his judgment has become increasingly . . ." He paused to search for the right word, and decided not to find it.

"Take for example, Nekipelov. Yes, he was a sluggish schizophrenic. You knew it, I knew it, and Borisov knew it. But Borisov also knew he was pushing the limits of scientific curiosity and medical ethics by performing insulin coma treatment on him. He could have used the more conventional treatment modalities — hydrotherapy, the phenothiazines." Zoubok stood behind Nekipelov's motionless body, adjusting the adhesive tapes around the intravenous tubes. "At this point I'm sorry I allowed him to do it. This is too expensive a price to pay for the future of scientific discovery."

Zeleneyev was incredulous. He had never heard such patently false words of contrition from Zoubok. He decided that he was more comfortable with the abrasive, authoritarian, self-assured Zoubok he knew so well from clinical grand rounds. It was clear that Zoubok was trying to alienate him from Borisov. How ironic, thought Zeleneyev. There are already significant substantive differences between us. He adjusted Nekipelov's catheter, annoyed with himself and with Zoubok because tomorrow, at the commission hearing, he would for the first time be in open disagreement with his boss, mentor, and friend.

"For some reason that I can't understand, Alexsandrovitch has been indecisive about the Vartanian case," Zoubok said.

Disgusted, Zeleneyev walked over to a desk drawer, took out a chart and handed it to Zoubok. "There, take it. You don't have to worry."

"The Eighteen PF." Zoubok was surprised and angry. "The Eighteen PF. You know there are restrictions on its use."

"Read it!"

"Why are you showing me this?"

"Because in this particular case you and I are not in disagreement. Please read the file."

Zoubok glanced over the file and broke into a broad smile. "You're right. I apologize. I think, for too long, we have had an unrealistic assessment of the Eighteen PF. I think the results should be admitted at tomorrow's hearing."

"I agree. Now if you would please excuse me, I should finish with the patient. They're coming to pick him up in a little less than an hour."

"Of course . . . of course. I'll leave you for now. If you don't mind, I'll take this chart with me. Keep up the good work, Dr. Zeleneyev. You have quite an impressive career ahead of you." Zoubok rushed down the hall, elated. The other two, he thought, would be much easier. Much, much easier.

Borisov raised his aching body slowly from the floor. He knew he was badly bruised. He reached into his pockets — the theatrical flier was still there, along with his wallet, money, and keys. He scanned the room. The bookcase was empty. The folder of reviews was gone. So was Sukhumi's photograph. Clearly, he had found something that was not meant for his eyes.

He ran his fingers quickly over his head and face. His nose was bleeding and he ached, but nothing was broken. Borisov got up slowly and walked into the next room. Natalya's nanny was also gone. Had her drunken stupor been staged? He doubted it when he recalled the incredible alcoholic stench she exuded.

As Borisov made his way toward town along the side of the dirt road, he wondered who had beaten him up and why. The obvious motive was that the assault had been intended as a warning. Stop investigating Natalya's background. Whatever happened to her in the past was off limits to him.

Borisov was pleased to see his dilapidated black Volga parked in front of the obelisk just where he had left it earlier that day. He opened the door, started the ignition, and drove quickly out of Novobrat, checking his rearview mirror every five minutes to make certain that he wasn't being followed. Yet he knew that from this moment on he would always be watched. And for the first time in his adult life he felt vulnerable.

Borisov's mind raced as he drove back to Moscow. Sukhumi was Natalya's *bogatyr*. And if she were correct, Sukhumi had been murdered. But who killed Sukhumi? And why? Was she being confined to keep the news of his death away from the public, or did she also know other secrets that had to be kept hidden? Who was the mysterious Donskoi? Was Zoubok involved in it at all? Zoubok certainly was political and manipulative and authoritarian. But above all else he was a scientist, a man of integrity. If he had wanted to imprison political dissidents he would have become the director of the Serbsky Institute.

What could he, Borisov, now say at the hearing? If he refuted his data, he placed his own credibility as a scientist in question. And his future as a reseacher. If Natalya were sane, how was it possible for the EEG readings to be abnormal? Of course, under severe psychological stress any latent schizophrenic trait would become more pronounced. But that would not be a very compelling argument. Not to a distinguished board of psychiatrists. On the other hand, as a senior clinician he had an obligation to his patient and his profession to state his clinical impressions. And despite her paranoid, histrionic, and manipulative traits, she was not, to his knowledge, in need of hospitalization. Especially not against her will.

He had to admit to himself that if Zeleneyev were correct about his irrational feelings toward her — his countertransference — then it was indeed increasing in intensity. He accelerated slowly, passing a police car and nervously anticipating a flashing red light.

What was the old fox up to, Ternowsky wondered. This was the first time in five years he and Tsarev had been asked personally by Dr. Zoubok to come to his office. The "Ukrainian scourge," as he knew Zoubok called him behind his back, was not only invited into the inner sanctum, but also asked to sit on a psychiatric commission to evaluate one of Borisov's patients. He wanted to ask what the hell was really going on. But he knew better.

"We should make more use of the blood studies. I think we can arrange it so that any suspected schizophrenic . . . no, better yet, anyone admitted to the hospital, would have a T-lymphocyte test."

"But," Tsarev interrupted hesitantly, "Dr. Borisov turned that proposal down some time ago. With your approval."

"Yes, yes, I know." Zoubok was annoyed to be reminded of his own words. "But that was before . . . A good idea sometimes looks even better after some serious consideration. At the end of the week, right after the psychiatric commission hearing, I will make it standard procedure for every patient admitted to Kashchenko to have T-lymphocyte tests." Zoubok took Tsarev's satisfied smirk as a sign he could be counted on. He turned toward Ternowsky with his most beneficent smile.

"How are things going with . . ." Zoubok paused, trying to pinpoint exactly what it was about Ternowsky that irritated him.

"With my chronic schizophrenics or my women's groups?"

"Yes, of course. I hear good things about your women's groups."

"As opposed to bad things about my chronic schizophrenics?"

"Of course not. Of course not. Simply that the work you are doing with the women is outstanding." Although he had been originally opposed to the concept, Zoubok was now grateful that he had deferred to Borisov's decision to go ahead with it.

"If you don't mind, I might suggest that you write an article on your group for the *Journal of Neuropsychiatry and Multiple Therapies*, of which, of course, you know I am the editor."

Ternowsky knew that Zoubok was waiting for a response. He said nothing. He might as well raise the ante, since Zoubok was the journal's editor.

"What would you say if we made your article the lead in the spring issue?"

"Interesting," Ternowsky said, nodding phlegmatically.

" 'Interesting'? I have heard more enthusiastic responses in my life." Zoubok paused to control himself. Now I remember, he thought, why I can't stand this peasant.

"What if I coauthor the paper with you?"

"Interesting."

"Still only interesting?"

"Only interesting."

"There is a vacancy coming up for the directorship of the Regional Psychiatric Hospital in the Ukraine. I have been asked to nominate several candidates. If I only put down one name, I would think that . . ."

"I would think so . . ." Ternowsky nodded in agreement.

Zoubok sat back in his chair and smiled contentedly. Self-righteous pig of a peasant.

"Hello, my dear, how are you feeling?" Donskoi, accompanied by Vladimir Panova, entered the hydrotherapy room, wearing a white lab coat. "I imagine you are still a little upset from the vestibulo-ocular examination."

Natalya noticed Donskoi staring at her naked body as he led her over to the table where she was to lie down. Perhaps there was a chance, she thought. A chink in his armor.

"I see you brought your *feldsher* along for protection."

Panova smiled in response.

"Why don't you come a bit closer to me, Leonid?"

Donskoi ignored Natalya's obvious attempts to make herself seductive. He walked over to a shelf and pulled out a large white canvas blanket with buckles hanging from straps.

"Your friend, Dr. Borisov, has just found out about your liaison with Sukhumi." Donskoi was matter-of-fact as he and Panova unfolded the canvas on the table alongside her.

Natalya pushed her leg against his. She held her breath. She disliked using her body to manipulate this man. But she had no choice.

"And why don't you say hello, Vladimir? Don't you talk. Or are you simply Donskoi's *petrushka*, a puppet?" Panova looked away.

"Please, Natalya. This type of behavior does not become you. At least if nothing else in these hours of duress — a little dignity. At least that. If not for yourself, at least for Sukhumi." He pulled away from her, fidgeting with the buckles on the wet pack.

"Are you going to tie me up?" she asked seductively. "Tell me, Leonid, is that what you like?"

Without warning, Donskoi raised his hand and slapped Natalya across the face, as surprised as she by his anger.

Panova appeared amused by Donskoi's apparent discomfort.

"I don't think you heard what I was trying to tell you." He regained his composure.

"Yes, I heard it." Natalya nursed her bruised cheek.

"Dr. Borisov has found out that you were placed in this institution for reasons other than problems with your marriage — or your mind." Donskoi took a cup filled with cold water and dropped it on the canvas.

Was it true about Borisov? she wondered. Had he really not known why she was incarcerated? But how could that be possible? He was Zoubok's deputy.

"You see what happens when I wet that canvas? It remains loose, large — should I say, unrestricted?" Donskoi took out a butane lighter from his pocket and passed the flame over the canvas. His tone became professional, as if he were lecturing to a group of students.

"When the canvas dries up, it shrinks." He paused to see whether Natalya reacted. She remained calm, just as he expected. "A wet pack, that's what we call it. Here, put your arms at your sides, and I'll just wrap it around you like this." With Panova's help the two men rolled her up in the canvas and buckled her in.

Natalya didn't offer any opposition. The wet pack felt oddly soothing. Protective.

Donskoi thought that she knew more than she did. Sure, she knew the broad outlines of the plan. Had Donskoi penetrated the group? But if he had, he wouldn't be wasting his time with her. Of one thing she was certain — Donskoi wanted to know the name of her contacts. But he would never get them from her.

Donskoi placed a large heat lamp alongside the table and turned it on. "The heat from this lamp will force the wet pack to dry quickly and constrict you. Just like a corset."

Natalya felt the lamp's heat permeate through the pack. Surprisingly, it relaxed her. Much of her dizziness and nausea had subsided while she lay anchored to the table. The room no longer felt as if it were spinning. She noticed a tightening sensation around her chest. Donskoi's voice sounded unusually soothing.

"If you permit me, I will be quite frank with you, in the clear expectation, of course, that you will be equally open with me," Donskoi continued. "To begin with, let me summarize our situation by stating a simple fact: there is a very important piece of information that you have that I want. It concerns the implementation of Sukhumi's plan. I want you to tell me who your main contact is. And where I can find the plan."

Donskoi turned the knob on the heat lamp, increasing its intensity. "Are you feeling all right?"

"Yes, thank you. It's very touching of you to be so concerned about my well-being."

"You know the goal of an effective negotiation is to bring the two opposing sides as close to each other as possible. And if you take a minute to think about it, we are really not that far apart. For example, I know the date that the plan is to go into effect — Soviet Day — November seventh, correct?"

"Why ask me if you are so certain of your information?"

"In any case, I can assure you that the members of the Politburo are fully prepared for any possible disruptive contingencies."

"Fine. Then why not let me go? I present no threat to you."

"Yes and no. I know the broad outlines of the plan. You know the broad outlines of the plan. But from this point onward, you know more than I do. And that is not fair. You know the names of the leaders, or, at least, the individual who can get you to the leaders and the plan. I don't. You may even know the specifics of that plan. So I feel quite embarrassed that I am so ignorant . . . so vulnerable. A little knowledge is indeed very dangerous. What I know now would force me to arrest and detain hundreds of Soviet citizens, many of whom would be innocent. Believe it or not, my superiors in the Politburo have specifically prohibited me from such preventive detention because they are extremely cautious men who do not want to harm the Russian people. Certainly not with the knowledge that Sukhumi is dead."

"Murdered!" interjected Natalya.

"Murdered . . . as you wish. I won't argue with you. If that news were to get out, I'm afraid we would have spontaneous protests. Possibly anarchy. The political murder of a popular leader, even in a closed system such as ours, is not acceptable. I find myself in the terribly awkward position of being trapped by my own ignorance. In two weeks — if I don't act quickly — I may also find myself embroiled in civil riots. So the spotlight is on you, Natalya. You see, I know for a fact that Sukhumi appointed you his courier in case of his death."

"You know that for a fact?" Her voice became strained as her chest tightened. "Where do you get your facts? From your KGB informers and spy network?"

"It was much easier this time. From Sukhumi himself."

"Do you really expect me to believe that Sukhumi told you about a plan?"

"So you don't believe me. What a shame."

"I no more believe that Sukhumi told you about a plan than I believe that Borisov isn't one of your stooges. Why would Sukhumi tell you anything about a plan?"

"Perhaps he wanted me to work with him."

"You?"

"Yes, me!"

"Then why are you torturing me?"

"That is a good question, Natalya. It seems somewhat paradoxical, doesn't it? But the fact is that I ultimately decided not to work for Sukhumi. That he was a danger to the Soviet Union."

"What a pathetic creature you are. I think you belong in this madhouse."

Donskoi turned the knob on the heat lamp to maximum strength.

Natalya had started to perspire. The binding grew tighter and it was becoming hard for her to inhale without pain. "You bastard."

"I wish I could take credit for this invention. But unfortunately it is as old as Hippocrates and Greek medicine. Psychiatrists in the Soviet Union use it frequently to calm their agitated patients. Don't struggle so hard. You'll find it more bearable if you don't move about so much."

"If . . . I . . . don't . . ."

"Don't speak either. It's clearly quite an effort for you. But I'm sure you can appreciate the fact that I really have no other choice. All I need is one name. Someone whom Sukhumi would trust as much as he trusts you. Perhaps here in Moscow . . . perhaps elsewhere. The person you were supposed to contact. Now who is it, Natalya?"

"All right." She was barely able to mutter the words through the barrier of pain. Donskoi leaned closer so that he could hear her fading words.

"Zoubok . . . is my contact."

He looked incredulously at her, then at Panova, who appeared uncomfortable as he watched the canvas tighten.

"You're lying, Natalya. You can't fool me. Zoubok works with me."

"How . . . do . . . you . . . know for certain?"

Donskoi tried to dispel the doubts that she had suddenly raised. She's right. How would he know? Zoubok could be her contact.

"And . . . *petrushka* . . . there. He, too, is my contact."

Donskoi laughed. He was relieved. Now he knew that she was simply trying to provoke him.

"Oh, by the way, I think it would be wise of you to make certain that Dr. Borisov does not pry any further into your situation. Otherwise he, too, will become a victim of Sukhumi's plans. I'm making you responsible for his well-being."

As she started to black out, she wondered how one of Donskoi's KGB stooges had penetrated the group. Did they know about Father Vakhtang? Was he still safe?

"Succinylcholine two-cc. IV," Zoubok ordered the heavyset nurse to prepare the frail woman lying before him for electroshock therapy. He still enjoyed administering ECT therapy himself. This was a difficult case; the patient for whom hydrotherapy, phenothiazine medication, and even insulin coma had not worked. Her paranoid delusions that the Politburo had conspired to have her son killed during his routine army tour of duty in Afghanistan had not diminished. "Let's cut the atropine dose in half and prepare doses of sodium barbital in increments of fifty milligrams. I'm concerned about her." Normally, Zoubok would not have accepted her as a potential candidate for ECT because her spinal x-rays had revealed osteoporosis, a significant loss of calcium. But he had to try to arrest her deteriorating mental condition before she destroyed herself or killed someone else.

He adjusted the metal electrodes on her temples and turned the dial on the black electrical transformer. The patient writhed on the table from the jolt of electricity.

"I think she had too much succinylcholine." Borisov stepped forward from his position in the doorway and examined the familiar face.

"You're right, Alexsandrovitch." Zoubok turned and ordered the nurse to prepare one cc. of succinylcholine, half the necessary amount for paralyzing the muscles. "You look upset. Is something wrong?"

"Yes, very much so." Borisov motioned toward the nurse.

Without another word, Zoubok nodded to her and she obediently left the room.

"We'll start with a new course of therapy. Double the amounts of atropine and sodium amytal, and make certain her feet and arms are tightly bound to the table."

Borisov adjusted the leather straps on the patient's ankles. "I think the KGB is trying to destroy Natalya . . . Mrs. Vartanian. And possibly me."

"Now wait a minute," Zoubok said. "Slow down, Alexsandrovitch. You're distraught. What has happened? So you received a traffic violation? And now the entire bureaucracy is against you?"

"I went to the town where Natalya lived, Novobrat. I saw evidence . . ."

"What evidence?" Zoubok repeated.

"Evidence that Natalya knew Anatoly Sukhumi. That she and Sukhumi . . ." Borisov paused.

"What evidence?" Zoubok repeated.

"That she and Sukhumi were . . . close friends. Perhaps lovers."

"Did you read a diary? Or love letters?"

"No. There were no letters. I went to the house where she lived as a child and saw her old nanny. There was a photograph of Sukhumi that was inscribed to her, 'With Love — Your *bogatyr*.' And, then, I was ambushed and beaten up by somebody who didn't want me there."

"Beaten up? My dear friend, I think you have an overactive imagination. Or a serious drinking problem."

Borisov stared at Zoubok, perplexed. Why would Zoubok deprecate his observations? Why didn't Zoubok believe him?

"Dr. Zoubok" — Borisov was angry as he injected the medications into the Y joint of the plastic tubing from the IV bottle — "ever since I was assigned to Natalya Vartanian's case, I've felt that I've been kept purposefully in the dark about the real reasons she was admitted to this hospital. Why is it that every time I turn my back I find that you've ordered some course of therapy about which I know nothing? Why, when I pursue any leads that might clarify the mystery surrounding her, am I followed by the KGB? And now, even beaten up?"

"I'm sorry." Zoubok's tone was serious. He stopped what he was doing and placed his arm around Borisov's shoulders. "I'm sorry that you feel hurt and betrayed by my lack of openness. I had no intention of keeping you in the dark about anything. But I can only tell you as much as I know, or should I more accurately say, as much as I am permitted to know." Zoubok paused, carefully monitoring Borisov's reaction. "What is this about your having been beaten up?"

"I think it was the KGB. But I just don't know. That's why I have come to you. There is no one else I can talk to about this." Borisov's anger subsided.

"Of course, of course." Zoubok's tone remained serious. "My friend, there are times when we must not ask too many questions or we shall never find any peace. As you know, the professional road that led me here was never straight or easy. There were many times when I agreed to demands or made concessions that I knew I would eventually regret. But I acceded. Because I knew that if I wanted the opportunity for success, and some modicum of happiness, I had to make concessions to the system. I did things. I didn't ask why. I just did them. I've learned to keep silent, and forget."

"But how do I explain Natalya's picture of Sukhumi? A KGB beating? Doesn't it mean that her delusions may not be delusions but an accurate description that there are certain people who want her incarcerated, here, at Kashchenko Hospital, because of information she has?"

"Do you want her released, Alexsandrovitch?"

"Of course. Especially if she doesn't belong here."

"That's right. So do I. Especially if she doesn't belong. But there may be mitigating reasons which we do not fully comprehend at present, but which may become more apparent to us at some later time. So for the present, it is best to remain silent. Treat her as you would any other sluggish schizophrenic."

"What mitigating reasons?"

"Alexsandrovitch, hold the respirator over the patient's face." Zoubok's interest returned to the patient.

"What reasons, Dr. Zoubok?"

"I'm going to increase the voltage. Watch for any unusual muscle spasms."

A frustrated Borisov watched silently as Zoubok turned the dial, sending the patient's body into violent spasms of muscular contractions that subsided minutes later with the crackling sounds of compressed vertebral fractures.

"Damn it! Why did this have to happen! Had I left her alone, she might have survived admirably. Now we'll have to treat her for paraplegia as well as paranoid delusions." Zoubok paused to assess whether Borisov understood his message, but Borisov had already left.

Chapter Twelve

"ALL I NEED is something or someone to verify what I have seen. What you have told me." Borisov stared at Natalya, confused by the silence and indifference with which she had greeted him. He closed the door, making certain that the KGB guards posted outside the door could not hear.

Natalya lay staring at the ceiling, angry for having allowed Donskoi to make her responsible for Borisov. Her life as she herself had described it to Borisov was a continual flight from responsibilities, and she liked it that way. She had taken care of her mother until she realized she was in a bottomless pit. No matter how much she gave, the more her mother wanted and needed. It was suffocating. So she ran away. But no matter how far she ran, she was no closer than one dependent relationship away. Her first husband, her second husband — each one was no different from her mother. Each had incessant needs for love, reassurance, support, refusing at the same time to recognize that she, too, had needs. Now a complete stranger had become her ward, her responsibility. Damn it!

"I have one more day to try to help you get out of this hospital. I know now that you do not belong here," he repeated, "but you have to help me. Otherwise, I have nothing to counter my own" — he stopped, realizing the irony of his words — "convincing data and arguments."

"Leave me alone!" Natalya tried to turn away from Borisov, but winced from a shift in the surgical adhesive tape around her chest.

"What's hurting you? Why are you holding your chest?"

Natalya ignored his concern.

"I'm fine. I was just examined a few minutes ago."

"You're lying." Borisov pulled up her gown and saw the tape around her chest, from above her breasts to a point just above her stomach.

"What happened? Who did this?"

"I fell. I was dizzy. And I fell, that's all. Go away, please. If you know what's good for you, go away."

"Was it Donskoi?"

Natalya remained silent.

"What have they done to frighten you into silence? Tell me! Help me! Otherwise you won't get out of here. We have one chance . . . tomorrow. A slim chance. But a chance. Help me. Give me the name of someone who can testify to your relationship with Sukhumi."

Borisov looked away. She looked so vulnerable that it hurt him. He yearned to hold her, to hug her the way her *bogatyr* must have. But there was little he could do if she was unwilling to talk to him. How could he persuade her to cooperate?

"This is not the time to tell you . . . or maybe it is. . . . Your mother is dying from cancer. According to her records, she has anywhere from a few days to a few weeks left to live. I thought you should know." He waited for her reaction.

It came slowly. Natalya turned her head and stared at him. She said nothing, but her eyes filled with tears. She bit her lower lip. Borisov sat down on the bed and took her in his arms.

Natalya felt Borisov's strong, warm hand caress her back. "Go away, Dr. Borisov . . . Alexsandrovitch. Please. They will hurt you. Donskoi will destroy you if you help me. He thinks you know too much already."

"Did he torture you again?"

"Yes. Wet packs. He warned me not to talk to you anymore."

"Why?"

"He will do something to harm you. I'm afraid."

"Natalya, will you help me? To help you?"

"No. Go away. I want to be responsible only for myself. I can't afford to worry about you. Otherwise I will never survive. If you leave me alone they won't bother you. Get out of here now." She began to cry, and he gathered her into his arms and held her. "Please, Alexsandrovitch, help me. Please," she sobbed.

Gradually her tears gave way to determination. "Get me out of here, Dr. Borisov. I must get out. I must see my mother. I must see her before she dies." She lay back on her pillows. "Please, Alexsandrovitch. Believe me when I tell you I must see her before she dies. I must."

"There is nothing I can do right now. You can't walk out of here. The KGB will stop you. Look at you. You are in no physical condition even to move. Every time you breathe, it hurts. You couldn't take four steps without being caught."

Natalya pulled him gently to her and whispered. "General Viktor Janowski, the retirement home on the outskirts of Moscow. Be careful."

Borisov gazed into her glistening eyes, and then bent

over and placed a gentle kiss on each. How beautiful she is, he thought.

"Do nothing to compromise the general," she said quietly. As Borisov left the room Natalya sank deeper into her pillows, thinking about what she had just done. General Janowski was a close personal friend of Sukhumi. He was someone with whom she could discuss their relationship. At this point in his life, he was apolitical and wanted no part of a conspiracy. But he knew Father Vakhtang because the three of them had grown up together in Tbilisi. She had sworn to Anatoly that she would never reveal any names. But she had no choice. This was her only chance. Her life now depended on one of the most politically naïve men she had ever met.

Borisov paid his fifty kopeks to one of the thirty cashiers and pushed through the turnstile of the Moskva Swimming Pool at 37 Kropotkinskaya Embankment. He was totally flabbergasted. Possibly two thousand bare bodies were at the pool on that cold morning. It certainly deserved its reputation, he thought, as the largest open-air swimming pool in the Soviet Union and all of Western Europe. Vapors of steam rose from the eighty-degree waters of the sprawling, white-tiled pool. The smell of chlorine was pervasive. A scene from Dante's Inferno — the fallen in pursuit of ablution and redemption. There was a decadent quality about it. Western rock-and-roll music played by balalaikas and guitars blasted from loudspeakers hanging on metal poles around the pool. All these people in a swimming pool on a cold day. Why weren't they at work?

How could he find General Viktor Janowski? The landlady of the state-bequeathed cooperative in which many retired military officials lived had described Janowski as a heavyset, bald man in his late sixties, always found biting on a filtered cigarette. Every day, sometimes twice a day, the general would visit the swimming pool.

Borisov asked several lifeguards whether they knew the general. A few thought they recognized the name, but weren't sure that they could recognize the man. Finally one lifeguard pointed to a man matching the general's description lying comfortably on a chaise longue, tanning his face with a sun reflector.

"General Janowksi?" Borisov carefully avoided shading the well-tended lady before him.

"Who wants to know?"

"My name is Dr. Alexsandr Borisov. I am the deputy director of the Kashchenko Psychiatric Hospital."

"You have the wrong person."

"Natalya told me to see you."

"Natalya? I don't know any Natalya."

"Natalya Nikitchenko Vartanian."

"Vartanian? Sorry, I still don't know anyone by that name."

"Sukhumi's friend."

Janowski lowered his sun reflector slowly, carefully studied Borisov's face, then raised the reflector to his face again. "Doctor, you have the wrong person."

"Natalya is in serious trouble. She is a patient at Kashchenko Hospital. To obtain her release, we must present some verification of her relationship with Sukhumi."

"Doctor, please let me be. I am a retiree on a comfortable pension from the state. I come here twice a day. In the evening I go out with my friends — also retirees — for a drink or two. I have a simple life, doctor. But it is enough." He lowered the reflector. "Do you understand me, doctor?"

"I understand that Natalya is in danger. And she desperately needs your help."

"Even if I were to know this woman, there would be very little that I could do for her anyway."

"Did she or did she not know Anatoly Sukhumi? And is Sukhumi dead as she claims he is?"

Janowski folded up his sun reflector and looked searchingly at Borisov. Suddenly, Borisov heard a familiar voice call his name. A slender man treading water at the edge of the pool beckoned to him. Janowski picked up his reflector and walked quickly away.

Borisov reluctantly turned around. No one knew he was here. He had been extremely careful, changing trolleys three times before boarding Bus Number 8.

"What are you doing here?"

"I told you that when I take my lunch I usually go to the park, as we did yesterday. Occasionally I come here." Vartanian pulled himself out of the water, grabbed a towel from poolside, and led Borisov to a long metal bar. "Wasn't that General Janowski?" Vartanian poured vodka into a shot glass.

"I don't think so." Borisov considered the coincidence of finding Vartanian and Janowski at the same place. Did Vartanian know Janowski? Was Natalya's room bugged? Or was Janowski under surveillance? And was Vartanian working with Donskoi?

Vartanian slapped his firm stomach muscles. "My mistake, then. Drink up! Vodka is good for you, doctor. Good for your arteries. But I needn't tell you." He placed his arm around Borisov's shoulders and turned him toward the diving boards. A man on the highest board was jumping into the water alongside a woman who had already jumped from a lower board.

"Now look at that. Who can honestly say that we Russians don't enjoy ourselves? That we only enjoy being miserable? Nonsense. What other people could swim in the middle of the day in this weather?" He squeezed Borisov's shoulder. "Tolstoy knew the Russian character." He paused.

When a Russian loves, then he must love without reason or limitations;

The Russian will never threaten in jest, so never threaten him unless you are very serious;

A Russian should be mad to the fullest extent possible, holding nothing back;

When a Russian punishes someone, let that person know from the nature of the punishment why it is he is receiving such treatment;

When a Russian eats, then he should eat as much as he wants.

Vartanian led him away from the bar and strolled back toward the poolside. "May I call you Alexsandr? I feel as if we are just beginning to get to know one another. We do have so much in common. I don't have to ask how my wife is doing because I'm sure you're taking excellent care of her. Tell me, what did you find in Novobrat? Anything of interest?"

Borisov didn't know how to answer the question. If Vartanian was working with Donskoi, he would already know what had happened.

"Come along, my friend, I want you to meet someone of particular interest to you. But I'm afraid I've made you uncomfortable?"

"Well . . ."

"Photographs?"

"Yes . . ." Borisov was surprised. "How did you know?"

Vartanian took Borisov's arm and they strolled like two old comrades. "My friend, I've known about Natalya and Sukhumi for quite a while. He is her *bogatyr*, as she calls him. Her superhero. Her Russian warrior."

"He is . . ." Borisov was perplexed by the use of the present tense.

"He is, of course. You don't think their relationship is over? Do you? Come, come."

Borisov stopped in his path, oblivious to the water being splashed on him from a vigorous game of polo.

"An excellent game. Truly Russian — masculine, aggressive, and definite. It suits our brusque, crass manners."

"I would hardly say you were either crass or brusque," Borisov replied.

"You are too kind. And too sensitive. But, of course, that is part of your métier." Vartanian laughed. "It would be like accusing a soldier in battle of possessing too much aggressiveness. Wouldn't it?"

"I imagine so." Borisov again began to question the serendipity of their meeting.

"I appreciate your sensitivity toward my feelings. There's not very much left for me to discover about my wife's infidelities, and, if I may be so presumptuous, her reasons for committing them. If I were to strip my wife of any of psychiatry's fancy diagnoses — schizophrenia, paranoia — what we would have left is simply a very, very insecure little girl who, underneath all that beauty, charm, and independence, wants what every little girl wants — a secure, stable, loving father." Vartanian grabbed Borisov's hands as if he were trying to reassure him of a very crucial point. "What I'm saying may sound very simplistic, very idiotic, and very Freudian. Yes, even I have read Freud. Don't be surprised. But the truth is that Natalya has been looking for an older man to take care of her. To love her in a way that she imagined a father would or should. Let us be honest. She has an infinite capacity to create the kind of world she needs. Haven't you already fallen in love with her?"

Borisov looked at Vartanian. The man was serious. There was no trace of teasing innuendo.

"What do you mean?"

"Come, come, doctor. You must then be the first male with whom she's entered into a relationship who was not, should I say, seriously affected."

Borisov was uncomfortable. He didn't answer. Instead, he fixed his gaze on the water polo players.

"How simple it would be if all adversaries could simply square off in some contest of prowess — water polo, soccer, wrestling. Sometimes I envy the old days of dueling, when conflicts were easily resolved. Believe me, doctor, I don't think any the worse of you. On the contrary, there is, if I may be so bold, a special bond between us now."

Borisov was annoyed at Vartanian's insistence that the two of them had something in common. He wanted to break off the conversation and pursue the general.

They walked through a cordon of blue-uniformed police, with long coats and furry hats, pushing back crowds. Vartanian pulled a plastic identification card from a pocket in his bathing suit and the police let them pass. As they walked into the locker room many of the officials recognized Vartanian, bowing their heads ever so slightly. At another cordoned-off area state television cameras and crews waited while incandescent klieg lights burned. Before Borisov could accustom himself to the glare, he was being introduced by Vartanian. An aide quickly gave Vartanian a package.

"Dr. Alexsandr Borisov, I would like you to meet the general secretary of the Communist Party, Anatoly Sukhumi."

"Dr. Borisov, it is nice to meet you." Before Borisov could respond, Vartanian handed him a pair of swimming trunks, adding, "Here, put them on. I hope you know how to swim."

"Yes, of course."

"Good," Sukhumi replied in that familiar robust voice. "Come join me in a swim. I'm taking a lesson from history and showing my fellow comrades that, like

Mao Tse-tung, I, too, am a good swimmer and in perfect health — contrary to nasty rumors that have been from here to there. Come!''

Borisov walked into a cabana and changed clothing. His pulse was racing. So Sukhumi *was* alive.

As they ran into the pool, Sukhumi stopped once to acknowledge the plaudits from the onlookers. He jumped into the water and swan freestyle in an area cleared by his guards. An incredibly handsome man, Borisov thought. He looks very much in person as he appears in the media. He had an impressive vitality. His swim strokes were powerful. Sukhumi beckoned to Borisov from the far end of the pool.

''I prefer to talk here, in the water. This way no one can overhear us.''

''I understand,'' said Borisov, catching his breath.

''How is she?''

''She's had a difficult time in the hospital. She claims that she has been tortured by one of your KGB.''

''Who is that?''

''Leonid Donskoi.''

Sukhumi began a slow breaststroke in deference to Borisov's heavy breathing. ''A fine man. Have you seen evidence of any torture?''

''Well . . . not directly. She has had wet packs and hydrotherapy and sustained some injuries. But they could be an unfortunate result from the therapies themselves which, quite frankly, are not innocuous.''

''I'm asking these questions because I'm concerned about her behaviour . . . her delusions. Please understand, I'm not criticizing you or your methods. They are, of course, none of my business. If Dr. Zoubok has faith in you than I have faith in you.''

''Thank you.''

''Vartanian assures me that you are an honorable man. Of course, we've done a little checking on you. Your father and mother were heroes of the Soviet Union . . .''

Borisov was offended to be treated like a schoolboy. There were so many questions that he would have liked to ask Sukhumi about Natalya, about their relationship, about power.

"I understand you're a member of the Party?"

"Yes."

"Good. Naturally you must keep what we say here between us, strictly between us."

"Of course. My professional ethics would require that." Two young women, screaming that they loved Sukhumi, tried to jump into the water, but were restrained by uniformed soldiers.

"You see, it's not easy being a leader." Sukhumi laughed. "All these women!" He shook his head. "But imagine, Dr. Borisov, imagine what happens when one of these women is terribly beautiful and seeks a liaison without any complications."

"Natalya?"

"Natalya. The wife of one of my most trusted assistants. He knows about it — she has cuckolded him before. You must believe me, I don't think any the less of him for it . . . it's simply very hard to control her. So for several years we had a liaison. That's all. Nothing more. No promises on my behalf, certainly. Nor did I expect anything from her. Except her discretion. Which became doubtful. And that is when our relationship began to deteriorate. On my instructions Donskoi put her under surveillance. To the best of my knowledge, he never exceeded his orders or his authority. Unfortunately, Natalya learned of the surveillance. She became angry, moody, suspicious, accusing him and some of my colleagues in the Politburo of trying to kill her. And, can you believe it, of trying to kill me too? For some reason she's been telling people that I am dead." Sukhumi's boisterous laughter attracted the applause of the onlookers. He waved back.

"All I can tell you is that she'd become increasingly erratic, possessive, and extremely unreasonable. She began to suspect everyone of foul play, including me. So with the help of her husband, and the good Dr. Zoubok, we were able to get her quietly and discreetly admitted to your hospital for much needed treatment. I didn't want the police or courts involved. I didn't want any official record of her admission. I only wanted the people who treated her to understand the extreme sensitivity of the problem. I know you understand and I thank you for your cooperation. I'm sure you will do what is best for your patient. I understand you have quite a bright future in Soviet psychiatry."

Sukhumi, in a burst of speed, swam to the water's edge and climbed out of the pool into the crowd of admirers.

Borisov remained in the water, frightened by the paradox that confronted him. If this man were Sukhumi, then Natalya was much sicker than he had imagined. But if she was right and Sukhumi was dead, his country was heading toward disaster.

Chapter Thirteen

THE AUDITORIUM WAS silent. Zoubok, Ternowsky, Tsarev, and Zeleneyev sat on one side of the amphitheater facing Borisov, Natalya, and her two nursing orderlies. The other rows of seats were empty. Standing in shadows in the rear were Donskoi and Panova.

Zoubok approached the podium and began to speak slowly from notes he had written. "By the powers vested in me through the legislation enacted by the Supreme Soviet in 1958, entitled *The Fundamentals of Criminal Legislation and Criminal Court Procedure*, and supported by the interdepartmental instructions coordinated through the Ministries of Justice, Internal Affairs, and the Procurator's Office, I hereby convene this psychiatric commission hearing to determine whether the patient, Natalya Vartanian, born Nikitchenko, is guilty of violation of Article Seventy of the Code of Criminal Procedure of the RSFSR. We are also to decide whether she is to remain at the Kashchenko

Psychiatric Hospital for further evaluation and treatment. Article Seventy of the Code of Criminal Procedure of the RSFSR states as follows: 'Anti-Soviet behavior is considered as *agitation'* " — Zoubok paused to assure that the word would be sufficiently emphasized — " 'or propaganda carried on for the purpose of subverting or weakening Soviet authority or of committing certain especially dangerous crimes against the state, or circulating for the same purpose slanderous fabrications, written or spoken, which defame the Soviet state and social system . . .' "

Borisov was on his feet immediately. "Dr. Zoubok, I beg to differ with you. There has never been any discussion of a violation of Article Seventy with regard to this patient. No criminal charges were ever pressed against her. There were no representatives here from the prosecutor's office nor is there a lawyer to represent the patient."

"Did you agree, only the other day, that we should not bring your patient through the formal legal system?"

Borisov realized how naïve he had been. Of course, Article 70 could be involved at any time prior to, during, or even after a hospitalization. It was simply a clinical judgment rather than a legal one. But had Natalya been officially admitted under a violation of Article 70, he could have been prepared for a legal argument, although the best legal defense was a psychiatric argument that the patient was nonimputable, imputability being the concept for criminal responsibility. In the long run the outcome would depend on whether she was actually mentally ill and whether she required further hospitalization.

Natalya broke into a fit of laughter. She tugged at Borisov's coat. "Tell me once again, Alexsandrovitch, about the pure scientific nature of this hearing."

Borisov didn't respond. He hadn't been able to see

her before the hearing, to tell her that Janowski wouldn't talk to him, and that Sukhumi appeared to be very much alive. What would she, what *could* she have said? He was thoroughly confounded. Perhaps the best thing after all was for her to remain in the hospital.

"In the instructions to the commission psychiatrists, I say that they may consider the following articles of *The Fundamentals of Criminal Legislation and Criminal Court Procedure* in determining the degree of the patient's willfulness or responsibility in committing her anti-Soviet behavior. Consideration might be given to Article Thirteen, a plea for self-defense or a plea for dire necessity, a certain uncontrollable impulse; or the insanity defense, Article Eleven, which sets forth the criteria for an insanity defense. By invoking Article Eleven the patient will be . . ." — he corrected himself without missing a syllable — "the patient found guilty under Article Seventy can then invoke the insanity defense under Article One hundred ninety, Clause Four, in order to receive compulsory treatment at Kashchenko Hospital."

Every member of the commission understood exactly what Zoubok was saying: If she's crazy — hospitalize her; don't send her to prison for her anti-Soviet behavior. It was as simple as that.

Borisov's interpretation of Zoubok's words was quite different. Zoubok was substantively changing the nature of the commission hearing. An official pronouncement had been made — anti-Soviet behavior. Even in Borisov's conversations with Vartanian and Sukhumi there'd been no mention of anti-Soviet activity. Rambunctious, willful, spirited, individualistic, irreverent — certainly — but not anti-Soviet.

"I now turn the podium over to Dr. Borisov, who will present his case in the standard report form. Mrs. Vartanian will then have the opportunity to make a statement on her own behalf." Zoubok glanced at Natalya for the first time. "May I remind my good colleagues that this entire hearing should take no more than one hour."

Borisov took the podium and began his presentation with a detailed history of Natalya's admission for depression and paranoia. He discussed her family history, her disintegrating marriage, a mother being treated for schizophrenia, a father who had abandoned her, and her embarkation on an acting career with its associated peccadilloes and eccentricities. He tried desperately to portray a woman who had some personality aberrations and some abnormalities scored by an objective test, but a woman who had committed no known acts of anti-Soviet behavior. Promiscuous, restless, lively, artistic, perhaps, but not an appropriate patient for a mental hospital.

He knew he was treading on very delicate ground. But he had to carry through on his commitment to help her gain a release from the hospital. So he minimized his findings on the EEG and made no mention of his findings on the Eighteen PF. Neither did he mention her persecutory delusions or her association with Sukhumi. The truth of the matter was that Zoubok was probably right, she was a sluggish schizophrenic. She had created such a mess in the upper circles of government that she was probably safest remaining in the hospital. But Borisov thought she'd be better treated on an outpatient basis.

As he spoke he was aware that his colleagues were restless and disappointed. For the first time they were witnessing him waffling over a diagnosis and presenting a less than convincing argument for his case. Should they release her or keep her in the hospital?

Only Zoubok sat unperturbed. The hearing was going better than he had hoped. He was tempted to look around to the two men standing near the top row but he didn't dare.

The absence of important information about her case was not lost on Natalya, who sat restlessly between her attendants. What about the other evidence — General Janowski, the physical torture? Borisov must be waiting for a more propitious time.

"What is this patient's diagnosis, Dr. Borisov?" Tsarev asked the first question.

"The tests show she may be a schizophrenic, of the sluggish type. But she could well be a personality disorder with strong paranoid, histrionic features."

Zeleneyev was annoyed. Borisov was attempting to minimize his scientific findings. His friend and mentor was discarding years of valuable research for an irrational countertransference. If I don't bring Borisov to his senses, Zeleneyev thought, who will? He girded himself for what he was about to do.

"Dr. Borisov, would you please tell the commission about the nature of the patient's delusions of persecution?"

"They involved people whom she knew."

"Who exactly did they involve and what were they trying to do?"

Borisov looked at Natalya. How could she understand his dilemma and his anguish? She glared at him.

"She felt her husband and a man named Donskoi, chief of Internal Security for the KGB, were trying to keep her in the Kashchenko Hospital for reasons other than mental health."

"What reasons?" Tsarev asked, realizing he had a new ally in Zeleneyev. Only Ternowsky was disturbed by the fact that there was nothing he could do to soften Zeleneyev's blows. He just didn't know enough about the case. Zoubok quickly realized that the less he said at this point, the more convincing his case would be. It was going as he had planned, a trial by Borisov's own colleagues. Better yet, close friends. The composition of the commission was certainly loaded in Borisov's favor.

Yet Zeleneyev, Borisov's protégé, would do the necessary dirty work.

"The patient felt . . ." Borisov started to reply.

" 'Felt'?" Zeleneyev repeated.

". . . feels that she was admitted to the hospital because she knows something that certain people didn't want her to reveal."

"Could you be more specific please, Dr. Borisov?" Zoubok interjected.

"She believed that certain prominent men . . ."

"Which prominent men?" Zeleneyev was annoyed with his mentor's uncharacteristic evasiveness.

"Her husband, the executive administrator to the Politburo . . ." he paused.

"Who else?" Zoubok asked.

"You. Dr. Zoubok."

"Me?" Zoubok replied ingenuously.

"Yes, you. You hypocritical, fat, lying slob!" screamed Natalya. She stood up and spat out the words, waving an accusatory finger first at Zoubok and then at Borisov. "And you! Is this what you call the 'purity' of the science of psychiatry . . . the 'integrity' of the psychiatric commission. Look at them. Tell me how impartial these barracudas are. Look at them, damn it. Can't you see it? They've already made up their minds. The diagnosis has already been written."

Zoubok shook his head, indicating to the two attendants that for the moment they should not restrain her.

"What is it, gentlemen, sluggish schizophrenia? No, better yet, paranoid schizophrenia? And the treatment, some of Donskoi's special torture?" She pointed toward the back of the auditorium. "Come out of the shadows, Leonid. Why don't you let the doctors get a good view of you so that they can see you're not a figment of my crazy imagination."

Everyone turned toward the back as a man came forward. His voice was soothing, apologetic. "My name is Vladimir Panova. I am sorry to interrupt your hearings. I am here as an informal observer for the patient's husband, Mr. Vartanian, who was unable to attend because of an exceedingly busy work schedule. Thank you for allowing me to be here." Panova sat down.

"Petrushka!" Natalya shouted. "Where is that snake who was sitting beside you? Did he slide out of here on his stomach?"

"Please take note of her behavior," Zoubok whispered to the other members of the commission. "Obstreperous. Abusive, Paranoid. Sees enemies where they don't exist. I think that will be very important for the record."

"Tell me" — Zeleneyev turned toward Borisov — "is this behavior and outburst typical of her previous behavior?"

"Somewhat."

"Somewhat? More? Less?"

"At times she has been very calm and reasonable. At other times she has been like this."

" 'Like this'?" Natalya shouted, her arms flailing as she spoke. "What do you mean? You would be screaming too, if you realized that there was no chance in hell of getting out of this . . . this . . . "

Zoubok nodded and the two attendants restrained her arms. When she started to bite they pulled her backward, tying her hands behind her back with a rough cord and placing a piece of adhesive tape over her mouth.

"Do we really need all this?" Borisov knew that such treatment would make her even more agitated. He turned to the attendants. "Please take it off."

The attendants looked at Zoubok, who nodded in agreement. They ripped the tape off brusquely. Natalya screamed.

"Dr. Borisov, who else was involved in this conspiracy to unjustifiably hospitalize her?" Zeleneyev continued.

"Me."

"Why you?"

"I presume because I am the doctor directly responsible for her psychiatric care. Therefore, I have the power to discharge her."

"Who else?"

Borisov paused. "You."

"Me? Could you explain to the commission why I have been accused of this conspiracy?"

"Because you are my deputy."

"Any other reasons?"

"Probably the fact that you were responsible for a lumbar puncture as a result of which she had a severely traumatic experience."

"As the result of my direct efforts?"

"No. Apparently this Comrade Donskoi replaced you in the room and did several lumbar punctures, which I understand were quite painful."

"Did you see any clinical evidence of multiple lumbar punctures?"

"Yes. I examined her the next day. There were two small puncture sites — both normal sequelae for a routine spinal tap. There was no evidence of papilledema. And no cervical rigidity."

"Did you find anything to indicate that she had been subjected to torture at the hospital?"

"Well, she had severe ocular nystagmus which she claimed resulted from a vestibulo-ocular test."

"Is that an unusual reaction to have after calorics have been done, doctors?"

"No. We frequently see that response to the test."

"So we can hardly call it torture, is that right?"

Borisov nodded in agreement.

"Could you tell the commission of any other alleged tortures?"

"Well, the patient is currently wearing a corset of adhesive strips to bind a broken rib she claims she sustained from a wet-pack treatment."

"Did she have a wet-pack treatment?"

"I didn't order one."

Zeleneyev picked up the chart. "There are two notations here — one for hydrotherapy. By the way, did she consider that torture?"

"Yes," Borisov replied hesitantly.

"And the other notation is for wet-pack therapy . . . both were ordered directly by Dr. Zoubok."

Borisov said nothing. He felt trapped. Whatever case he could muster in Natalya's defense looked less and less credible.

"Would it be fair to say, Dr. Borisov, that almost every routine test that Natalya Vartanian received here was perceived by the patient as a mechanism of torture to elicit some secret information from her? Is that right?"

Borisov nodded.

"Please, for the record, speak up."

"Yes, that is right."

"What would you say about a patient who perceived every normal hospital procedure as a method of torture and considered every doctor who was associated with her in a professional way as an enemy?" The emphasis on the word *professional* was not lost on Borisov. "What do you call a patient like that?"

"Suspicious."

"Please, Dr. Borisov, let us not be so coy. What exactly do we call them?"

"Paranoid."

"Simply paranoid?"

"No!" Borisov was enraged. "Enough, Yuri, enough! You've made your point."

Disturbed by the reaction he had provoked from his friend, Zeleneyev's tone softened. "I'm sorry, Alexsandrovitch." Perhaps he had pushed too hard. But he wished

Borisov could hear himself. He simply wasn't reasonable. And it wasn't at all like him to be so indecisive. Zeleneyev had to save Borisov from himself.

"So far you've given us the portrait of a patient with a documented family history of schizophrenia, and a personal history earmarked by delusions of persecution, mood swings, erratic behaviour, and a frame of reference that views simple medical procedures as lethal and terrifying. What are we to believe? I ask you and the members of this commission, what would you think if I had brought you a case like that?"

Zoubok decided to put an end to Borisov's foolish resistance. "Dr. Borisov, may I remind you that for less evidence than this — I might add significantly less evidence — you insisted on the admission of Mr. Nekipelov to this hospital. Would it be fair to say that Mrs. Vartanian's findings were indicative of schizophrenia?"

"Yes."

"Could you be more specific? For the official record?"

"EEG, EMG readings were positive for sluggish schizophrenia. CSF fluid normal."

"T-lymphocytes?" Tsarev asked.

The question made Borisov smile. "No, I'm afraid T-lymphocytes were not done."

"Any other tests?" Zoubok asked.

"Yes," Borisov replied. "We did the Eighteen PF psychological assessment."

"And?" Zeleneyev asked, knowing full well the response.

"She was found to have features consistent with a paranoid personality — a lot of suspiciousness, increased anxiety, strong need to dominate, and marked histrionic features."

"Dr. Borisov, what would make you think that this patient was anything other than a sluggish schizophrenic with paranoid features?" Zoubok asked.

"Her mental status revealed someone who was oriented to time, place, and person. And although she appeared suspicious and anxious, her paranoid ideations could be related to fears as to what might happen to her. And" — he paused, knowing there was no other way out — "and there was evidence that she was telling the truth."

For the first time, the members of the commission looked perplexed. Ternowsky was worried that Borisov was jeopardizing his professional reputation. His judgment and scientific objectivity were in question. The hearing was no longer only a consideration of the patient's sanity. His friend was now on trial. The worst part about it was that he couldn't do anything to help him. Zeleneyev, too, had to fulfill his professional obligations.

"What evidence?" Zoubok walked toward the podium, avoiding Natalya's gaze.

"I had discovered some evidence that corroborated certain parts of her story."

"What could that be, Dr. Borisov? That you and I were in a conspiracy to hospitalize her for reasons other than her obviously deranged personality? For someone who is allegedly involved in a conspiracy to hospitalize her, you are trying very hard to get her out." Zoubok raised his voice and stretched his arm toward Natalya in an accusatory and dramatic fashion. "No one in this room can doubt your sincerity and commitment to your patients."

"Thank you, Dr. Zoubok."

"Don't thank me, Dr. Borisov. You have only yourself to thank for whatever happens to your patient. But whatever may happen to her will result not so much from a lack of effort on your part but from her own pathology."

Why is he trying to vindicate me now, Borisov wondered.

"What evidence did you find?"

"She informed me that she had had a close personal relationship with Anatoly Sukhumi. I found a photograph to corroborate that statement."

"What else?"

"She told me that she was admitted to the hospital because Sukhumi had been killed. Whoever was responsible for Sukhumi's death had her committed here in order to keep her silent about the murder, and who needed to find out what else she knew about it. And other matters."

"What other matters?" Zoubok asked.

"I don't know."

"I ask you again. What made you think then or now that she is not mentally ill and in violation of Article Seventy?"

Borisov became angry. He was being asked to make a judgment that had nothing to do with her mental competence.

"She had never, to the best of my knowledge, presented herself in manner or speech as anti-Soviet. She has said nothing against the state or its officials."

"Then what do you make of her accusation that members of the Politburo or others within the Soviet government have plotted together to kill General Secretary Anatoly Sukhumi? Is that not treasonous? To accuse your collective leadership of trying to kill one of its own members? If that is not anti-Soviet then I must be completely mistaken about what constitutes anti-Soviet behavior. Do the other members of this commission consider what Dr. Borisov has told us to be indicative of the patient's anti-Soviet behavior?"

Zoubok looked at Zeleneyev, then at Ternowsky, who in turn looked at Tsarev, who simply nodded his head.

"There's your answer. Apparently none of your colleagues thinks of her as free from a violation of Article Seventy."

"Did you find any proof of Sukhumi's death?"

Zeleneyev asked, knowing full well that Borisov had spent the day before tracking down further evidence to substantiate Natalya's story.

The room fell silent again. This was the moment that Natalya had been waiting for. The answer to this question would vindicate her. She sat on the edge of her chair. Borisov looked at her and she could see his eyes glisten. Then he turned his head away and faced his friends on the commission.

"No."

"Did you try?" Zeleneyev's tone was supportive.

"Yes."

"What happened?"

"I met . . . Sukhumi."

Borisov winced as he saw Natalya's reaction to his answer.

"Does that make your patient's statement about the death of Sukhumi a product of a deranged imagination?"

Borisov shrugged his shoulders. "There are many strange aspects of this case. . . ."

Natalya stood up and started to walk toward the door. Her guards followed closely behind her. She stopped in front of the podium and spoke calmly to Borisov. "Should I thank you, doctor, for having given me a moment's hope? Perhaps that was the worst of the last few days. That for a brief time I thought I could trust you. Of that I am guilty."

"I am sorry. I would like to see you leave the hospital."

"Why? I am probably better off in here." She looked around the auditorium. "Here at Kashchenko Hospital, the bastion of Soviet psychiatry. The Mind Palace. At least here I'm familiar with my captors. Out there I don't know who they'll send after me. Just for the record, Dr. Borisov, did you ever meet the person I told you about?"

"Yes. But he claimed not to know you. Nothing you have said has proven to be true."

"No, doctor. Everything I told you up to now is true. Completely true. You just weren't able to prove it."

"What about Sukhumi? You said he was killed."

"He was."

"But I swam with him."

She leaned toward him. "Sukhumi did not know how to swim." She blew him a stage kiss. "I forgive you, Alexsandrovitch. You tried. Come, Misha and Pisha." She turned toward the commission members. "Gentlemen, I have been in the theater for a long time. But I must congratulate all of you, particularly you, Dr. Zoubok, for having given a magnificent performance of an impartial board. I suggest that your manager, Mr. Donskoi, take you all on tour around the Soviet Union. It's a very impressive performance." She left the auditorium.

Zoubok closed the hearing. "The commission of experts has formally found the patient Natalya Vartanian to be in violation of Article Seventy of the RSFSR Code, guilty of anti-Soviet behavior. Her official diagnosis is sluggish schizophrenia with strong paranoid features. The patient will be involuntarily committed to Kashchenko Hospital and will receive the necessary organic therapy under Article One hundred ninety, Clause Four, of the RSFSR Criminal Code.

"Gentlemen, thank you for your participation. In particular, mention should be made of Dr. Zeleneyev's excellent questioning. Dr. Borisov, I want to commend you for your care of this patient. But I think you need a rest. From this moment on the patient will be under my direct supervision. Dr. Zeleneyev will administer the day-to-day orders." He turned again to Borisov. "Alexsandrovitch, I order you to take a week's vacation, starting tomorrow. Go, enjoy yourself. Dr. Zeleneyev, prepare the patient for a course of insulin coma therapy."

Chapter Fourteen

BORISOV TOOK THE icon down from its shelf in the bedroom closet. He needed an escape from what had happened. He had never before been dismissed from a case. Never! Looking at the oilcloth package, he noticed it was wrapped differently from the way he had left it. He quickly unfolded the corners of the cloth. He didn't have to study the statue at length to conclude that something was wrong. The gilded edge around the Madonna's head had been darkened with black paint. So had the eyes of the Christ Child. Borisov's hands shook. Someone had broken into his apartment. Who could have done it? And why? Who would take the time and effort to desecrate the icon in a way that was so subtle? He was more angry than afraid.

Borisov took a book from the shelf and looked through the index. Somewhere he had read about lines of black painted across Byzantine icons. He found what he was looking for. In the early Byzantine period, when icons were first introduced in the churches, priests who objected to the gaudy gilded portrayals of the Madonna darkened those parts of the head with pieces of carbon wood as a warning to the heretics. The lesson was intended to teach greater reverence and appreciation for the sacred image of the Holy Mother and Child. The Infant's eyes were also darkened so that the Christ Child should not be a witness to the desecration of the Holy Mother.

Those icon makers who failed to heed the warnings were beheaded in their sleep by the priests who acted in the name of God. Borisov's eyes filled with tears. She was lost to him forever. This beautiful Madonna, upon which he had worked for so many months, was now ruined. Clearly, the markings were a warning. And as he looked at the icon the message became clearer — stay away from Natalya.

He picked up the etching utensils and the vial of acid. The more he scraped, the more scratches he made on the icon. A few drops of acid resulted in a froth of black paint that left a residue on the parched material. There was nothing he could do to restore the icon.

He tried to scrape the fragments of black pigment from the eyes of the Christ Child. What if Natalya was right? What if he were part of a conspiracy to keep patients incarcerated within the confines of Kashchenko? As Zoubok's tacit co-conspirator. Zoubok could not maintain the viability of the hospital without doctors like him or Zeleneyev or Ternowsky. And its integrity depended upon more than their simple cooperation. It depended upon a fierce, almost blind devotion to Zoubok, to his theories, and to the general tenets of Soviet psychiatry. Borisov never questioned them. There was never a need. But if Natalya was right, he was simply a stooge. For Zoubok, and for the system. There to implement and propagate whatever "they" said. Sufficiently critical to be convincing to whoever might care to judge.

Damn Natalya, he thought. She had forced him to question his values, his professional ambitions, his personal hopes. How was she able to do it? Was it her seductiveness? Her irreverence? Her spontaneity? Perhaps being Georgian gave her the imperative to be argumentative, suspicious, manipulative, devious, strongwilled. And yet how easily all these traits seemed to fit into the category of sluggish schizophrenia. There was a fine line between an individual's idiosyncrasies and pathologies — a distinction that might not exist without men like him and Zoubok. He cursed himself for accidentally piercing the thin metal sheet of the Christ Child's eye. Funny, he had felt so good after Zeleneyev tried to explain the positive feelings he, Borisov, had for Natalya. Absolved of guilt. Relieved. Liberated. He had learned something about himself. In some uncanny way the emotional tension he experienced when he was with Natalya increased his self-questioning and self-doubt. It was frightening, yet, at the same time, exciting.

He again stuck the probe through one of the Christ Child's eyes, as if there was nothing else he could do now but destroy them. Damn, he said aloud, throwing down the metal instrument. He could only brood over the day's events, and his yearning for Natalya. His pain. His sense of failure. His doubts. His love. He could no longer look at the icon. Whoever had desecrated it had inflicted more than physical damage. He grabbed his coat and left his apartment.

He walked quickly along Gorky Street, certain that he was being followed. What difference did it make anyway, he thought. What could he do about it? Nothing.

He walked through Manege Square to Pushkin Square, where he entered the Pechora Café. A popular hangout among the more daring students and young professionals, it was one of the "forbidden" dollar bars accepting hard currency and catering to foreigners.

A cacophony of voices shouting in different languages greeted him. Boisterous American farmers from Oklahoma here to sell their wheat, tight German businessmen from Stuttgart eager to sell an automobile plant, uncomfortable Finnish salesmen trying to market their furniture suites. All waiting for a courtesy call. In the meantime there was nothing else for them to do except to sit, drink, and stay out of trouble. Only a handful of Russian men and half that number of Russian women were there.

Occasionally Borisov would frequent the café to immerse himself in foreignness, in drink, in music, in unintelligible conversation. All of which helped him escape from himself, from his inner turmoil. He moved among the customers, smiling, nodding his head. A group of Germans offered him a drink as an act of "imperialist friendship." He took it, thanked them, and continued through the crowded, smoke-filled room toward the dance floor. The Polish jukebox, a cheap version of a 1950s American model, was replete with multicolored blinking lights. The thunderous drum beat of some 1970s rock-and-roll record, combined with the alcohol, anesthetized him.

After several hours, Borisov had had enough. With slurred speech he asked a man dressed in a dark overcoat who was standing near the door whether he was following him. If so, he invited the man to accompany him home. The man scurried away.

The night air was brisk. It felt good. Borisov started to cross the street and laughed at his stumbling gait. He pretended he was a toreador and challenged the oncoming Volgas, Zhigulis, and Moskvichs to charge his imaginary cape.

Suddenly a motorcycle policeman in a blue uniform appeared in the middle of the street as he waved on the last bull. "You are in violation of the public nuisance code. If you offer any resistance you will be charged with hooliganism, which carries a penalty of several weeks in prison." Despite protestations, Borisov was forcibly escorted to the officer's sidecar and taken to a Vytrezvitel.

The Vytrezvitel — a police station where public drunks were normally kept for one night, charged a ten-ruble fine, and warned never to repeat the behavior — was located a few blocks from the café. It was a dilapidated building run by supernumeraries and ex-alcoholic police officers who prided themselves on making an encounter there so unbearable that no one, even in a drunken stupor, would want to return.

Borisov gagged as he was thrown into a cell, on top of two men engaged in a mock knife fight, feinting, threatening, boasting what they could do to one another once they were out of prison. The cell was ten by fifteen feet, and contained seven men in varying stages of inebriation. Two men were leaning against the rough, naked stone walls, vomiting with uncanny ease, as if all they had to do to sober up was to expel the contents of their stomach. Several men, their pants soaked with urine, lay in excrement, oblivious to all but the imperative for sleep.

The fight stopped momentarily as the men turned their attention to Borisov. The one called Reshat, a beefy, short Tartar with a harelip, a large protruding stomach, and a foul temper, spat at the newcomer. "Look what we have here. The inspector general of prisons."

Borisov backed off.

"Let me see your identification." The beefy man's cohort, the one with whom he had just been fighting, grabbed Borisov's shoulders from behind. Without any provocation, Reshat punched Borisov in the stomach. "Who are you? One of them?" Borisov shouted and waved his arms in the direction of the guards who were close by, amused by the commotion. Reshat, a three-time offender of Article 206 of the RSFSR Code, hooliganism, was no stranger to the Vytrezvitel. Inspired by the catcalls of encouragement, he punched Borisov several more times.

It was impossible to break the man's hold on him. As Reshat came closer for another punch, Borisov raised his right foot and slammed his knee into Reshat's groin. The man holding Borisov was so surprised by his friend's painful scream that he released Borisov's shoulders. Borisov pulled away, clasped his hands tightly together, and swung at the man's face. The man fell backward, clutching his jaw.

The guards now cheered Borisov, until an unshaven middle-aged sergeant opened the cell door and pulled Borisov out. He took Borisov down the hall to a room with a large two-way mirror, a small wooden table, and one unsteady metal chair, onto which Borisov was pushed. "You have been charged with a violation of Articles Seventy and One-ninety of the Criminal Code of the RSFSR.

"That's nonsense." Borisov cleared his throat, which tasted of bile. He was doubled over with pain. What was going on? The charges were outrageous. These were the same ones with which Natalya had just been charged.

"Nonsense?" The sergeant struck Borisov across the face with the flat of his hand. "Who do you think you are? You don't speak that way to an official of the Soviet police. If I say you are in violation, you are in violation. You are guilty of systematically writing and disseminating false and slanderous materials against the Soviet government."

Standing up, indignant, confused, Borisov shouted back, "You're crazy!"

The sergeant slapped Borisov twice across the face. "We will have to teach you some manners! Do you admit to writing slanderous material?"

"No." Borisov fell into his chair. He was drunk,

angry, and his stomach hurt terribly. All he wanted to do was to go home and fall asleep.

"I have here evidence of your conspiracy against the state." He raised a crumpled piece of paper.

"Let me see that." Borisov reached for the paper.

"Don't touch state property without my permission!" The sergeant shoved Borisov back into his chair.

"State property? It's nothing but a plain piece of paper with scribbling."

The sergeant threw him off the chair onto the floor. Borisov wondered where this was meant to lead. Slander? Defamation? Against the Soviet Union? It was utterly crazy. Drunkenness, fine! He'd accept the appropriate accusations, indictments, and fines. But the rest was nonsense. Borisov decided to try a more restrained approach. He stood up, brushed himself off, and quietly sat down.

The sergeant also seemed to have quieted abruptly. Even his physical appearance changed. He pulled out a pack of Pani, a slim, filtered cigarette favored by senior members of government, and lit it.

"Take one, Dr. Borisov. I think it will calm your nerves."

Borisov took a cigarette. This was the first time his name had been spoken since being brought to the Vytrezvitel.

"Please, Dr. Borisov. We may act and look like peasants, but I am surprised that you should be so easily deceived. By the way, let me compliment you on the way you handled yourself in your cell."

"Thank you."

"However, you will not be able to fight yourself out of this room. Believe me."

"I have no intention of resisting. But quite frankly, neither do I intend to allow you to make false accusations. I am a Soviet citizen, the son of two heroes of the Soviet Republic and . . ." — he paused, disgusting himself by what he was saying —". . . and I am a distinguished member of the Academy of Scientists and the Communist Party."

"Are you equating the scientific prestige of the Academy with the egregious undertakings of those political farts in the Communist Party?" The sergeant laughed.

Borisov was stunned by the heavy-handed irreverence.

"Come, come, doctor. I certainly can't have shocked you. Can you seriously tell me that those political toads in the Communist Party are equal in stature and accomplishment to that august body of researchers and scientists like yourself?"

No, Borisov thought, he wouldn't be baited into agreeing. With the slightest hint of agreement he would be trapped.

"Now, now, doctor," the sergeant continued coyly. "Silence? What do we have here? Do I interpret this as resistance? Wouldn't you doctors at that hospital consider that negativistic behavior? Antisocial?"

"No," Borisov replied flatly.

"No?" The sergeant slammed his fist on the table. "Doctor, I can hold you on charges of perjury. Lying to an official of the State Security." He smiled cruelly. "Do you know what the sentence for perjury is?"

Borisov shook his head.

"Ten to fifteen years. Now, doctor, can you tell me truthfully, as the distinguished psychiatrist you obviously are, that you consider silence as negativistic behavior?"

Borisov's face flushed, but he remained silent.

"Upset? Perhaps you need one of those medicines you give out so freely."

Borisov started to stand but was pushed back down.

"Don't. That would be very, very foolish. Now, doctor, if silence is not negativistic behavior, what is?"

Borisov watched the man's face. His eyes had a

malevolent intelligence so characteristic of Russian peasants from the Ukrainian region. He was no ordinary policeman. His handling of Borisov was too agile. Too facile in the way he was switching his moods and approaches. And too informed about psychiatry.

"Answer, please!" The man shouted in Borisov's right ear. "What are the negativistic behaviors for which you put people away?"

"Self-destruction. Suicide."

"Suicide? Interesting. What do you consider self-destructive?"

"Self-mutilation. Drugs. Alcohol." No sooner had Borisov said the last word than he realized the consequences.

"Alcohol?" The sergeant repeated Borisov's words as if he had just been served a sumptuous meal.

"Severe alcoholism."

"How long do you incarcerate someone for such a self-destructive behavior as alcoholism?"

"It depends on how long the person has been drinking, how much he drinks, and how much damage was inflicted to his body and his mind."

"Well?"

"Well, what?"

"Answer those questions, please."

"There has to be sufficient damage to the liver and the brain to create a complete picture of a deteriorated body with auditory and/or visual hallucinations."

The sergeant leaned forward over his clenched fists and spoke matter-of-factly. "Not all alcoholics have to be that deteriorated to be incarcerated in your hospital, do they?"

"No."

"So an acute state of intoxication with a history of drinking could be sufficient reason for incarceration."

"Yes. We could hospitalize on the basis of what you've just described."

"What, then, stops me from incarcerating you here for a sufficiently long time to cure you of your alcoholism?"

"I am not an alcoholic!"

"But how can you say that, doctor? We picked you up on a routine sweep of the city."

"I wasn't just picked up by chance. I was followed and targeted by one of your agents." As soon as the words were out Borisov was sorry.

"Which agent? We have no agents here. We are a simple police station. And why would we want to follow you?" The sergeant leaned over so that his face almost pressed against Borisov's.

"Never mind."

"Which agent?" He tapped Borisov's chin contemptuously. "Describe him to me."

"Short man. Nondescript features. I didn't get a very close look at him."

"I see. So you thought you saw someone whom you thought looked like an agent — whatever they are supposed to look like. Furthermore, you have the presumption to conclude that I had some other motive to have you picked up. What could that motive be, doctor?"

Borisov replied wearily, holding his head in his hands, "I don't know. I want to go back to my cell."

The sergeant jerked Borisov's head upward, not allowing him a moment's respite. "I think we have evidence here of a visual hallucination mixed with a strong tincture of paranoia. Now, doctor, of course I am not an expert like yourself, but it looks like we have a clear mental problem. Alcoholism, possibly paranoia, or both. In any case, you should not be allowed on the outside until you are much better." Without warning or reason the sergeant swung his massive hand across Borisov's face, knocking him to the floor. "We've just added attempting to strike a security officer to the list of hooliganism, public nuisance, alcoholism, slander, perjury, and uncooperative behavior. And we still have the possibility of adding serious mental illness." He grabbed Borisov by the lapel, lifted him up, and slammed him against the wall several times.

Borisov attempted to defend himself but the sergeant thrust his thick muscular arms upward, breaking Borisov's lock around his neck, and threw him against the wall once more. A knee into Borisov's groin, and he fell onto the floor, screaming in agony.

"Enough." The door to the room opened and another man walked in.

The sergeant stepped out of the room with alacrity.

"Dr. Borisov, please. Take your seat." The man offered him his hand, lifting him up from the floor. "I apologize for the overzealous nature of the sergeant. Poorly trained police often confuse questioning with interrogation. They think and act as if they were judge, jury, and prosecutor." The man had witnessed the interrogation through the two-way mirror, and knew that the "sergeant," a middle level KGB agent, expert in cross examining witnesses, had done well. Years of experience questioning tipsy foreign diplomats and businessmen wandering aimlessly on their way back toward their hotels had paid off. A convenient method that the system had perfected for culling intelligence data, compromising enemies, and evaluating potential agents. Yes, from the moment a foreigner left the detoxification center he was a potential Soviet agent. Sometimes the man was embarrassed by the ease with which he could recruit agents, using the simplest of all human weaknesses — drink. Now sex, that was more complicated but far more exciting. These psychiatrists could learn a thing or two about human nature, he thought, from all the interviews he had personally conducted over the years.

The man took particular pleasure in watching Borisov under stress. He didn't do too well. He responded too quickly. Underneath that cool, collected exterior Borisov was a Russian Slav, with all the emotionalism that only vodka . . . or pain . . . can elicit. Had Borisov only remained silent a little longer he might have brought the interview within his control.

"It is amazing how the pain of physical punishment can often serve as an effective relief for the unrelenting anguish of an interrogation, particularly one based on a series of arbitrary premises." He spoke with an air of detached arrogance. "Is there anything I can get you?" He tried to help Borisov to stand up but was rebuffed. "It's so hard to control the quality of the people working for you. I'm sure you must encounter a similar problem at the hospital."

"Who are you?" Borisov asked suspiciously.

"Oh, forgive me for being so inexcusably gauche." He extended his hand. "I am Leonid Donskoi."

Borisov looked at the meticulously dressed, diminutive man before him. Urbane, cosmopolitan. Natalya had described him accurately. "What is it that you want from me?" Borisov wanted to ask for a glass of ice water to soothe the tearing sensation within his stomach, but he wouldn't give Donskoi the satisfaction.

"Please, Dr. Borisov, don't jump to any conclusions. There is really nothing I want from you. It's simply a matter of a series of incidents mounting into this one unfortunate episode."

"What is it that you want, Comrade Donskoi?" Borisov repeated. "I'd like to get home. I'm tired, and, as you can imagine, not feeling well."

"Of course, of course. I understand completely." He lifted Borisov from the chair, helped to straighten his clothing, and led him out the door, past the fetid row of steel-barred cells. He pointed to the overnight derelicts, with obvious contempt. "Create an arbitrary law that no alcoholics are allowed into the street after a certain hour, and you create enough work for several thousand."

Borisov walked with difficulty. He avoided the envious stares of the men behind the bars.

"Dr. Borisov, you and I are not very different. We both serve the same function — servants of the social order created for the specific purpose of maintaining a modicum of law and order. I say 'modicum,' because, like any viable system, there has to be allowance for some deviation within that system. Even such a repressive regime as that of our glorious USSR can still tolerate some noticeable anti-Soviet behavior so that things will function relatively smoothly."

Outside, Borisov shielded his eyes from the blinding morning light.

"You see, Dr. Borisov" — Donskoi held on to his arm as they continued to walk down the street — "I allow for some flexibility in my approach to deviance. If one is drunk, I simply lock him up for the evening, barring some unforeseen exigencies, and then release him the next day. However" — Donskoi's voice turned icy cold — "if he's diagnosed as a paranoid schizophrenic, then the burden of proof falls upon him to prove that he's not. In my system he has a chance to prove he's not an alcoholic. Or a deviant. In *your* system there is no way for the individual to prove your doctors wrong. Once he's labeled insane, the label remains forever. Even if his aberrant behavior were to cease, it's simply termed a remission. But nothing else changes. Neither the label, the condition, nor the way you think about him. For the rest of his life he'll stigmatized with your diagnosis. As appropriate or inappropriate as it might be."

Borisov knew that Donskoi was not waiting for a rebuttal.

They walked down several blocks to the Pechora Café. Donskoi ordered and paid for two black coffees. "I thought you might enjoy this little touch of dramatic irony — returning to the scene of your crime. With your bailiff. You see, in many ways I may, on the surface, appear brutal in the way I deal with antisocial behavior. But I am far more humane than you or your colleagues, who quietly but systematically and scientifically elicit information from the deviant which will invariably lead to his *execution*, so to speak. Accomplished without their knowledge or consent, of course. At least, I give my victims an opportunity to call in members of the judicial system to protect their interests."

Borisov felt constrained to answer. He was impressed by the compelling nature of Donskoi's argument. But the notion that the patient, or the victim, as Donskoi called him, was without any recourse was too galling.

"I disagree." Borisov was surprised by the civility of his tone.

Donskoi laughed. He tapped Borisov's arm patronizingly with his finger. "Excellent . . . I want to hear what you have to say."

"We have mental health commission hearings, where the patient can argue for his or her release."

"Of course. Like the one you had for Natalya Vartanian. Fair. Impartial. Scientific."

"So you were there! She was right!"

"In a matter of speaking. But what difference does it make if she was or was not right. Your tests proved her conclusively insane. Even you found it hard to argue against your scientific findings. Your EEG, GSR, and Eighteen PF. What difference does it make if she is or is not being persecuted? Your tests have already preordained her to a specific course of action. In my system, the citizen has a fighting chance to avoid the consequences of retribution. Simply admit the mistake and cooperate. As you well know, we Russians are extremely forgiving. And I am no less Russian than the next person. But where's the point of redemption in your system? Even if Natalya were to admit she's insane and was willing to work with you as a psychiatrist, you'd still continue to treat her in the same manner as if she were totally uncooperative and defiant. You'd give her those medications that would make her compliant or soporific. Or you might subject her to your well-researched insulin coma therapy.''

Borisov flinched. "What do you want?"

Donskoi raised his arm, and a black Zilenko pulled up in front of them. Donskoi motioned Borisov forward, inviting him to enter the back seat. They rode in silence until they arrived at Warehouse 10, a dilapidated building close to the outskirts of town.

Donskoi knew his way through the dark labyrinthine hallways lined with dying patients, screaming for pain medication. He led Borisov into a small room where a young Greek Orthodox priest was giving a patient the last rites. When the priest saw the men approach the bed he stepped quietly aside.

"There he is," Donskoi said, pointing to the patient on the bed, "Vladimir Nekipelov, the product of your medicine. Your system. He will soon die because you were so certain that you had discovered a new method for proving a questionable scientific diagnosis. Not satisfied with the impertinence, you were somehow even more determined to try a new therapeutic technique for what was, at best, a questionable behavioral condition. An alcoholic. A vagrant. In my system he would have simply spent one disturbed night at the place you just left. But he would have remained alive. To panhandle, if you please." Donskoi paused for effect and spoke softly. "You asked me what I wanted from you. So I say to you, look carefully at Nekipelov and think of Natalya."

Chapter Fifteen

BORISOV HAD DONE everything possible to dissuade Zeleneyev from continuing his preparations. But it was no use. The orders had come directly from Zoubok. First, an intramuscular injection as a priming dose. Second, insulin intravenously, according to their newly developed course of treatment.

He was now certain that he had to get Natalya out of the hospital. Otherwise, she would never leave, at least not with any semblance of her personality intact. She had been right all along. There was a conspiracy, and he, Borisov, had been used as a foil for Donskoi's machinations. But was he any better than Donskoi? Certainly, by using a medical system replete with tautologies and circular definitions, and *ex cathedra* statements concerning normal and abnormal behaviour, he appeared more legitimate and acceptable to the outside world. But in reality, wasn't he an agent of the state who maintained law and order by minimizing aberrant behaviour patterns? Last night's inebriation could become tomorrow's sluggish schizophrenia. No, Natalya didn't require change. The system did.

Borisov broke into a cold sweat. The palms of his hands felt clammy. He counted a pulse of one hundred and forty. He was more frightened than he had ever been in his life. What he had to do to get her out of the hospital would have to be done quickly, illegally, and probably against her own will. There was little chance of convincing her that he was on her side.

"What do you need with sulfazine?" the pharmacist looked quizzically at Borisov. "I haven't stocked that drug since 1956. Khrushchev personally denounced it as an integral part of Stalin's inhumane treatment of psychiatric patients and political prisoners. I threw out every bottle we had."

"Of course, of course." Borisov tried not to be defensive. "But I need it for some animal experiments."

"How important is it?" The pharmacist had been at the hospital for forty years and was used to the impulsive demands of the research staff, "those scientific prima donnas," as he called them. "I think I can find something for you that may be just as good." The pharmacist disappeared into a back room and returned with two dusty brown bottles. "Here are the two principal ingredients of sulfazine — a four percent solution of sulfur and peach extract. I don't know how good they still are. They may have lost their potency over the years."

Borisov inspected the bottles closely. This was their only chance. He thanked the pharmacist and took the bottles to his laboratory, a few doors down from the Organic Therapy Unit. Here, amidst bunsen burners, wooden shelves overflowing with thick bottles of chemicals, and black slate desktops, Borisov felt complete. Only in this room could he integrate the fragments of his life — teacher, clinician, administrator, and researcher. It was here, on laboratory mice, that he had developed his diagnostic techniques and therapeutic modalities for sluggish schizophrenia. It was here in the quiet solitude of this underequipped, dark, smelly room that he had fulfilled his personal aspirations, and his professional obligations to a system that had always been protective and supportive, demanding in return only integrity and loyalty. Now integrity no longer seemed essential to the system. Loyalty no longer seemed important to him.

As he mixed the sulfur with the peach extract, in a four percent base of alcohol, he trembled. He had just embarked on his first act of defiance against the very community that had nurtured him. Now, he was about to destroy all that he had achieved. For moral integrity? No. He wouldn't try to deceive himself. It was his desire for Natalya, more than anything else, that compelled him to take such drastic action.

Borisov watched the two chemicals settle into a compound. He took a syringe and pulled back the plunger, making certain to extract only the 1-1/2 cc. required for the test. He went into the small room adjoining his laboratory, brought out a few cages of squealing black-and-white mice, injected the newly created sulfazine into a mouse, and waited. For the first five minutes the mouse ran aimlessly around the cage. Within seven minutes it fell down, dead.

Borisov cut the dose in half and injected it into another mouse. As he watched, the mouse's behaviour became progressively more agitated. He looked at his watch — three minutes, five minutes, ten minutes. Fifteen minutes later the mouse had settled into a highly excited, but normal pattern of activity. Ten more mice gave Borisov the same results. He had found the right mixture. Now all he had to do was to multiply the dose by a factor of four. Natalya would receive 3 cc.'s of this pearl-gray liquid in place of insulin.

Borisov took a standard vial of insulin and withdrew its contents, substituting his newly prepared sulfazine mixture. After thirty minutes the mice exhibited no further side effects. He meticulously cleaned up the lab and returned the mice to the animal room. In the Organic Therapy Unit he substituted the insulin bottle that contained his compound of sulfazine for the one that Zeleneyev had marked with letters NV — Natalya Vartanian.

Borisov glanced at his watch. He had at least twelve hours before the hospital staff would learn that he was "on vacation." So he continued his usual practice of calling the night physician covering the hospital to warn him of any potential problems with a patient. He informed the doctor on call that he, Borisov, had a patient by the name of Natalya Vartanian who had been spiking very high fevers over the past two days. "If the patient develops one or all of the following symptoms — fever over 104.5 degrees Fahrenheit, marked chills, severe muscle aches, headaches, nausea, vomiting, or photophobia — call me immediately. It might be typhoid. We might have to transfer her immediately to the Infectious Disease Unit at Botkin Hospital."

Hanging up the telephone, Borisov felt comfortable that the night physician would follow his orders. It was standard operating procedure. But would his plan work? The entire scheme was replete with risk; would the medicine be given to Natalya? Would it work as desired, during the night? Could he really manage to get her out of Kashchenko and to a nonsecurity hospital without incident?

The next call he placed was to the chief of the Infectious Disease Unit at Botkin, informing him of the possibility of an admission during the night of one of his top-priority patients who must receive the utmost of discretion and care because of her husband's high standing in the government. As expected, the chief responded with the alacrity of someone eager to service the state elite.

Borisov placed a group of medicines he would need to counteract the effect of the sulfazine in his medical bag and went to the financial office to collect his past month's salary. He asked for and received an additional draw of five hundred rubles for the "holiday" he was going on, collateralized against his pension fund. Because of his seniority, there were no questions asked. Unfortunately, to say goodbye to his friends — Ternowsky, Tsarev, and, of course, Zeleneyev — would be too dangerous. For him and for them.

Walking to his car, he stared for the last time at the unkempt grounds, the patients walking aimlessly, the overflowing garbage cans.

A third of his life had been spent here. He would be leaving behind an important part of himself.

He forced his thoughts back to the plan he was piecing together. What was missing? The sulfazine should work within four to six hours; the clinical reaction should mimic typhoid fever; the night physician should inform Borisov of the problem; Natalya should be transferred to the Infectious Disease Unit at Botkin where he would be waiting to whisk her away. But then to where? Probably Leningrad by car, and then a ferryboat to Finland. And freedom.

But to leave Moscow and travel through the USSR he would need two interior passports. He already had one for himself. Now he needed one for Natalya. He also couldn't forget his membership card to the Communist Party and a set of clothing for Natalya, or, at least an overcoat, until he could find something suitable.

Borisov drove home quickly. He glanced frequently

in the rearview mirror to see if he was being followed. He didn't think so. But he could never be certain.

Natalya pulled more forcibly on the leather straps binding her wrists to the bed. The more she strained the more it hurt. What will happen to me next, she wondered. Donskoi and his minions had won. I am now officially declared insane. They can now do with me whatever they want without fear of attracting undue attention. And no one will know. She imagined her friends and acquaintances wondering where she was, and someone languidly responding that they had heard that Natalya was hospitalized in a psychiatric institution. "But you know her," they would say, "she always was a little bit unstable. Just like her mother."

The thought that she was just like her mother frightened her. What if they are right? Those tests with the needles and wires say I'm crazy. Maybe I do belong in this *pskhushka*, strapped down like a mad dog. Damn you, mother! Where are you now that I need you? You never gave a damn about me. You only cared about yourself.

Natalya called for water but no one came. Her throat was dry and hoarse. She felt hot. Terribly hot. Her muscles began to ache with an intensity she could not understand. She fantasized that Zoubok and Borisov were pulling her legs in opposite directions. Her husband and Donskoi were pulling at her arms.

"Anatoly," she sobbed. "Anatoly." A blur of images began to race across her mind: Sukhumi, her mother, her father. Borisov.

She cried silently. My mother is dying, my *bogatyr*. She's dying. I want to see her. She's going to leave me alone like you did . . . like he did. Why does everyone leave me? "What have I done?" Natalya cried out in the darkness of the room.

The present faded away and her mind was flooded with theatrical scenes. The cardboard outline of a ship called the *Imperial* stretched out before her across a stage as men in nondescript uniforms climbed up the side toward the deck. Was it a scene from *Intervention*, a play in which she had a small, but important, role? It had played four months in Moscow at the prestigious Vakhtangov Theater. How Anatoly had complained about the drab, unadorned theater, with its wooden folding "undertaker's chairs." But how enraptured he had sat through the four hours of the performance, reliving a time with which he was intimately familiar — the intervention of Western imperial allies at Odessa during Russia's darkest hours after the Russian Revolution. He made her promise to take him to more plays of that kind. She sobbed at the thought.

She tried to visualize him seated in the audience at Chekhov's *The Three Sisters*. Where was he? She couldn't see him. Instead, she saw a banquet scene from Gogol's *Dead Souls*. As a child her mother had taken her to see it at the Moscow Art Theater. She had whispered theatrical names, Stanislavsky, Meyerhold, names which would only become significant to her years later. A group of men dressed in dark clothing with somber expressions of grief peered down at the comrade's dead body. Who was it? Sukhumi? Her Anatoly? Or was it *The Optimistic Tragedy*, in which she played a highly emotional role of a patriotic woman at the Kamerny Theater. She began to scream, invoking Zoubok, Stanislavsky, Meyerhold, Donskoi, Borisov, Sukhumi, momma, poppa, as the door to her room opened slowly. "I must go to Tbilisi," she cried.

Passing it slowly over the yellow flame of the candle, Borisov blurred the Ministry of Health insignia, hoping that an official glancing cursorily at the passport would mistake it for the Ministry of Interior designation. So far, he was surprised to discover how simple the counterfeiting process could be. Tearing off a piece of tin from the corner of the Madonna and Child icon, he copied a design from his own passport which bore the words Ministry of Interior/Internal Passport and brushed some black ink lightly over the embossed letters and patterns. Only the most distinct features of the ministry's seal were not identifiable. Very carefully, he pressed the inked imprint onto the aged yellow paper. He then substituted an old ribbon for the new one in his typewriter and inserted the paper. As he typed the state's questions, he gently dabbed the paper with his fingers until the letters were sufficiently smudged. He inserted the number 632407 by hand, at the top of the passport, and answered the questions he had typed in longhand. Borisov smiled with satisfaction. So far it looked genuine.

But a recent photograph of Natalya? How would he be able to get one? He sat at the table, running his hand nervously through his hair. Without a picture there was no chance of making the passport look completely authentic. And without the internal passport there was no chance of escaping Moscow. Where could he obtain a picture? He recalled the theatrical leaflet with her picture he had found in the cabin. But where was it? He ran to his closet and found the pocket in which he had left it. Creased, but very usable, he thought.

From the highest shelf in the closet he took his Polaroid camera, a token of friendship given him on his visit to the United States by a senior representative of the American Psychiatric Association. Of all his cameras, including the secondhand Leica he had bought on his last vacation to Dubrovnik, he cherished the Polaroid most of all. He had hardly used it, however, for fear of not being able to acquire more of the special film it required.

He stretched the flier between two books, took a picture of Natalya's photograph, and waited nervously the few minutes it took to develop. The likeness was remarkable. Borisov cut the picture so that it fit into the lower part of the right-hand page and stamped it with the ersatz seal from the Ministry of Interior. Passing the page gently over the flame a few times dried the seal. It looked authentic!

The telephone rang, interrupting his self-congratulations. Borisov checked his watch before he picked up the receiver. Two thirty in the morning. The familiar voice of the night physician at Kashchenko Hospital gave him the long-awaited news that Natalya Vartanian had become feverish, markedly delusional, and manifested both auditory and visual hallucinations. She had to be completely restrained. The bad news was that the Infectious Disease Unit at the Botkin Hospital would not accept her because she sounded too emotionally disturbed. "That's absurd," replied Borisov. "She's only deranged because of her febrile, typhoidlike condition."

"Typhoidlike?"

"Well, we don't really know until the blood cultures are taken, right?" Borisov replied defensively. "Please stay by the phone. I will call you in a few minutes." He had to make certain that Natalya was transferred to Botkin Hospital.

Instead of apologizing for having awakened the chief of the Infectious Disease Unit at Botkin in the middle of the night, Borisov feigned indignation. "If this is the type of service I can expect from one of my esteemed colleagues, I have no other choice than to send this prominent patient — and others like her — to a local regional medical hospital where they'd have to wonder why the Botkin didn't take her."

The point was clearly made. An apology was offered and Borisov was assured that his patient would be transferred to the chief's own private service, where Dr.

Borisov could participate as freely as he wanted in her treatment. To make further amends, he would send one of the hospital's ambulances to pick her up immediately.

"I would appreciate it if her private guards, who are government *apparatchiki*, are placed in immediate quarrantine, away from the patient for at least twenty-four hours." Would this request sound parenthetical?

"Don't worry, Dr. Borisov. We'll take care of everything. Please forget our earlier misunderstanding. It's always a pleasure to work with you."

Borisov listened to some predictable words of praise for his work with Dr. Zoubok and returned the compliments. They were accepted with hypocritical modesty.

The return call to the night physician at Kashchenko was sufficient to have him prepare the patient for transfer to Botkin Hospital. Borisov ordered her to be wrapped in a hypothermia blanket, to lower her temperature, and given 75 milligrams of phenothiazine intramuscularly to diminish her agitated behavior. He hung up the phone and for the first time that evening took a deep breath and exhaled slowly.

His moment of relaxation was interrupted by a knock on the door. Who could it be at 2:45 A.M.? Borisov remained silent, hoping the person would leave. The knocks became louder. Donskoi? The KGB? Had they known all along what he had planned and were they now going to stop him? Borisov stood transfixed. The doorknob started to turn. Someone was trying to force his way into the apartment.

Chapter Sixteen

"ALEXSANDROVITCH, YOU SON-OF-A-BITCH. Open up."

Borisov rushed to open the door.

"Ternowsky!" Borisov's voice choked with fear and surprise.

"You didn't think you could fool this Ukrainian *kulak*, did you?"

"Come in." Borisov gestured Ternowsky into his apartment. No one else was in the hallway.

"The cashier at the hospital is one of my friendly informants — a fellow Ukrainian. He knows I'm a good friend of yours and told me about your money withdrawal for your forthcoming . . . vacation." He wrinkled his brow as if deep in thought. "Why don't you be hospitable and offer a breathless friend some vodka?"

Borisov went to the credenza and brought back a bottle of vodka. Ternowsky took a swig. "Where are you going, my friend?"

Borisov was reluctant to answer. What if Ternowsky were here on orders from Zoubok?

"All right. So you don't trust me. I don't blame you. My performance at the commission hearing was less than admirable . . . or supportive. But forget your thick Muscovite pride and accept the humble apology and assistance of your close friend and colleague." He placed his arms around Borisov's shoulders. "Remember, my friend, it was you who seduced and recruited me to this cosmopolitan inferno. It's only fair that I help you to leave."

Borisov laughed at the contagious good will this simple man always generated. "But Yuri, it's three in the morning."

"My friend, I'm not asking you what you are about to do. Obviously you're reluctant to tell me." He held Borisov at arm's length. "Let me say goodbye the way two good friends should." He pressed Borisov toward him and embraced him tightly. "You will need a bit of help," he said. "It will be impossible to hide in Moscow. Especially with her. She's too sick."

Borisov pulled back. "How did you know?"

"I know how your mind works. And now I know how your heart works." He hugged him once again. "I'm so glad for you. I'd always felt that for too long your life was ruled by your mind. And now" — he pulled back — "it will be ruined by love. But what better way to go? Please, my friend, let me help you."

"Who else knows?"

"No one. I swear to God."

"I don't want you to get into trouble. You have a wife and children."

"They know I love them. And they also know that I love you. If I didn't help you in your hour of need then I'd never forgive myself. And I'd become intolerable to live with. So it's both to their benefit and yours that I help you."

Borisov couldn't resist Ternowsky's entreaties. Borisov had hired him for the very reasons Zoubok disliked him. To his very soul he was a true Russian peasant — shrewd, practical, and affectionate. Yes, he thought. I could use his help. Ternowsky had a strong instinct for survival.

They agreed that Ternowsky would drive so that Borisov could concentrate his full attention on caring for Natalya. Depending on her condition, they might need an overnight stop. But Ternowsky would leave them in the morning. Once Borisov had gathered up his medical bag, the internal passports, his money, and an old overcoat for Natalya, they left to drive to Botkin Hospital.

"Would you be offended, my friend, if I try to warn you once more against taking her out of the hospital?"

"No, I won't be offended. But you know me better than that. Once I've made up my mind I don't change it."

"She'll be safer in the hospital. At least they'll try to keep her alive."

"As a vegetable, like Nekipelov. They'd already begun the insulin coma therapy when I left. I can't risk her going through even one minute of it. I could lose her at any point. At any point."

"What if she really belongs there?"

"Andreivitch, if you don't want to help, tell me now. Please don't do me a favor. I already have too much on my mind."

"My friend, I'll say no more."

Botkin Hospital was a massive compound of seven eight-story buildings with all the austere solemnity and dilapidation that befitted a one-hundred-year-old institution. The hospital was slated to be moved to new quarters on the outskirts of Moscow while the present plant was transformed into a chronic care center. But that was the future. For the moment, the walls were peeling and the corridors were crowded with patients on stretchers. It reminded Borisov of a civilian evacuation center during wartime.

On their way to the fourth floor of Building 2, Borisov and Ternowsky were stopped by two wooden doors that opened and closed electronically upon voice identification of the visitor.

"Shit," muttered Borisov. "This is not what I'd expected. I thought this was an open unit, accessible to anyone."

"Please identify yourselves," a voice crackled over the loudspeaker.

"Dr. Borisov and Dr. Ternowsky from the Kashchenko Psychiatric Hospital coming to see a recently transferred patient, Natalya Vartanian."

"One moment, please."

Borisov peered through the round, wire-mesh windows and saw a stern-looking male attendant check a clipboard.

"I'm sorry, but we do not have a patient by that name."

"What do you mean?"

"There is no patient by that name."

"Let me in," Borisov yelled through the mesh. "I would like to see the names for myself." The plan is already falling apart, he thought. The chief of the unit became frightened and decided not to transfer her after all.

"Maybe she was admitted under another name," Ternowsky suggested.

"But I only gave them Natalya Vartanian."

"You know what bureaucracies are like. Try it."

"My mistake." Borisov shouted into the voice box on the wall. "The patient's name is Natalya Nikitchenko."

Suddenly the wooden doors leading into the Infectious Disease Unit opened. The attendant checked

Borisov's and Ternowsky's hospital identification cards and pointed to a room at the end of the corridor. The patient's personal bodyguards, they were told, were in a room directly across from hers in mandatory quarantine.

Hospital rules, Borisov thought. Thank God for hospital rules.

They walked down the hall, Ternowsky several paces ahead of Borisov. As he passed nonchalantly by the guards' room he saw two men seated at a table playing cards, but with a good view of Natalya's room. They were talking and drinking, complaining to each other about not having personally received orders from their superiors about the transfer, and about the poor telephone service at the hospital. Ternowsky walked back toward Borisov and summarized the situation; they needed a diversion.

Borisov looked around the corridor and saw several gray bins of clean hospital uniforms. Taking off their overcoats and placing them over the bin they quickly dressed themselves from head to foot in green cloth cap, body gown, and shoe covers, as if they were prepared to perform major surgery.

Ternowsky entered the guards' room and introduced himself as the chief of the service, enjoying the stunned expressions on both men's faces when he ordered them to lie down on their respective beds so that they could be examined for contagious liver and spleen problems, similar to some found in other patients on the ward. Initially the guards resisted, insisting that they were not patients but healthy security officials entrusted with the personal safety of the sick patient across the way. Ternowsky, however, would not be deterred. He replied that the microbes of disease were not particularly impressed by their credentials. If they insisted on being invincible, it was fine with him. It would simply mean that, when the inevitable happened, he would have two less patients to worry about.

It worked as planned. Ternowsky sufficiently frightened the men into lying on the beds, stripped down for a proper examination.

When Borisov saw the guards' door close, he entered Natalya's room and removed his face mask. A deep sadness overcame him as he took her limp hand and felt her thready, rapid pulse. She was still febrile. He touched her moist forehead. She was hot — maybe 103 or 104 degrees Fahrenheit. He checked the rubber hypothermic blanket beneath her. Damn, it wasn't working. He would have to lower her fever quickly or she might sustain brain damage. Her breathing was rapid and shallow but she didn't seem in respiratory distress. What shocked him most of all was the ashen color that had washed away her naturally vibrant hue.

Natalya opened her eyes but was too weak to pull her hand back from the green monster before her.

"Who are you? And what do you want?"

Those were the most reassuring words Borisov could have heard.

"I'm glad to hear that you're feeling better."

"Oh, it's you," she said faintly.

"We don't have too much time," Borisov said. "I've come to take you out of the hospital. I've had you transferred from Kashchenko here to Botkin Hospital. You are in the Infectious Disease Unit so that it will be easier for me to take you away."

"Take me away?" With great difficulty, she pulled herself into a sitting position on the bed. "Take me away where?"

Borisov was relieved that her mind was clear and that the effects of the sulfazine were obviously waning. The night physician had followed his orders. "I'm sorry, but there's no time for a discussion."

"Is this another instance of your well-known technique of unrealistically raising patients' hopes and then disappointing them?"

"Look, I don't blame you for mistrusting me."

"Mistrusting you? My dear doctor, there's nothing you can say or do that will convince me that you aren't one of Donskoi's louts."

He was becoming annoyed. Perhaps it would have been better if she were unconscious. He sat down on her bed and looked her straight in the eye. "We don't have time for this. When dawn comes, Zoubok and Donskoi will find out that I had you transferred out of their jurisdiction. They won't like that. The fact that you don't like me or trust me is unfortunate but understandable. For whatever it's worth, I've been discharged from the hospital because I wouldn't let them continue the insulin therapy Zoubok recommended. Because I believe that you were admitted for the reasons that you said. So right now, there are three lives at stake — yours, mine, and my friend next door, Dr. Ternowsky, who's keeping your security guards occupied while I try to get you out of here."

"To where?" Her voice was still skeptical.

"To Leningrad and then Helsinki. I want to get you out of the Soviet Union as quickly as possible. You'll never be safe here again."

"Helsinki?"

"You're wasting time."

"Last time you offered me freedom I was handed to a jury of your peers who committed me. Thanks! But I prefer captivity. It's more dependable. At least I know they mean what they say."

Borisov stood up. He would have to act quickly. There was no point trying to reason with her. At least not now. "I'll be back," he said as he left the room.

Borisov walked across the hall and beckoned to Ternowsky, who was busily palpating one of the guards' spleens for any possible enlargement.

"We have a couple of problems. She won't go. And we're going to have to get past that guard."

"Leave the guard to me. When you hear a scream coming out of this room, quickly get off the ward. Head straight to my car. I'll join you there."

Borisov returned to Natalya's room with an extra scrub suit. "Put this on now."

She looked first at the scrub suit and then defiantly back at him.

"Put it on, damn it." Behind him, Borisov could hear Ternowsky calling the security attendant to help him. The way was clear. It had to be now. They had only a few minutes before the guard would return to his post.

Borisov rushed over to the bed. With one single movement he tore off the flimsy hospital gown. When Natalya screamed, he slapped her. "Don't fight me. I have to get you out of here," he hissed. Too exhausted to resist, Natalya allowed Borisov to pull on the baggy scrub suit, which made her look as if she belonged on the hospital staff. She was able to put on her own shoes, but as soon as she tried to stand she slid onto the floor.

Borisov lifted her and held her tightly under her armpits in order not to aggravate her shoulder and rib wounds. "Try to walk. The more convincing you look, the easier it will be." As they maneuvered down the corridor, Borisov put on one of the overcoats and placed the other on Natalya's shoulders. They heard another loud scream.

"What was that?"

"A Ukrainian physical exam," Borisov pressed the button to release the electronic doors. They walked quickly down the empty corridors. The day shift had not yet begun to arrive.

Borisov was considerably less anxious as they crossed the threshold into the parking area. A garbled announcement came over the hospital paging system that a patient had escaped. All unauthorized personnel were ordered to the main security office for questioning. An exhausted Natalya climbed into the back seat of Ternowsky's car, as five police cars came screeching up to the front entrance of the hospital.

"Get down." Borisov pushed Natalya's head beneath the window line as Donskoi and Panova rushed into the hospital.

In silence Borisov changed into his clothes and helped Natalya roll the trouser legs of the scrub suit so that nothing showed beneath the coat. "The police are checking all the cars," Borisov whispered. He opened his door and crept out of the car. He pulled Natalya from the back seat by her collar and dragged her behind a concrete embankment. They lay side by side, flat on the ground, the beam of a guard's flashlight coming within meters of discovering them.

"Well, Dr. Borisov," Natalya said with difficulty, "you're beginning to be convincing."

Suddenly she felt a hand tap her on the shoulder. She froze.

"We meet again, Mrs. Vartanian." Ternowsky crouched down.

"Yes. Hello," Natalya said with relief.

"The only way out of this parking lot" — Borisov surveyed the area — "is by car. We'll have to get by that roadblock they've just constructed in front of the hospital. If we walk out they'll catch us. With a car, we might have a chance."

They crawled back into Ternowsky's car when the search of their area ended. Ternowsky took the driver's seat.

"Alexsandr, if you really want to help me, then I must get to Tbilisi."

"Tbilisi?" Borisov was annoyed by the presumption of her request. "Look around you. What do you see?"

"Police. And doctors. Frequently one and the same."

"Listen." Borisov spoke from a crouched position in the back seat next to Natalya. "We'll be damn lucky if we just get out of here alive. And it will be close to a miracle if we ever reach Leningrad. Every road, train station, subway, airport, will be covered, now that they know you've escaped. They won't let you get out of Moscow — let alone to Tbilisi. Every road covered by police, internal border guards, KGB. How do you expect to get there?''

"I must get to Tbilisi."

"If you argue any longer we might as well wait until the police come and pick us up."

Ternowsky drove the car toward a group of soldiers standing alongside a makeshift barricade and waited in a line of cars to reach the inspection point. When a young policeman stuck his head through the car window and asked Ternowsky for his identity card, he pressed his foot all the way down on the accelerator and broke through the barricade, followed by a blast of gunfire.

He sped down Michurinsky Prospekt past the modern buildings and bright floodlights of the Olympic Village.

Through the rearview mirror Ternowsky saw that they were being followed by a large black Zil. A few meters behind were two police cars whose flashing red lights illuminated the dark night.

"By the way, does anyone have any suggestions about which way we should go?" Ternowsky swerved to the left, barely missing a car making a right-hand turn from Lomonovsky Prospekt.

"Continue down past Moscow State University until you reach Vorabyovskoye Highway, then make a left onto Komsomolsky Prospekt," Natalya directed.

"Just as you wish."

"Where are we going?" Borisov was fearful. They couldn't proceed much farther at this speed. Soon they would have to veer off to some side street and try to lose Donskoi. But where would they go? Every neighborhood in Moscow was closely patrolled by local militiamen who recognized anyone not belonging in their area. There were few places where one could hide without sooner or later being reported as a stranger or a hooligan.

"Does anyone know a good hiding place at the university?" Ternowsky raced the car past the sprawling campus of Moscow State University with its neo-Gothic Stalinist architectural behemoths. He glanced nervously through the back window. Donskoi kept a steady two-car distance behind them. Never coming closer or falling back farther. He suddenly had a feeling that Donskoi was more interested in following them than in apprehending them.

"Too late. We've just passed the university."

They approached the six-lane Vorobyovskoye Highway. If Ternowsky turned right he would be heading toward Leninsky Prospekt and Gorky Park. If he went to the left he would be driving parallel with the course of the Moscow River toward the Kiev railroad station. He ran a red light, cutting across oncoming traffic, and swung the car toward the left. Donskoi's car was no longer in the mirror. "Good news. I think we've lost our friend Donskoi. He needs more balls than he's got to keep up with me."

Borisov looked back. Ternowsky was wrong. Donskoi was there. He had simply fallen behind far enough to be inconspicuous. The two police cars were back there too, but their red lights had been turned out. Clever, thought Borisov. This way Donskoi can pick up not only Natalya but anyone else she tries to contact. They would have to get rid of Donskoi before they proceeded any farther.

"Andreivitch, I am worried about you." Borisov leaned forward. "You have risked everything for me. For us. Will you be all right if Natalya and I jump from the car?"

"I'd be worried that you two had broken your neck."

"Be serious. Where will you go? What will you do?"

"I told you. Don't worry about me! I'll lose those *apparatchiki* behind me and head straight toward Leningrad where I have some friends."

Borisov could only hope that the consequences for Ternowsky would not be too severe.

"Soon you will be entering Beronhkovskoya Naberezhnaya. Bear right. And gradually diminish your speed so that we can leave without your stopping the car."

"You're crazy, Alexsandrovitch. You'll kill yourself . . . and her."

"Within a couple of miles the road closely parallels the Moscow River. It's still dark and Donskoi is still far enough behind that he may not see us leaving the car. From here we can get to the Kiev station and head south." Borisov was careful not to mention exactly where he was going, for fear of further jeopardizing Ternowsky. From Kiev, he calculated, he and Natalya could go either southeast toward Kharkov through Rostov-on-Don and straight down toward Tbilisi, or they could proceed in a southwest direction toward Odessa and make their way eastward by land or by boat on the Black Sea toward Tbilisi. The best thing he could do to assure Natalya's cooperation was to acquiesce to her demand to go to Tbilisi.

"Listen, my friends, if by any chance you get to Kiev, try to find my family. They live a few blocks off the Percherskaya Lane, the Monastery of the Caves. The Ternowskys will take good care of you."

"Are you sure *you'll* be all right?"

"I told you. Don't worry about me. I've been chased by the police since I was ten. Plenty of experience and plenty of rubles to buy off the necessary officials. I'll be fine."

"A few more meters," Borisov replied, saddened by the realization that this would be the last time he would ever see Ternowsky. "You know I can never thank you enough, my friend."

"Take care of yourself, Alexsandrovitch. I'll miss you."

"Slow down along that curve of the road. It's dark enough there so that Donskoi won't notice our exit."

"You mean I didn't lose him?" Ternowsky slowed the car to ten miles per hour. "Well, let's see how far I can lead him toward Leningrad. Now get out."

"Thanks." Borisov opened the back door and grabbed his black bag. He pushed Natalya out first and jumped immediately behind her. They rolled down a steep, grassy embankment and hid behind a clump of bushes near the edge of the river. Borisov reached out for Natalya. She could barely stand, and she shook with fatigue, fever, and pain. He buttoned her overcoat and helped her walk toward the river.

"Where are we?" she asked, holding tightly onto his arm.

"Not far from the Kiev railroad station. Across the river from Plyushchikha Ulitza."

"My head is burning."

"I know." Borisov reached into his bag and gave her two pills — aspirin and a phenothiazine compound that would help lower her temperature and reduce the aching. She swallowed them without hesitation.

Suddenly they heard the sound of screaming sirens above them and the shrill voice of Donskoi ordering his men to search the bushes. They both fell flat to the ground.

"We can't stay here. We've got to find a safe place to stay for a couple of days."

They crept down towards the river's edge, where several rowboats were pulled up on shore. Two fishermen were already making preparations for a dawn push-off. She pointed to the dark, cold, choppy waters. They both knew this was their only chance of escape. They crept over to the first rowboat of the group.

Natalya sat in the back as Borisov slid the boat into the water and started to row vigorously.

Midway across the river they heard the first deafening round of shotgun fire aimed at them.

Chapter Seventeen

WITH THE SOUND of gunfire receding behind them, Borisov and Natalya scrambled out of the boat as it touched land. They ran up the steep wooded embankment.

"Follow me." Natalya grabbed Borisov's hand and led him through the shadows of Plyushchikha Ulitza. They walked quickly down the block, passing once familiar stores and restaurants. For a brief moment Natalya could almost forget that they were still in danger. She stopped to catch her breath and began to tell Borisov of a world afforded the senior members of government that she once had enjoyed and even now missed. As they walked, she spoke compulsively of an elite society with access to special privileges, Western merchandise, and unusual services that could easily rival "the decadent opulence of czarist times." She felt rejuvenated. There was the Transagentsva Travel Bureau, which booked her yearly ski trips to Yugoslavia, and which was owned by the Georgian proprietor of the Pechora Café, frequented by her jazz musician friends and theatrical colleagues. Borisov couldn't understand how the people working at the fashionable hairdresser, The Witch, managed to supply her and her friends with "necessary drugs" for their "all-night parties." According to Natalya, the amphetamine pills came from a central veterinary supply depot and hashish was brought in by Russian soldiers on leave from Afghanistan. How could she speak so fondly of her past, he wondered. A past he was having a hard time accepting. French pastries delivered on a weekly basis to her house from the Metelitsa pastry shop, the only one in Moscow with a summer terrace. Gifts sent anonymously from the hard-currency Vesna gift shop for services rendered by her husband. Could such decadence and self-indulgence exist in the Soviet Union, he asked himself. Now? In the 1980s? As a senior member of the psychiatric community he was entitled to special privileges — his own apartment, his own car, six weeks vacation (of which he would only take four) and special seats reserved under Zoubok's name at the Bolshoi Theater or the Moscow Art Theater. He liked to enjoy an all-night vodka party as much as anyone. And from time to time he wasn't above giving a policeman a couple of rubles to forget a traffic violation. But what he was hearing about from Natalya was a life-style of a totally different magnitude, something he had been led to believe no longer existed, something that allegedly belonged to another era, or to a decadent capitalist system. If only half of what she was describing was true, the system was thoroughly corrupt — and so was Natalya. Perhaps he had made the biggest mistake in his life by giving up his livelihood and his country for a woman who could speak so animatedly about Jupiter, a film shop that sent her a new Leica camera every year in gratitude for the customer referrals she had made.

Yet he couldn't help but love this beautiful, sensuous, intelligent woman who had made him experience more in one week of his life than in the other forty-odd years. But there was also something less obvious about her that made him love her. From the first time he met her, he had sensed a quiet sadness, a deep yearning for someone to penetrate the surface glitter, to fill a darkened soul with warmth and light. And, with the need to love. Sukhumi had been able to reach her in that special way. But could he? Could he quiet her restlessness, her neurotic need to live life to the fullest? What would happen to them now?

He grabbed her hand. She squeezed his, knowing that she had lost him during a considerable part of her reminiscences. But it didn't matter. They would have a lot of time together. She would tell him everything.

Natalya pointed to a group of dilapidated single-story buildings, once the private mansions of court nobility. "Down there is Arbat Ulitza. That's where one of Moscow's greatest actresses lived."

"Who was that?"

"Natalya Nikitchenko."

Borisov laughed. "Not only Moscow, but the greatest actress in all Russia."

"Thank you. Thank you." She bowed and clapped in the traditional theatrical fashion with which an actress showed her appreciation to her audience.

Suddenly Borisov pulled her back into the shadows, pressing her body tightly against his. A police car passed by slowly.

"I don't think he saw us," he said with a nervous tremor in his voice.

She looked into his face. His eyes were soft and caring, unlike those that had looked at her one long week before. She wanted to kiss them. But something inside her made her pull away.

"Anything wrong?"

"No . . . yes . . . I just don't know if I can continue without some rest."

She led him past the majestic Mayakovsky Theater, with its ornate 1930s stone decorations, past the Moscow Conservatory of Music, to a plain six-story apartment building, only a few blocks north of the thirty-story skyscraper of the Foreign Ministry.

Dawn was breaking over General Janowski's apartment building. Borisov recognized the concierge as the woman who had directed him to the swimming pool to find Janowski. She, in turn, knew Natalya from her previous visits.

Natalya knocked on the general's door.

"General Janowski?" There was no answer. She knocked again.

"General Janowski? Are you there?"

"Yes?" Janowski opened the door, nervously eying his three early morning visitors.

"It's me. Natalya."

"Yes, Natalya, of course, how are you? I'm sorry I'm not able to invite you inside. But I'm not feeling very well and I really must get back to bed." He tried to close the door but Borisov's arm held it open.

"Please! We need a place to rest."

"I think the best thing for you to do is leave *now*."

Natalya traced Janowski's gaze to the concierge and immediately understood. Within a few minutes the concierge would telephone Donskoi that they were here and have them all arrested — she, Borisov, and Janowski.

"Go home to your sick mother," Janowski tried again to close the door. "Pray for her. Don't forget her garments."

The door closed. Natalya and Borisov walked downstairs and hurried down the street.

"He was trying to warn us."

"What did he mean by going home to your sick mother? And not to forget her garments?"

"It's important — now even more than before — that I return to Tbilisi. Because of what you told me a few days ago. My mother *is* dying."

Borisov held her. She buried her face in his chest.

"She made me swear a long time ago that when she died she would be buried with dignity, wearing the elegant clothing of her youth." Natalya's voice was almost inaudible. "You understand, don't you?"

Borisov nodded in agreement, but felt certain she was lying. He could only hope that as greater trust between them developed, Natalya would reveal the truth.

Natalya dried her eyes on his shirt and started to walk in the direction of her own house — only two blocks away.

"What are you doing? Have you gone mad?" Borisov grabbed her.

"No. If we can get to my house I think I know of a way to insure our escape to Tbilisi."

"What do you mean?"

"You'll see. Trust me."

There was nothing else he could do.

"But we'll never get in. Donskoi will have his men watching the house."

"There are more ways into a house than the front door."

She led him down the narrow, cobblestoned Arbat Street, where writers and court princes once rode their horses for sport. She was back home. For a while, at least. She relished the sight of the stately mansions and manicured gardens that lined the street, which had a long time ago belonged to the aristocracy and now were allocated to senior Party officials. It was an area replete with a history with which she liked to identify. Vakhatangov Street crossed Arbat after several blocks; it was named after a famous director whom she admired. Pushkin had lived just a few houses down from her own. The side streets where she shopped, filled with small stores passed on from one generation to another, had been named for their trade speciality: Cook Street was famous for its specialty foods, fashionable bakers were found on Fancy Street, unusual utensils could be purchased on Silversmith Street.

About halfway down the street they stopped. Borisov was right. Two security agents were guarding the front steps. Natalya steered Borisov into an alleyway leading to the property abutting hers. As she had hoped, the neighbor's gate had been left unlatched. They walked quietly through the overgrown garden along a high fence of wide wooden planks. Natalya stopped and slapped at a few of the planks with the heel of her hand until she felt one give.

"It's still here," she breathed. "Thank God. It's loose. We can slip through."

They squeezed through the narrow opening and crouched down toward the side of the house. They saw no other guard. Borisov's heart pounded.

The house was a magnificent three-story structure in nineteenth-century restoration style. The mansion shone in the morning's light with a pristine elegance that reflected the nineteenth-century taste for grand proportions and French pedigree. Rows of slender, rectangular windows dominated the façade. The three center French windows, shadowed by their hemispheric arches, led onto a black wrought-iron balcony marked with the rusted chancres of time and neglect. Two large cypress trees on either side of the house swayed gently in the morning breeze.

Natalya anticipated Borisov's reaction. "Incredible, isn't it? You could house twenty to thirty families in there. Wait until you get inside."

Borisov felt the anger well up within him again, an anger rising from self-righteous intolerance of gross inequities, and from the sense that no matter what future he and she might have together, there was a part of her life to which he could never belong.

"How do we get inside?"

"I'm sure we can open one of the windows. There are no locks on any of them. Quickly!"

Borisov tried the windows until he found one that he was able to open and they climbed inside. There seemed to be no one there.

The opulence of the gilded baroque furniture in the foyer and on each landing was overwhelming. Borisov stopped to gaze into the dining room, an intricate, elegant pastiche of a Louis XVI sideboard, beneath a modern tapestry, and willow-green contemporary Sèvres bowls placed alongside Limoges porcelain on a nineteenth-century English table. Yet, it all seemed to fit together. Bokhara and Isfahan Persian rugs covered the highly polished inlaid wood floors. Large eighteenth-century French paintings hung on the walls. So this is what it is like to live as a senior government official, Borisov thought. What more was there for members of the Politburo to receive?

Natalya went directly to her husband's room, a chamber full of pictures of Vartanian and prominent Soviet officials. The room was furnished with eighteenth-century drawing-room pieces with red flowered uphol-stery, a pattern that also covered the walls and the bed. A large Bordeaux Bokhara rug covered most of the floor but clashed oddly with the colors in the rest of the room. Sounds of running water came from the adjoining bathroom.

Natalya rifled through the clothes in a nineteenth-century French armoire adorned with a glossy painting of cherubs taunting a satyr. She found what she was looking for, a nine-millimeter Makarov pistol, and made certain the silencer was in place and the clip filled with its complement of eight bullets. She sat down on her husband's bed while Borisov paced nervously around the room.

Vartanian walked into the room.

"Hello, my dear husband. Come in. Welcome me home."

"Well, my dear. It's so good to see you back to your . . . old self . . . so quickly. And I see you have brought along the medical staff. How do you do, Dr. Borisov."

Borisov nodded.

"Please make yourself at home." Vartanian indicated a worn leather chair. "Try it. It's really quite comfortable. It belonged once to Marshal Alexander Berthier, one of Napoleon's generals."

Borisov declined the invitation.

"Well, you must be quite hungry and tired after your" — Vartanian paused to consider his words carefully — "escape."

"I see you've taken to wearing silk smoking jackets since you put me away."

"Tsk, tsk . . ." Vartanian reached into his pocket for cigarettes. "You don't mind, do you?" He lit the Pani without any trace of discomfort. "May I offer you one?" he asked Borisov.

Borisov ignored his question.

"I want you to tell Dr. Borisov why you hospitalized me." Natalya's voice rose in anger.

"I'm sure you must have told him. Why repeat a boring tale?" He smoked the cigarette thoughtfully. "We once had a good marriage, didn't we, darling?"

"Stop the nonsense," she replied, pointing the gun straight at his midriff.

"Then our marriage turned sour. You played around, and so did I. You became agitated, paranoid, hostile, and all those other lovely postures women assume when they feel grieved, injured."

Natalya cocked the gun. "Zhores, don't say foolish things. Because I will use this gun. And since you taught me how to use it, you know quite well that I will not miss."

"Darling, I know this may not be the most opportune time to tell you this, but you definitely don't look well."

Natalya fired a shot. The bullet went past Vartanian's

right shoulder and wedged itself in a wall in the corridor.

"I've asked you a question, Zhores. And I want an answer."

Vartanian inhaled deeply. "All right. After Sukhumi's death, you became an extremely dangerous woman. Rather than send you to prison, Donskoi came up with the idea of having you committed to a psychiatric hospital so that whatever you might say about Sukhumi and his death could be automatically discounted as the ravings of a madwoman."

Natalya sighed, as if a great weight had been lifted from her very soul. She whispered something into Borisov's ear, handed him the pistol, and went down the hall to change out of the scrub suit.

Borisov was impressed by her escape plan. It was extremely dangerous. But, feasible and clever. Just like Natalya, herself. He instructed Vartanian to lie down on the bed. It would be difficult for him to flee from a reclining position.

"How did Sukhumi die?" Borisov placed the barrel of the pistol against Vartanian's temple.

"Don't worry. I'm not interested in becoming a dead hero. You can put the gun down."

Borisov let his arm drop to his side and said, "Natalya claims he was killed."

"You could say that. The job killed him, so to speak. Sukhumi wanted the country to go in a certain direction. More open — economically and politically. Greater decentralization. But like all new ideas, there are barriers. In this case these barriers were certain members of the Politburo who felt particularly threatened by Sukhumi's approach. I thought it was worthy of a trial — but I was overruled. Personally and professionally, I had a high regard for Sukhumi. He was far more intelligent and creative than those old farts in the Politburo with their paranoid suspicions of one another. Unfortunately for Sukhumi, his desire to liberalize the Soviet Union was one of the few issues around which a majority of the members of the Politburo could agree on a course of action. To preemptively kill Sukhumi before they suspected he would kill them."

"How do you know all this?"

Natalya returned, wearing woolen slacks and a heavy cardigan sweater. "Answer Borisov's question — you vermin. Tell him how a snake like you gets to know everything about everything."

"Please, darling, remember that you once enjoyed the bountiful advantages of my privileged status. I am the executive administrator for the Politburo. And, although I have no official standing within that body, I am, nevertheless, closely connected to all the paperwork and information that is involved in running it. Donskoi, who was personally assigned the frightful task of killing Sukhumi in the most inconspicuous way possible, was to report to the Politburo through me. And as much as I opposed the decision to kill our general secretary, I nevertheless obediently carried out their instructions. With great misgivings but no hesitancy."

"How could you! You scum." Natalya lunged at Vartanian, but was restrained by Borisov.

Vartanian started to raise himself up from the bed, but returned to his reclining position when he saw Borisov pull back on the barrel and heard the bullet drop into the chamber.

"Please continue."

"Donskoi's execution of Sukhumi had a certain Dostoevskian quality to it — based on that peculiar human delusion that one can commit a perfect crime, if only one plans it carefully enough. Patent nonsense, especially if the death is to appear natural. If one can say nothing else about Donskoi, I think it fair to say that he's a genius at his job. He outlined a plan for murder that was sublime in its simplicity. A sick man who, by temperament, is always concerned about his health, is convinced by his doctor to take just a little bit more medication to prevent future problems. Although this man might be wary of death plots directed against him, this same man is the very last person to suspect that the medication he is already taking — which by the way has already proven effective — could be a weapon of death. The plan was brilliant in its conception. Except for one minor flaw. It did not take into account Sukhumi's insistence upon Natalya's presence at the birthday party. The rest I think you may have learned from Natalya. Sukhumi was taken to a clinic run exclusively for members of the Politburo and their immediate families and whose doctors, unlike yourself, are completely corruptible." Vartanian paused and looked at his watch. "Where was I? Yes, of course. We now have the scene where Sukhumi accuses the doctor and Politburo members of murder. Remember, as the daughter of a doctor, she knows what an increased concentration of nitroglycerin can do. Our heroine also knows that the slightest squeeze can send that extra lethal amount into the blood stream. Causing immediate death. In any case, it was decided that she should be flown back here and placed under my care, which was supplemented with ten KGB security guards. It was decided that 'house arrest' would be a more humane, if not effective, means of keeping her out of public circulation and giving her a decent interval of time to regain her strength."

"You goddamn liar! They didn't kill me only because they wanted something from me. The KGB was interrogating me here in this very house. And they didn't want to send me to Lubyanka Prison or the Serbsky Institute because it would have become a legal mess."

"Perhaps that is so. In any case, she escaped — somehow managed to scale herself down the second-story window onto the garage roof, and then sneak by the guards — disguised as an old woman. There were those in the Politburo who wanted her apprehended and sent to the Gulags, but Donskoi insisted on hospitalizing her at Kashchenko." Vartanian turned toward Natalya. "Please believe this, if you believe nothing else. I had no desire to harm you by having you hospitalized. I simply wanted to contain the damage that you were capable of doing if left unbridled. I thought the hospital was the lesser of all evils."

"Tell me why Natalya is considered so dangerous." Borisov watched Natalya pace nervously around the room.

"In Russia, anyone who knows anything he should not know is already a danger to the system. The fact that she knows that Sukhumi is dead is dangerous. He was immensely popular. Many *apparatchiki* in the military, the police, and in the bureaucracy gave him their personal allegiance. Sukhumi ruled with a charisma unlike that of any other leader we've had. It motivated people. He took a system that had been faltering ideologically, economically, and bureaucratically and turned it around — without using force or brutality. He was beginning to rid it of the corrupt, the inefficient, the lazy. All of this without reverting to old Stalinist techniques — Gulags, midnight arrests, mass killings of citizens. This is quite a remarkable achievement. Can you imagine how the Soviet people would react if they knew that their beloved leader was dead? Or worse yet, murdered by one or several of his colleagues in the Politburo? Protests. Conflagrations. Riots. I know. I witnessed the minor protests that arose all over the Soviet Union when Khrushchev was summarily dismissed from his position as Party secretary. Now suppose these loyal people learned that Sukhumi had tried to give them more personal freedom and greater economic liberalization . . . before he was murdered. What do you think would happen, my dear Dr. Borisov?"

"So that's why you created a new Sukhumi?"

"Of course. Take an actor who is normally used as his surrogate by the KGB and who closely resembles Sukhumi — and sift him through our normal manipulation of the press. We can maintain the illusion that he is alive for several years, if we have to. It takes a considerable effort. But, I assure you, we can manage it."

"But you couldn't manage Natalya."

"Those who were opposed to Sukhumi could not afford to kill her, at least not before she gave them certain secrets he had told her. Who were the people involved in his scheme to take over the Politburo? How were they going to implement his plans? So that's where you came in, Dr. Borisov. A dedicated researcher and clinician with the most impeccable credentials, treating Natalya for an all encompassing disorder called sluggish schizophrenia. Through you and your medical skills we were hoping to find out what she knew, while at the same time having her officially — and unofficially — discredited as being insane. Who would believe her rantings? You see, doctor, your innocence serves the purposes of those who want to implement what you would consider *their* evil deeds."

"Bastard." Natalya slapped his face.

"My . . . my . . . my." Vartanian ran his hand over his cheek. "What would you say, doctor? Wouldn't you call that poor impulse control?"

"I would say that she was justifiably angry." Borisov pulled Natalya away from Vartanian and sat her on a chair. He walked over to the window and looked down at the crowds of people on their way to work. At the bottom of the hill was a roadblock where the police were making spot checks of pedestrians and motorists. He turned toward Vartanian.

"Get dressed. And make sure you bring your special identity cards with you. We're going to take a little trip to the country. And you're going to be our chauffeur."

After Vartanian dressed, they left the house, climbed

into the front seat of his new seven-passenger gray Chaika, and drove cautiously through the rear alleyway. They'd driven only a quarter of a mile when a policeman waved the car to a stop.

Borisov poked the gun concealed beneath his jacket into Vartanian's right side. "Don't be clever, Vartanian. I can assure you that Komsomol taught me more than the glories of communism and the intricacies of building a latrine."

"I'm surprised at you, Dr. Borisov. If I wanted to sabotage your mission and kill myself in the process I would have simply crashed into one of these lamp posts." Vartanian rolled down his window.

"Get out of the car and let me see all of your identity cards." The young policeman kept his right hand on his unfastened leather holster cover.

"Such impudence! I'll do no such thing." Vartanian handed the policeman his identity card through his window. "If you don't let me through immediately, I will make certain that you spend the next five years of your puberty patrolling Siberia."

The police officer stared at the card. His demeanor and voice immediately changed. "Please forgive me. Had I known who you were, I would have waved you right through."

He stepped aside and waved the car on. As the car sped away the young officer phoned the Central District Office, reporting a description of the Chaika sedan, license plate ZEK-4020, and its occupants — one Politburo member and an unidentified man and woman. The vehicle, he said, was heading south, in the direction of Ochakovskoye Highway. That message was immediately relayed to Donskoi and Panova.

Donskoi and Panova raced across Kalimina Prospekt, down the empty lane earmarked for official use only, turning left onto the Kutuzovsky Prospekt. Panova had been correct after all. Borisov and Natalya had gone to her house. Donskoi had thought that her house arrest would have discouraged her from doing so. She certainly had no interest in seeing her husband again. He returned to his preoccupation with the Janowski incident. The concierge had telephoned him and relayed the entire contents of Janowski's curt, seemingly innocent, conversation. Even after having interrogated Janowski intensively, Donskoi had learned nothing more than what he had already known: Natalya's mother was a terminally ill psychiatric patient. Donskoi had cross-referenced all of Janowski's responses with the central files at KGB headquarters. They checked out. Most important, he was politically clean. An ex-soldier without ambitions other than to live a quiet retiree's life. In any case, if Donskoi wanted to detain him in the future, he knew where to find him.

Panova looked at him quizzically.

"Don't worry. I'm all right." He kept going over and over the general's words to Natalya. Go home. Return to your sick mother. Pray for her. Don't forget her garments. But what had the general meant? Natalya's mother had acquired religion in the latter years of her life. But, Don't forget her garments? What garments are relevant to a half-crazed dying woman? Why would General Janowski transmit that message at that particular time? It had to be a code.

Donskoi recalled how, with an extra-sensitive electronic bug, he had heard Natalya mention General Janowski's name to Borisov, in the hospital just before Borisov went to Novobrat. He really hadn't expected to pick up anything of importance in his routine electronic surveillance of her room. In fact, routine surveillances, including those placed on Panova and Vartanian, usually revealed nothing but petty gossip. Most Soviet citizens, and even foreigners, expected certain places to be bugged. And a heightened state of general awareness provides less valuable information for the KGB than one might expect. So he hadn't expected Natalya to say anything significant. General Janowski was a reputed World War II military hero who was an old Georgian friend of Sukhumi's. From time to time they would drink together. But that was about it. General Janowski was well known as someone who deplored politics. On numerous occasions he had refused Sukhumi's impassioned invitations to enter the government as a senior statesman. But Natalya had specifically told Borisov to talk to him. He had to know something.

"Vladimir, what do you make of General Janowski's statement to Natalya, 'Go home. Return to your sick mother. Pray for her. Don't forget her garments?' "

Panova banked a sharp left turn onto Novopublyovskoye Highway, a heavily traveled truck route that ran perpendicular to the Ochakovskoye Highway. He tried to remain alert for Vartanian's Chaika, while he considered Donskoi's question. After three years of working together, Panova had learned to respect Donskoi's professionalism, even if he disapproved of his indulgent and decadent personal life. They worked well together. Perhaps because Donskoi wasn't threatened by Panova's private views that over the years the KGB had been transformed into an elite club of opportunists and cynics. Panova called the KGB the Kontora Grubykh Banditov: the Office of Crude Bandits. Donskoi humored him and his self-righteous attitude and promised him that in any new regime he, Donskoi, would personally appoint Panova inspector general of a newly reorganized KGB. Yes, he enjoyed his working relationship with Donskoi, except for the unnecessary sadism Donskoi sometimes brought to a particular assignment. Like this assignment. An expert in interrogation and assassination, Panova had always felt that agony need not be prolonged one second longer than absolutely necessary. A KGB assignment should be emotionally neutral. Accomplish it as efficiently as possible, then go on to the

next assignment. There was no room in this profession
for private indulgences.

"Vladimir, do you think the general's words were
related to Sukhumi's plans?"

"I'm not sure. Let's consider his statements separately.
There seem to be three basic parts to his warning. The
first is that Natalya should return home as quickly as
possible."

"She does have a dying mother."

"Yes. But we're also less than a week away from
Soviet Day, when our tanks, missiles, and artillery units
will be paraded through Red Square in front of the
Politburo reviewing stand. You are certain that Sukhumi's
plan is to be carried out then?"

"Of course. Yes." Had he been mistaken to have
confided his knowledge about the implementation of
Sukhumi's plan to Panova? He hadn't told him how he
received the information, and Panova knew better than
to ask. He had merely told Panova the date.

"I agree with you. I think that in some way
Janowski's urging her to return to Tbilisi is related to
the November seventh deadline."

"And the other two statements?"

"The statement about praying may refer to remaining
at her hospital bedside where Natalya might meet her
contact."

"Yes. Perhaps. And the third instruction?"

"Wait. I think I see them — a gray Chaika about six
car lengths down. What do you want me to do?"

"Do you think they've seen us?"

"No. I doubt it. But I think they are heading for
trouble."

"What do you mean?"

"The right rear tire is wobbling. Do you see it?"

"That wheel is either going to fall off or the tire is
going to burst. Stay back here awhile. Let's see where
they take us."

Panova pulled behind a blue model GAZ-56 truck hauling an overload of building bricks.

Donskoi picked up the microphone on the dashboard and ordered central headquarters to relay directly to him the night's tape recordings from Vartanian's house. Maybe there was something on those tapes that could give them a clue about General Janowski's warning.

"The third instruction, the one about not forgetting the garments, is the one that makes the least sense. Is she really to bring her clothes? Is Natalya to go to a place where her mother's clothes are located?"

"Do you think Sukhumi may have entrusted Natalya's mother with the plans?" It was a possibility that he had not yet considered. Or perhaps Natalya's mother was to send her elsewhere. A place related to cloth. Like a store, a tailor shop. But what about praying? To a church? For a holy garment?

"I don't know," Panova replied. "It would be too risky to entrust valuable information to a certifiably insane woman. Furthermore, we don't know whether Sukhumi and the mother knew each other."

"They may have." Donskoi adjusted the sound on the car radio as the Vartanian tapes were played. "On the other hand, it wouldn't have been unlike him to take such a high-risk option and use her insanity as an effective camouflage against anyone considering her a serious conduit for the plan."

Donskoi paused and focused his attention on the conversation between Vartanian and Borisov. He heard several things that infuriated him — Vartanian's reference to his admiration for Sukhumi; the reference to Donskoi as "reprehensible," and the sheer stupidity of Vartanian's blank disclosure of how Sukhumi had been murdered. Admittedly, Vartanian was under duress. But what Donskoi was hearing, in effect, was the confession of someone who wanted to be caught. Of someone who wanted to be relieved of the burden of his guilt — guilt by association in the killing of Sukhumi. It was a phenomenon he was familiar with, from many interrogations. Once they confessed they felt better. And they kept talking.

"Try to catch them. I want Vartanian. He has just become too dangerous."

Panova passed the truck and rapidly gained on the Chaika. Vartanian turned onto a ramp leading to the Ochakovskoye Highway. But the faster the Chaika went, the more the right wheel wobbled. When Vartanian veered off into a dirt road, the car traveled for several minutes until the wheel finally fell off. The Chaika came to an abrupt stop in a cloud of smoke and dust.

Natalya and Borisov were already in the woods when Donskoi raced out of his car. He took aim with his Tokarev TT33 pistol, but, despite its range of forty feet, he missed. He reloaded eight rounds of bullets and pursued them into the woods. The underbrush was thick and he was too unfamiliar with the terrain to gain on them. From now on, he would have to anticipate their moves, not follow them.

Donskoi returned to his car, opened the trunk, and removed a crowbar. He approached Vartanian, who was being questioned by Panova. He raised the crowbar into the air and brought it crashing down on Vartanian's skull.

Chapter Eighteen

"FOR THE LAST time, where did they go?"

Fidgeting uncomfortably on the metal chair, Ter-nowsky looked at Donskoi and then at the metal tray in front of him with its five-gauge intravenous needle, bottle of D5W, and glass syringe filled with insulin. The Organic Therapy Unit was dark. Three patients lay in varying stages of yellow and red coma. Panova and Zoubok looked on.

Donskoi gently caressed the forehead of a comatose patient. "Don't you ever wonder what these poor creatures must be thinking, suspended in time and life. It must be very lonely. But, they're lucky. Unlike us, they don't feel any pain."

"They were headed toward Tbilisi."

"Are you certain?"

"No. I'm not certain. But that's what she was arguing with him about when they got into the car."

"What do you mean?"

"Borisov wanted to go to Helsinki, through Leningrad. She insisted that he take her to Tbilisi. He thought it would be an impossible undertaking. But she insisted."

Donskoi looked at Panova. "Use both our computer and our agents in Tbilisi to compile a list of the names of all the churches and priests within twenty-five miles of the city, and a list of names of any legal or illegal operations having to do with the selling, manufacturing, or purchasing of any type of garments." The contact point for Natalya was definitely in Tbilisi. But where? At her mother's psychiatric hospital? At a church? At a clothing store? And with whom? A doctor? A priest? A factory manager? If he could only decipher Janowski's words.

"Did Natalya say anything about wanting to see her mother?"

"No."

"Anything about praying? Or garments?"

"Leonid, is this relevant?"

Donskoi glared at Zoubok with contempt. "When I want your opinion, I will ask for it."

Zoubok walked over to Donskoi and whispered, "Don't talk to me that way. Not in front of my staff."

Donskoi approached Ternowsky and took his face between his hands.

"Tell us, my dear Dr. Ternowsky, whose staff you are really on."

Zoubok's eyes darted between Donskoi and Ternowsky. Why had Donskoi demanded that he be present for Ternowsky's interrogation? All he had been told was that he would learn where loopholes existed in the hospital administration, that had allowed Natalya to be transferred without Zoubok's knowledge.

"Tell your omniscient, all powerful boss, who prides himself on knowing every detail of this hospital's operations and who, despite repeated warnings from me, could still assure me that everything would turn out all right. Go ahead, Ternowsky, tell this self-proclaimed god of science, this brilliant administrator and medical director who allowed my patient to escape from *his* hospital — tell him for whom you are working."

Ternowsky tried to pull his head away from Donskoi's tight grip.

"If you insist on remaining mute, I will be happy to accommodate you. Dr. Zoubok, please give me the intravenous needle. I don't think Dr. Ternowsky is yet convinced that I am a man of my word."

Zoubok refused to pick up the syringe. "This hospital is not your Lubyanka Prison. Here, in *my* hospital, there will be no more KGB interrogations. Or political incarcerations." Zoubok's face flushed scarlet. "Unless you are formally arresting Dr. Ternowsky for complicity in the escape of Natalya Vartanian, I insist that you let him go."

"I would listen if I were you."

"Don't threaten me, Leonid. I've worked with you up to this point because I had to work with you. No more. We *both* have our political patrons in the Politburo. The hospitalization fiasco is your mess. I never wanted her here. In fact, you might want to consider resigning your post as chief of Internal Security." Zoubok walked out of the room, slamming the door behind him.

Donskoi released his grip on Ternowsky. He spoke with a repentant tone. "Why did you help Borisov that night?"

"He is my friend."

"Friendship is a precious commodity that neither you nor I can afford."

"I have no regrets. I would help him again if I could."

"You had an assignment."

"I completed my assignment. I told you everything

that had transpired up until that evening. That's what I had to do. No more, no less. What I did later that evening I did on my own. To help Borisov."

"Touching. Very touching. But inexcusable." Donskoi caressed Ternowsky's face and spoke with an awkward, forced smile. "You've been too good an . . . employee, for too many years, to lose your valuable services over a minor transgression. I have something far more important for you to do." He looked at Ternowsky's face, searchingly. "It involves your *bête noire*, Dr. Zoubok." Donskoi outlined his plan. "Is your family still living in Kiev?"

"Yes."

"Good! Does Borisov know about them?"

Ternowsky hesitated.

"Yes or no."

"Yes." Ternowsky understood the implied threat.

"Good. Then I will apprehend our friends in Kiev."

"Come on, hurry." Natalya reached up and grabbed Borisov's hand. He pulled her into the bright yellow wooden boxcar marked on both sides with faded red stenciled letters: MOSCOW — KIEV — ODESSA. As was customary on long freight trips, the two sliding wooden side doors were left open to provide ventilation for the perishable merchandise. But on the trip south from Moscow to Odessa, there were usually very few, if any, perishable items. Certainly no foods that would have to be consumed within forty-eight hours; otherwise they would have been placed in the attached metal refrigerator cars located in the middle of the twenty-car caravan. During his childhood, when Borisov would accompany his mother to the factories she'd helped design, each located near a major railroad terminal, he had become fascinated with the anatomy and protocol of suburban and long-distance trains. They reflected a particularly Russian obsession with traveling in the proper style. These trains connected the major cities between terminals, stopping at small stations along the way. The suburban trains had only one class of tickets — *zhestkiy* — meaning hardclass, wooden seats. On the long-distance trains like the one they were on, there were two classes of tickets: the less expensive coach cars which could have wooden or padded seats, and the *coupé* — expensive two-to four-person compartments with sleeping berths. Even here, there were two degrees of luxury: the *zhestkiy vagon*, the cushionless car where one rented bedding from the conductor, and the *myagky vagon*, the soft car with built-in padding. How Russian, thought Borisov, to complicate a simple pleasure like riding trains into an elaborate exercise of choices. In the long run what difference did it all really make, he wondered. He felt a certain restlessness welling up inside.

"Welcome to our home for the next few days. A step down from your Arbat Street house, I'm afraid." Borisov closed the boxcar door.

"It's lovely. Our very own *myagky vagon* without conductors to interrupt our privacy." In the darkness she pressed her body against his.

Borisov's hands moved over her breasts, her buttocks, her thighs. They undressed each other, as they both sank to the floor. And beneath the protective warmth of their overcoats, Natalya guided him carefully into her.

She felt a quick surge of pleasure released within her. It had been so long.

Natalya ran her fingers through Borisov's soft, flaxen hair. "Soon you'll need a haircut. I wish I had a pair of scissors with me."

He pulled her closer to him and began to kiss her on the lips and neck.

She pulled his head down onto her breasts and kissed him, whispering, "Thank you." They lay together in the semidarkness, watching the moonlight pierce the wooden slats of the boxcar wall.

"Tell me about ex-wife. Was she pretty?"

"Do I detect a note of jealousy?"

"Perhaps."

"Some thought her beautiful. She wasn't as beautiful as you. Nor as passionate. I think she was always running away from something or someone. So, in turn, I simply withdrew into my work. I'd spend twelve to fourteen hours a day at the hospital. When I came home I'd work on my icons. Restoring. Making them even more perfect than they were. Recently, every time I worked on the Madonna I was restoring, I thought of you."

"You must promise never to treat me like some type of Madonna. A Madonna is something you can't touch. Someone who isn't real." She lowered her head and slowly kissed his nipples, his stomach, and the twitching muscles of his thighs.

Zeleneyev turned toward Ternowsky and congratulated him for having prepared this complicated case so well. He looked down at the heavyset sixty-five-year-old lying before him on the table. The patient's head was completely wrapped in gauze bandages. Zeleneyev picked up the chart and reconfirmed the unusual nature of this emergency, proud that Ternowsky had asked him to administer the electroshock therapy. Originally a patient of Zoubok's, the notes in the chart indicated that he had been transferred to Ternowsky's care because he had once before been treated by Ternowsky — when the patient was the regional director of the Ukrainian Communist Party. The chart indicated that the patient had tried to kill himself by jumping from a five-story building during a bout of severe depression and had been operated on only two days before for reconstruction of his fractured cranial bones. There was great concern among his colleagues in the Ukrainian Communist Party, as well as in his family, that he would try to commit suicide again, once he recovered from the operation and realized that his first attempt had failed. Zoubok wanted him shocked immediately.

This was not the first time Zeleneyev had shocked suicidal patients after surgery. It was a standard procedure, and more often than not there were no serious complications. However, this patient had a history of severe ventricular arrhythmias, so that, according to Zoubok's notes, "great care should be taken to avoid any further cardiac complications." The chart indicated that the patient had been appropriately premedicated with Lidocaine, an antiarrhythmia drug.

Zeleneyev checked the notations on the IV bottle of 5 percent dextrose and water. The muscle relaxant, mucous inhibitor, and anesthesia had all been administered. All that remained was to apply the shock paddles to both temples.

Focusing on the chart, Zeleneyev missed the patient's desperate eyes, the panicked screams suppressed by the bandages. This patient knew the ECT procedures by rote. He tried to force his fingers and toes to respond to a surge of adrenaline he willed to his extremities. But the excessive dose of muscle relaxant had completely blocked any neurochemical transmission to his muscles, and he was totally paralyzed. He tried to yell, "Zeleneyev, stop! You have the wrong patient!" But he knew that all that Zeleneyev heard was a reassuring silence.

It had all been prearranged. Simply. Methodically. And so quickly, Zoubok thought. Soon after he left the Organic Therapy Unit, he had been arrested and detained in the hospital by Donskoi. An intramuscular injection of succinylcholine administered by Ternowsky had paralyzed him, and, lying inert on the table, Zoubok could only watch as Panova forged medical orders. It not only had medical legitimacy, but it appealed to Donskoi's sense of irony that Zoubok would end his life at the hands of the doctors he trained. Zoubok would be wrapped in gauze bandages to disguise his identity. Patient care was to be supervised by Ternowsky, who frequently replaced the busy Dr. Zoubok, and who would make certain that Donskoi's plans were implemented. No heroic measures were to be undertaken to save his life in a "crisis." Zeleneyev was unwittingly recruited by Ternowsky to provide the professional backup expertise required to explain the sudden death of this high-risk patient. The body was to remain untouched and removed only by the clergy, to be buried in a Ukrainian church. After a few hours, the hospital staff would receive the tragic news that Zoubok had died in a car accident. His body had been burned beyond recognition. Memorial services would be held the next day at the Academy of Science. All so simple. And logical. Donskoi had learned well the basic lessons of medicine that Zoubok had taught him — doctors will perform whatever procedures are ordered from above, without asking too many questions.

Zoubok felt the cold, greasy metal paddles hug both his temples. Within seconds the electrical current tore through his brain, throwing his muscles into fitful contractions, slapping his body mercilessly against the metal table, snapping his spinal column, and drowning him in an aspirated pool of saliva. Zoubok's eyes closed for the last time.

There was something within her that frightened him. A part of her that clung to the memories of the past, no matter how painful. A part of her that was obsessed with Sukhumi and the need to implement his plans regardless of the consequences.

As they walked along the narrow road parallel to the train tracks, Borisov held Natalya around the waist. The past two days on the freight train had permitted them their only carefree moments to explore each other's fears, hopes, desires. Yet as they approached the outskirts of Kiev, Borisov felt a certain unease. The closer he came to understanding her, the more elusive she became.

They strolled hand in hand, comfortable in their anonymity, walking past the buildings of Kiev University, painted red in honor of the students who had died in the 1917 October Revolution. The broad, tree-lined boulevard of Novo Novodnitska was on their way toward Pecherskaya Lane, the Monastery of the Caves. Resting at a hotel before continuing their voyage to Tbilisi would have been impossible. Each time they would be asked to show their internal passports to the concierge who, in turn, would pass them on to the police. So they decided that the best place to stay would be with Ternowsky's family. If Ternowsky had escaped safely, his relatives would be expecting their arrival. However, if he had been captured . . . or tortured . . . he might have revealed that they were heading toward Kiev. Donskoi could be waiting for them. They had both decided that it was a risk worth taking. They were exhausted and needed a place to rest.

Borisov was not used to the significantly warmer climate, but it came as a pleasant surprise. He walked along the broad, sundrenched promenades with his overcoat slung over one shoulder. Such informality was unusual in Moscow. And although Kiev was a major industrial and cultural center, it had a relaxed pace that Borisov savored. Completely rebuilt after World War II, Kreshchatik, the principal boulevard, often termed the "Champs-Elysées of Kiev," attracted shoppers whose grocery bags contained items not found in Moscow — succulent capons; rich red kielbasa made from real pork, not the sausages that Borisov was used to eating in Moscow; a surfeit of various spices which would enchance dishes such as *vareniki*, small dumplings filled with sour cream, and *medovik*, spiced honey cake; as well as colorfully decorated bottles of Livodia and Mossandra wines. The abundance of color and light cheered Borisov. As much as he loved Moscow, he had to admit that it appeared drab and gray in comparison to Kiev. Where else could he see a pretty young red-haired woman wearing multicolored bell-bottom pants, talking to a well-dressed young man with a characteristic rich, full Russian beard, long-sleeved patterned shirt, and an ersatz American cowboy hat? Natalya assured him that if he loved Kiev, he would adore Tbilisi.

Natalya dragged him over to a poster pasted on a kiosk, an advertisement for the famous Ukrainian opera *Zaporozhets Za Dunayem*. It was a story she knew well; the tale of a Ukrainian wife who beats up her Cossack husband, reflecting the popular impression that if a man appears timid and indecisive, he must then have a Ukrainian wife. "Let's see it tonight."

Borisov laughed, reminding her that the only thing they could see were possible escape routes toward Odessa, and from there eastward toward Tbilisi. He had to admit that it would sadden him not to be able to enjoy the sights of Kiev.

They continued along the boulevard paralleling the gently flowing waters of the Dneiper River. On the left bank the city was a flat plain covered with factories and skyscrapers. On the right bank, hills dominated the landscape, punctuated only by an overpowering bronze statue of Saint Vladimir holding a cross and gazing across Trukhanov Island toward the suburb of Darnitsa, where golden wheat fields embraced the seething orange steel ingots manufactured at the steel factories working overtime. Legend went that at the spot where the statue stood, Saint Vladimir had baptized the entire population of Kiev. It was here in Kiev, Borisov knew, that Christianity had its first major success, sustaining the relentless onslaught of Crimean Tartars. They recognized the famed Monastery of the Caves, a complex of churches, cathedrals, and monuments centered around the twelfth-century church of the Redeemer of Berestov, built as a burial site for the princes of Kiev. The Ternowsky family lived just around the corner.

Ternowsky's parents lived in one of the five high-rise buildings arranged in a semicircle that had been built expressly for the purpose of relocating cooperative farmers who wanted to work in the factories. But which building? They all matched Ternowsky's description — twenty-two floors, pale yellow brick buildings, dotted with balconies covered by orange awnings, and crisscrossed by a hideous lattice of metal fire escapes. And, like Moscow, Kiev had very few telephone directories. Someone's address remained, for the most part, private. The only way to find the Ternowskys, Borisov concluded, was to check the hundreds of names on the mailboxes in each building. Natalya took the right side of the lobby of the first building; Borisov took the left. But before he could finish reading down the first column, he felt someone tap his shoulder.

"May I see your identification card, please?"

Cold sweat formed along his backbone. Slowly he reached into his jacket pocket and took out the internal passports. The policeman, a man close to retirement age, Borisov judged, examined the passports carefully, glancing across the lobby at Natalya, who had just gestured at Borisov to indicate that she had found the name. The policeman made some notations on a piece of paper. His voice was gruff. "What brings you here? It looks like you've traveled quite a distance."

"We came down by train from Moscow. We're visiting some friends here."

"May I see your train ticket, please?"

Borisov searched his empty pockets, looking more distraught as the seconds flew by.

"My God. Where could I have put them?"

"Perhaps in your bags. Where are they?"

"We left them at the train station."

"Do you have the tickets for them?"

"Natalya," Borisov yelled across the lobby. "Do you have the train tickets? Or the tickets for our luggage? This policeman wants to see them."

Natalya immediately understood the problem. She would have to do something to distract his attention. As she walked across the lobby she suddenly fell to the ground. Borisov ran to her, as a crowd gathered around.

The policeman bent down. "Come with me!"

"Can't you see? She's not well."

"We have the necessary accommodations for her. Please come with me."

Natalya got up slowly, looking groggy and dazed. She turned toward Borisov. "Do you have my pills?"

"No, I'm afraid they're in the baggage."

As they started walking toward the front door, a heavyset, round-faced woman in her mid-sixties, wearing a red checkered babushka, ran up to them screaming. "Come! Come! There's been a serious accident outside. I believe some people have been injured."

An old man in his late sixties, the driver of a four-seater gray Volga, was screaming at the younger man, the driver of a six-seater black Chaika, for being reckless, stupid, and insolent. The second man, in his early thirties, was smartly dressed in blue jeans and a T-shirt printed with English words. He started to push the old man against the car, accusing him of being senile and blind.

When a fight started between the men, entangling the policeman and the burgeoning crowd, the moon-faced woman with the red checkered babushka spoke to the couple in a whisper. "Follow me. Quickly. Please!" She led them down a staircase to the basement of the building, moving briskly along long tunnels filled with ducts, pipes, and wires which connected all the apartment buildings in the complex. They accompanied her up two flights of stairs. Once inside her apartment she looked sternly back and forth, at each of them.

"Welcome, Alexsandrovitch!"

The woman gave Borisov a big, sloppy kiss on his right cheek. Without waiting for a response, she walked over to Natalya and repeated the kiss. "Welcome, Natalya Nikitchenko. Welcome! Call me Matushka." She looked at their bewilderment. "You don't know who I am? That good-for-nothing son of mine didn't tell you? Andrei Ternowsky? I'm his mother."

Borisov took both of her hands into his. "Matushka. You have no idea how happy you have just made us."

Suddenly there was a knock on the door. Help was too much to hope for, Borisov thought. But why must happiness be so fleeting? "Is there a back way out of here, Matushka?"

The rusted fire escape leading down two floors to the ground behind the building was in poor condition. At some points Natalya could see that it was hanging loose from the building. "Wait out there until I tell you to come in. But be careful! The fire escape is not very sturdy. It can only hold a few people at a time."

They watched from the fire escape as Matushka opened the door and warmly embraced the two men who entered the room. She retrieved her two guests.

"I want you to meet my husband, Simon Ternowsky, and my youngest son, Ivan. These are the two men who started the fight in the street. Not bad for amateur actors?"

"Their performance certainly convinced the policeman," replied Borisov.

They all embraced each other.

"Andreivitch gave us a good description of both of you," Simon said, ushering them into a living room that also served as an extra bedroom. It was a typical communal apartment where one or more large families shared a common bathroom, kitchen, and even bedroom facility. Borisov appreciated the warm, crowded quality of the living room which was a pleasant contrast to the cold, stylized expansiveness of Vartanian's house. The room was dominated by an expandable oak table with a plastic cover, surrounded by an assortment of metal and wooden chairs in need of repair and a frayed green convertible couch. Framed family pictures interspersed with an occasional icon covered a peeling, peach-colored wall. The only luxury was a Japanese stereo set, constructed from disparate component parts.

"But I must admit, he never came close to describing your beauty," Ivan said, staring at Natalya admiringly. "Please excuse me, but we Ukrainian men are used to plumper women." He pointed to his mother, who in turn slapped him affectionately on the buttocks.

"Did I not produce two handsome sons?" she asked.

"Please sit down. Matushka, bring out some food — they must be starving." Simon pulled out the two finest chairs for his guests.

Matushka brought out tray after tray of Ukrainian delights. "The crispest of dumplings, filled with the sweetest sour cream," said Simon, obviously proud of his wife's cooking. "Deep-fried matchstick potatoes. Our finest Livadia wine. And you must try some spiced honey cake. She baked it only this morning."

"And you must eat everything on the table — otherwise you will hurt my parents' feelings."

"What does your shirt say?" Natalya asked.

"Do you read English?" Ivan stood up and threw out his shoulders proudly. His white T-shirt was printed with a large red heart surrounded by bold black lettering. "It says 'Virginia is my lover.' "

Borisov laughed. "No, Ivan. I think it reads 'Virginia is for lovers.' "

"Does it mean that if people are lovers they should go

to the United States? To the State of Virginia?" Natalya asked, laughing freely. She squeezed Borisov's hand beneath the table.

"Well, I suppose I should tell my friends that all the women in the State of Virginia love me," Ivan concluded.

"Where did you get the T-shirt?" It was close to impossible for a Russian citizen to buy American-made items, other than at the Beryozka shops, the shops accepting only hard currency.

"Ivan is a gambler, a hooligan, and a drifter. And a wonderful son who can get you anything your heart desires." Matushka pointed at various objects around the room. "Clay figures from Kymkovo, amber jewelry from Lithuania, Vologda handmade lace."

"Please, momma, you make me sound like some petty thief."

"But you are my petty thief," Matushka replied, squeezing her son's handsome, dark face with her fat fingers.

"I'm a merchant seaman. Right now I work as a captain's assistant on a hydrofoil, the *Raketa*, which travels at sixty miles an hour from Kiev to Dnepropetrovsk, down to Zaporozhye, to Kherson, and to Golaya Pristan on the Black Sea." He paused. He had been waiting for Natalya's and Borisov's reaction. It came as expected. "I've already made plans for you to come on board tomorrow evening. Andreivitch told me that you had to get to Tbilisi. I've gotten work on a boat that will take you from Golaya Pristan around the Black Sea to Batumi. It will leave you about two hundred miles west of Tbilisi." He paused. His voice became somber. "Andreivitch was arrested a couple of days ago. No one knows where he is."

Natalya, turning to Matushka said, "You have wonderful sons. How can I ever thank you enough?"

Matushka embraced Natalya, pressing her firmly against her large bosom.

"We Russians are too sentimental," Simon shouted, standing up. "Ivan, put some of your dancing music on."

Ivan put on a rock-and-roll tape. A male voice screeched in English.

"Rolling Stones?" Natalya identified the group with great satisfaction. She walked over to Borisov and took his hand. "Come dance with me." Her slender hips swayed slowly, provocatively from side to side to the persistent drum beat.

"I can't do this," Borisov replied good naturedly. "Come here, Ivan, take my place."

"I learned to dance from some Polish girls from Bialystok. That's all we did on board ship on a two-week cruise." Ivan felt uncomfortable with Natalya. He had never seen such a beautiful woman.

"Ivan, put on some of our good Russian music. This noise gives me a headache," Matushka interrupted. "Simon, help me clean up the table. Let these two travelers get some sleep. They must be exhausted. I've prepared our bedroom for our guests. They will need rest."

Strained protests were overruled. In the bedroom, as Borisov turned off the night light, Natalya whispered, "More and more . . . I . . ." She didn't finish the sentence. Curled against him she fell soundly asleep, until they were awakened by heavy banging on the apartment door.

Chapter Nineteen

THEY RAN THROUGH the maze of pipes in the tunnels beneath the apartment complex. Ivan led the way through the darkness. Borisov and Natalya followed, grateful for what the Ternowsky family had done for them. Their lives were in jeopardy. If caught, Donskoi would send them all to one of the prisons in the Gulag — if they were lucky. Moments before, Natalya had heard Donskoi's familiar voice shouting through the front door to "open up for the police."

Donskoi and Panova had rushed into the bedroom just as they were fleeing down the flimsy fire escape. She smiled as she recalled the image of Donskoi and Panova holding on to the metal railings of the fire escape as it pulled away from the building and fell to the ground. Too bad it was only on the second floor. No one had been injured.

How had Donskoi known that they would be there? Realizing that Ternowsky must have been interrogated brought back scenes of her own torture. Poor Ternowsky, she thought. She didn't blame him at all. She would have confessed too, if Donskoi had threatened to harm her family. But what if the Ternowskys knew all along that Donskoi was coming to apprehend them? And they were simply holding her and Borisov until Donskoi's arrival? This sudden thought sent a chill down her spine. But if that were the case, why was Ivan going through this frightening charade of escape — at considerable risk to his own life? Whatever the truth, she and Borisov had no choice but to follow Ivan's lead.

Natalya gagged as they rushed through sections of broken pipes and sewer backups. At the end of the last tunnel, Ivan opened a steel door leading to the parking area on the opposite side of the Ternowskys' building, far away from the concentration of police. His gray Volga was waiting for them, just as he had said.

The three of them began to relax only as Ivan turned the corner of Lesya Ukrainka and Zolizhichna, two blocks from the harbor. Both Natalya and Borisov were enthralled by the eerie picture of this alien nautical world of shimmering floodlights, crowded piers, imposing steel cranes arching over fishing trawlers, cruise liners, cargo ships, and even the nuclear-powered *Lenin*.

They ran through a crowd of Russian tourists milling about the entrance to the three-story Rechnoy Vokzal passenger terminal which jutted into the water. On either side were large passenger liners crowded with tanned vacationers recently returned from the Black Sea. Donskoi, Panova, and five uniformed policemen were only a few hundred feet behind.

Ivan led Natalya and Borisov up a concrete staircase to the first floor, where giant metal containers were being loaded onto various ships. He pulled on the latch of each container until he found one that opened. The room-size container was loaded with piles of wrapping blankets and small wooden crates of white Georgian wine marked KAKHETIZSKOYE 8. The three of them climbed in. As Ivan swung the door shut, they heard Donskoi and his men opening and closing the other containers.

Ivan checked his watch. "You have four minutes left to board a hydrofoil that will take you down to the Black Sea and straight on to Batumi, Georgia. If you don't make this one, there won't be another one until tomorrow evening." He paused. "I'll create a diversion to allow you enough time to board the *Raketa*. Then just buy your tickets and present your passports. I don't think you'll have any problems with Donskoi once you get on board."

"How did you know his name was Donskoi?" Borisov asked.

"No, don't tell us." Natalya's voice was despondent.

Ivan sighed deeply. "We knew he was coming. Andrei called and told us. Donskoi wanted you lavishly entertained so that you wouldn't suspect anything until he came. I'm sorry."

"Why are you helping us to escape?" Natalya asked. "Or is this still another trap?"

"No, it's not a trap. Before he had to hang up, Andrei quickly said 'help them' in our village dialect. I know how he feels about you, Dr. Borisov. I know he didn't want to hurt you."

"He worked for Donskoi?"

"Yes. For some time. I beg your forgiveness for my brother."

Borisov nodded, but he could not believe what he had just heard.

Ivan checked his watch again and opened the door.

"Why are you doing this?" Natalya asked.

He smiled. "Because it's the right thing to do."

The door swung open and Ivan ran out, making a considerable amount of noise. Donskoi and his men followed him, leaving Natalya and Borisov to race down to the ground floor and run up the ramp of the hydrofoil *Raketa*. Just as Ivan had predicted, the captain sold them two tickets to Batumi, Georgia, and examined their internal passports. The crew started the engines and the *Raketa* lifted up out of the water, then flew over the waves at great speed, accompanied by the shrill, high-pitched sound of the motor. Natalya and Borisov stood on its deck, watching the flashing red lights of the police cars disappear into the haze.

The captain was a laconic man whose principal passion was the hydrofoil, and who long ago had learned never to ask questions to which he didn't already know the answer. He brought the passengers kielbasa sandwiches and glasses of hot tea. In a few hours the *Raketa* would arrive at Dnepropetrovsk. The boat would go on to Galoya Pristan on the Black Sea and then straight to Batumi, Georgia, with a few stops on the way. There were sleeping cabins below for anyone who wanted one — for an extra charge, of course.

Borisov and Natalya walked the deck, holding each other tightly around the waist. The shimmering outline of Kiev dissolved into the silvery brilliance of the full moon. They nodded to the captain as he moved above the deck, greeting his passengers. Borisov had always been told that the Russian sailor was a special breed; a man who was an individualist by temperament and who believed in the simple philosophy of live and let live. It was no accident that the 1905 Russian Revolution against the czar was initiated by the sailors of the *Potemkin*. Who else in feudal Russia would have dared to defy the moral and political sanctity of the crown? Who else could have been exposed to the liberalizing influences of the West and translated that experience into a defiant political act? Yes, thought Borisov, they were unusual men. And so was Ivan. A seemingly carefree, whimsical, young man, enamored with the crass materialism of the West. Yet he had sacrificed himself so that Borisov and Natalya could escape. What made him do it? Was it simply, as he had told them, because it was the right thing to do? Perhaps it *was* another trap, lulling them into a false sense of security just to betray them when they least expected it.

Borisov felt angry and violated. Andrei had known that for Borisov the sanctity of friendship was absolute. They had shared a bond of intimacy and trust that was rare between two men. What had made Andrei an informer? Money? Upward mobility? Power? What promises did Donskoi have to make to entice Andrei to inform for him? As hurt as Borisov was, he felt sorry for his friend. Ternowsky had to compromise his integrity. That wasn't replaceable. Borisov searched desperately for ways to rationalize Andrei's betrayal. Maybe it wasn't only his fault. Maybe it was the fault of a system that continuously pitted one person against another, forcing each individual into a permanent attitude of paranoia where the only emotion that could be trusted was fear. Centuries of foreign invasions and internal repression had certainly left an indelible imprint on the Russian soul. *Kto kovo*, who would be on top of whom, a game of daily life in which none of the players could trust anyone else.

"Are you all right?" Natalya asked.

"I'm all right."

Borisov took her by the shoulders and held her at arm's length.

"You know, you mean a lot to me," he said.

"I think I know that."

"Perhaps . . . perhaps not. I don't think you realize just how much you mean to me."

"Then tell me."

"I fell in love with you the minute I saw you. But I know that you're used to that type of infatuation. You're so certain that men can't resist you. I'm not as certain about myself when I'm with you. Or about your feelings for me."

Natalya remained silent. Borisov took a deep breath.

"In the hospital, treating patients or doing research, I always felt totally in control of my own life. Without doubts. And now I've given all that up."

"Why did you give up *everything?*"

"For you. My love for you. For me. Because of my disgust with myself for having accepted certain compromises in my life, in my profession. After I met you, I began to ask myself some basic questions. What did I really want? Why did I want it? What was I willing to pay for it? You forced me to ask — and answer — other questions. Were you really insane? Did you belong in the hospital? Did I believe what you had to say about Sukhumi? Once I had the answers to those questions, it was no longer right for me to remain at Kashchenko — or in psychiatry in the Soviet Union. I can't support a system that's so corrupt, immoral . . . and terrifying. Once I made the decision to help you escape . . . quite frankly, it was the only decision I could make."

"Thank you." She kissed him.

"Do you want to talk about Sukhumi?"

She turned away, wrapping her arms around herself. "Truthfully?"

"Yes."

"No. Not yet. I'm not ready. He's still very much a part of me. Despite Donskoi, despite everything. I survived the hospital. I wanted to live because of him."

"And now?"

"Listen to me. It takes time. I've just met you. Within the last two weeks you and I have been through hell. I owe you my life. I need you. And in my way, I love you. But I need time." She looked up at him sadly.

"When my father left me, I was a young, impressionable teenager. I went into a severe depression, blaming myself for having driven him away. For years I thought there was something wrong with me. I wasn't lovable. Otherwise my father wouldn't have left us. At the time,

I never thought that his reason for leaving could possibly be related to his terrible relationship with my mother. And my mother certainly never blamed herself. I created a new personality for myself. I was flippant, gay, carefree. And totally indifferent to the attention and love that men showered upon me. I swore that no man would ever do to me what my father had done — walk out. Reject me. I would make certain that I would always be in the position of strength." She paused, surprised at her own honesty. "Until I met Anatoly Sukhumi." She stopped. She couldn't go any further. Not now, she thought. Not until we reach Tbilisi. Then she would see. She lay her head against his shoulder. "Let's go to bed." Borisov put his arm around her. She felt reassured. She was beginning to feel secure that here was a man who wouldn't leave her.

They made love that evening as if they had discovered each other for the first time.

Donskoi lingered over his drink at the café on the pier, cursing Ivan's successful ploy. He knew he had to change his strategy. Otherwise he would always be trying to catch up to Borisov and Natalya in some infernal cat-and-mouse game. He would go straight to Tbilisi, wait for them there.

He turned toward the manacled Ivan and looked at him with a quizzical smile. What was he going to do with this American hustler? Could he transform him into an effective *golubchik?* Perhaps too much independence and rebelliousness. But a worthwhile challenge. He had been successful with Andrei. That had taken some time and effort. Anyway, he thought, in every good Ukrainian there is a potential traitor to Russia. What better way to eliminate a future problem than to coopt the more fractious ones now. He unlocked Ivan's handcuffs and informed him that he was free — on one condition, of course . . .

Chapter Twenty

DONSKOI AND PANOVA descended from the Tupolov 104 onto the tarmac at the military airport. They entered a black Volga that took them to La Boutique, a small shop in the center of Tbilisi. Panova had pared his list of eighty-five churches, priests, retail clothing stores, wholesale garment manufacturers, religious artifact distributors, and black marketeers down to fewer than ten likely sources of information, beginning with Ilya Irakly, an experienced Georgian smuggler and the owner of La Boutique.

La Boutique was as pretentious as its French name indicated. A small room, fifteen by twenty feet, it had been decorated by its owner in red wallpaper, red upholstery, and red carpeting based on a photo in a five-year-old copy of *Vogue*. The room was filled with unopened cartons.

"What have you been . . . 'retrieving' . . . lately?" Donskoi looked contemptuously at the heavyset man before him, whose beefy fingers were covered with diamond rings.

"I'm truly sorry, sir. You have the wrong impression of me. I'm simply a small businessman who buys and sells a few pieces of merchandise now and then."

Donskoi ripped open a carton and pulled out a pair of blue jeans. He thrust it into Irakly's face. "Where in the Soviet Union were these manufactured?"

"Well, they're . . . not exactly . . ."

"Speak, Mr. Irakly. I can't hear you too well." Donskoi signaled Panova to open the other boxes.

"Please, gentlemen. Take care. Some of my inventory is delicate."

"Would we ruin your inventory, Mr. Irakly? You mean like this?" Donskoi took a switchblade from his jacket, cut strips of blue denim from the pants in one box, and flung them at Irakly.

"Please, gentlemen, how may I help you?"

"Now that's a very smart question. I will ignore what I see about me if you tell me the whereabouts of your co-conspirators."

"Co-conspirators?" Irakly took a handkerchief from his pocket and wiped his forehead. "I don't even have a partner. My wife, God bless her, died three years ago. She was the only one, besides myself, who knew anything about this business."

"All I want are the names of your contacts in Tbilisi." Donskoi picked up another pair of blue jeans and began to cut them up.

"Contacts? What contacts? I don't know what you're talking about."

"The leader of the group. The one who will implement the plan." Donskoi spoke with certainty, although he had no idea where the conversation might go. But it was a scene that he and Panova had perfected, and it frequently resulted in important leads.

"I have some shipments of blue jeans coming from West Germany on November fifth. And another arriving on the ninth. But nothing, I swear to you, absolutely nothing else coming for several months."

"Not blue jeans, you idiot. The plans. Who is your contact?"

"From time to time some bureaucrats come into the store during their lunch hour to buy a French-made shirt . . . or a Japanese radio. But I have no plans." Irakly stood and walked over to an opened carton. He pulled out a white silk shirt wrapped in cellophane. "Here, take one."

Donskoi tore open the cellophane and ripped off the sleeves.

Irakly ran to another box. "Perhaps you like it in another color. Blue. Brown. I see that you are a man of refined taste. I have a shipment of fine Italian-made suits coming in at the end of the month. I'd be happy to set aside several for you and your companion."

"You buy and sell icons, don't you?"

"Yes, of course. Would you prefer some original icons?" Rushing to another carton, he took two icons from the box. "Which one do you prefer? I have some from the seventh century, ninth century. They're very valuable, I assure you. Take one. Take all."

"Where did you get these icons?"

"It's all very straightforward and legal. Believe me. From time to time the prelates from the local parishes ask their priests to sell an icon to get money for their parishioners. Or to repair the church. And so they bring the icons to me, and I sell them to foreigners. That's the way I've been doing business for years."

"Have you ever heard of a church where there may be garments of special importance? Of great significance?"

"A church with garments? What type of garments?"

"You tell me. Special garments."

"I woud love to be of assistance to the authorities, but I am not acquainted with any special church garments. At least not here in Tbilisi. Near Sionskaya Street, on the left side, there is the Cathedral of the Assumption."

Panova shook his head, indicating to Donskoi that it had already been investigated by local KGB agents and dismissed.

"On the left bank of the Liera River there is a rocky hill with a small church on it. I've been in it once. There's nothing much there. I think the priest once sold me an icon. I can't remember the name . . . it starts with *M* . . ."

"Metekhi Chapel," Panova interrupted. "There's nothing there."

"Wait. On Shavtelli Street, on the main thoroughfare of the Old Town, there's Anchickhati Church. The priests there wear fancy vestments. And they sell me quite a few icons in order to pay for them."

Panova nodded his head. "Our people have already checked that out. Nothing."

Donskoi motioned to Panova. "Have all this confiscated. Let's go to the next parasite on your list."

As Panova and Donskoi started to exit the store, Irakly almost tripped over a carton as he ran toward them. "Gentlemen, I forgot. About thirty miles to the west of here, on the Georgian Military Highway, there is a small church at an old excavation surrounded by all kinds of artifacts and tombs. Occasionally, a play is performed there. It is rumored that they have a piece of cloth that once belonged to Christ. Once again, I can only say that it is a rumor. You know how rumors spread."

Before he could finish his sentence, Donskoi and Panova had left the store.

She held Borisov's waist tightly as they raced along on a refurbished World War II Harley-Davidson motorcycle. Tbilisi lay before them; the snow-capped peak of Mount Mtatsmenda behind them.

The ten-hour journey on the *Raketa* had been quiet and soothing. And as soon as they landed in Batumi she began to feel as if she had never left Georgia and the towering peaks of the Caucasus that dominated the rich fertile valleys scattered with green tea plantations. And Rustaveli Boulevard. How beautiful it was with its luscious sycamore trees, its majestic hotels, and its terracotta buildings. She had asked Borisov to slow down at the end of the boulevard, just before the enormous statue of Mother Georgia holding a sword in one hand, a cup in the other. It was here that it had all started, she told him. Here in this nineteenth-century Moorish-style building, with its golden domes and red minarets — the Paliashvili State Opera, she had received her first acting lessons. From there she had gone on to perform with the Rustaveli Drama Company in *Romeo and Juliet* in the theater just down the street.

It was all so hard to believe. Only a month before she had been in Tbilisi with Sukhumi. Two weeks later, the Kashchenko Hospital, destined for permanent incarceration. But saved by the doctor who had treated her, and with whom she had fallen in love.

What would he say when he found out she had lied to him? How would he feel? Yet he might not have wanted to help her if he knew. When they bought the motorcycle in Batumi from the ship's mechanic, he thought she was hurrying to see her dying mother. But she knew this part of the country better than he. The route they were on would take them to the tiny village of Mtskheta long before they reached the Tbilisi Neuropsychiatric Hospital.

Suddenly Borisov steered the motorcycle onto the side of the road.

"Where are we going? This road seems to be veering away from Tbilisi. Did we want the Georgian Military Highway?"

"This is the road we want."

"It can't be. The sign back there . . ."

"I know. I know." She got off the bike and walked around to face Borisov. "I must get to the village of Mtskheta as soon as possible."

"Why?"

"Because I have to meet someone who will tell me where I can find the plans Anatoly Natalya had written out for the overthrow of the government."

Borisov stared at her in disbelief. "What's this person's name?"

"Father Vakhtang. He's an old childhood friend of Sukhumi's."

"Why you?"

"Sukhumi needed a courier. I have no political interests. And he trusted me completely. It was that simple. I am supposed to present his plan to the leader of the coup."

"Do you know the leader?"

"No."

"Do you know what the plan is?"

"No."

"Do you know where the plan is?"

"No. That's why I've been in such a hurry to get to Tbilisi."

"Why didn't you tell me this before?"

"Fear."

"Fear of what?"

"Of you."

"Natalya, I can't believe that you still don't trust me. Did you *ever* intend to see your mother?"

"Please don't be angry with me. It's not easy for me to trust anyone."

"What about your mother?"

She shook her head.

"Are you afraid to see her?"

She turned away. He grabbed her and turned her toward him.

"I want you to see your mother. Before we see Father Vakhtang. And I want you to say goodbye to her. Once you can do that, you'll be able to say goodbye to Sukhumi. And then, and only then, will you begin to trust yourself. And then me. Goddamn it, Natalya, she's dying!''

How odd, Natalya thought, as she walked across the expansive grounds with Borisov. The place didn't look very different from Kashchenko Hospital. She went into the administration office and was given directions to a dilapidated building toward the rear of the hospital grounds where terminally ill patients were housed. Her mother's ward.

They found a frail woman with hollowed alabaster cheeks and porcelain blue temples who scarcely seemed alive. Her once sparkling hazel eyes were clouded by cataracts created by the prolonged administration of phenothiazine medication for her schizophrenia.

Borisov stood unobtrusively in the shadows in the back of the room, watching silently as Natalya tried to talk to her mother.

"Mother, it's me, Natalya."

The eyes looked through Natalya as if she were transparent.

"He left me." Her voice was raspy.

"Who, father? Yes, he did, mother. Father left both of us."

"He was a handsome man. Strong. Virile. Dark."

"Do you know where he went, mother?"

"He became a famous writer."

"But father was a doctor."

"He held me in his arms and we made love all night long."

"Mother, do you know who I am?"

"He was strong. Handsome. Dark. He spoke like Pushkin."

"Mother. Listen to me! It's Natalya!"

"Oh, my, was he handsome. A handsome Georgian." She looked at Natalya as if she were a sympathetic old friend. "But he was already married. I believed him when he promised me that he would divorce his wife and marry me. He lied.''

"Mother, who lied?"

"I gave my life for him. I gave up my husband, my daughter, so that I could be with him. He said he loved me . . . my husband . . . you know, he was a doctor . . . a very famous clinician . . . he was even nominated for the Academy of Sciences in Moscow."

Natalya didn't interrupt her mother's ravings. Her father had been a simple, ordinary general practitioner whose patients were primarily the farmers and peasants of Tbilisi.

"When I left my daughter, she was only five. I left her with my husband. He was a doctor, you know. I had no intention of returning. I had run away with my writer who had become very, very famous. We ran away to Moscow. For several years we lived in a little town, outside the city called Novobrat. I made jewelry . . . silver jewelry. He wrote poems and plays. We were very happy. Very happy." Her voice drifted off, lost in the past. She seemed to sink into her bedcovers. "He left me all alone." She reached for Natalya's shoulders, and tried to raise herself as her anger mounted. "He left me. I hate him."

Natalya looked at her mother with pity. A victim of her own passion. She had sacrificed everything for a man who had abandoned her. The similarity between mother and daughter was not lost on her. A history of two failed marriages. Abandoning one man after another until she had fallen in love with the one man who eventually abandoned her. Death was no excuse.

Borisov's strong hands clasped Natalya's shoulders.

"I only want one thing."

"What's that?"

"My daughter. My beautiful sweet child Natalya." She started to fumble on the side table, and handed Natalya a picture.

Natalya and Borisov looked at it. There was her father, handsome, swarthy, in his early thirties, dressed in white, holding a beautiful child of about six years on his lap.

"No man will ever do to her what they have done to me."

"What have they done to you, mother?"

"He tried to stop me. How dare he? I was her mother. My husband was a fine doctor. But a terrible man. He told the judge that I was not fit to be her mother. Can you imagine that? I was not fit to be her mother." Natalya gently wiped the tears from her mother's eyes. "He took me to court, requesting a divorce and custody of *my* baby. What a fool he was. The judge found me attractive. So I invited him out for a picnic. He was naïve, my husband. The judge not only refused him the divorce, but gave me my little girl. And my fine doctor was ordered out of his own house." The old woman began to laugh wildly, oblivious to the fact that her own daughter had just adjusted her bedcovers, kissed her on the forehead, and walked quietly out of the room.

Tears rushed down her cheeks. "It was so unfair. Hating my father all these years for having left me. I wish I could find him. I wish I could ask his forgiveness." Borisov held her, quietly, comfortingly, in the dimly lit corridor.

As Natalya and Borisov walked through the massive carved-oak doors of the Sveti Tskhoveli Cathedral, she thought of the many times her mother had brought her here to worship during Easter Sunday services. It was one of the oldest churches in Georgia, dedicated to the Twelve Apostles, and possessed a cloth remnant of the shirt of Jesus. The church was crowded. A handful of devout old women knelt in front of the ornate altar. Groups of tourists milled about examining the frescoes of the nativity scene adorned by glimmering icons.

Borisov walked over to examine a group of icons hanging on a wall while Natalya interrupted a priest dressed in a brown hooded gown as he was about to light the candles. "Could you tell me where Father Vakhtang is?"

"A few hours ago he was taken by the KGB." The statement was matter-of-fact. The priest kept lighting candles.

"Oh, my God. Did they say they'd bring him back?"

"He'll be back whenever God wills it!" The priest moved quickly to another group of candles.

Natalya found Borisov quickly. "Donskoi and Panova have taken Father Vakhtang. That means they will learn that he is my contact. And they will be returning here for us. I know it."

"Do you think the plans could be here?"

"It's possible. Sukhumi loved to spend time here with Father Vakhtang. Talking. Playing chess."

"Then a copy of Sukhumi's plans could be hidden somewhere in this church."

Natalya took Borisov's arm and tried to pull him toward the closest exit.

"Take it easy," he whispered. "If the plans are here, we will miss them if we move too quickly."

Borisov returned to the wall of the twelfth-century icons. He was overwhelmed. The Oriental influence in the Byzantine figures of the three martyrs — Procopius, Demetrius, and Nestorius — was impressive. The eyes of all three were larger than natural size, expressing the artistic concept of the arrival of a new spirit. The icons themselves had been retouched discreetly. It looked as if only the golden lines of the martyrs' robes had been regilded. The background had been left untouched.

In the middle of the group of icons stood Demetrius of Salonika, a man draped in a green cape against a red background. A fifteenth-century Greek icon. Strange, Borisov thought. Why should an icon made by the Greeks in the fifteenth century be included in this collection? He stepped closer to the wall. Etched on one side of the saint's golden halo were the letters alpha sigma. And on the opposite side he read the letters beta, omega, gamma, alpha, tau. He couldn't make out the two remaining letters. The Greek letters raced through his mind. Alpha sigma . . . Anatoly Sukhumi. Beta, omega, gamma . . . *bog* . . . *bogatyr*. Borisov trembled with excitement.

He pulled Natalya near and whispered. "The Greek icon, the one with the green cape. It's there. I'm certain." He gingerly took the icon down from the wall. Taped to its back were four typed sheets of paper. There it was . . . Sukhumi's plan.

They walked outside the church and hid within a secluded alcove amidst the archaeological ruins. They read the documents, hoping the papers would tell them what to do next. The first was a letter to Natalya:

My dear Natalya,

By the time you read these plans for the liberalization of the Soviet Union (do you think that sounds too pompous?), I'll either be by your side or I will be dead, murdered by my rivals in the Politburo, Misha Kostenchik and Field Marshal Oleg Rusanov. So you ask me for the fortieth time — why didn't I round up all those members of the Politburo whom I suspected of trying to assassinate me and murder them. The answer is as simple as it will be frustrating to you. The time was not right. I did not have enough support from the other Politburo members. Or from certain crucial members of the military whom I am presently trying to persuade to back me. It is simply a question of timing — as are most political events. A planned assassination, without the proper support, implemented at the wrong time, could be catastrophic. Since I am racing against time (so they don't kill me before I kill them), I have developed a formal scheme, the details of which no one knows except me — and now you. Even my dear friend Father Vakhtang only knew the exact location of these papers which he has led you to. In case something were to happen to you, he was to take the plan to my designated surrogate, whom I will tell you about shortly. Father Vakhtang understood that I could not use him as a liaison to the group of five men who are responsible for implementing my plan. These men would only trust someone who was completely apolitical and who was closer to me than anyone else in this world.

I am entrusting you, solely, to deliver this letter to Admiral Dmitri Bovin, commander in chief of the Soviet Navy. He was expecting my personal visit before November 1 on board his destroyer, the *Potemkin II*, anchored one mile west off Batumi. Failing that, he knows to expect your arrival, which should be no later than November 4, the time he would be engaged in routine naval exercises in preparation for Soviet Day.

Deliver these plans directly to him on board his ship. He, in turn, will contact the other four principals. After that you may remain with him to witness what shall be or he will help you to escape through Turkey to freedom in the West. This decision is up to you.

I had originally designed this plan with the clear intention of personally implementing it, in conjunction with trusted subordinates. But in case Misha and Oleg are clever enough to catch me off guard, you will be my contingency.

None of the five members of the elite council, including Admiral Bovin, have been entrusted with all the details of the plan. They must come together and share each other's knowledge. This plan is the blueprint that will allow the five to integrate their respective parts into a coherent strategy. If any of the five is captured and tortured, his limited knowledge of the plan would be without value. This way none of the other five could be tempted to usurp the powers of the other four.

For all the reasons stated above, I have designated you to be my personal emissary to Admiral Bovin and the Council of Five, as I will call them.

I hope there will be no need for your exclusive services and that all goes well on Soviet Day. And I hope that we will always be together, my darling.

Your *Bogatyr*

Tears streamed down Natalya's face as she glanced over the next page. Borisov glanced around to make certain that no one was watching them.

Sukhumi Plan: Code Name Gorodki

Objectives: (1) Assassination of Politburo members Misha Kostenchik and Field Marshal Oleg Rusanov. (2) Immediate destabilization of present Soviet regime through tactical cooperation of power in key strategic cities: Moscow, Leningrad, Kiev, Tbilisi, Odessa, Riga, Omsk, Vladivostok. (3) Immediate establishment of a new regime comprised of predesignated military and bureaucratic personnel, personally selected by General Secretary Anatoly Sukhumi. (4) Termination of Soviet occupation of Afghanistan. (5) Reestablishment of détente with the United States.

Time: November 7, 9:45 A.M., military parade on Soviet Day. Loyal troops will congregate in Moscow and in other key cities without attracting undue attention.

Tactics: (1) During the military parade three elite naval marine units (Sixth Riga Division, Second Leningrad Unit, Fifth Odessa Division) under the direct command of Admiral Dmitri Bovin (code name Crayfish) will redeploy themselves around the Politburo reviewing stand so that all members of the Politburo will in effect be taken hostage. Field Marshal Oleg Rusanov and Misha Kostenchik are to be executed on the spot as a clear signal to the other members of the Politburo of what will happen to them if they do not cooperate. Transport remaining Politburo members to military barracks on Lesnoya Street for interrogation. (2) Two Army divisions — Category I troops — Seventeenth Tbilisi Division, and Fourteenth Kharkov Division under the command of Major General Boris M. Milovidov (code name Cannon) are immediately redeployed from the Red Square parade to Dzerzhinsky Square to KGB headquarters and Lubyanka Prison where all KGB functions will be immediately transferred directly to Major General Milovidov. A list of loyal KGB personnel (see appendix KGB) will replace the following operational staffers of the Fifth Chief Directorate responsible for suppressing dissent within the USSR; the Eighth Directorate operating all electronic eavesdropping equipment, the First Department responsible for external operations against the United States and Canada, and all appropriate replacements of key personnel of the six thousand cover agents operating under the First Chief Directorate will be made immediately; the Second Chief Directorate responsible for the surveillance and recruitment of American travelers to the USSR will be combined with the functions of the Third Department, presently engaged in targeting British citizens. (3) GRU Military Intelligence functions will be transferred to civilian control directly to Deputy Minister Boris Frunze, who will coordinate his functions with Major General Milovidov. (4) The Soviet Ministry of Internal Affairs (MVD), responsible for internal order and security within the USSR, will be dismantled and all newly appointed personnel (see appendix MVD) will be distributed into the following autonomous regional divisions: Estonian SSR, Latvian SSR, Lithuanian SSR, Moldavian SSR, Georgian SSR, Armenian SSR, Azerbaijan SSR, Kazakh SSR, Uzbeck SSR, Turkmen SSR, Tadzhik SSR, Kirghiz SSR, Russian Soviet Federated Socialist Republic. (5) The following Air Force units, 457th Tactical Wing Command stationed in Kalingrad, 787 Backfire Bomber Command stationed in Mogilev, 611 Fighter Bomber Command comprised primarily of SU-17, SU-24, and MIG-17 fighter bombers deployed in and around the Moscow region, will immediately secure all relevant civilian airports and military airbases designated in appendix Airbase. Air Force operations will be coordinated under Air Marshal Yuri V. Grechko (code name Sentry) in close coordination with Admiral Dmitri Bovin and Major General M. Milovidov. (6) In a combined Army/Navy/Air Force operation under the troika command of Milovidov/Bovin/Grechko all strategic and tactical nuclear weapons will be secured, and inventories reduced by the following amounts:

(1) STRATEGIC NUCLEAR WEAPONS

	Present	*Reduction*
Intercontinental Ballistic Missiles (ICBMs)	1,398	700
ICBM warheads	6,170	3,000
Sea-launched ballistic missiles	969	500*
*(SLBMs)		*(Reductions include actual decrease of numbers of submarines of the following classes: Delta II SSBN Delta I SSBN Delta III SSBN Typhoon SSBN
SLBM warheads	1,809	900
Strategic Bombers	150	75
Bomber warheads	300	150
Total strategic missiles	2,367	1,150
Total strategic warheads	7,300	3,700

(2) THEATER NUCLEAR WEAPONS IN EUROPE

SS-20s (90 targeted on China)	345	170
SS4s, SS5s	260	130
SS12s, SS22s	120	110
SS-N-5s	30	15
TU-26 Backfire Bombers	100	50
TU-16s, TU-22s	435	220

(7) The Fourth Army Mechanized Division, Category I and II troops stationed in Kalinin-Novogorod under the command of Brigadier General Volker Maluta, will secure all major highway arteries in and out of Moscow as well as the principal railroad terminals: Volokolamskoye Highway, Leningradskoye Highway, Mozhaiskoye Highway, Mira Prospekt, Ulyanovskoya Street, the Leningrad train station, the Kiev train station, the Riga train station, the Kursk train

station, and the Paveletsky station. (8) The Ministry of Economics and Agriculture will be combined into one decentralized organization where control will be in the regional offices of the thirteen republics. Collective farms will be restricted into economic-incentive units allowing farmers to work primarily for themselves. Industrial factories will also compete on the basis of a Western free-market model, growing or dying on the basis of their individual profitability — see appendix Yugoslav Economic model. (9) Martial law with an 8:00 P.M. to 8:00 A.M. curfew will go immediately into effect, during which time anyone found in the streets without permission will be incarcerated. Over a five-day period the curfew restrictions will be eliminated and in place will be a new constitution guaranteeing the Russian citizens their complete rights and privileges as free men. The Gulag prison camps as well as the Special Psychiatric Hospitals (including the Serbsky Institute) will be permanently closed. And all prisoners and inmates, if appropriate, will be granted complete amnesty and relocated back home. All religious freedoms will be guaranteed, including the right to attend a house of worship and maintain religious schools. (10) Deputy Secretary Leonid Gladkov will become the new minister of Propaganda and Information. He will assume control of all media: including television, radio, newspapers (crucial *Tass* and *Pravda* personnel will be replaced), movies. Personal Sukhumi message (see appendix) to the Russian people will be broadcast around the clock in order to explain the new revolution and alleviate anxieties.

Natalya and Borisov quickly read the part of the appendix listing the key military and KGB personnel to be involved in Sukhumi's plan.

Military	Code Name
Major General Boris M. Milovidov	Cannon
General A.S. Shaposhnikov	Star
Marshal Yuri V. Grechko	Sentry
Admiral Dmitri Bovin	Crayfish

They stopped reading suddenly and looked up at each other, completely incredulous.

Leonid Donskoi   Fork

"I hope you're enjoying it. I so much look forward to sharing your reading pleasure." Donskoi was standing several feet away. Panova was directly behind him, his Makarov pistol drawn.

"Your friend Father Vakhtang was singularly un-cooperative. I'm afraid he became a martyr to his silence. A courageous man. I admire a man who is not afraid to die for his belief. Pity though. If only he could see us now with the plans. At least he was spared the humiliation of finding out that he died for nothing. And by the way, don't ever try to hide near a church again. Parishoners gossip too much."

"Bastard."

"Now, now, Natalya. Let's not get sentimental. We have too much important business to transact."

"How could you? You son-of-a-bitch. Sukhumi trusted you."

"Well, I'm terribly pleased that you've acquired the list of conspirators. Now, who else is on it?"

"Don't you know?" Borisov asked.

"No. That's why I have pursued you from Moscow to Kiev and all the way here. Sukhumi entrusted me with very limited information. But he did entrust you to me. He told me that if anything were to happen to him you would be the courier, delivering the plans to the leaders of the coup, who would contact me."

"I don't believe you," she shouted, shaking with rage.

"It is a pity you didn't believe me that day in the hydrotherapy room. Think how much anguish you'd have been spared. If only you had told me then the whereabouts of the plan."

Natalya started toward him. Borisov pulled her back. "Scum."

"Are you referring to me or Sukhumi?"

She tightened her grip around the sheets of paper.

"How different do you really think I am from your beloved *bogatyr?* Tell me that, Natalya."

"What do you mean?"

"I play both sides. I'll admit that. Three months ago Sukhumi came to me and offered me the job of director of the First Department of the KGB, which is responsible for all external operations against the United States and Canada, if I were to join him in a coup staged against Kostenchik and Rusanov scheduled for November seventh. The offer was attractive; but I was completely unable to assess the feasibility of the coup or the merit of the overall plan because I was not allowed to read it. I told him that I would be interested in the benefits of a successful opportunity. Then, to cover my flank, I informed Kostenchik and Rusanov of Sukhumi's offer. They, in turn, offered me a better job — director of the KGB itself — if I would keep them informed about Sukhumi. Now who could blame me for keeping my options open for as long as possible? You would have done the same. It is, as the capitalists say, 'good business practice.' As November seventh drew closer and I heard nothing else from Sukhumi, I presumed that a successful coup was unlikely. Without betraying myself to Sukhumi, I decided to side with Kostenchik and Rusanov. The rest, of course, you know."

"But why did you have to kill him?"

"You may not choose to believe this, but I was opposed to killing Sukhumi. However I am afraid that Kostenchik and Rusanov, who are, well, rather *nervous* men . . . overreacted. They felt it was necessary to kill him before he killed them. And quickly. With Sukhumi dead, the possibility of a successful coup would diminish dramatically. Enough to enable them to uncover the other conspirators. As you well know, Natalya, Sukhumi was a master politician, playing one person against the other until he could achieve his desired goals. I like to think of myself as possessing some, if not many, of his professional skills.''

"How dare you compare yourself to him.''

Donskoi cocked the hammer of his TT-33. "Natalya, let me tell you something else. Something I should have told you a long time ago. Except I saw no need to. Who do you think had you hospitalized at Kashchenko?''

"You did! I ran away from my house arrest — and you thought you could interrogate me more effectively in a psychiatric hospital.''

"That's true. Yet I could have sent you to the Serbsky Institute, which is run directly by the KGB. Or, better yet, why didn't I send you to Lubyanka Prison, where I would see you every day? It's just below my office. Or the Gulag, where I wouldn't even have to worry about your escape?''

"Because if you had sent me to the Gulag prisons, I could have starved or died from the cold. Then you would have learned nothing. At Lubyanka and the Serbsky Institute you would have had the risk of exposing yourself to your colleagues' inevitable questions regarding your detailed knowledge of the plan, and the very embarrassing question of how you knew that I was the courier. If I were your superior at Lubyanka or Serbsky, where I presume they are far more sophisticated in the methods of interrogation than they are at Kashchenko, I would have immediately been suspicious that you'd conspired with Sukhumi.''

"Bravo! Natalya! Bravo! It's uncanny how lovers think alike.''

"What do you mean?'' Borisov asked.

"That's exactly how Sukhumi reasoned when he proposed that I incarcerate Natalya in Kashchenko,'' Donskoi answered. "If he were to be killed, I had to protect her from Kostenchik and Rusanov. She would at least be kept alive there. He knew Zoubok personally, and, despite his obvious political ambitions, Zoubok was a man of extraordinary clinical integrity."

"He was?"

"Yes. He was . . . he is dead. An unfortunate accident. As I was saying, Sukhumi had always admired Zoubok for refusing to become director of the Serbsky Institute. Sukhumi knew that Natalya would fare better under Zoubok's care than in one of our prisons. Once I had chosen sides, it was not difficult to convince my political allies to have Natalya incarcerated at Kashchenko."

"Liar." Natalya tried to pull away from Borisov's grasp.

"I must admit, my dear Natalya, that without Sukhumi's initiative I might never have had the idea of interrogating you while at the same time covering my intended collusion in Sukhumi's conspiracy. And do you know what else, Natalya? In hindsight, I think that he never really intended to give me a post in his new regime. He simply wanted to entice me so that I would be sufficiently interested in protecting you, were anything to happen to him."

Natalya slumped against Borisov's chest and cried. Sukhumi had gambled with her life. She felt betrayed, even though Sukhumi had done it to save her life.

"Don't you see, we were both manipulated by your *bogatyr*. I was simply recruited into his plan so that I could act as an insurance policy for your future survival when and if he were to die. Incredible, isn't it? And now please . . . the papers."

Borisov handed him the sheets. As Donskoi skimmed the plans and read further lists of conspirators, he broke out into raucous laughter.

"What's so funny?" Borisov asked.

"Ask my close colleague and friend Panova — the Arrow."

The barrel of Panova's gun now pointed at Donskoi.

"What blandishments did Sukhumi offer you?"

"The same ones he offered you."

"Of course. I should have guessed. But think, my friend, why should people die for this nonsense?"

"What do you mean?" Panova grabbed the papers.

"That plan cannot be effected. It would take three Sukhumis to implement it by November seventh. The elite naval marine units — the Sixty Riga Division, the Second Leningrad unit — are nowhere near the Soviet Union. They are now deployed in the Middle East. The 457th Tactical Wing Command has been stationed on the Chinese border. And half the military personnel he mentioned couldn't work with the other half unless Sukhumi were personally present to mediate their incessant arguments."

"You're lying." Panova cocked his pistol.

"Vladimir, you know me better than that. Call up headquarters in Moscow and ask them the location of those units."

"Why should Sukhumi have developed a plan that wouldn't work?" Borisov asked.

"It would work. At least enough to create a bloodbath. The tactical maneuvers describing the redeployment of certain air force and army units loyal to Sukhumi could precipitate the beginnings of a revolution. Perhaps — a civil war."

"It still doesn't make any sense," Borisov said.

"Politically, it most certainly does. Sukhumi wanted to frighten his opposition. And he did. With a bluff. He probably thought he could outmaneuver Kostenchik and Rusanov with a well-planted scenario that would convince them that he had a sufficient number of military and security personnel behind him to stage a coup. What better way than to recruit your own chief of Internal Security, myself, who you know is as duplicitous as yourself. Sukhumi was betting on the fact that his opposition in the Politburo would be cowed into submission. He merely miscalculated. And they overreacted. Much as you are doing now. Panova, please, don't make a foolish mistake.''

"And if you're wrong, Leonid?''

"You'll always have another chance for a revolution. The key military units of all the armed services convene in Moscow on November seventh every year.'' As Panova took aim, Donskoi grabbed for his own TT-33, but fell to the ground with Panova's first shot.

Panova reholstered his pistol, took the plans, glanced through them, and handed them back to Borisov. "Only Admiral Bovin could say whether this schedule could be effectively implemented.''

"What about calling headquarters as Donskoi suggested?'' Natalya asked.

"Those are elite units whose whereabouts are kept secret. Anyone without the authority to know, like myself, would only arouse suspicion.''

Panova led Borisov and Natalya out of the church to his car. They drove in silence toward Batumi.

Donskoi was right, Natalya thought, as she leaned her head against Borisov's shoulder. Sukhumi had manipulated everyone for his own personal gain — his political self-aggrandizement. The master politician. He had used her to neutralize Donskoi by convincing him that his political future, no matter which side won, would in part depend on his keeping her alive. Donskoi had been used by both Kostenchik and Sukhumi to keep the channel of communication open between them, so that in some way each would know what the other was doing. He had become a double agent, serving two masters at the same time without peril because it served each master's needs. Only this time Sukhumi had miscalculated his control over Donskoi. And he had paid with his life for that oversight. Natalya suddenly felt relieved. Relieved of the burden of having to sustain the memory of a love Sukhumi had desecrated with his ambitions.

"Forget the plan," Natalya whispered. "Give it back to Panova. Let him take it to Admiral Bovin. Donskoi was right. The plan is nothing more than a formula for national disaster. We'll go to Turkey. Then to the West."

"Fine. If you wish. But how long will you be happy thinking of the opportunity you might have had to change the course of Russian history?"

"Why me? Give the plans to Panova. He can pass them to the admiral."

"No," Borisov interrupted. "Sukhumi made it quite clear in his instructions. No one but you can hand those plans to Admiral Bovin. Otherwise, there is no way for the admiral to attest to their authenticity. It's you, Natalya. You alone. In your most important performance."

"And what if I don't want that responsibility? It was never mine to have. That responsibility belonged to Sukhumi. It's all part of that . . . that egoist's need to reaffirm his importance. Even in death."

Borisov took her face in his hands. "You are right to be angry with him. He used you as he used all people. Zoubok. Donskoi. Me. But what he did to you personally is no longer important. What he can still do for Russia is what matters now. His soul, his vitality, his thoughts live on in a plan — a dangerous but courageous plan to transform — to humanize — Soviet society."

The car stopped in front of a wharf on the outskirts of Batumi. Panova helped Natalya and Borisov descend into a rented motorboat. He pointed to a group of gray destroyers on the horizon, gathering for normal naval maneuvers for Soviet Day. "The largest destroyer, the one in the middle, is the *Potemkin II*. Give those plans to Admiral Bovin and tell him that Arrow will be awaiting his instructions and that Fork is dead. Good luck.''

As the motorboat pulled away from the dock, Natalya stood alongside Borisov.

''Do you love me?''

''Yes. More than ever.'' He realized that she now needed him in the way he had hoped. Not to cure her. Not simply to help her forget her *bogatyr*. But to love her.

''Which way, Natalya?'' Borisov asked. ''The decision is yours. I love you. I will go with you whichever way you choose.''

She watched the shoreline disappear. The solitary figure of Panova became increasingly smaller. Nothing had really changed, she concluded. Panova had just killed Donskoi. Now he would have his chance to play the game of power. *Kto kovo.*

Natalya grasped Borisov's arm tightly. She was tired. Tired of death. Tired of sacrifice.

''Turkey,'' she replied. ''To the West. To freedom.''

ABOUT THE AUTHOR

Dr. Steve R. Pieczenik is a Harvard-trained psychiatrist who received his Ph.D. in International Relations from M.I.T. He is a practicing psychiatrist who was Deputy Assistant Secretary of State for Management (1976-79) and Director of International Activities at the National Institute of Mental Health, where he negotiated major mental-health agreements with the U.S.S.R. An expert in the files of Soviet psychiatry and Soviet behavior, Dr. Pieczenik is also recognized worldwide as a leading international crisis manager and hostage negotiator.

FREE!!
BOOKS BY MAIL
CATALOGUE

BOOKS BY MAIL will share with you our current bestselling books as well as hard to find specialty titles in areas that will match your interests. You will be updated on what's new in books at no cost to you. Just fill in the coupon below and discover the convenience of having books delivered to your home.

PLEASE ADD $1.00 TO COVER THE COST OF POSTAGE & HANDLING.

- -

BOOKS BY MAIL

320 Steelcase Road E.,
Markham, Ontario L3R 2M1

210 5th Ave., 7th Floor
New York, N.Y., 10010

Please send Books By Mail catalogue to:

Name _____
(please print)

Address _____

City _____

Prov./State _____ P.C./Zip _____

(BBM1)